THIS IS A FAIRY TALE OF
BLOOD AND BULLETS.

IT IS THE STORY OF TWO WOMEN AND THREE
MEN WHO CANNOT DIE.

MOSTLY.

THEIR NAMES ARE
ANDY, NICKY, JOE, BOOKER, AND NILE.

NILE JOINED THEM. BOOKER LEFT THEM.

THIS IS WHAT HAPPENS NEXT...

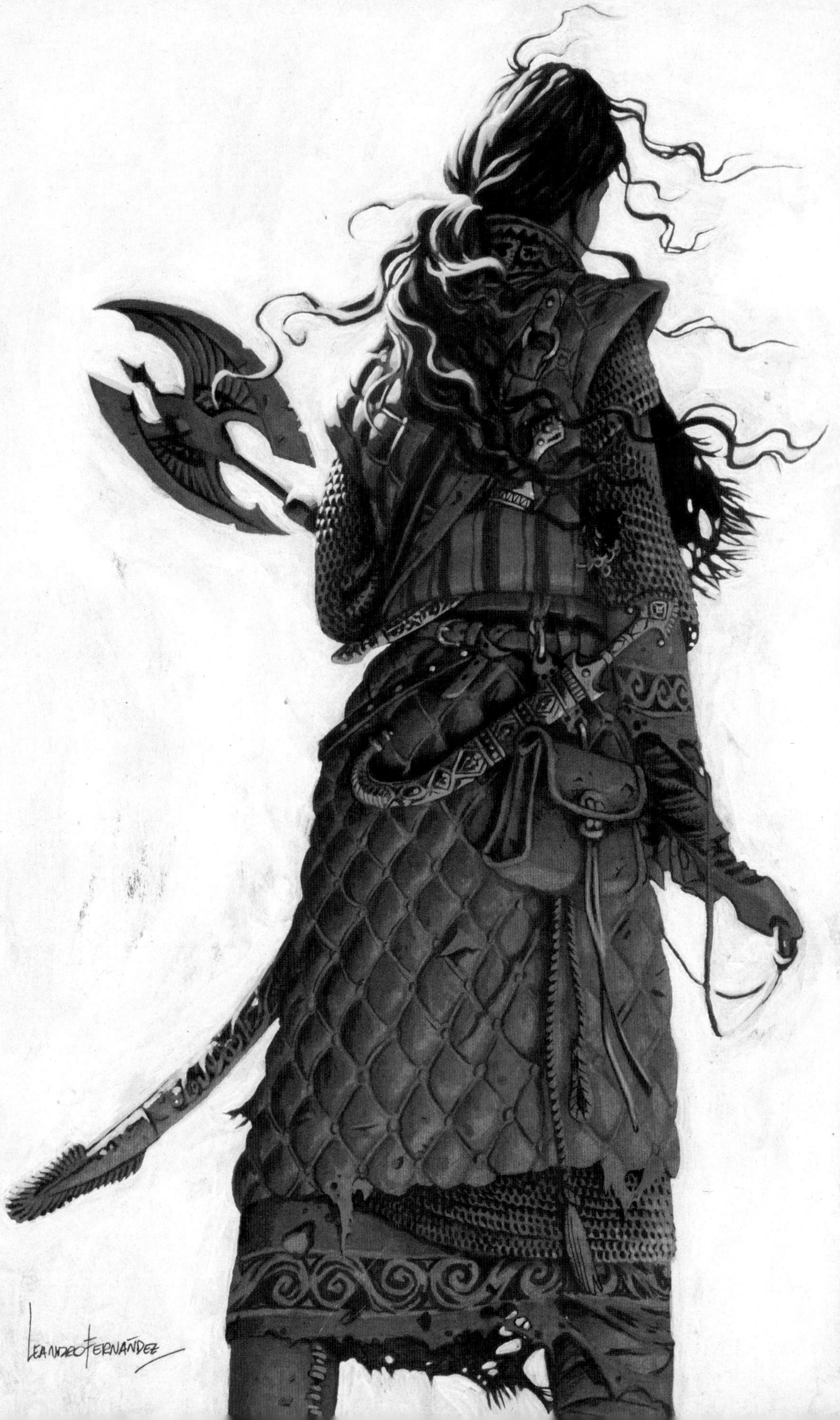
LEANDRO FERNÁNDEZ

THE OLD GUARD™
BOOK TWO: FORCE MULTIPLIED

written by **GREG RUCKA**

art and cover by **LEANDRO FERNÁNDEZ**

colors by **DANIELA MIWA**

letters by **JODI WYNNE**

edited by **ALEJANDRO ARBONA**

publication design by **ERIC TRAUTMANN**

THE OLD GUARD, BOOK TWO: FORCE MULTIPLIED. First printing. September 2020. Published by Image Comics, Inc. Office of publication: 2701 NW Vaughn St., Suite 780, Portland, OR 97210. Copyright © 2020 Greg Rucka and Leandro Fernández. All rights reserved. Contains material originally published in single magazine form as THE OLD GUARD: FORCE MULTIPLIED #1-5. "THE OLD GUARD," its logos, and the likenesses of all characters herein are trademarks of Greg Rucka and Leandro Fernández, unless otherwise noted. "Image" and the Image Comics logos are registered trademarks of Image Comics, Inc. No part of this publication may be reproduced or transmitted, in any form or by any means (except for short excerpts for journalistic or review purposes), without the express written permission of Greg Rucka and Leandro Fernández, or Image Comics, Inc. All names, characters, events, and locales in this publication are entirely fictional. Any resemblance to actual persons (living or dead), events, or places, without satirical intent, is coincidental. Printed in the USA. For international rights, contact: foreignlicensing@imagecomics.com. ISBN: 978-1-5343-1377-4.

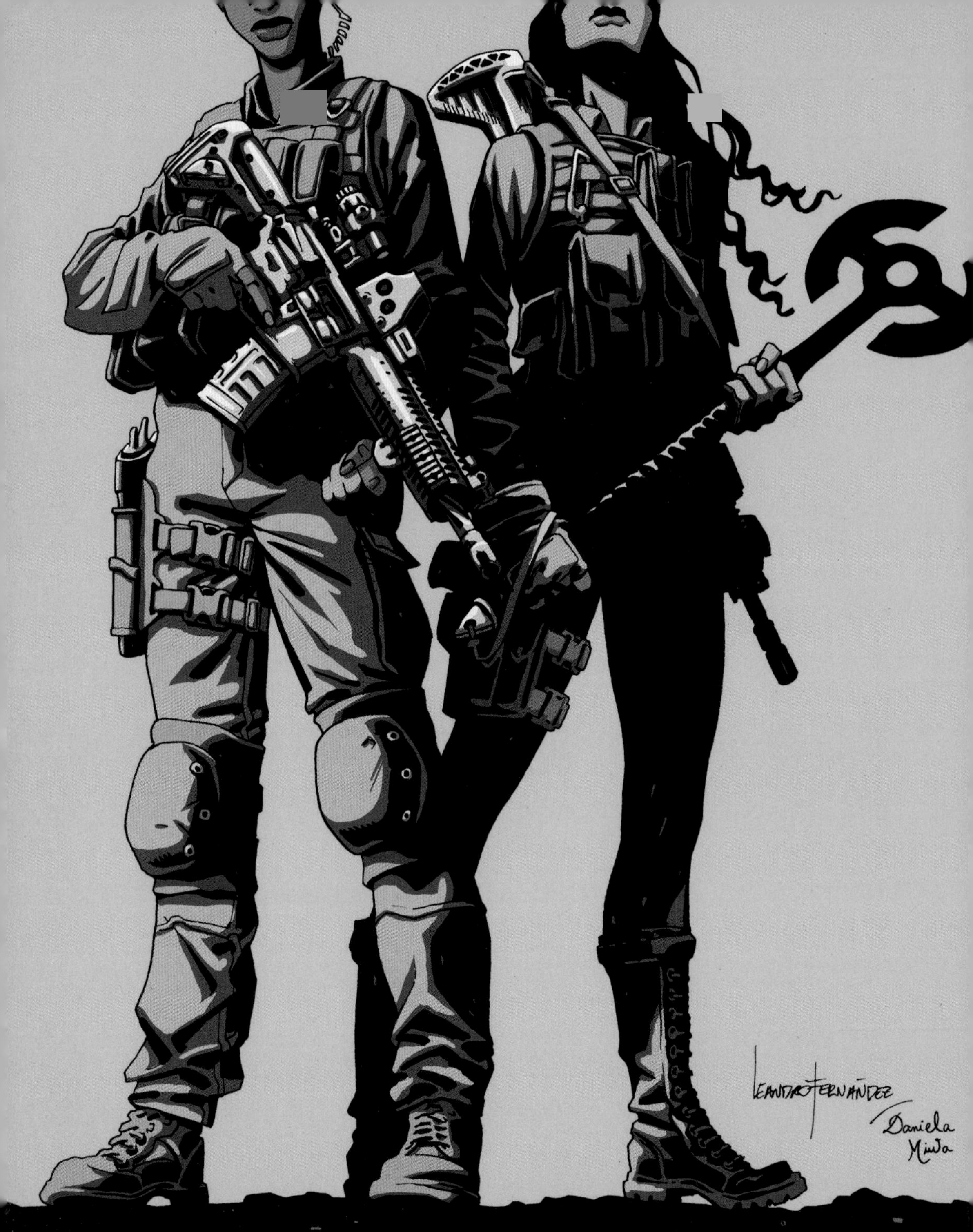
LEANDRO FERNÁNDEZ
Daniela Miwa

CHAPTER ONE

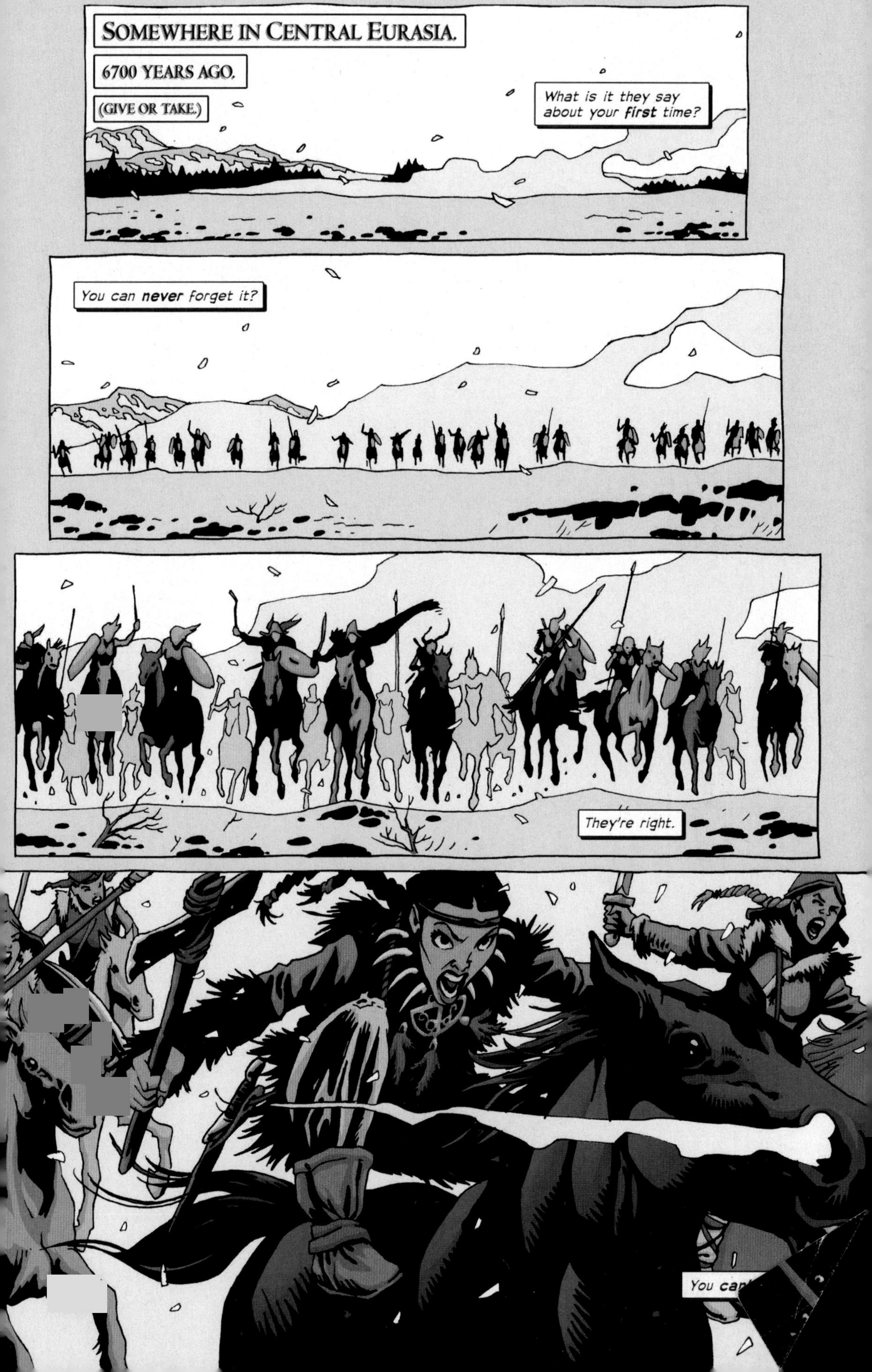
SOMEWHERE IN CENTRAL EURASIA.
6700 YEARS AGO.
(GIVE OR TAKE.)
What is it they say about your first time?
You can never forget it?
They're right.
You ca

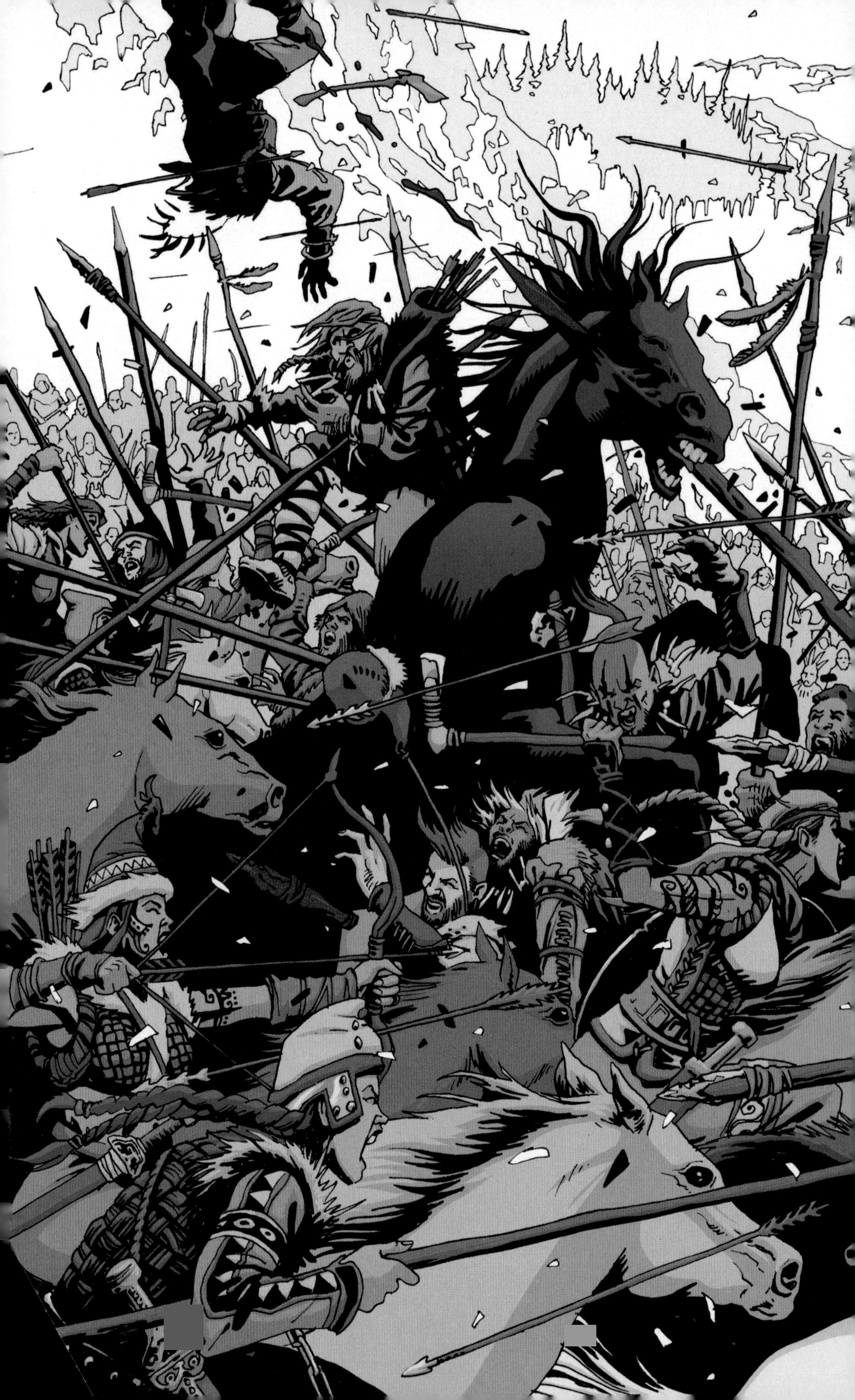

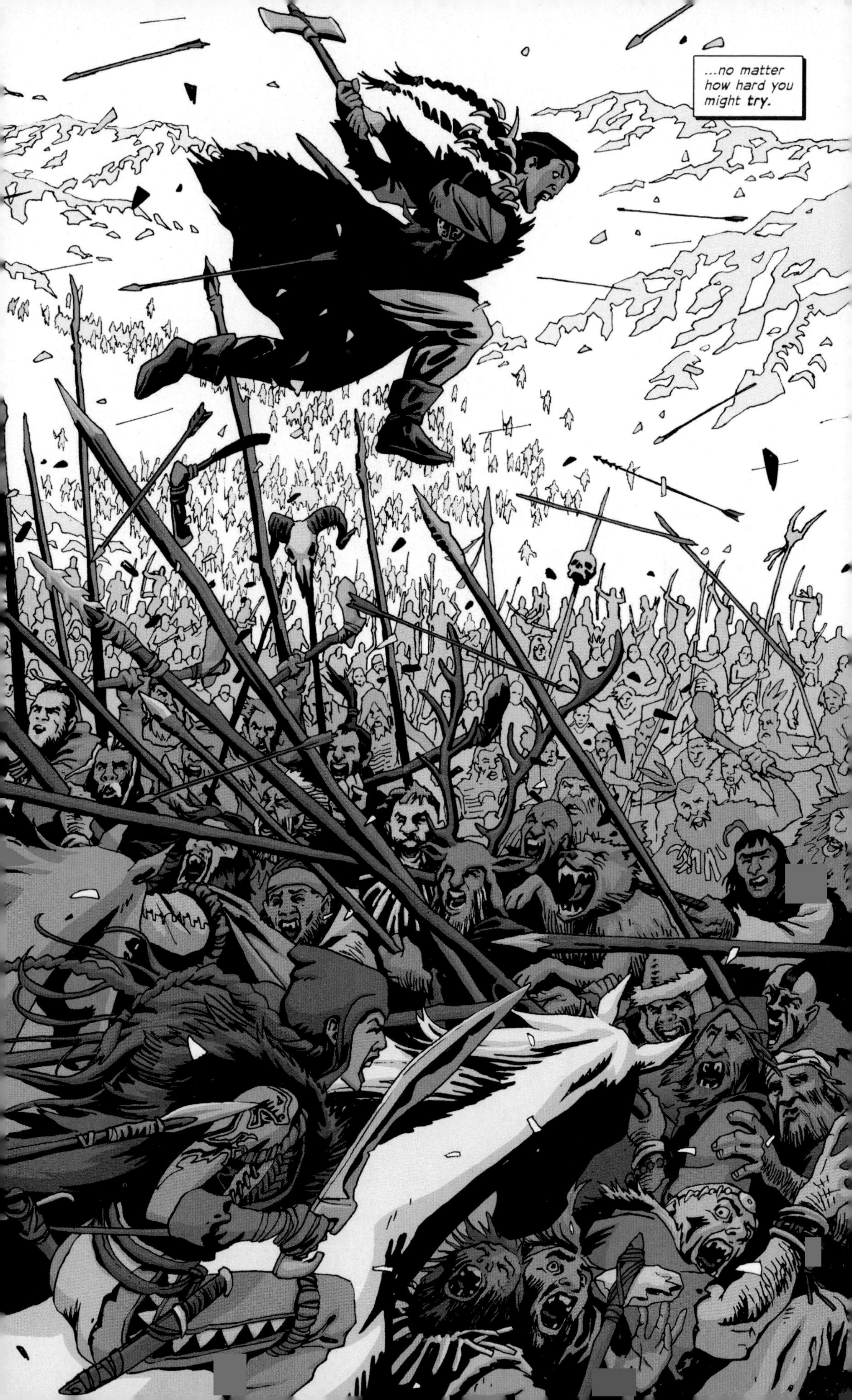
...no matter how hard you might **try.**

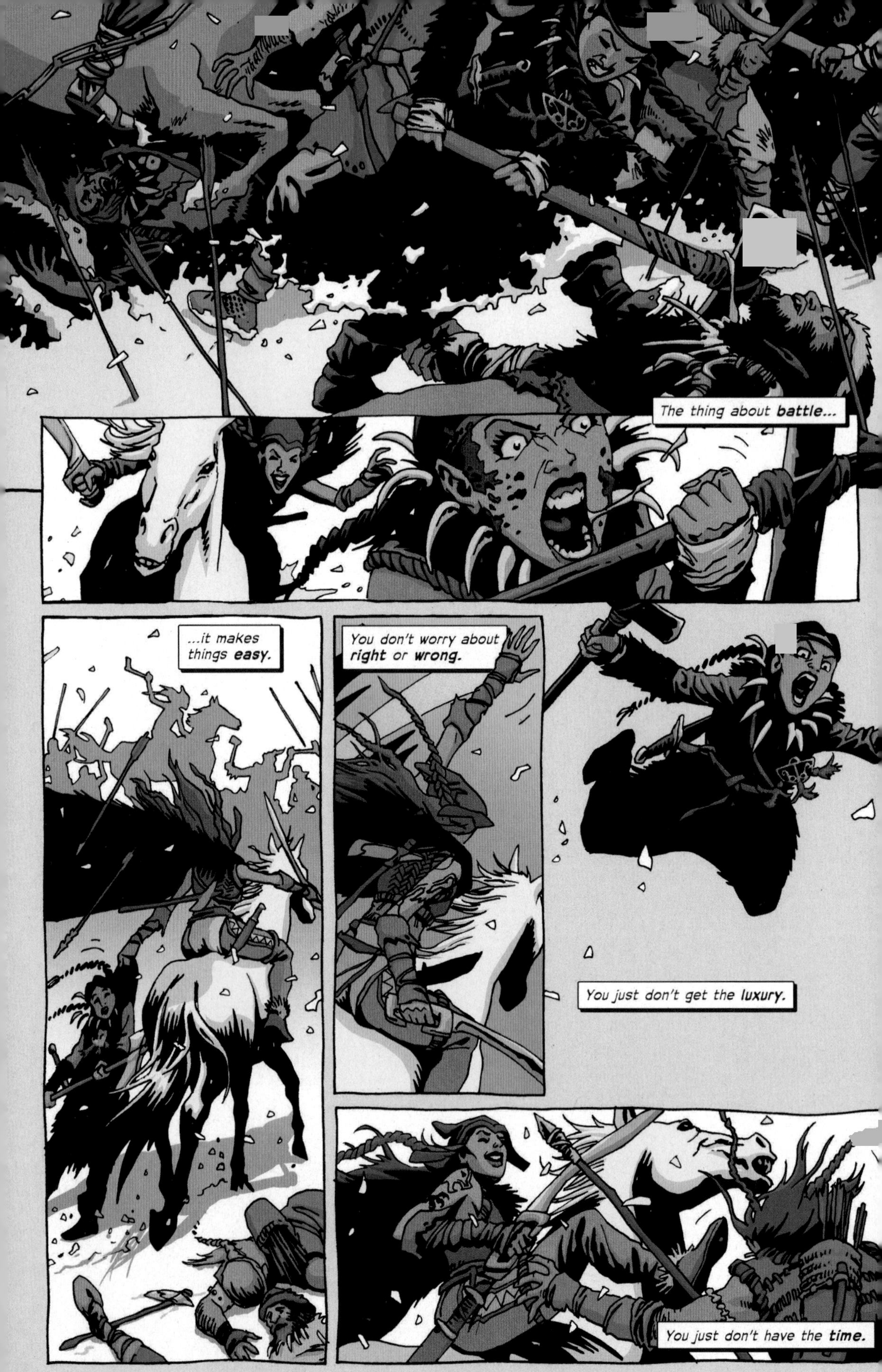
The thing about battle...
...it makes things easy.
You don't worry about right or wrong.
You just don't get the luxury.
You just don't have the time.

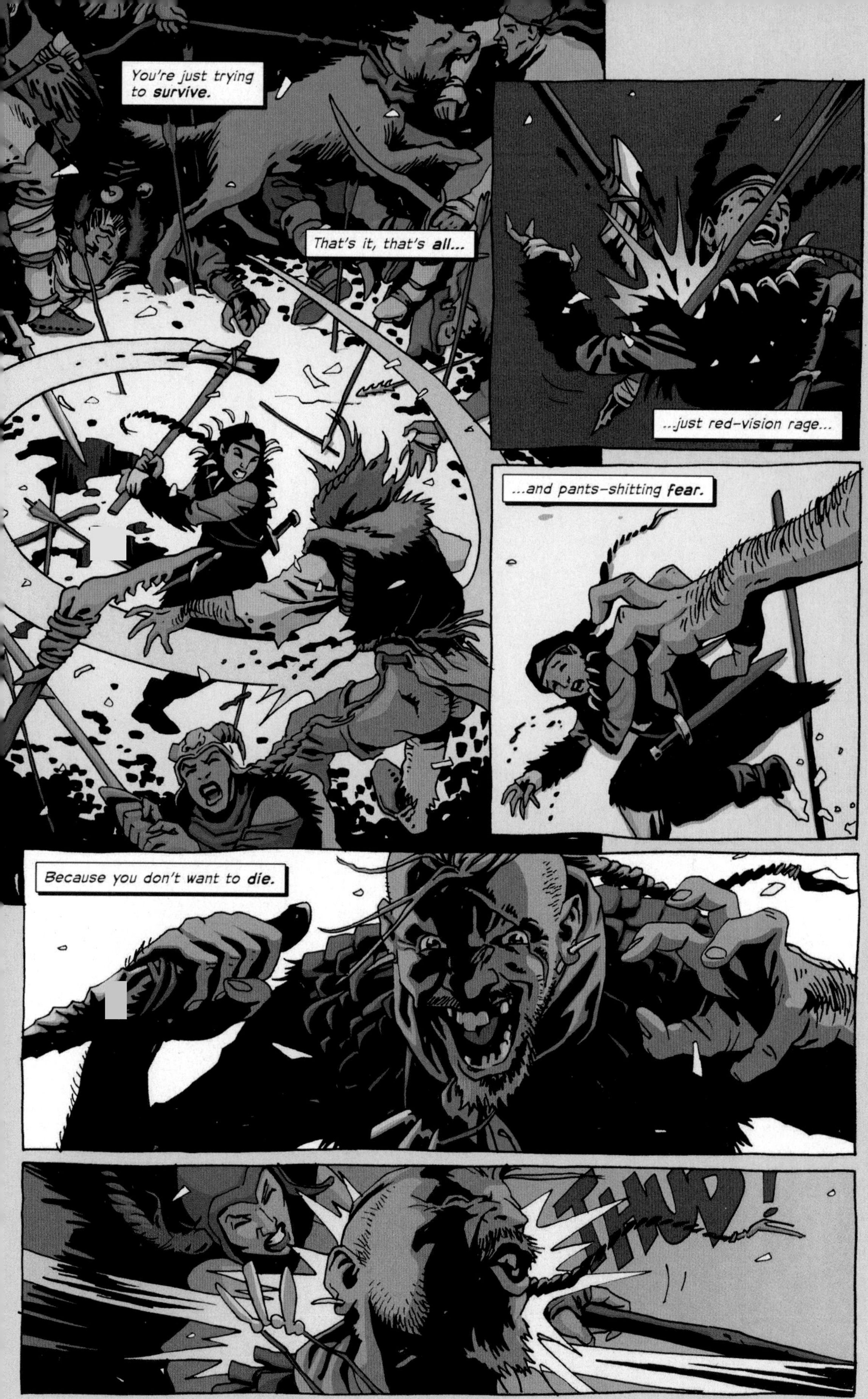
You're just trying to survive.
That's it, that's all...
...just red-vision rage...
...and pants-shitting fear.
Because you don't want to die.
THUD!

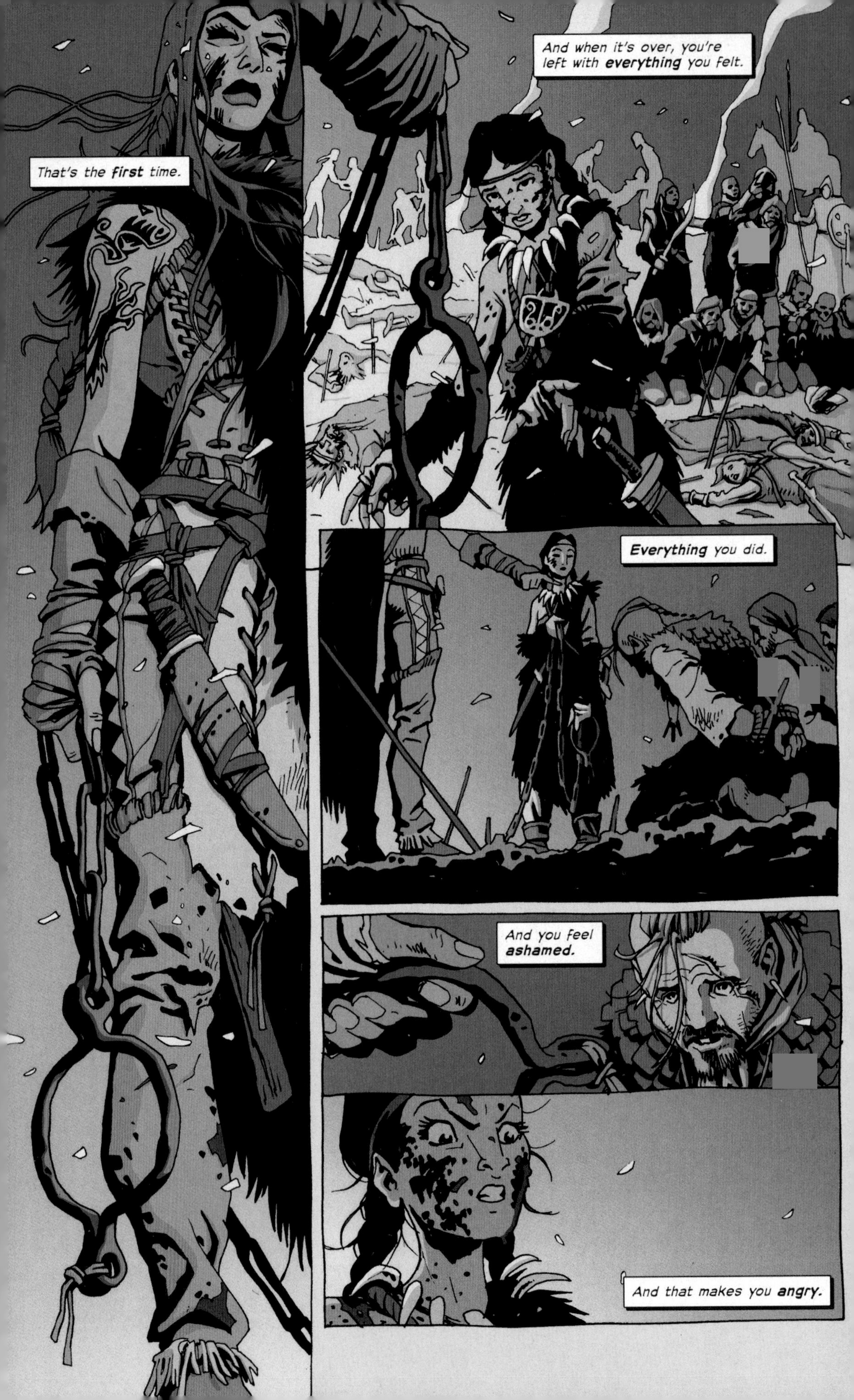
That's the **first** time.
And when it's over, you're left with **everything** you felt.
Everything you did.
And you feel **ashamed.**
And that makes you **angry.**

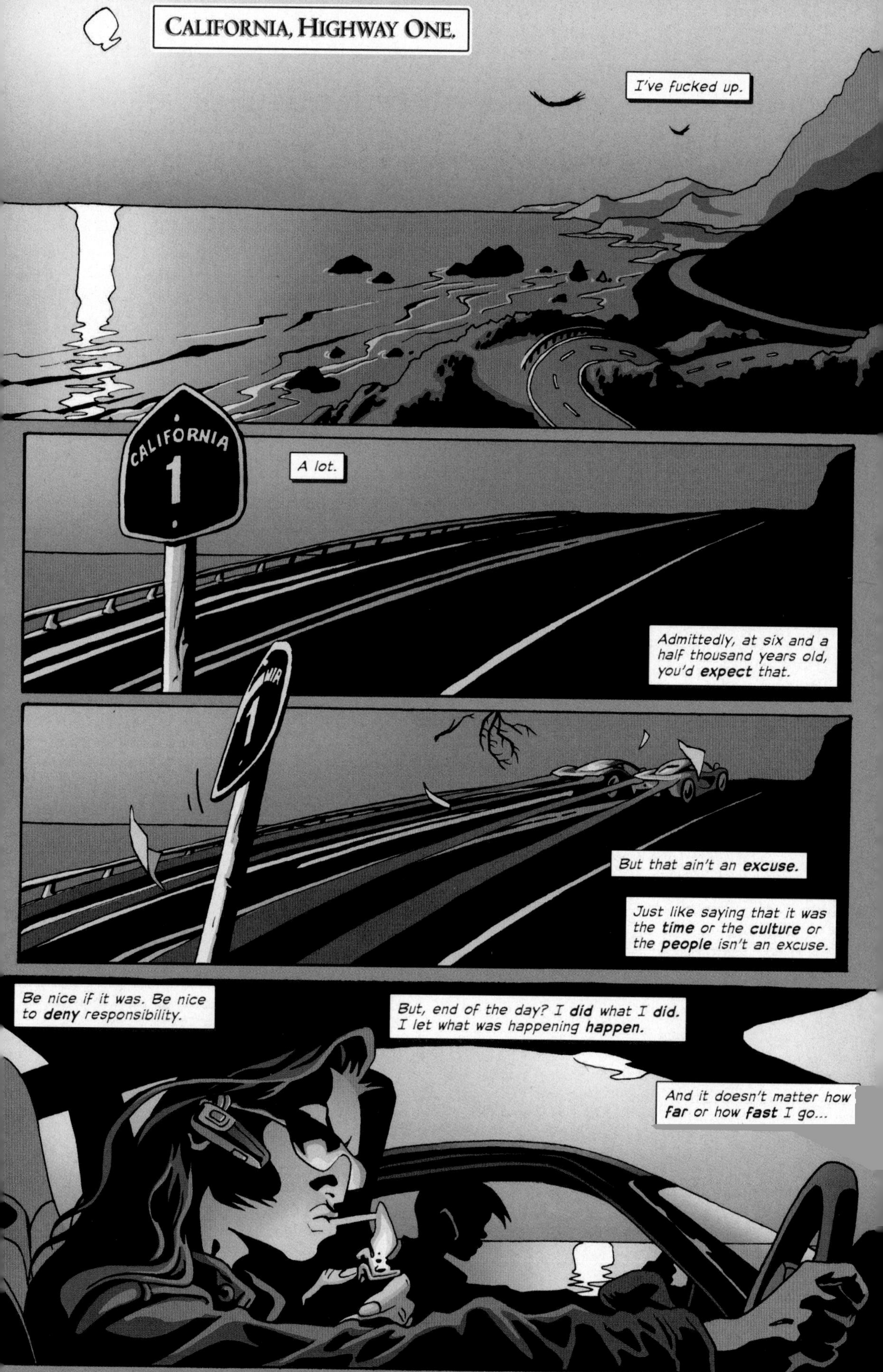
CALIFORNIA, HIGHWAY ONE.
I've fucked up.
CALIFORNIA
1
A lot.
Admittedly, at six and a half thousand years old, you'd expect that.
But that ain't an excuse.
Just like saying that it was the time or the culture or the people isn't an excuse.
Be nice if it was. Be nice to deny responsibility.
But, end of the day? I did what I did. I let what was happening happen.
And it doesn't matter how far or how fast I go...

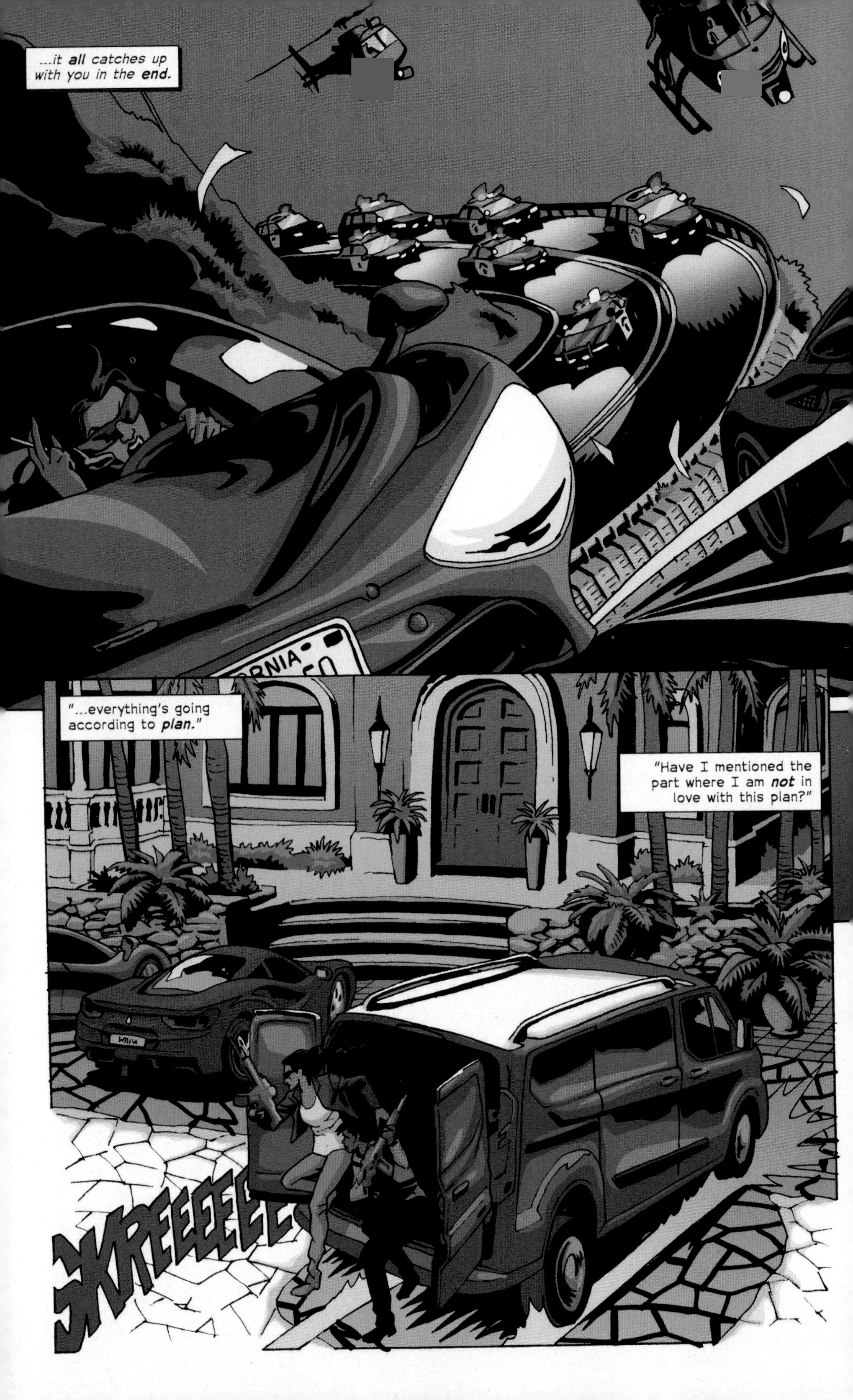
...it *all* catches up with you in the *end.*
"...everything's going according to *plan.*"
"Have I mentioned the part where I am *not* in love with this plan?"

Just **had** to steal the **cars**, didn't you, Andy?

Yeah, I don't think it's the **cars** that did it, Nile.

Just relax...

"Several times, yes, Nile."

POP

KRAK

KRAK

POP

KRAK

BOMM

POPOP

BUDDA

BUDDA

ABUDDA

BUDDA

BUDDA BU

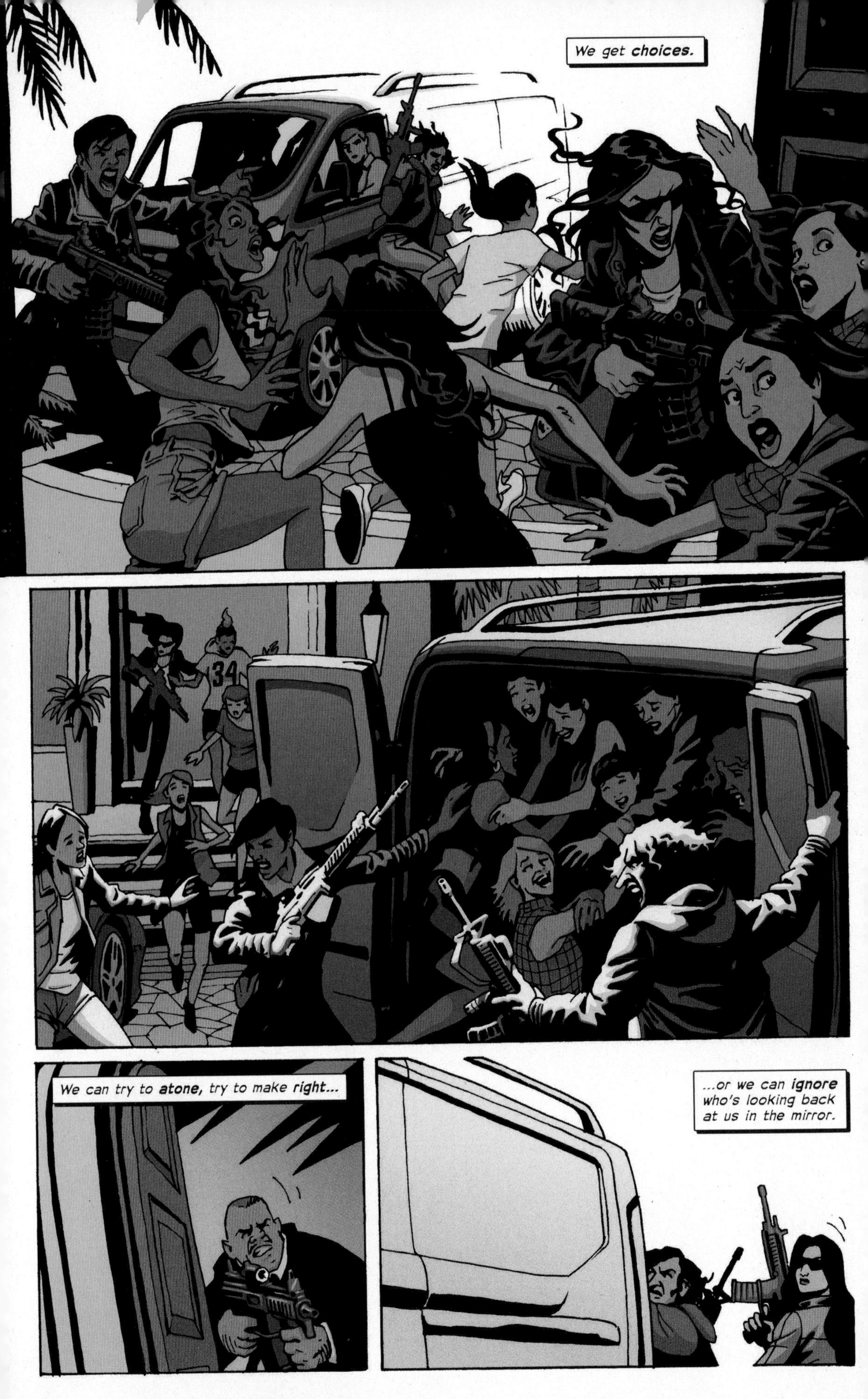
We get choices.
34
We can try to atone, try to make right...
...or we can ignore who's looking back at us in the mirror.

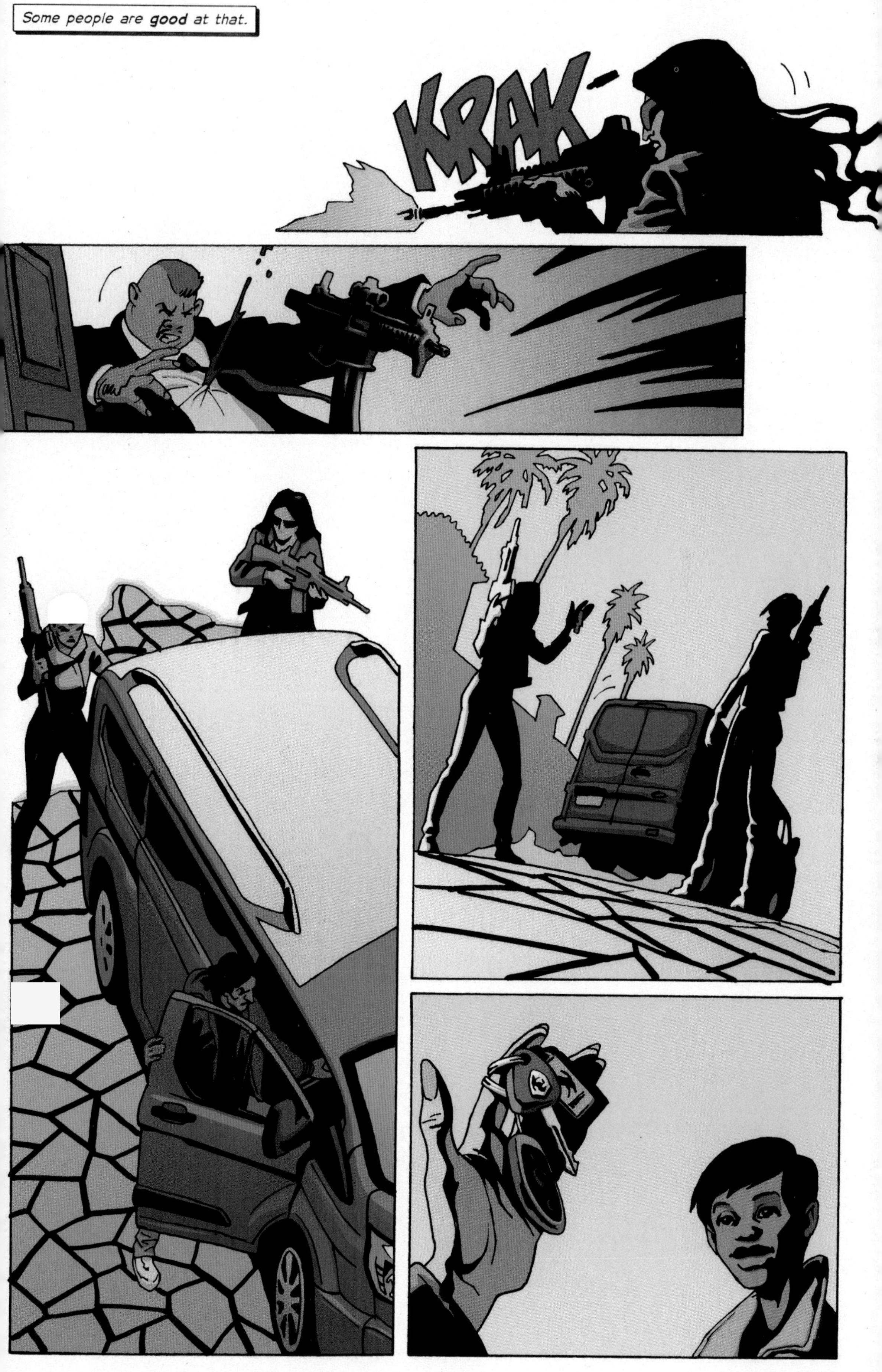
Some people are **good** at that.
KRAK

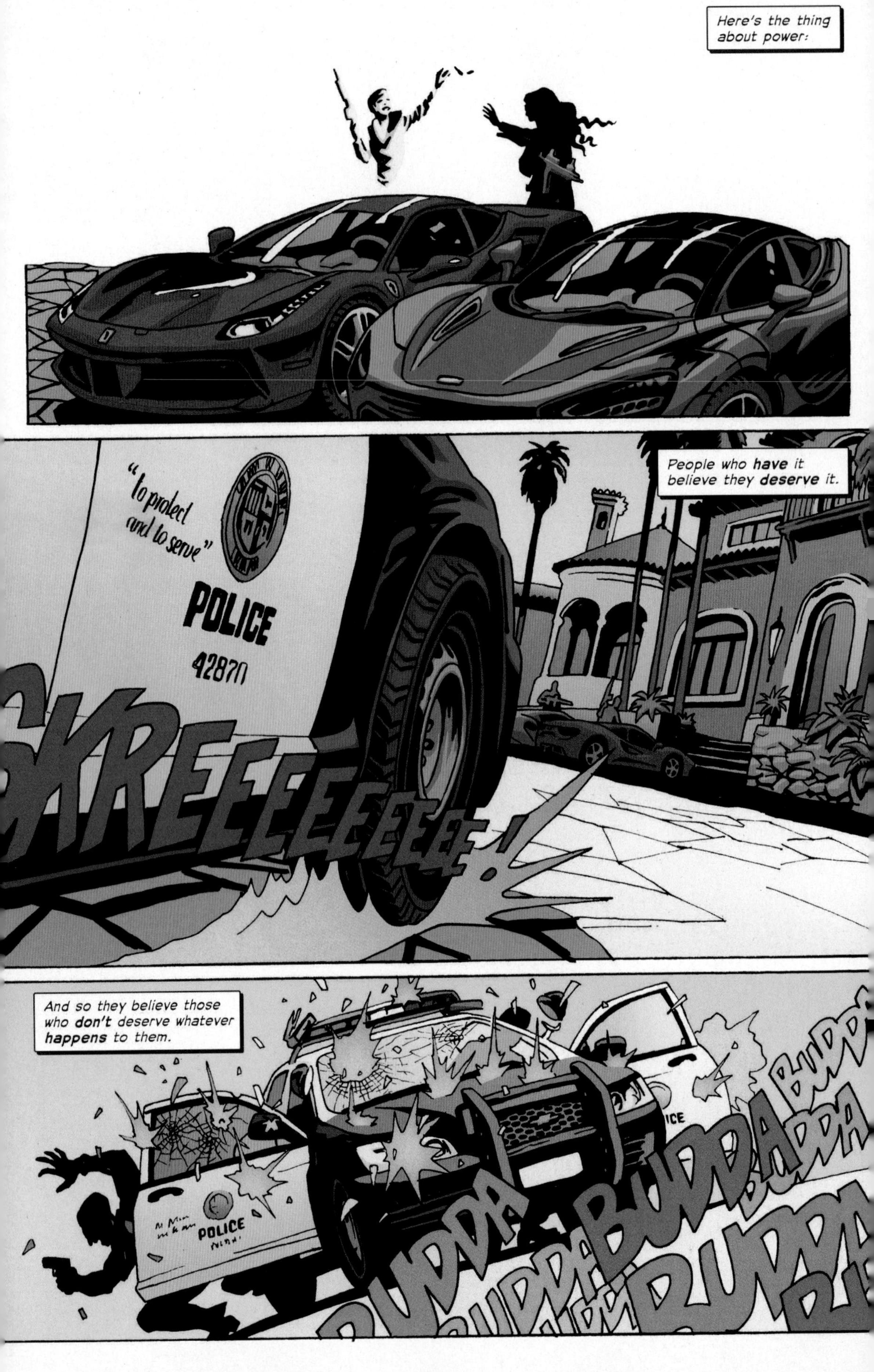
Here's the thing about power:
"to protect and to serve"
POLICE
42870
People who **have** it believe they **deserve** it.
And so they believe those who **don't** deserve whatever **happens** to them.
POLICE

People who **have** power will do **anything** to **keep** it.

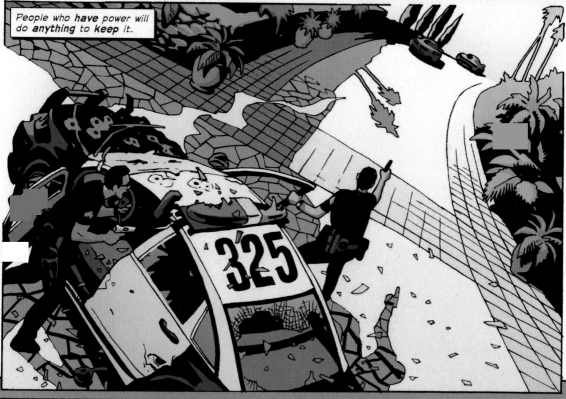

And they'll do whatever they can to **convince** you that you're better off that way.

How many you think are following us?

It's **not** the ones **behind** us I'm worried about...

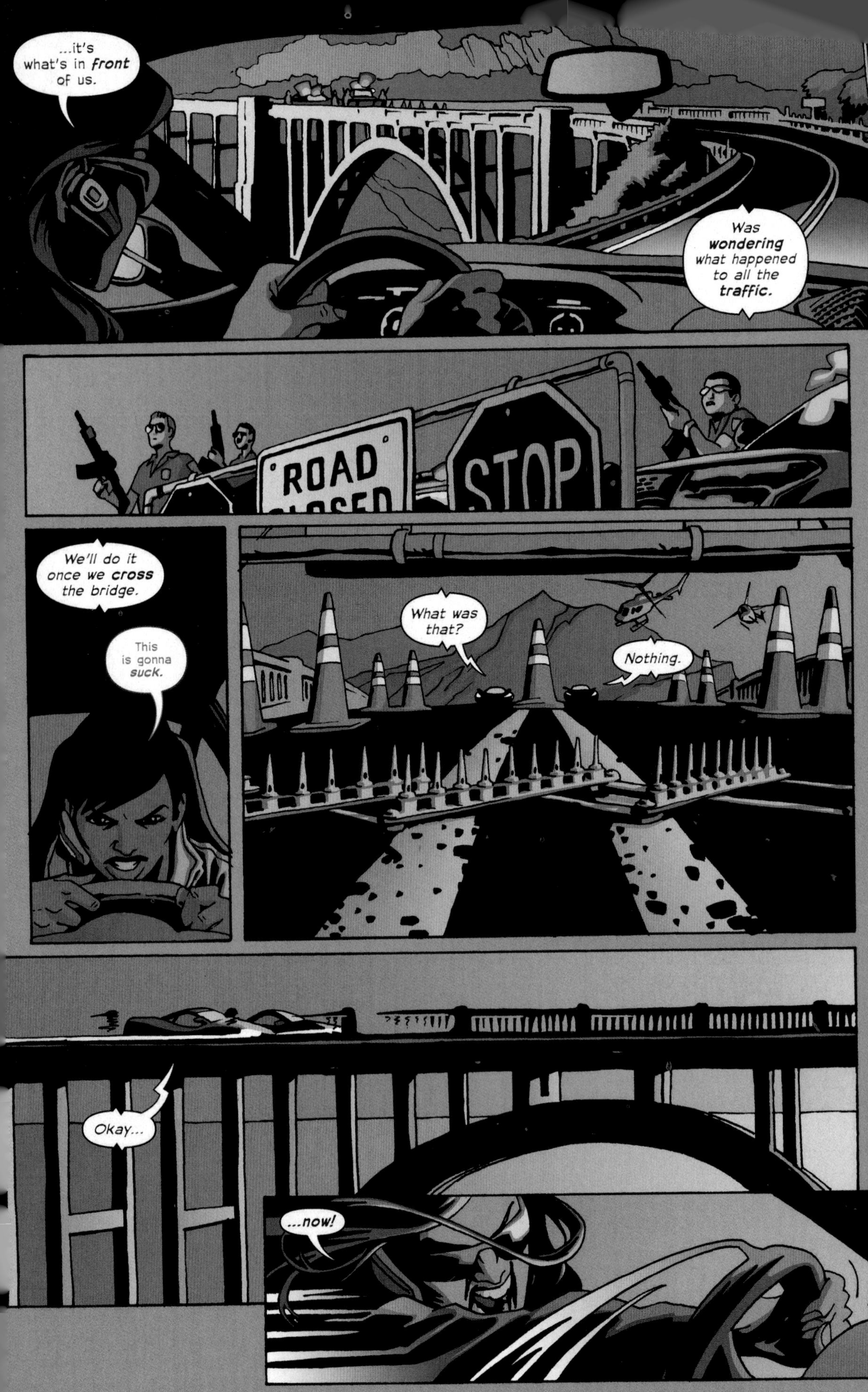
...it's what's in *front* of us.
Was *wondering* what happened to all the *traffic.*
ROAD
STOP
We'll do it once we *cross* the bridge.
This is gonna *suck.*
What was that?
Nothing.
Okay...
...now!

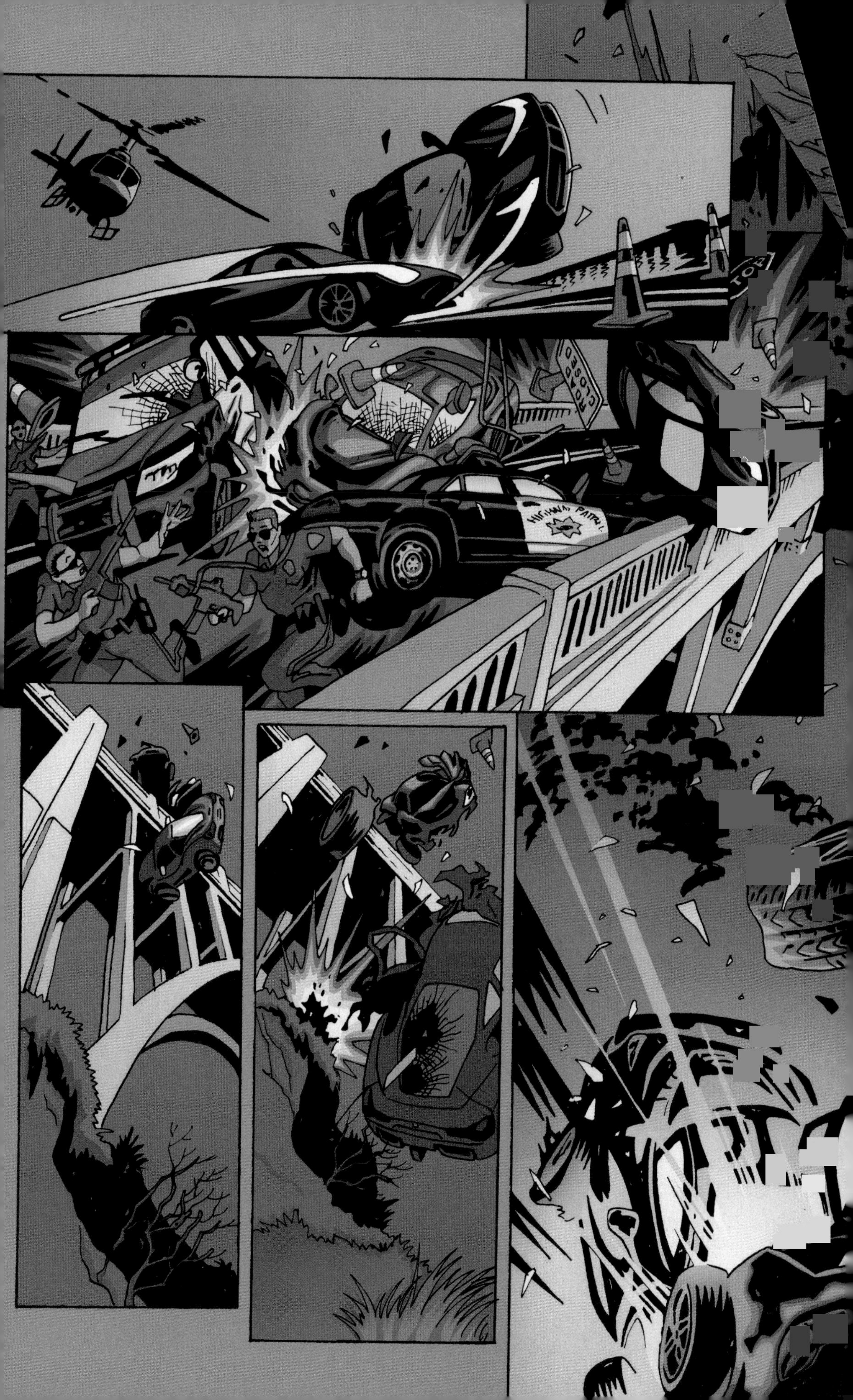
ROAD CLOSED

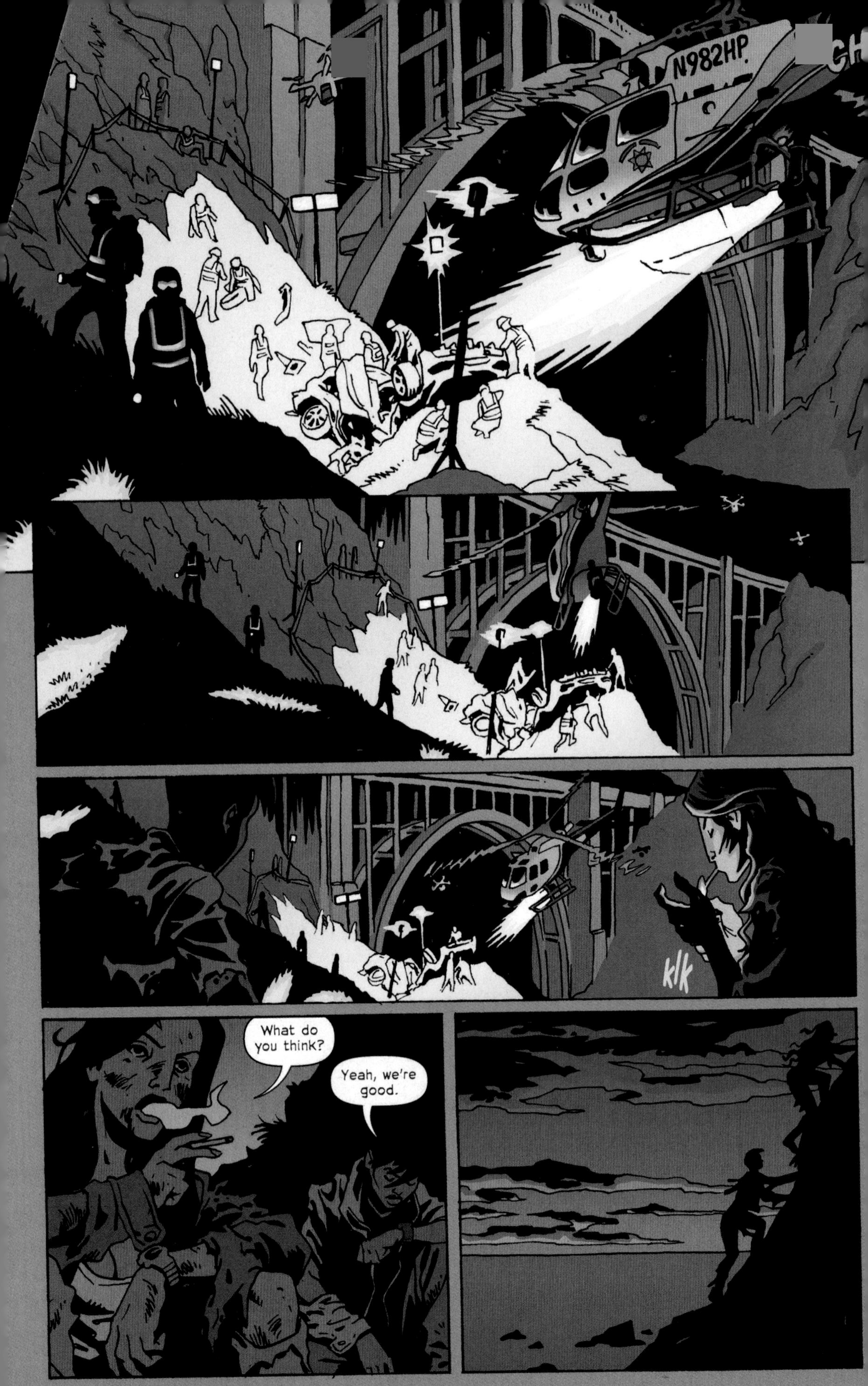
N982HP
klk
What do you think?
Yeah, we're good.

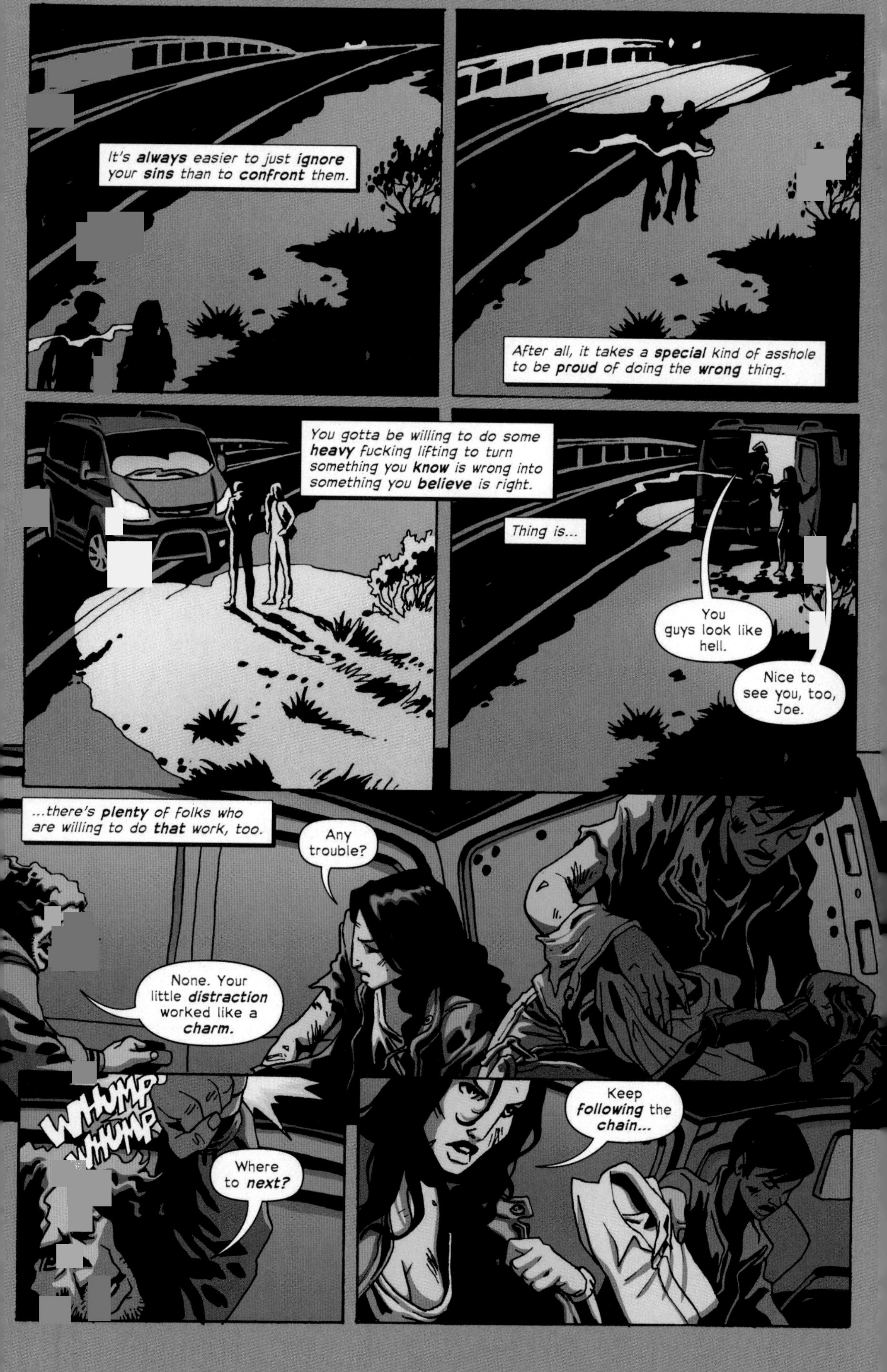
It's always easier to just ignore your sins than to confront them.
After all, it takes a special kind of asshole to be proud of doing the wrong thing.
You gotta be willing to do some heavy fucking lifting to turn something you know is wrong into something you believe is right.
Thing is...
You guys look like hell.
Nice to see you, too, Joe.
...there's plenty of folks who are willing to do that work, too.
Any trouble?
None. Your little distraction worked like a charm.
WHUMP! WHUMP!
Where to next?
Keep following the chain...

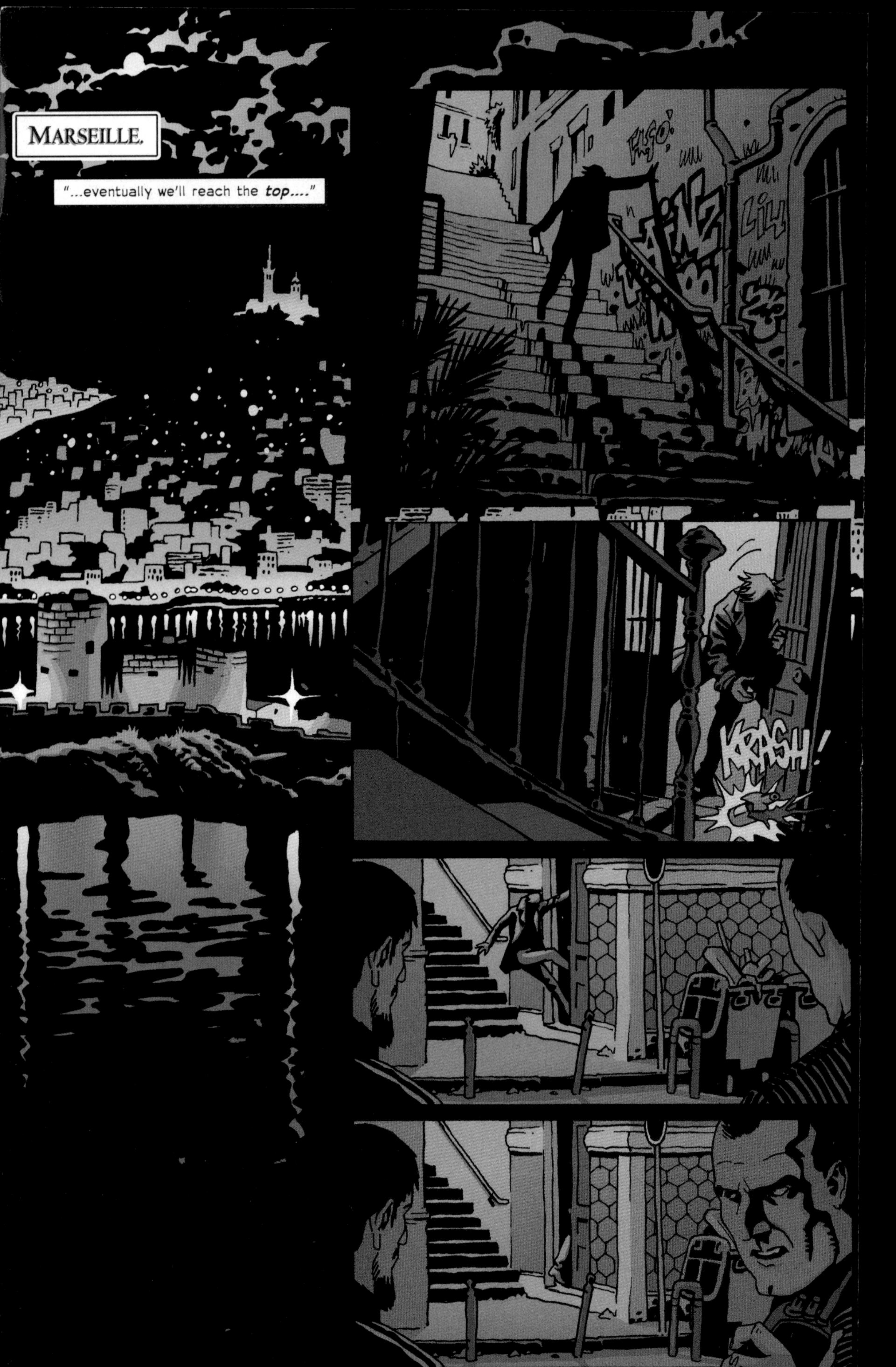
MARSEILLE.
"...eventually we'll reach the *top*...."
KRASH!

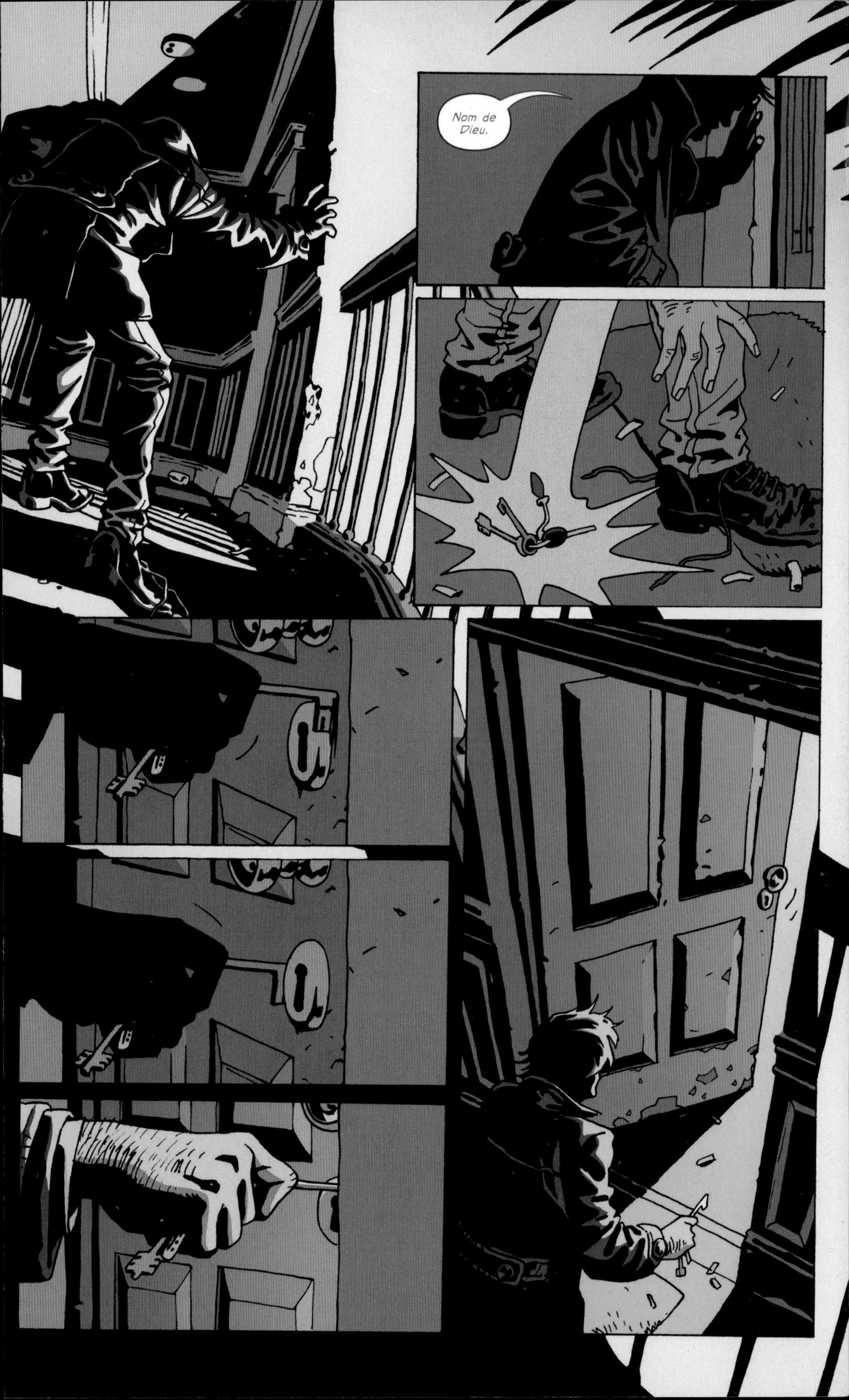
Nom de
Dieu.

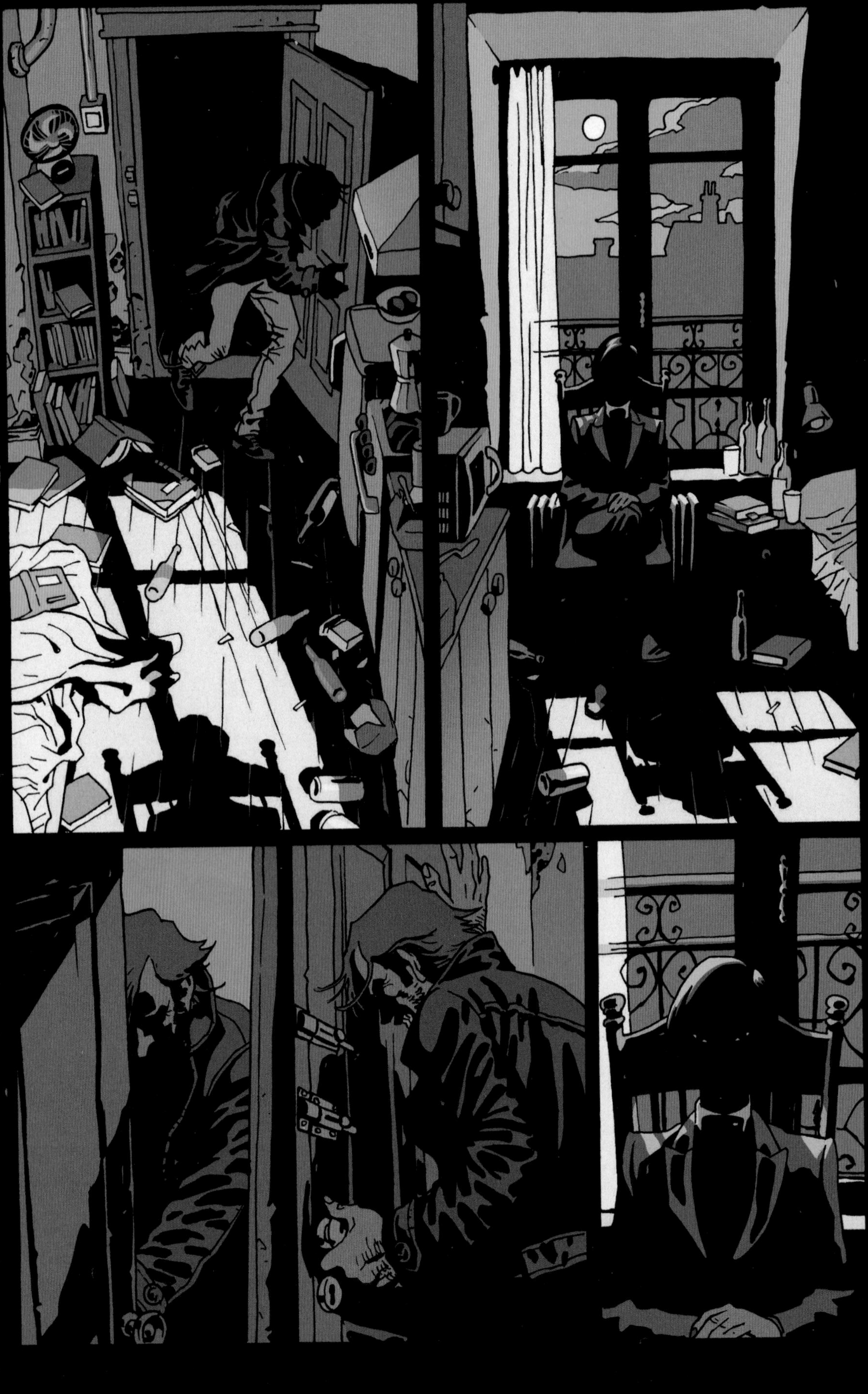

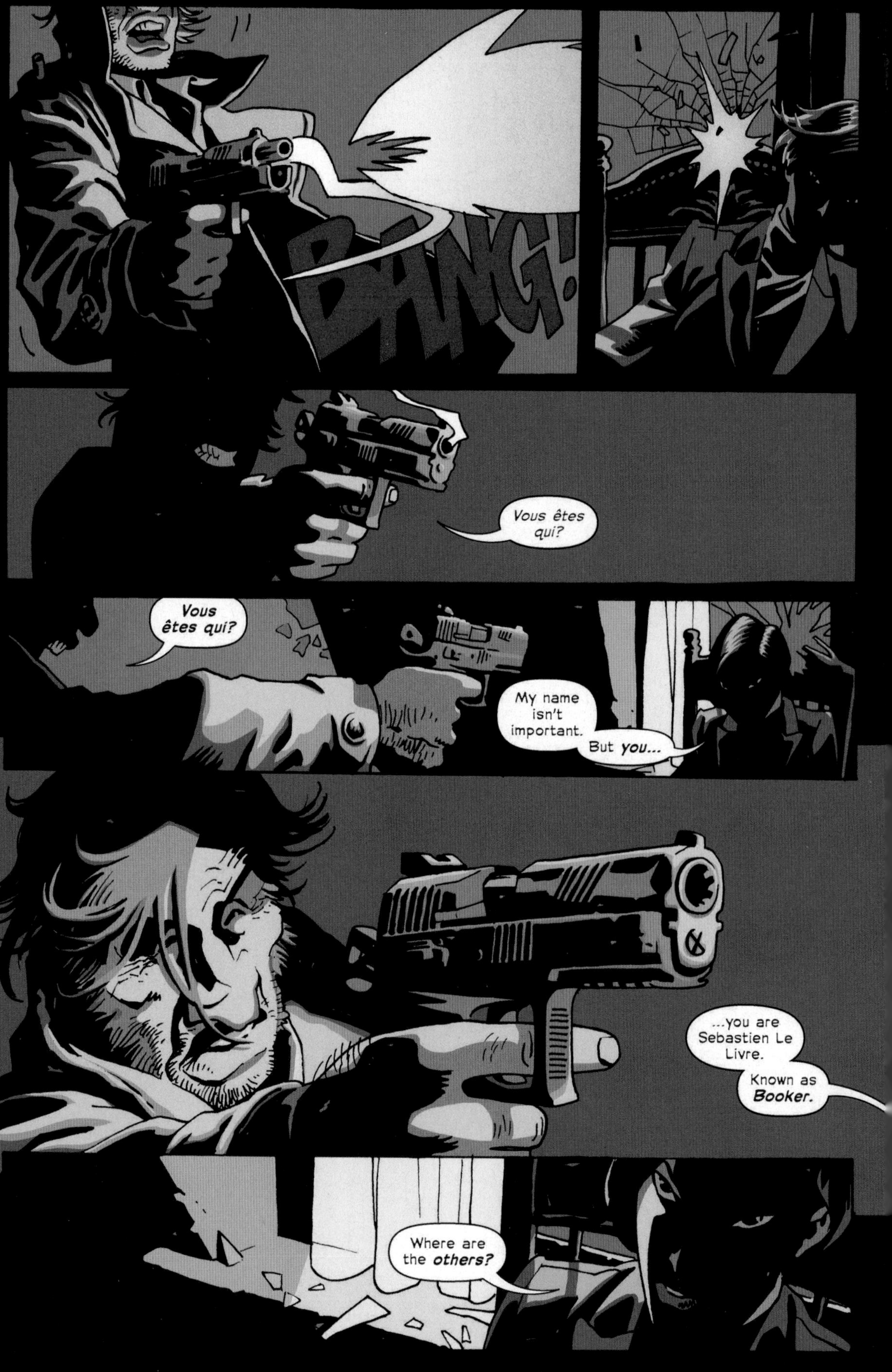
BANG!
Vous êtes qui?
Vous êtes qui?
My name isn't important.
But you...
...you are Sebastien Le Livre.
Known as Booker.
Where are the others?

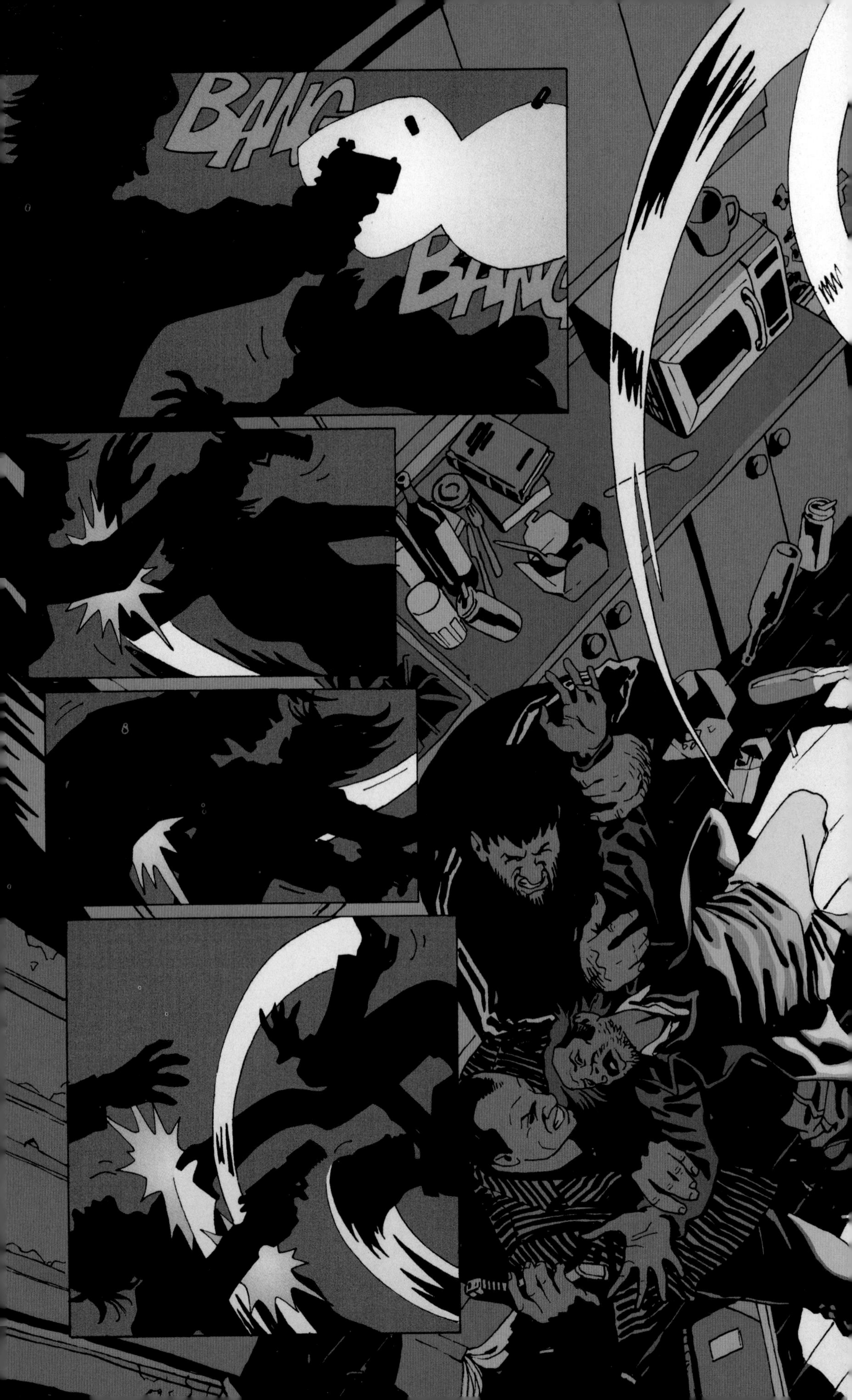
BANG
BANG

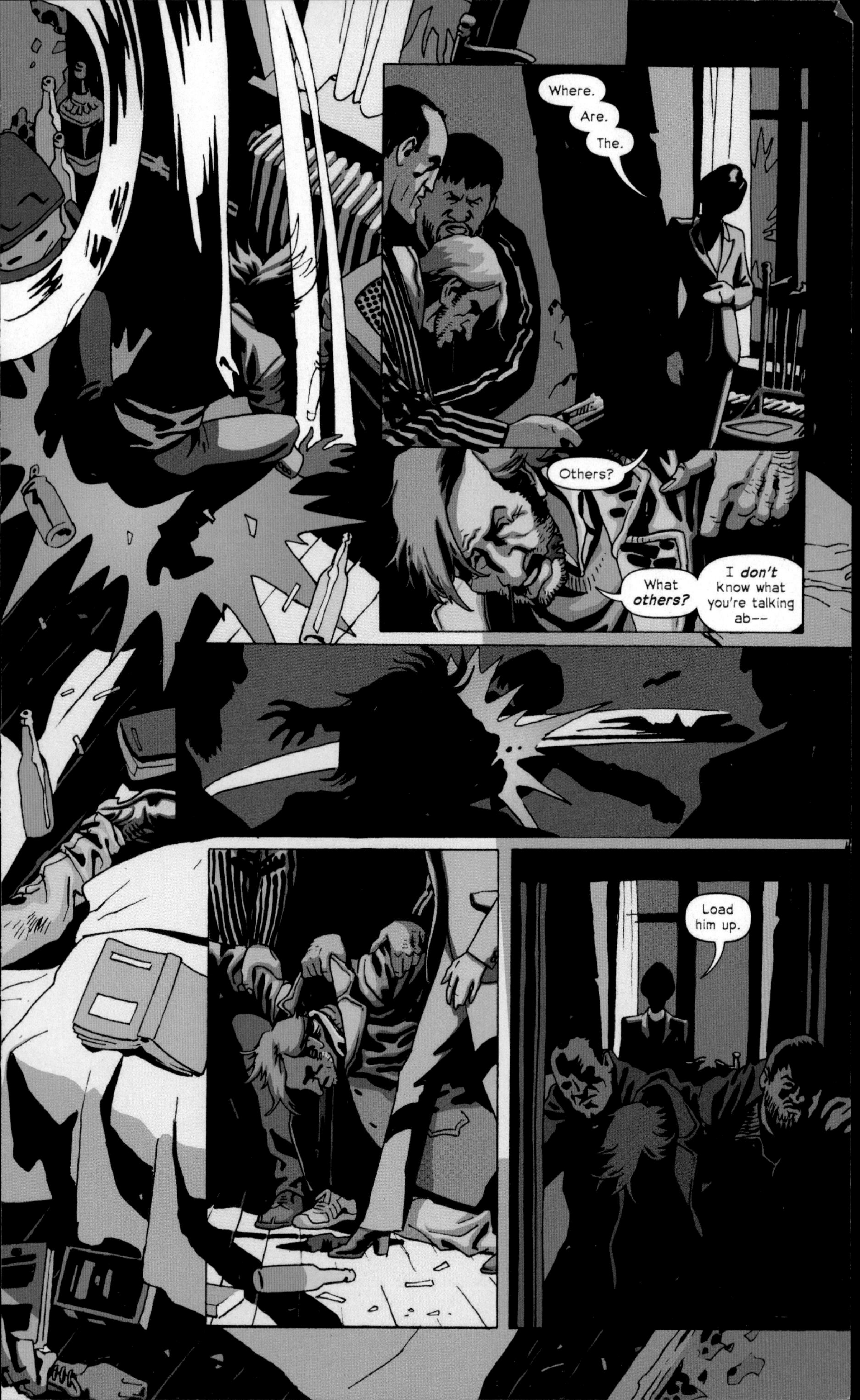
Where.
Are.
The.
Others?
What *others?*
I *don't* know what you're talking ab--
Load him up.

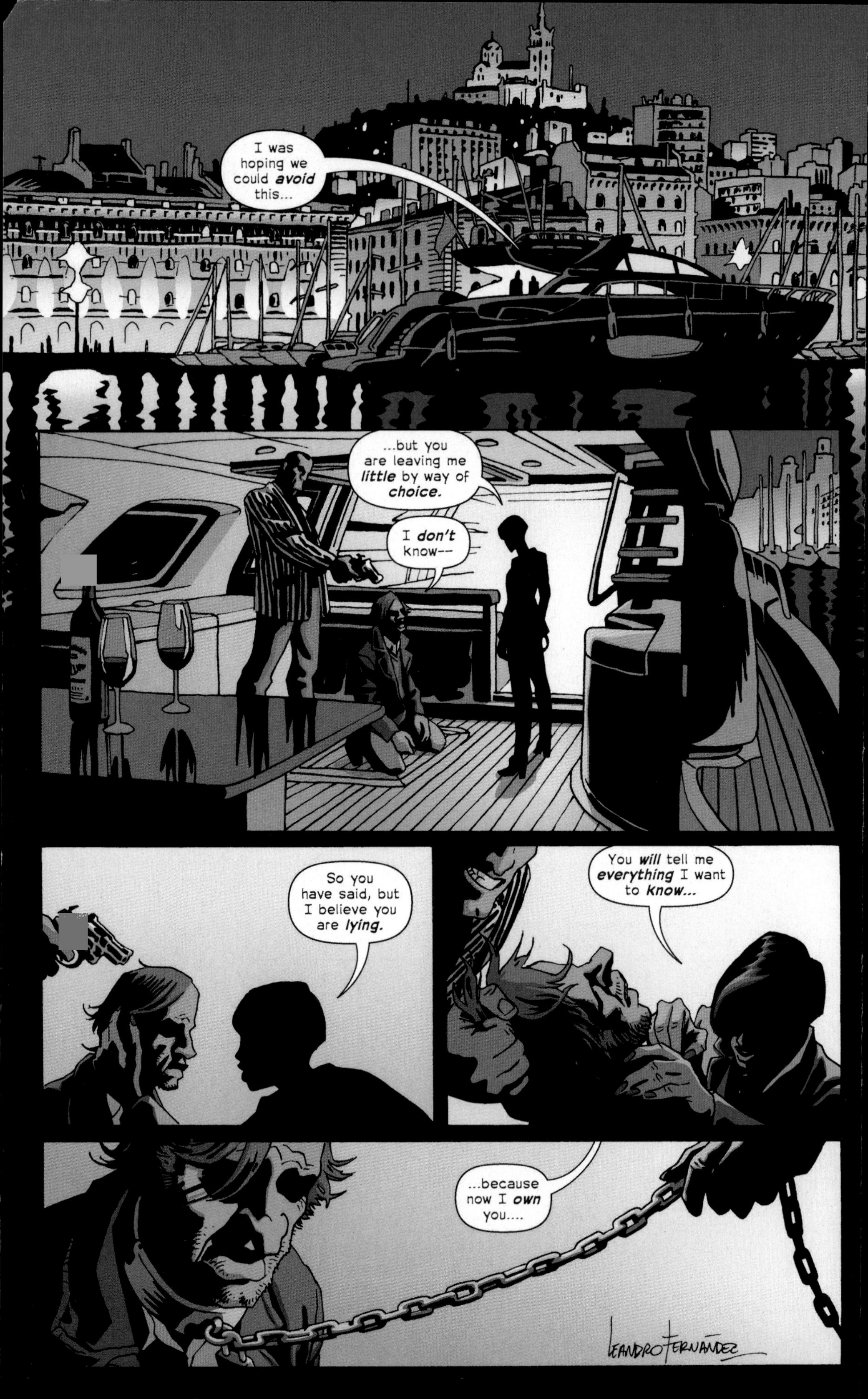
I was hoping we could *avoid* this...
...but you are leaving me *little* by way of *choice.*
I *don't* know--
So you have said, but I believe you are *lying.*
You *will* tell me *everything* I want to *know...*
...because now I *own* you....
LEANDRO FERNÁNDEZ

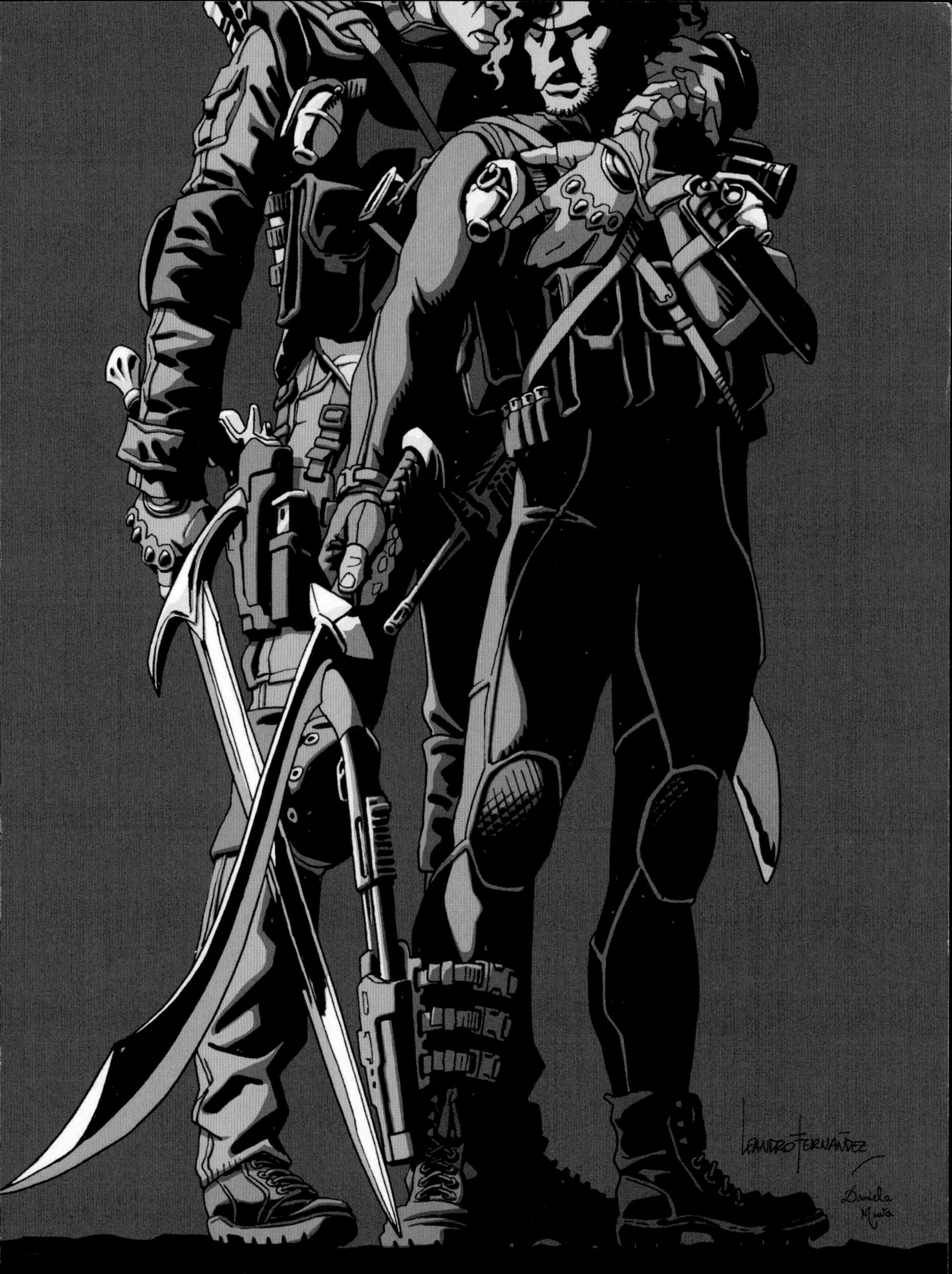
LEANDRO FERNÁNDEZ
Daniela Miwa

CHAPTER TWO

"EVIL BEGINS WHEN YOU BEGIN TO TREAT PEOPLE AS THINGS."

~SIR TERRY PRATCHETT, I SHALL WEAR MIDNIGHT

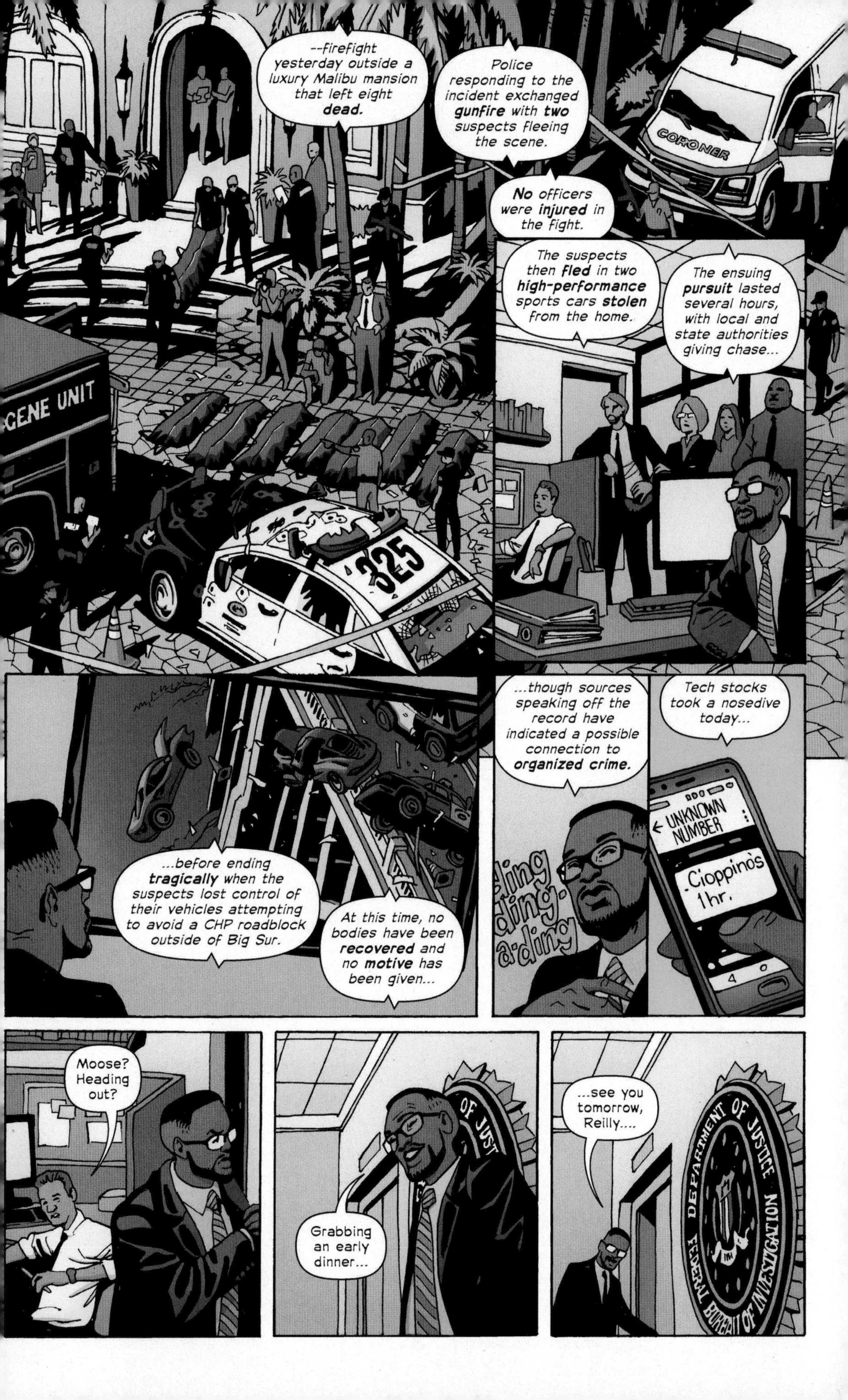

--firefight yesterday outside a luxury Malibu mansion that left eight **dead.**
Police responding to the incident exchanged **gunfire** with **two** suspects fleeing the scene.
No officers were **injured** in the fight.
CORONER
SCENE UNIT
325
The suspects then **fled** in two **high-performance** sports cars **stolen** from the home.
The ensuing **pursuit** lasted several hours, with local and state authorities giving chase...
...before ending **tragically** when the suspects lost control of their vehicles attempting to avoid a CHP roadblock outside of Big Sur.
At this time, no bodies have been **recovered** and no **motive** has been given...
...though sources speaking off the record have indicated a possible connection to **organized crime.**
Tech stocks took a nosedive today...
ding ding-a-ding
← UNKNOWN NUMBER
Cioppino's 1hr.
Moose? Heading out?
Grabbing an early dinner...
...see you tomorrow, Reilly....
DEPARTMENT OF JUSTICE
FEDERAL BUREAU OF INVESTIGATION

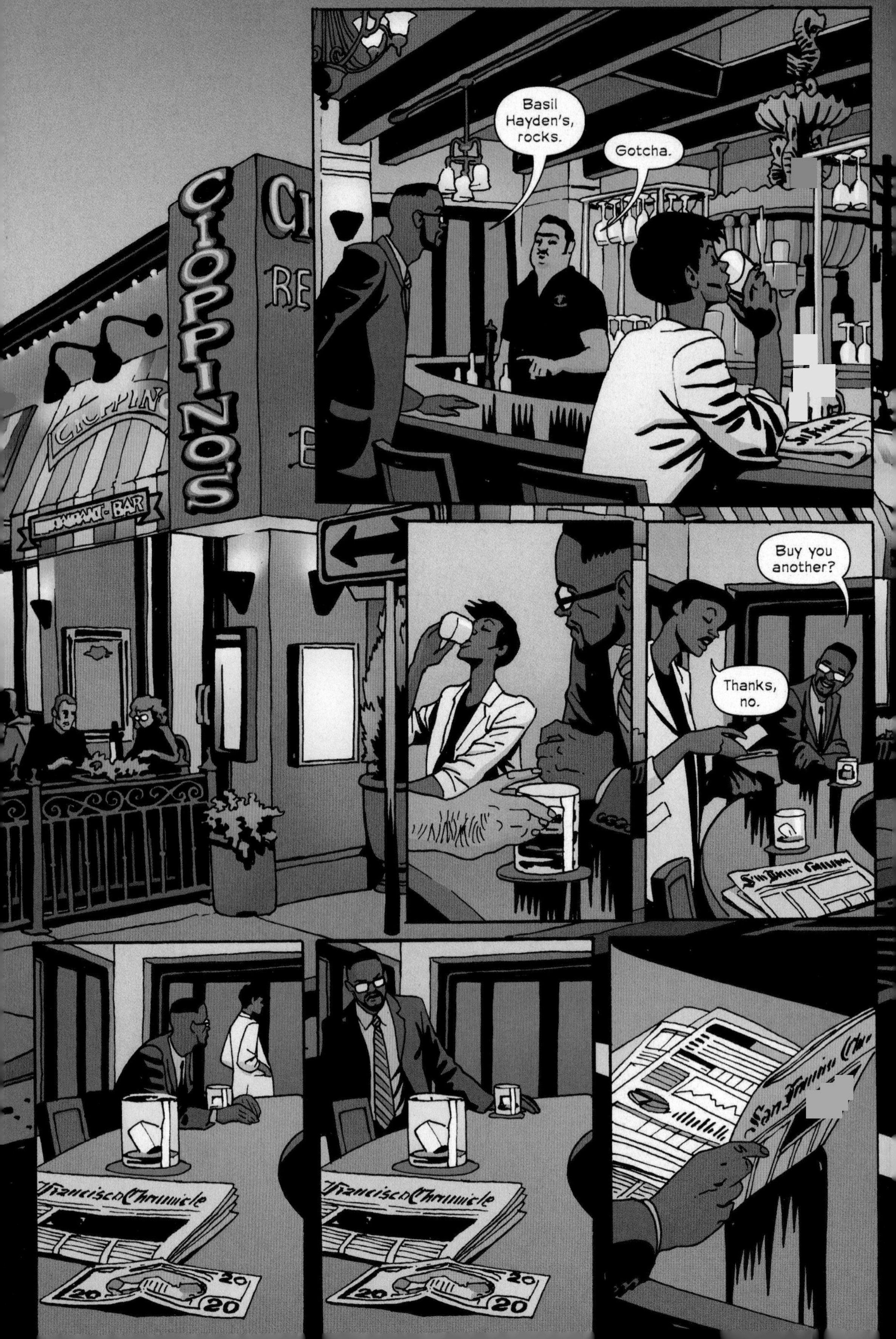
CIOPPINO'S
BAR
Basil Hayden's, rocks.
Gotcha.
Buy you another?
Thanks, no.
Francisco Chronicle
Francisco Chronicle

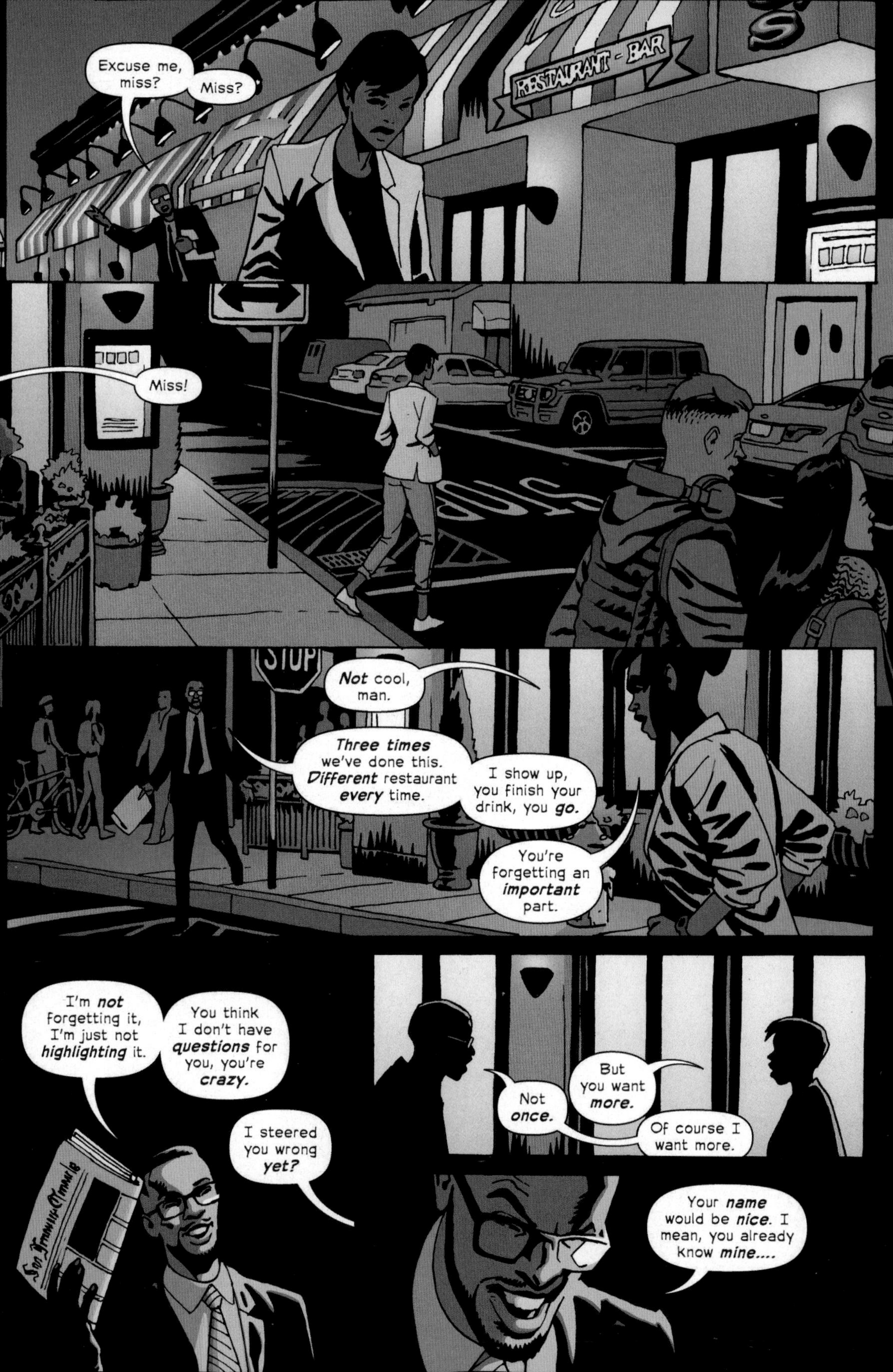
Excuse me, miss?
Miss?
RESTAURANT - BAR
Miss!
STOP
Not cool, man.
Three times we've done this. Different restaurant every time.
I show up, you finish your drink, you go.
You're forgetting an important part.
I'm not forgetting it, I'm just not highlighting it.
You think I don't have questions for you, you're crazy.
I steered you wrong yet?
Not once.
But you want more.
Of course I want more.
Your name would be nice. I mean, you already know mine....

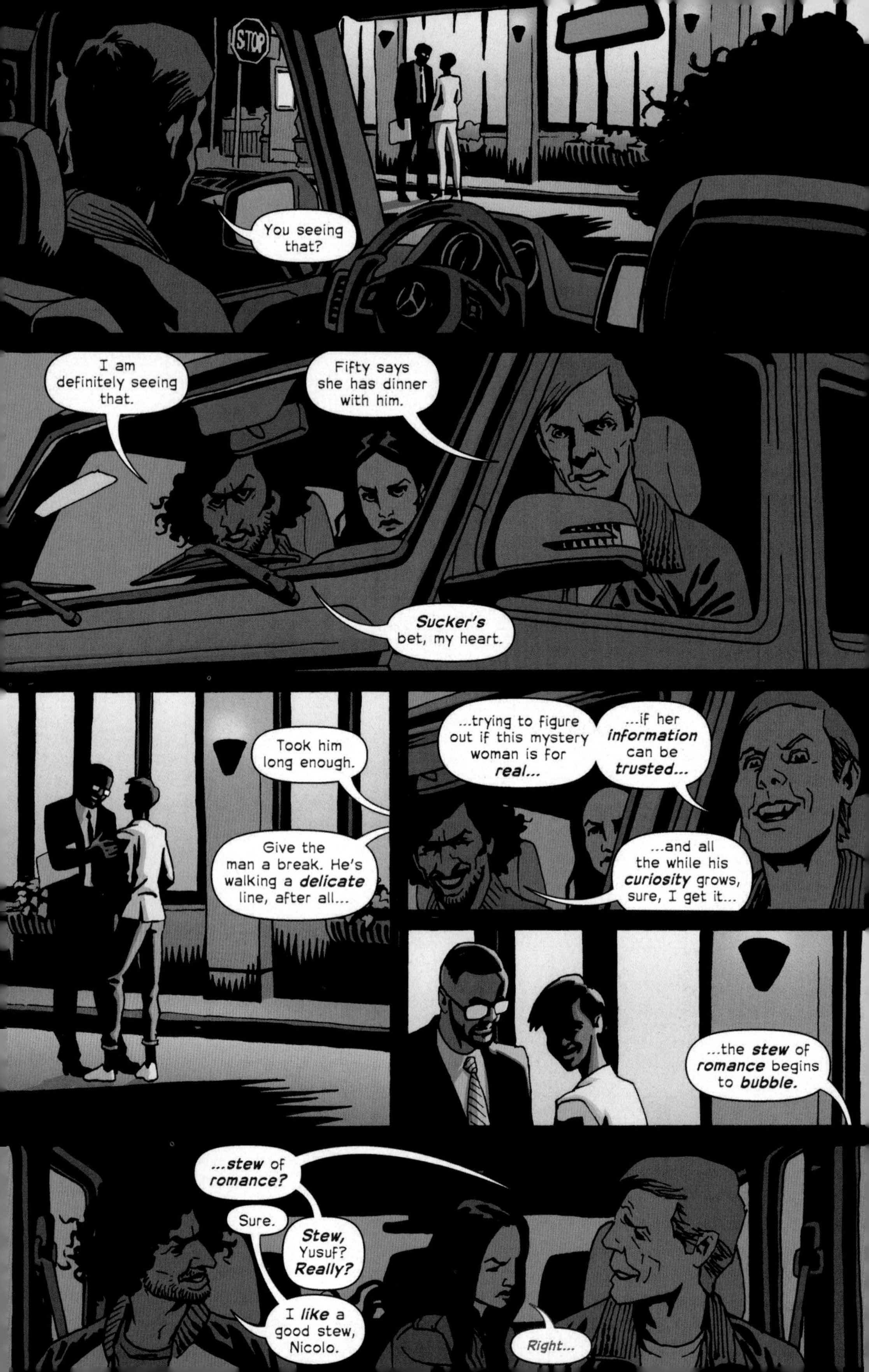

You seeing that?
I am definitely seeing that.
Fifty says she has dinner with him.
Sucker's bet, my heart.
Took him long enough.
Give the man a break. He's walking a *delicate* line, after all...
...trying to figure out if this mystery woman is for *real...*
...if her *information* can be *trusted...*
...and all the while his *curiosity* grows, sure, I get it...
...the *stew* of *romance* begins to *bubble.*
...stew of *romance?*
Sure.
Stew, Yusuf? *Really?*
I *like* a good stew, Nicolo.
Right...

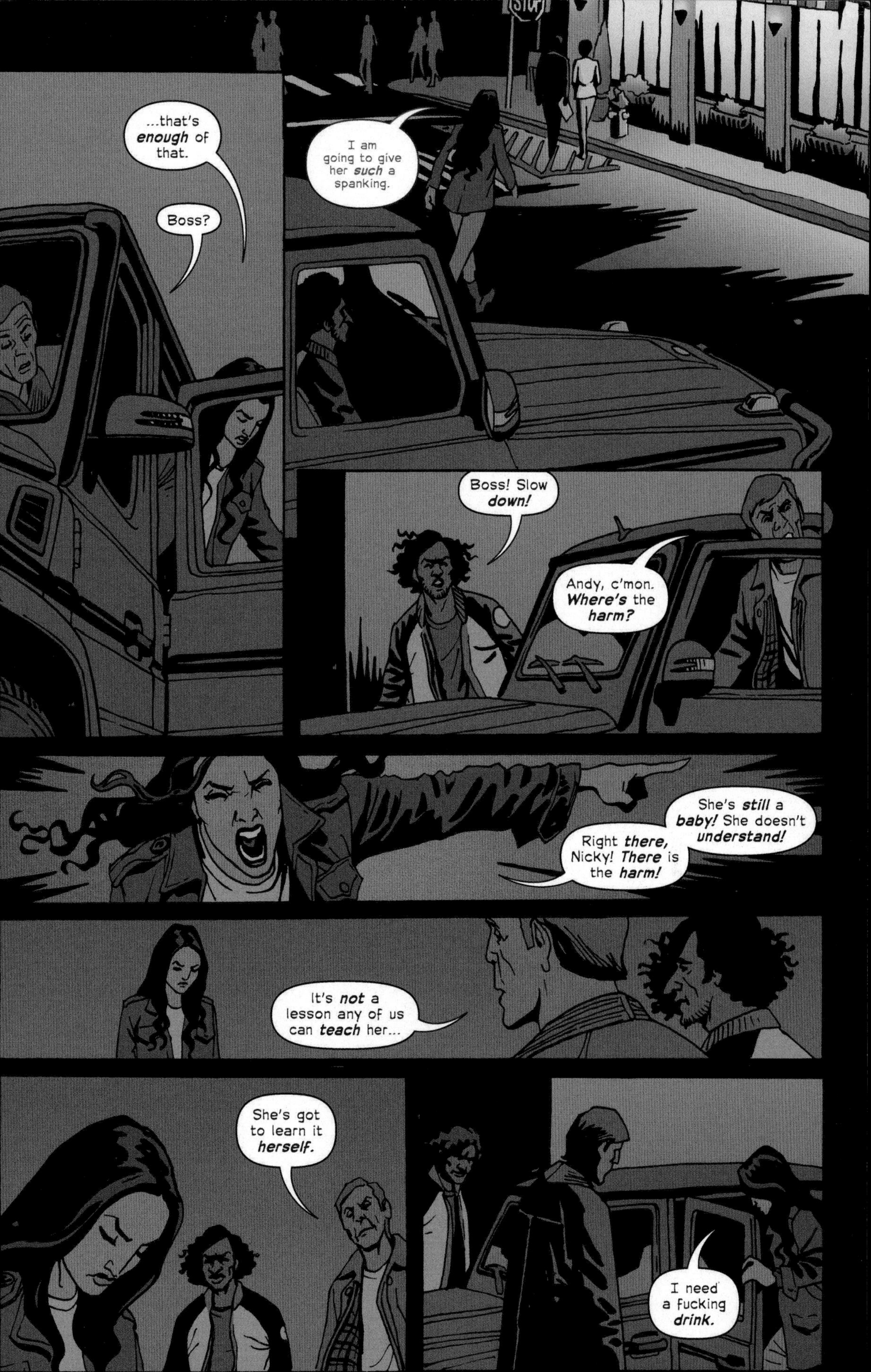
...that's *enough* of that.
Boss?
I am going to give her *such* a spanking.
Boss! Slow *down!*
Andy, c'mon. *Where's* the *harm?*
Right *there,* Nicky! *There* is the *harm!*
She's *still* a *baby!* She doesn't *understand!*
It's *not* a lesson any of us can *teach* her...
She's got to learn it *herself.*
I need a fucking *drink.*

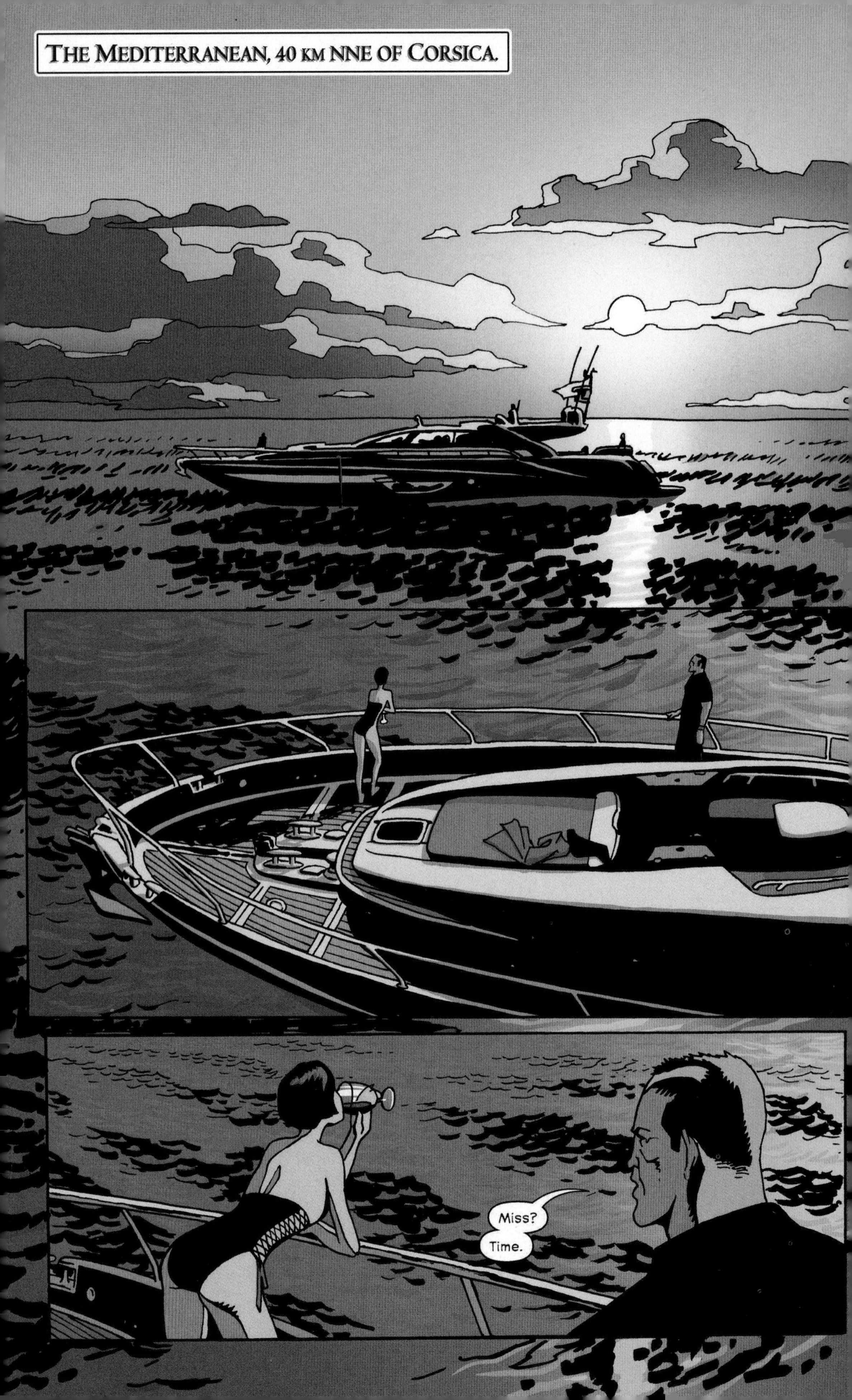
THE MEDITERRANEAN, 40 KM NNE OF CORSICA.
Miss?
Time.

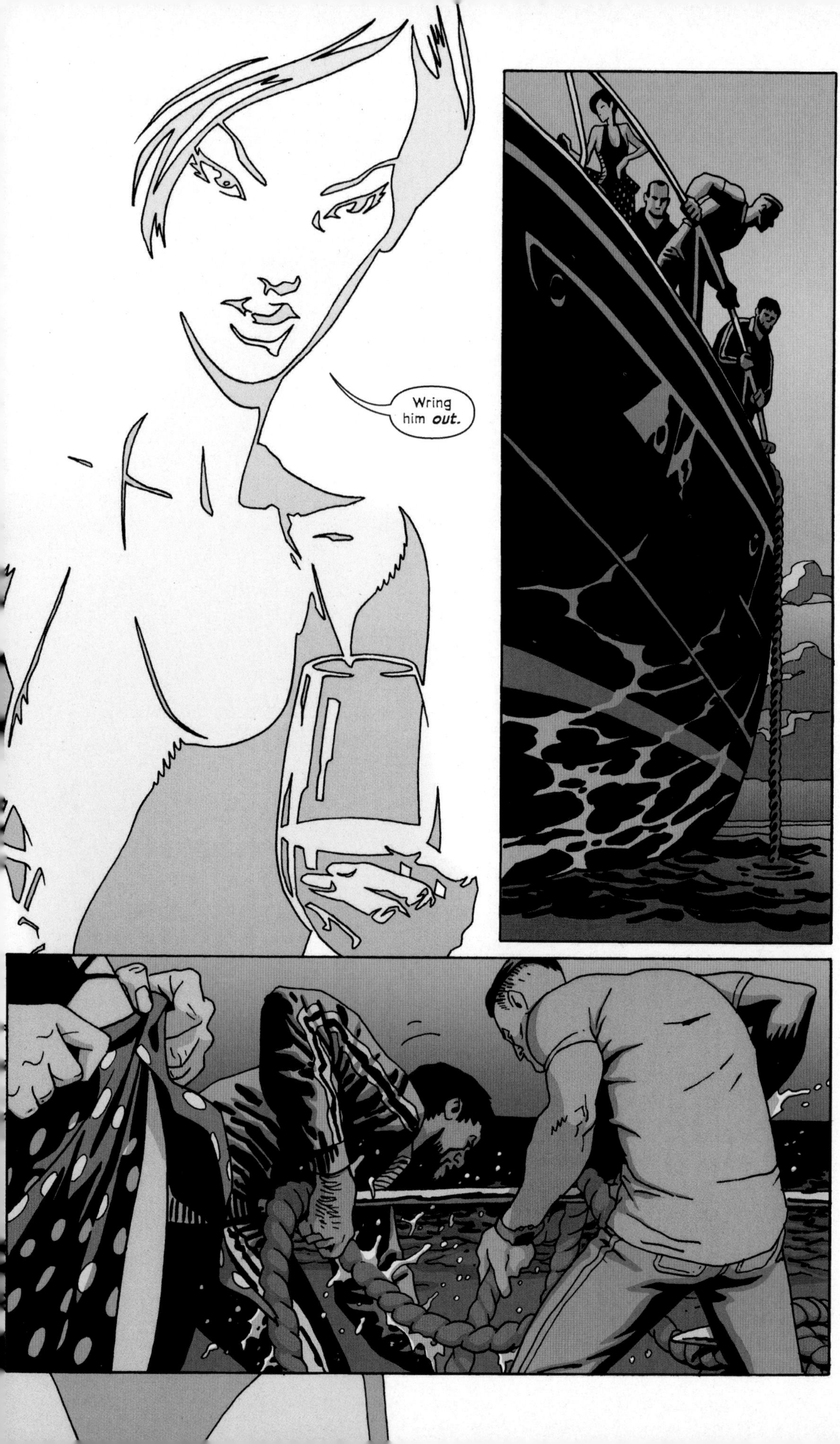
Wring him out.

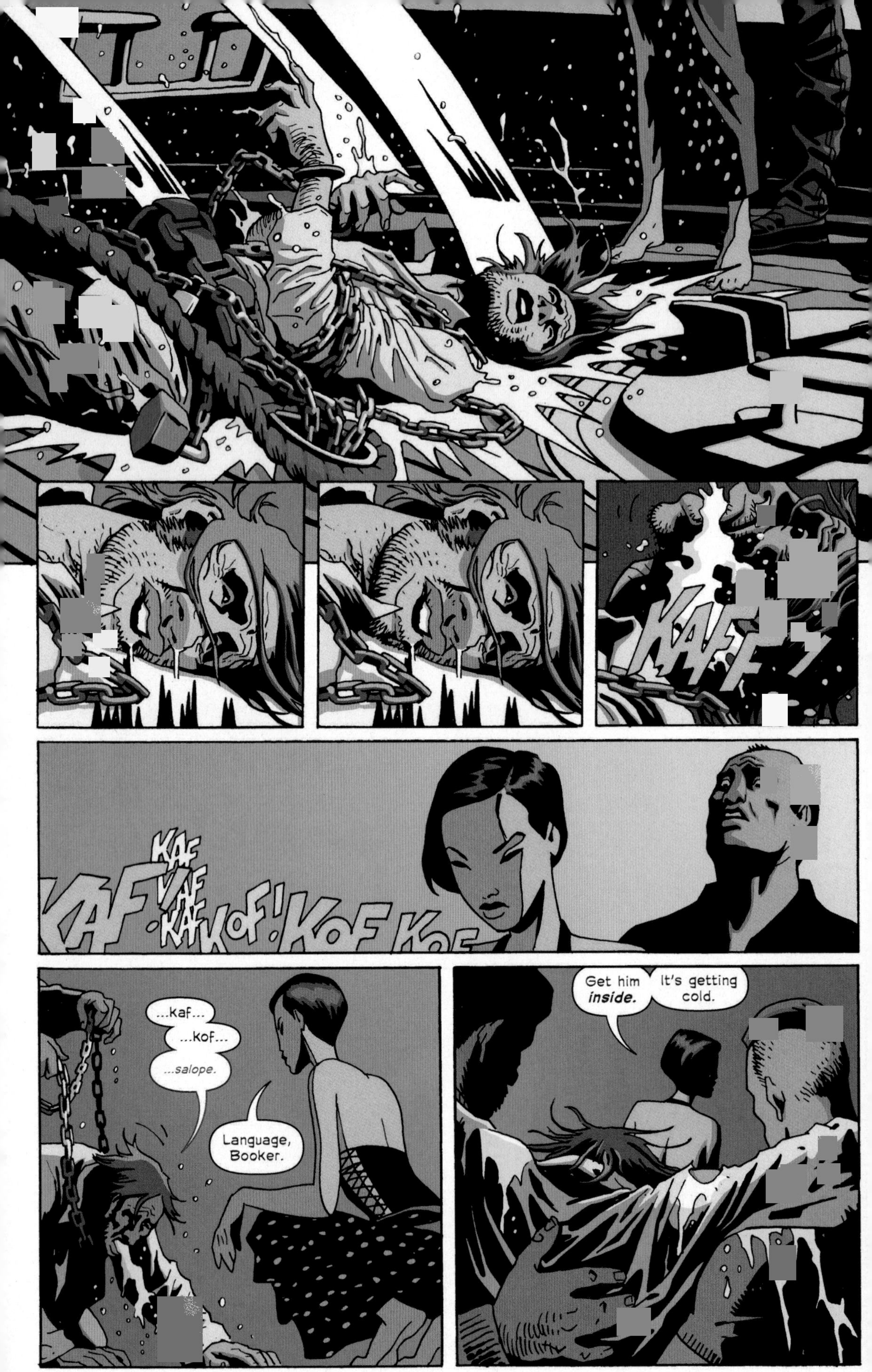
KAFF
KAF
KAF KOF! KOF
...kaf...
...kof...
...salope.
Language, Booker.
Get him *inside.*
It's getting cold.

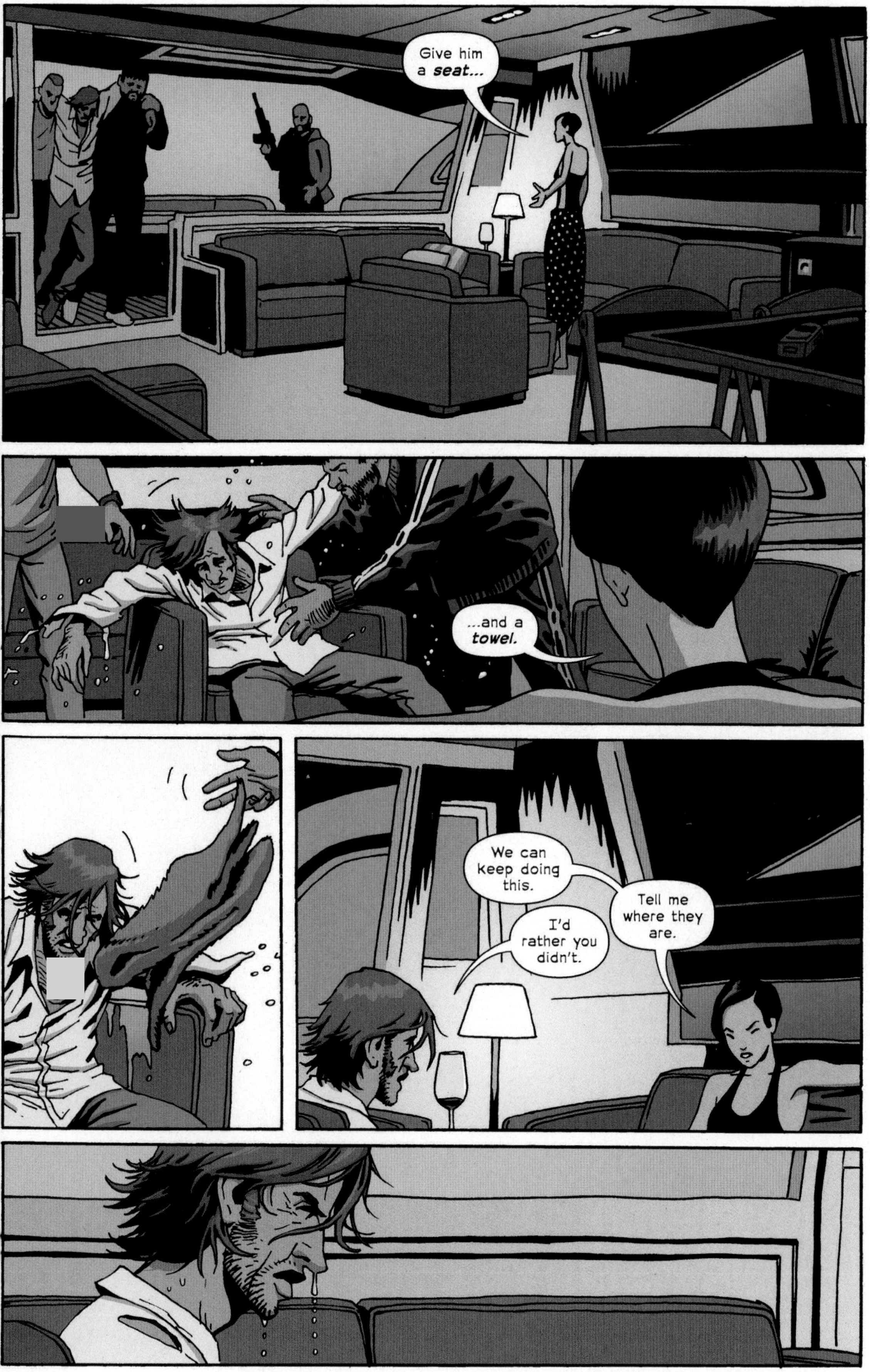
Give him a seat...
...and a towel.
We can keep doing this.
I'd rather you didn't.
Tell me where they are.

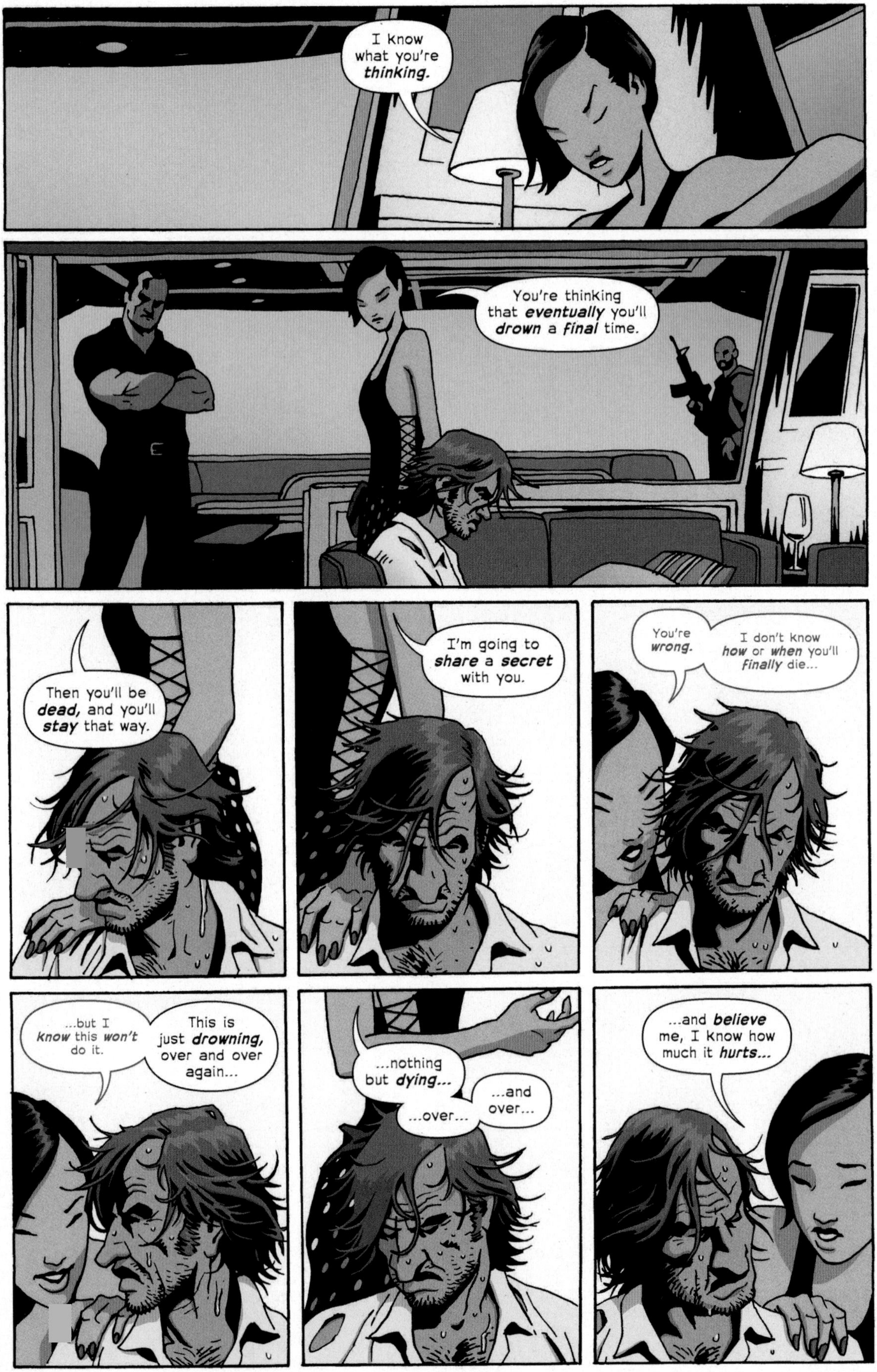

I know what you're *thinking.*
You're thinking that *eventually* you'll *drown* a *final* time.
Then you'll be *dead,* and you'll *stay* that way.
I'm going to *share* a *secret* with you.
You're *wrong.*
I don't know *how* or *when* you'll *finally* die...
...but I *know* this *won't* do it.
This is just *drowning,* over and over again...
...nothing but *dying...*
...over...
...and over...
...and *believe* me, I know how much it *hurts...*

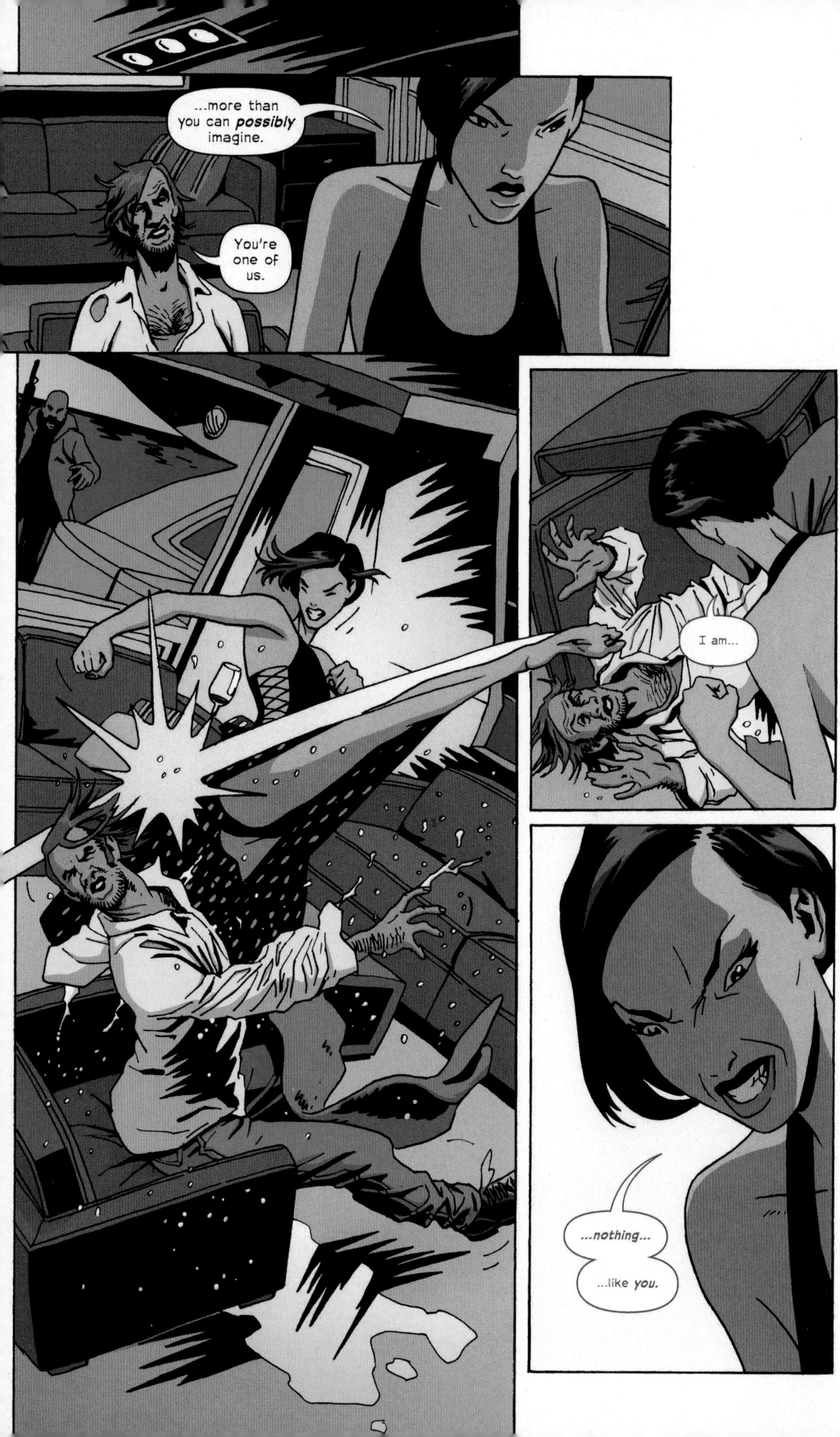
...more than you can *possibly* imagine.
You're one of us.
I am...
...nothing...
...like *you.*

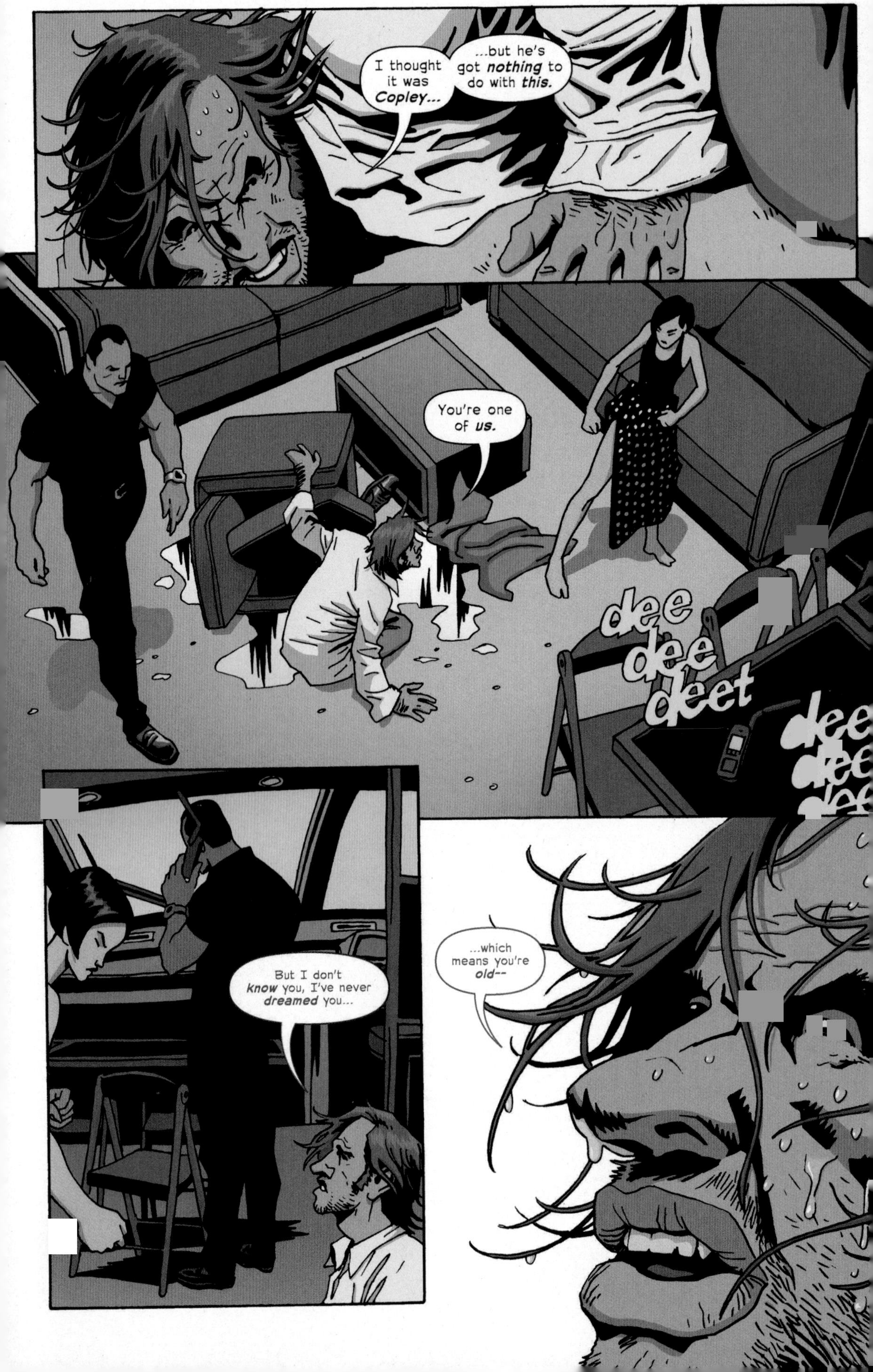

I thought it was *Copley...*
...but he's got ***nothing*** to do with ***this.***
You're one of ***us.***
dee dee deet
dee
But I don't ***know*** you, I've never ***dreamed*** you...
...which means you're *old--*

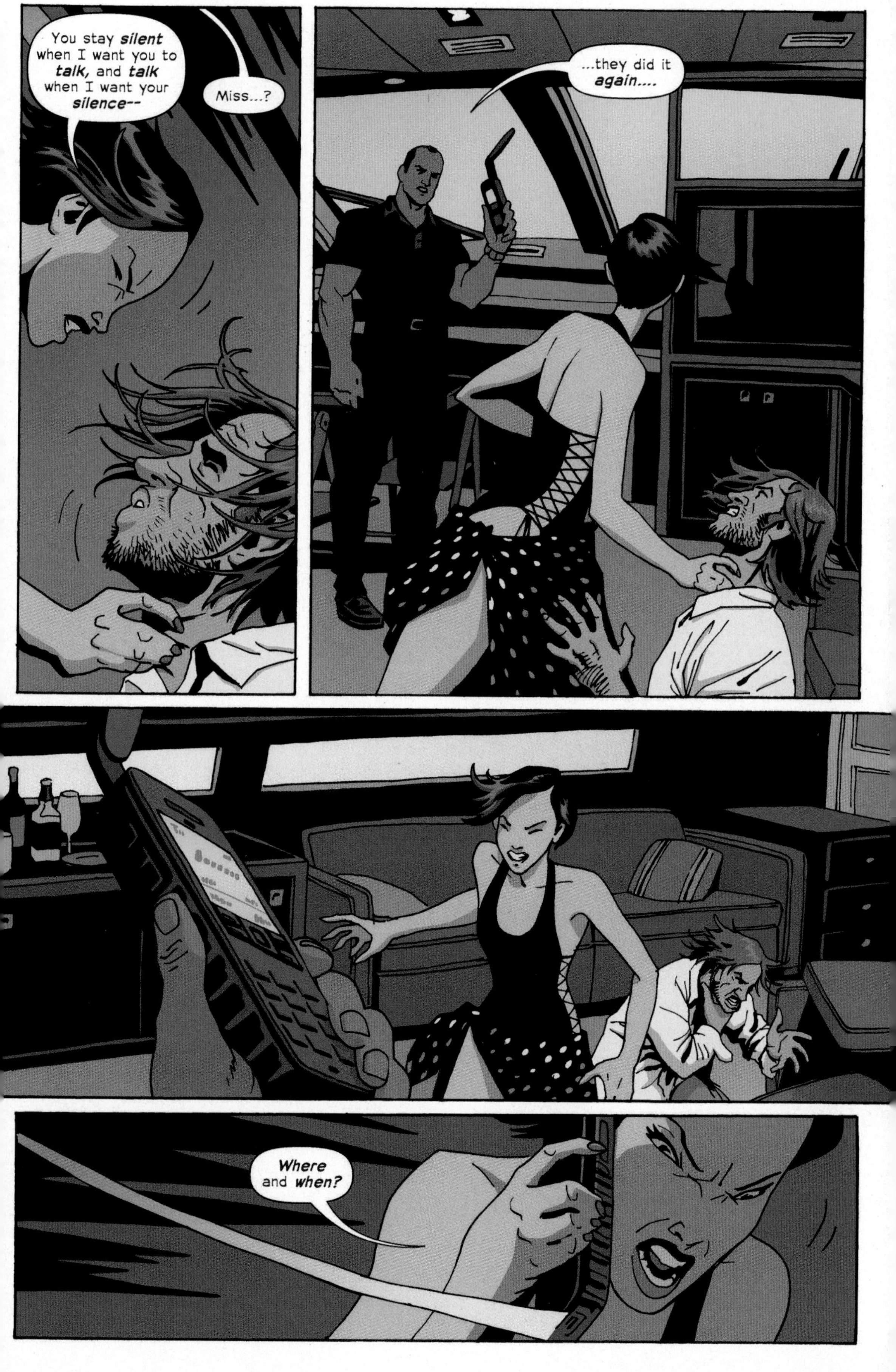
You stay *silent* when I want you to *talk,* and *talk* when I want your *silence--*
Miss...?
...they did it *again....*
Where and *when?*

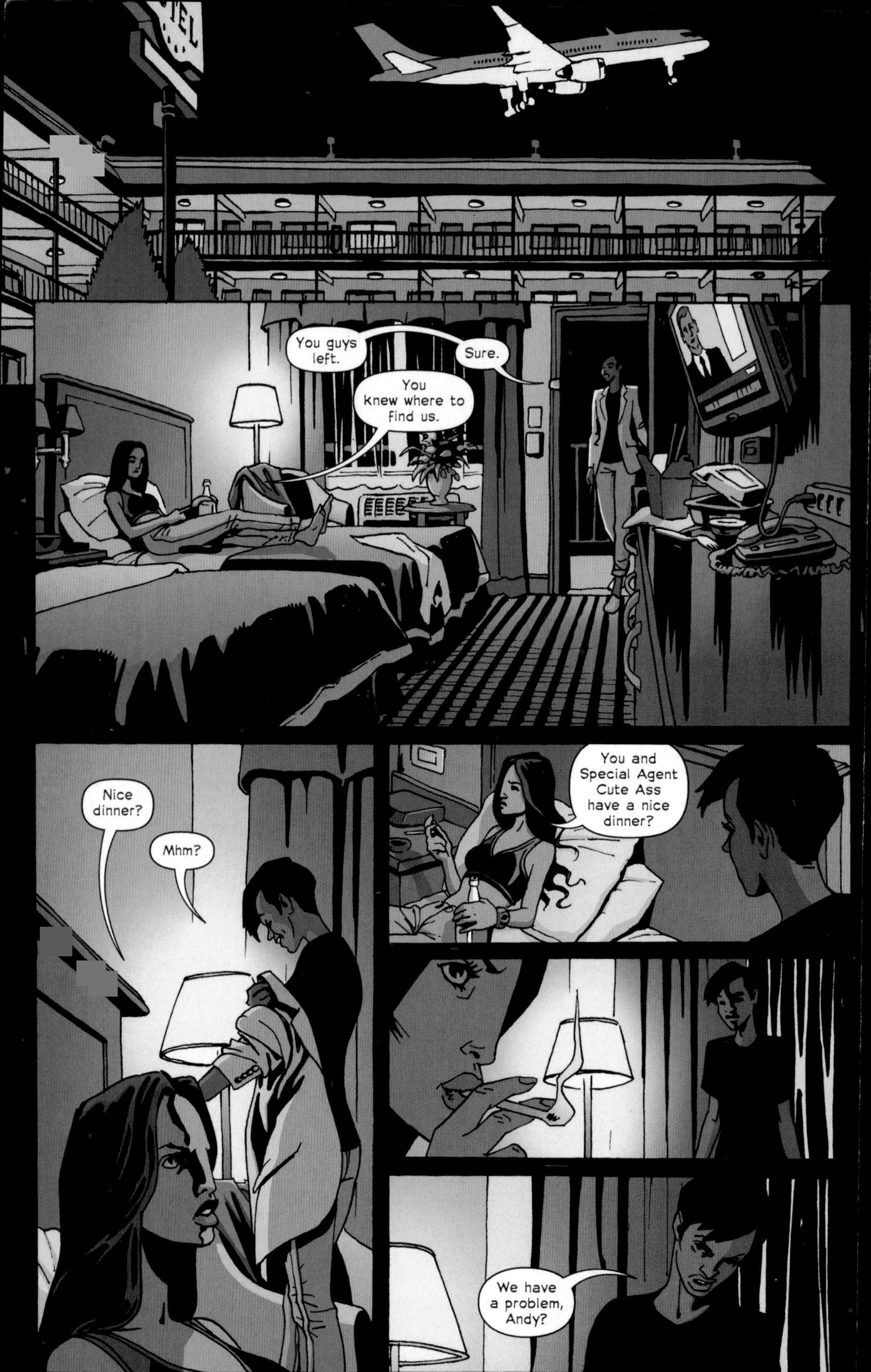
TEL
You guys left.
Sure.
You knew where to find us.
Nice dinner?
Mhm?
You and Special Agent Cute Ass have a nice dinner?
We have a problem, Andy?

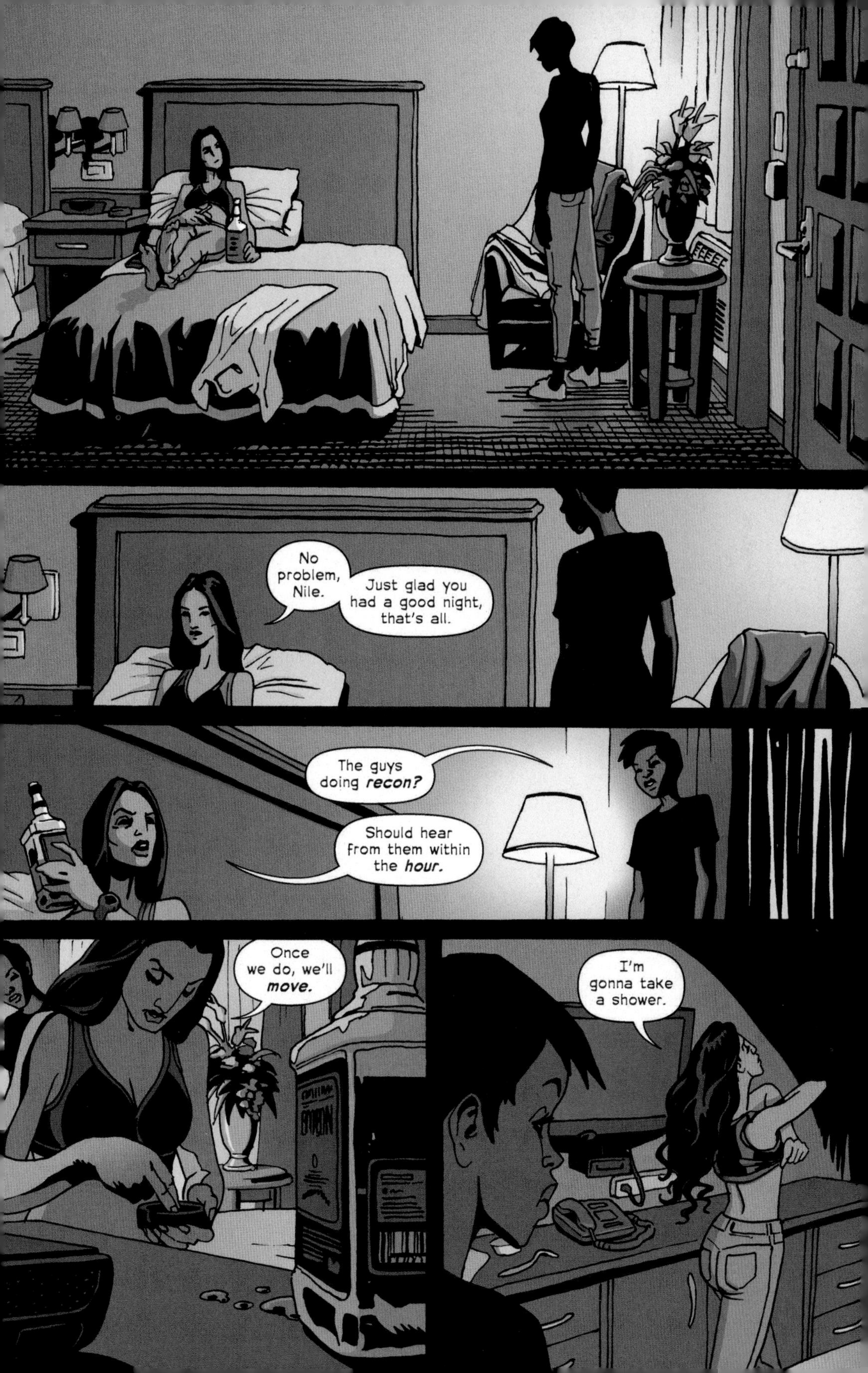
No problem, Nile.
Just glad you had a good night, that's all.
The guys doing *recon?*
Should hear from them within the *hour.*
Once we do, we'll *move.*
I'm gonna take a shower.

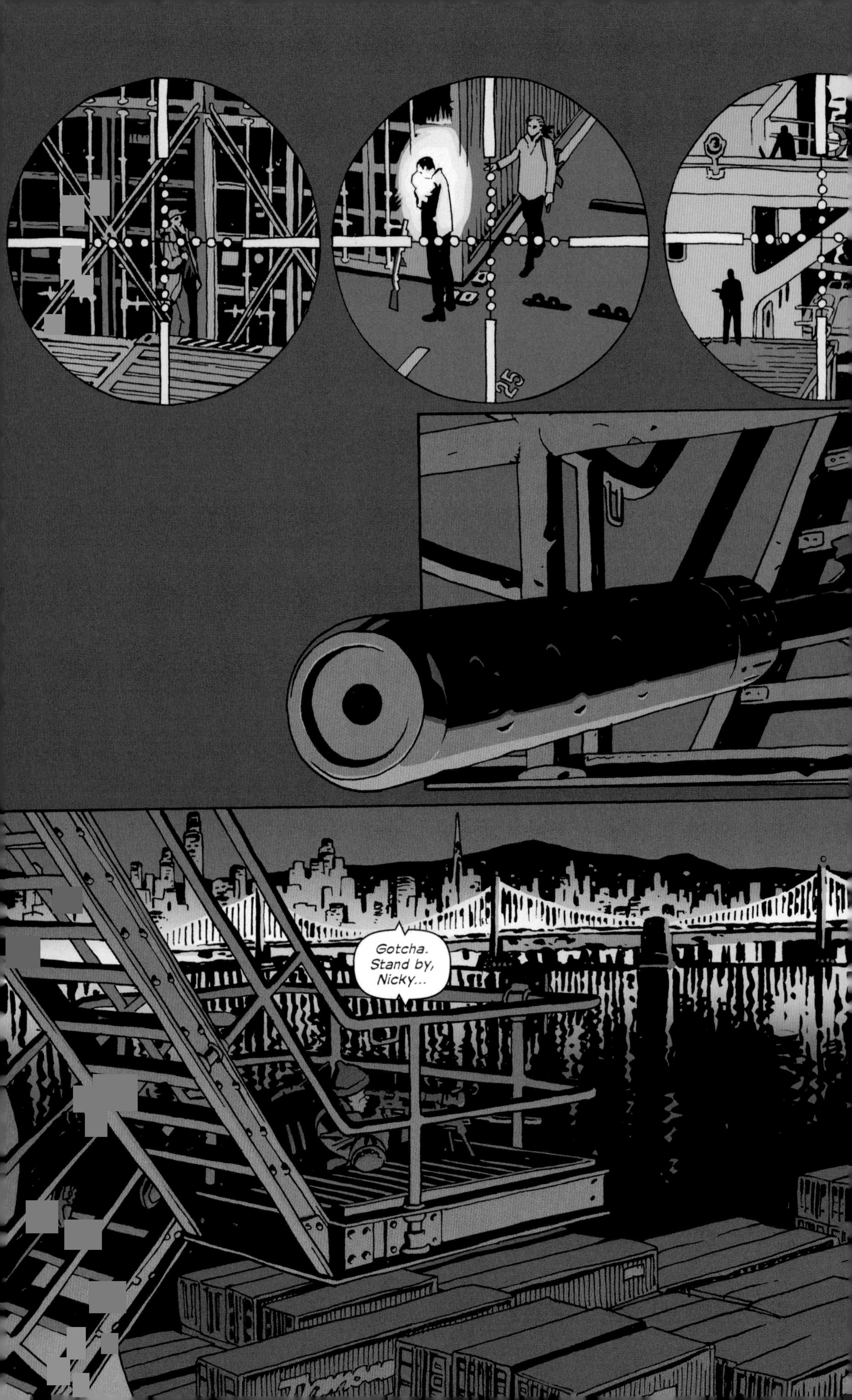
25
Gotcha. Stand by, Nicky...

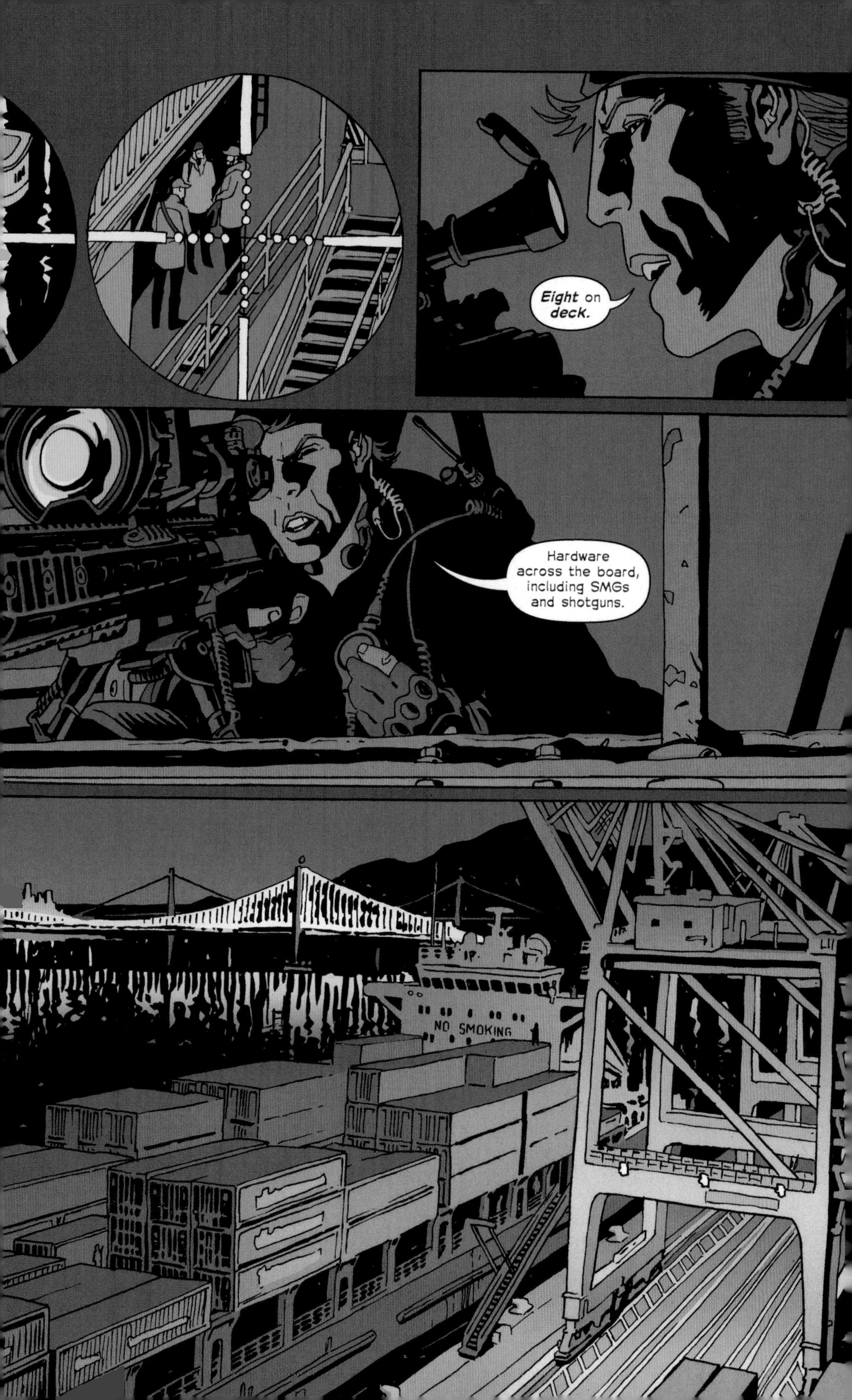
Eight on *deck.*
Hardware across the board, including SMGs and shotguns.
NO SMOKING

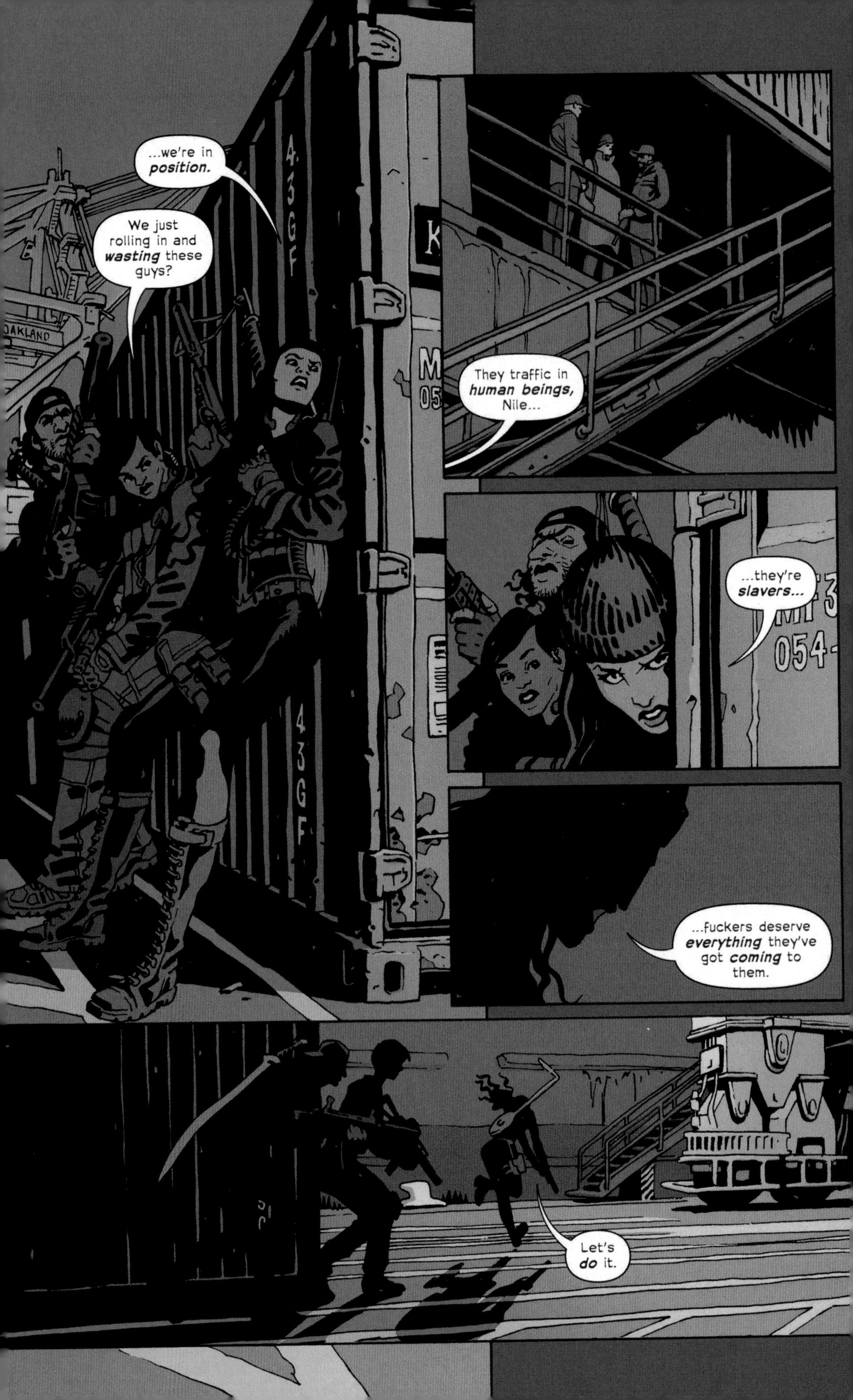
...we're in *position.*
We just rolling in and *wasting* these guys?
They traffic in *human beings,* Nile...
...they're *slavers...*
...fuckers deserve *everything* they've got *coming* to them.
Let's *do* it.

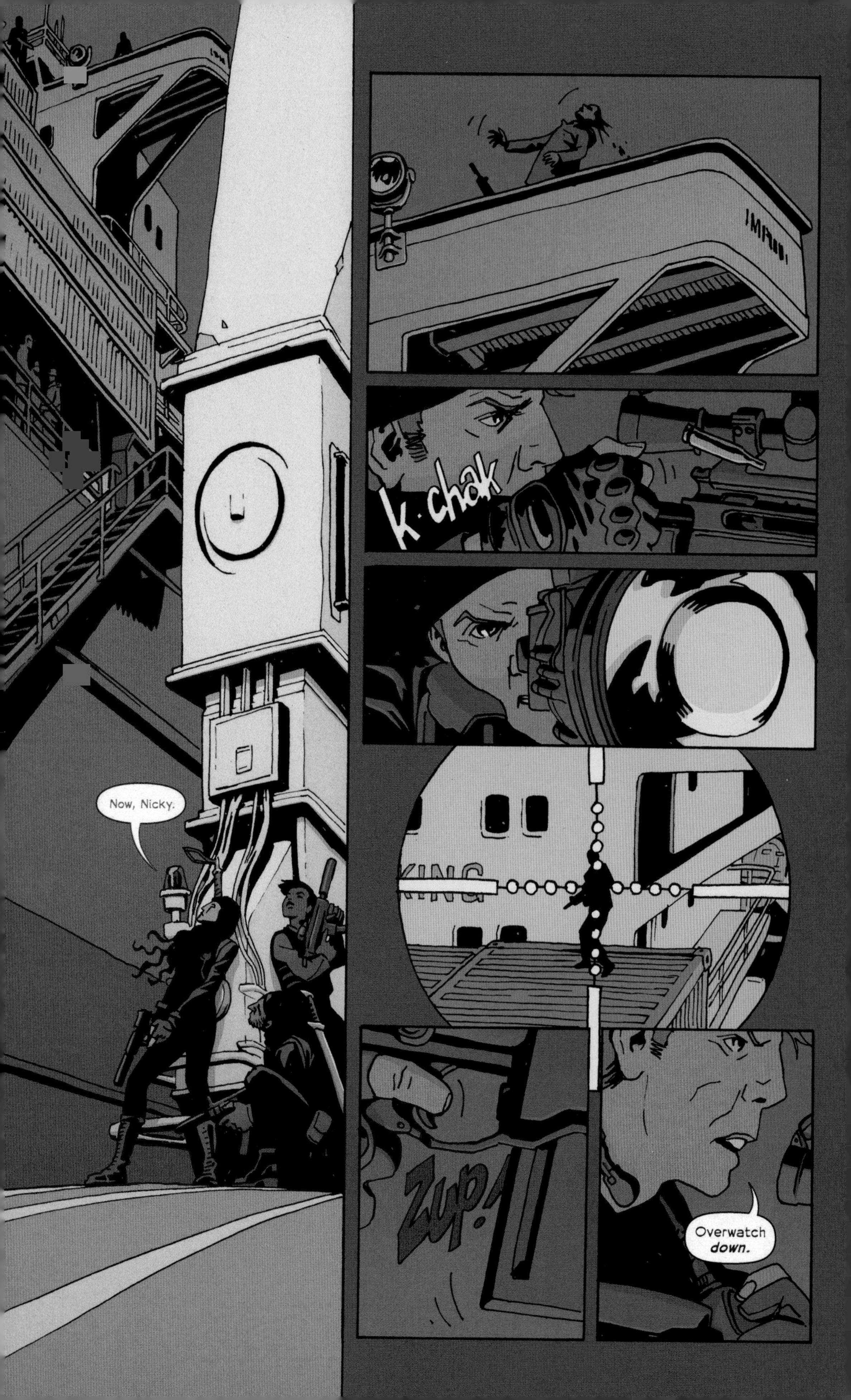
Now, Nicky.
k·chak
Zup!
Overwatch
down.

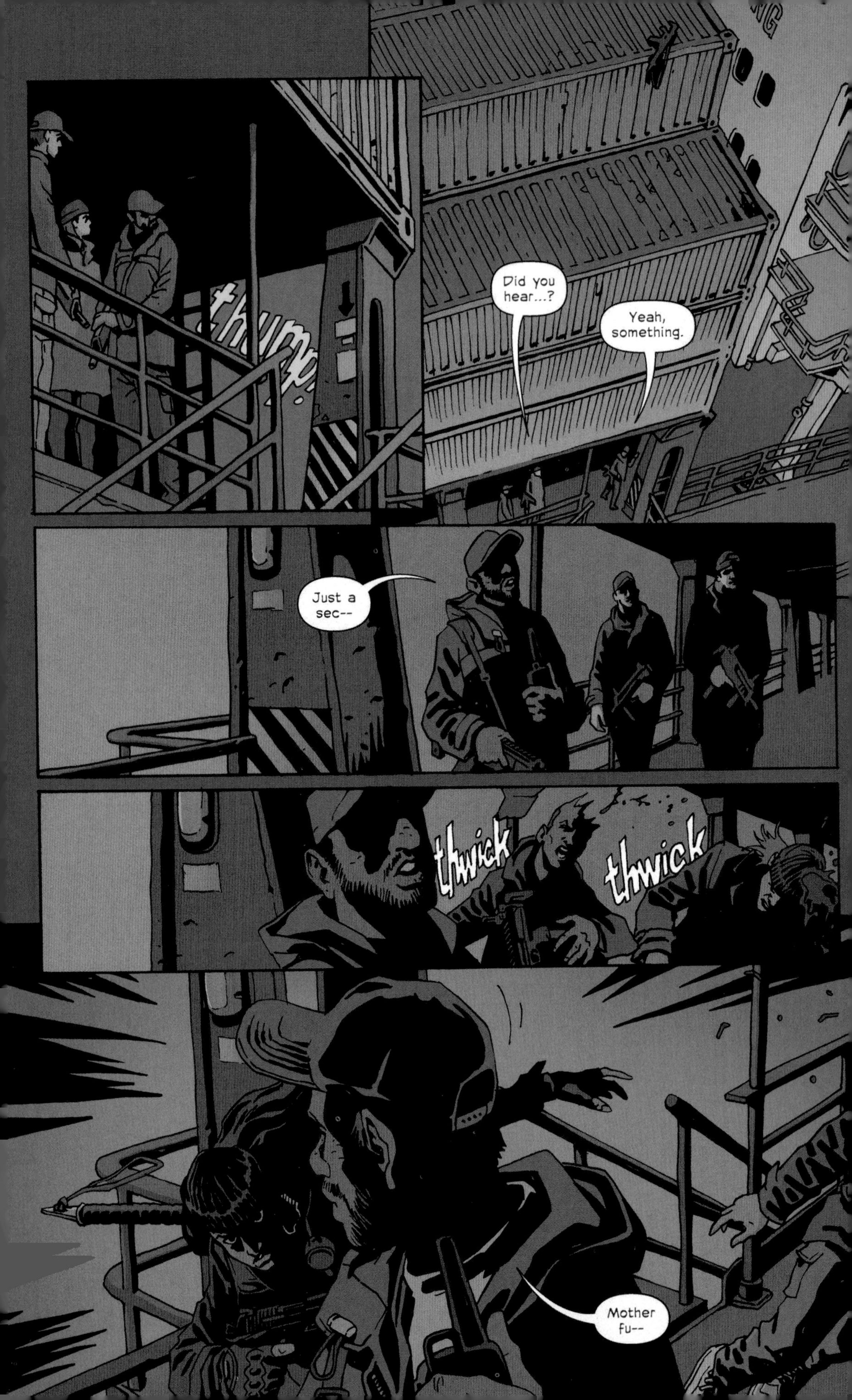
thump
Did you hear...?
Yeah, something.
Just a sec--
thwick
thwick
Mother fu--

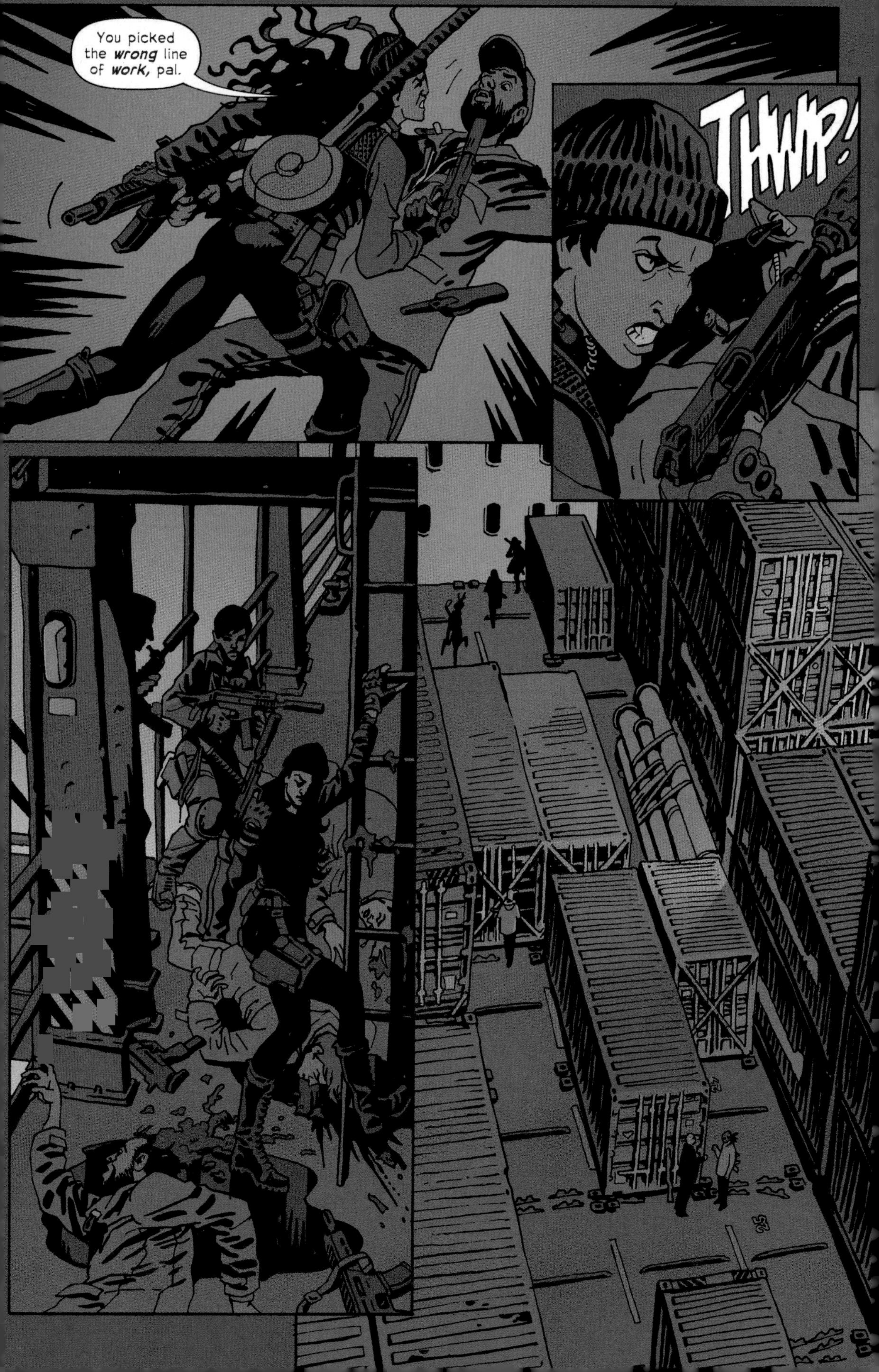
You picked the *wrong* line of *work,* pal.
THWIP!

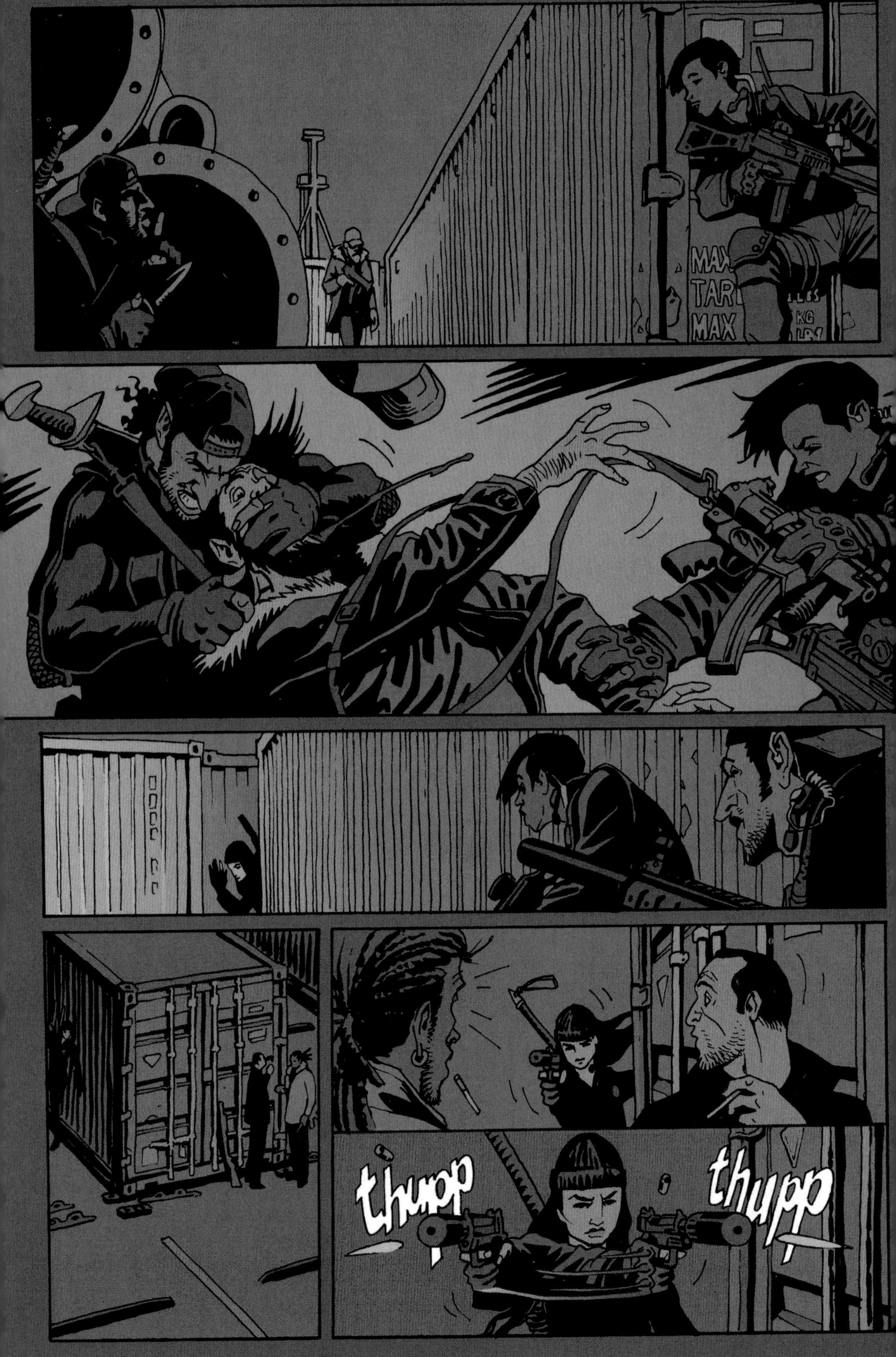
thupp
thupp

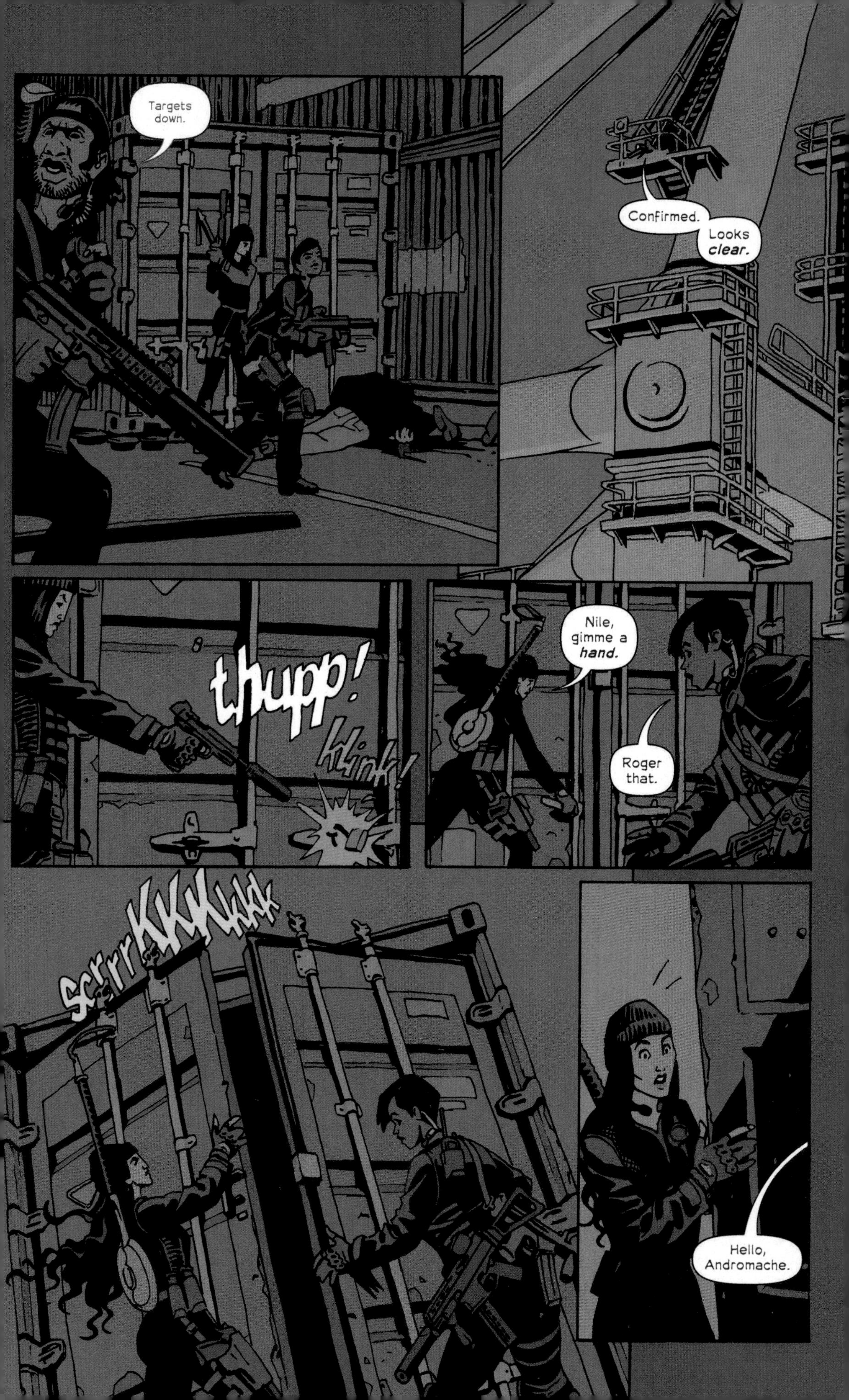
Targets down.
Confirmed.
Looks *clear.*
thupp!
klink!
Nile, gimme a *hand.*
Roger that.
Scrrr
Hello, Andromache.

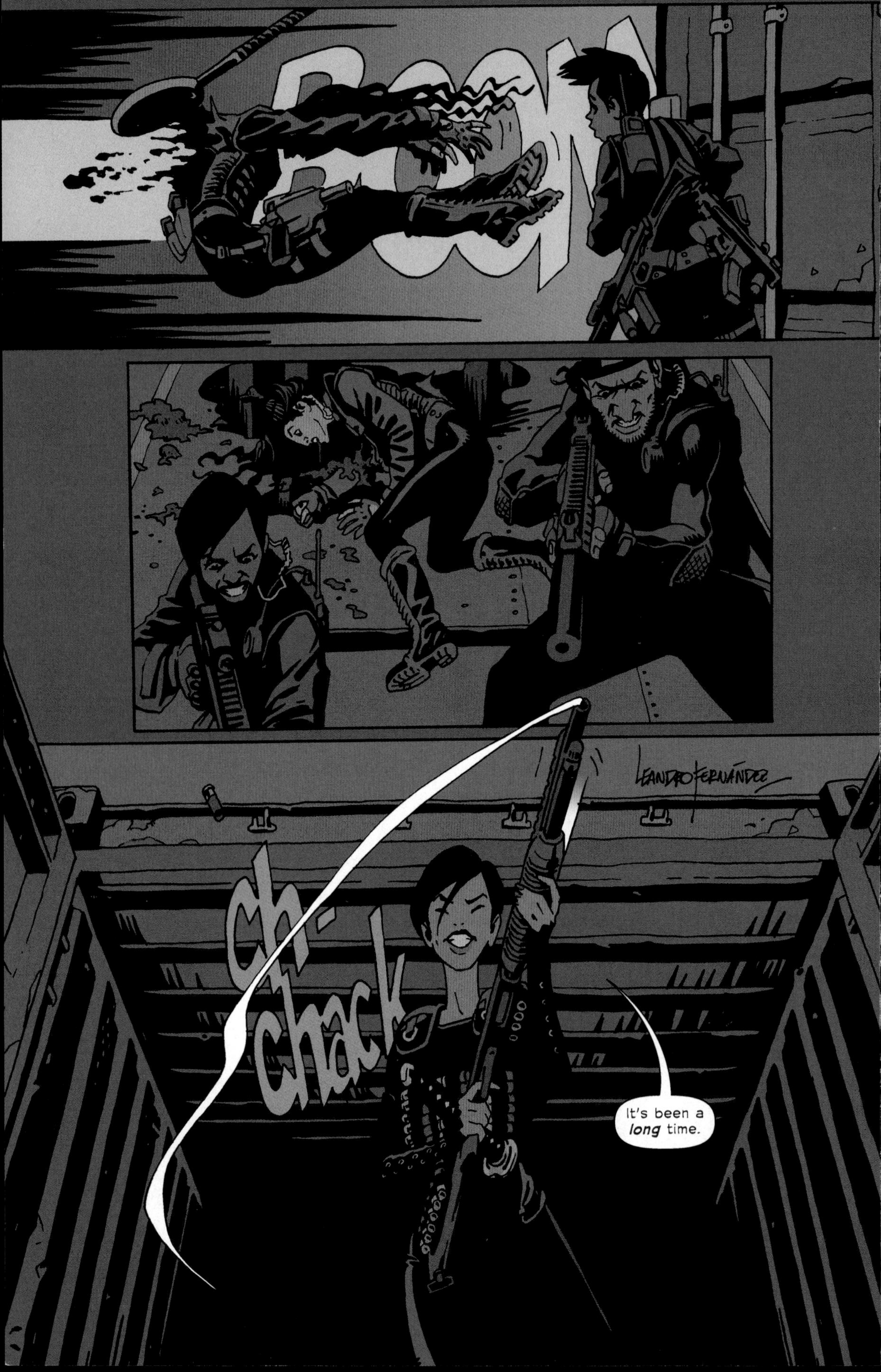
BOOM
LEANDRO FERNÁNDEZ
ch-chack
It's been a *long* time.

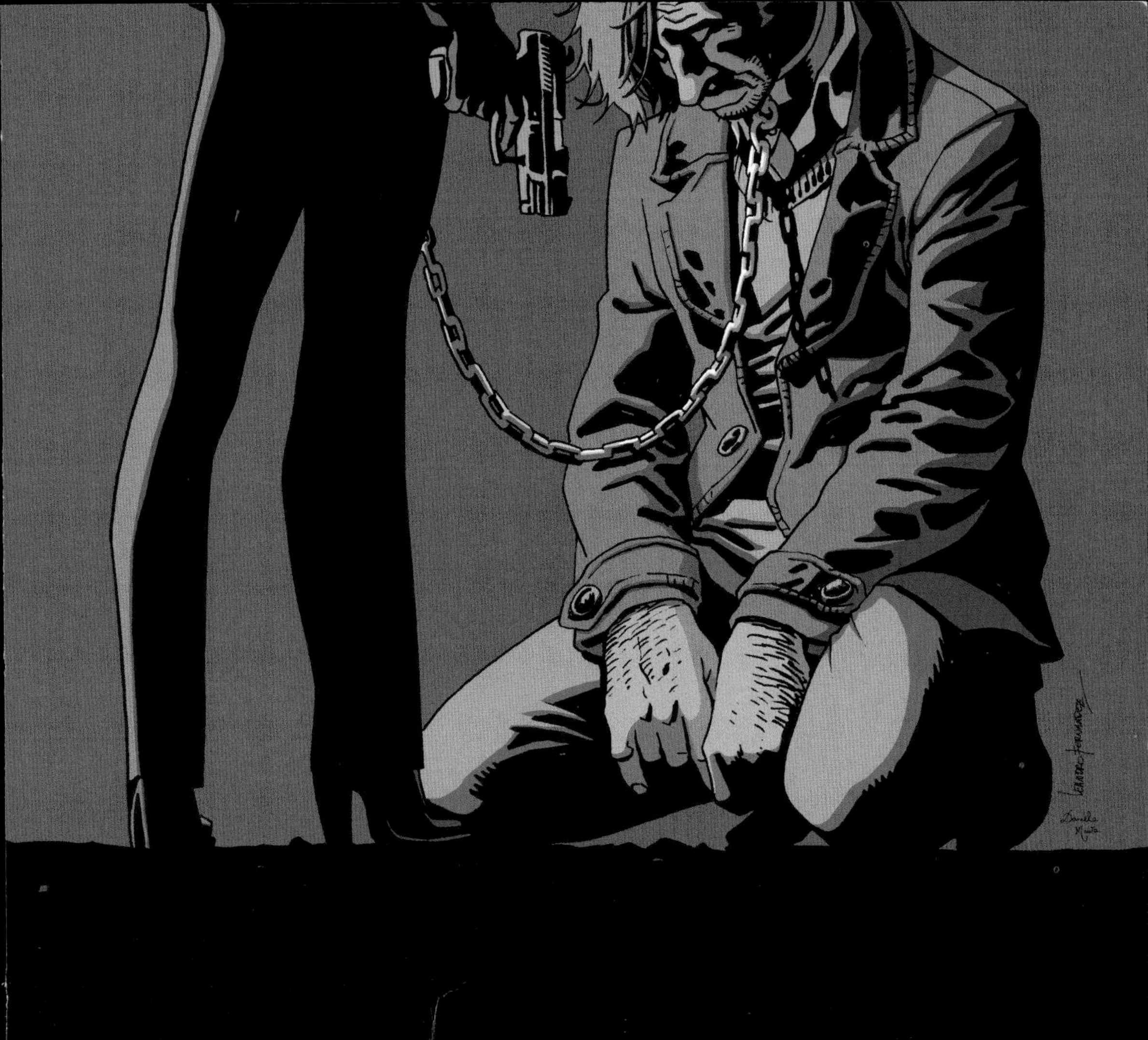

"Every saint has a PAST,

and every sinner has a FUTURE."

~Oscar Wilde

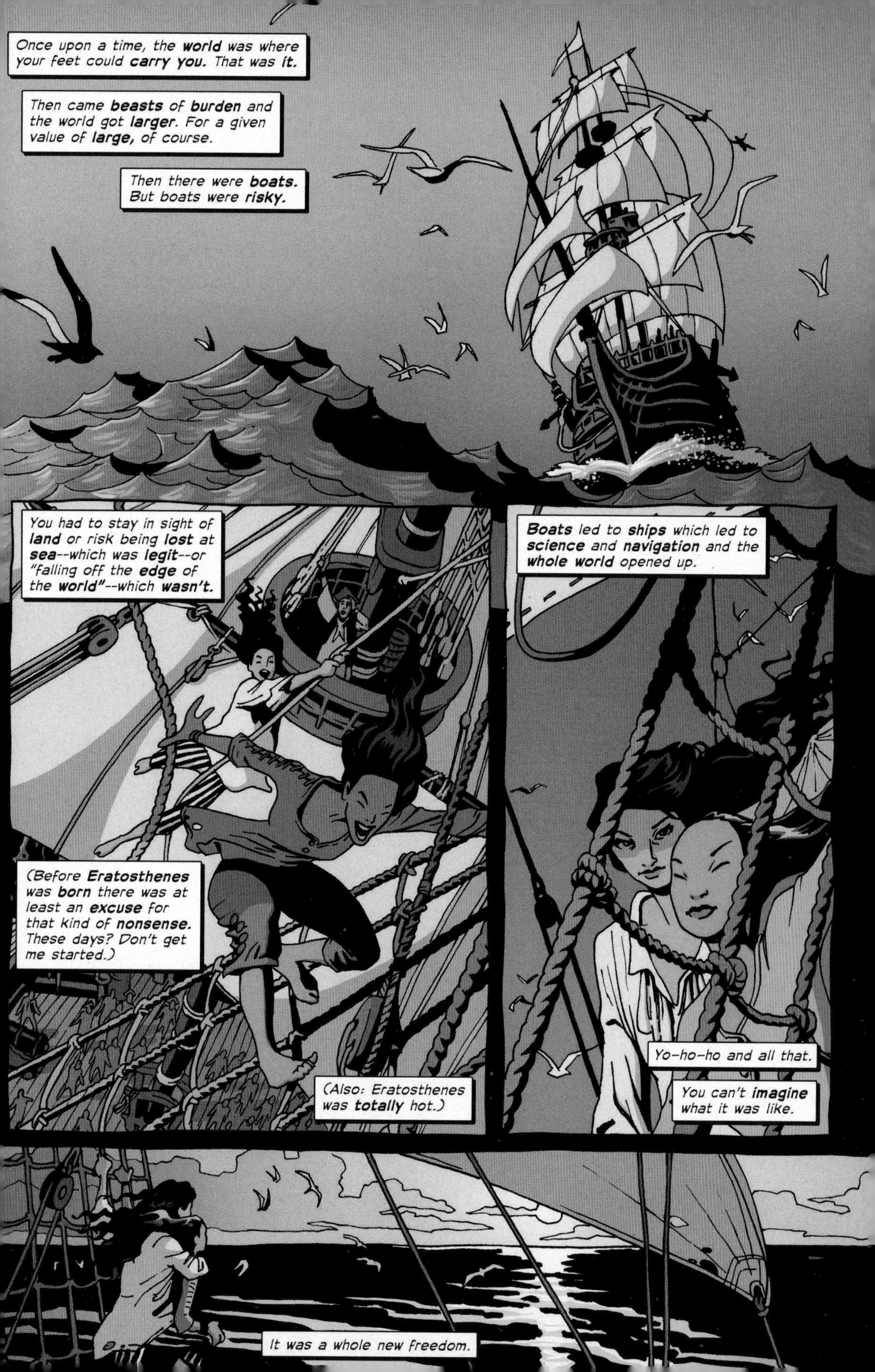
Once upon a time, the world was where your feet could carry you. That was it.
Then came beasts of burden and the world got larger. For a given value of large, of course.
Then there were boats. But boats were risky.
You had to stay in sight of land or risk being lost at sea--which was legit--or "falling off the edge of the world"--which wasn't.
(Before Eratosthenes was born there was at least an excuse for that kind of nonsense. These days? Don't get me started.)
(Also: Eratosthenes was totally hot.)
Boats led to ships which led to science and navigation and the whole world opened up.
Yo-ho-ho and all that.
You can't imagine what it was like.
It was a whole new freedom.

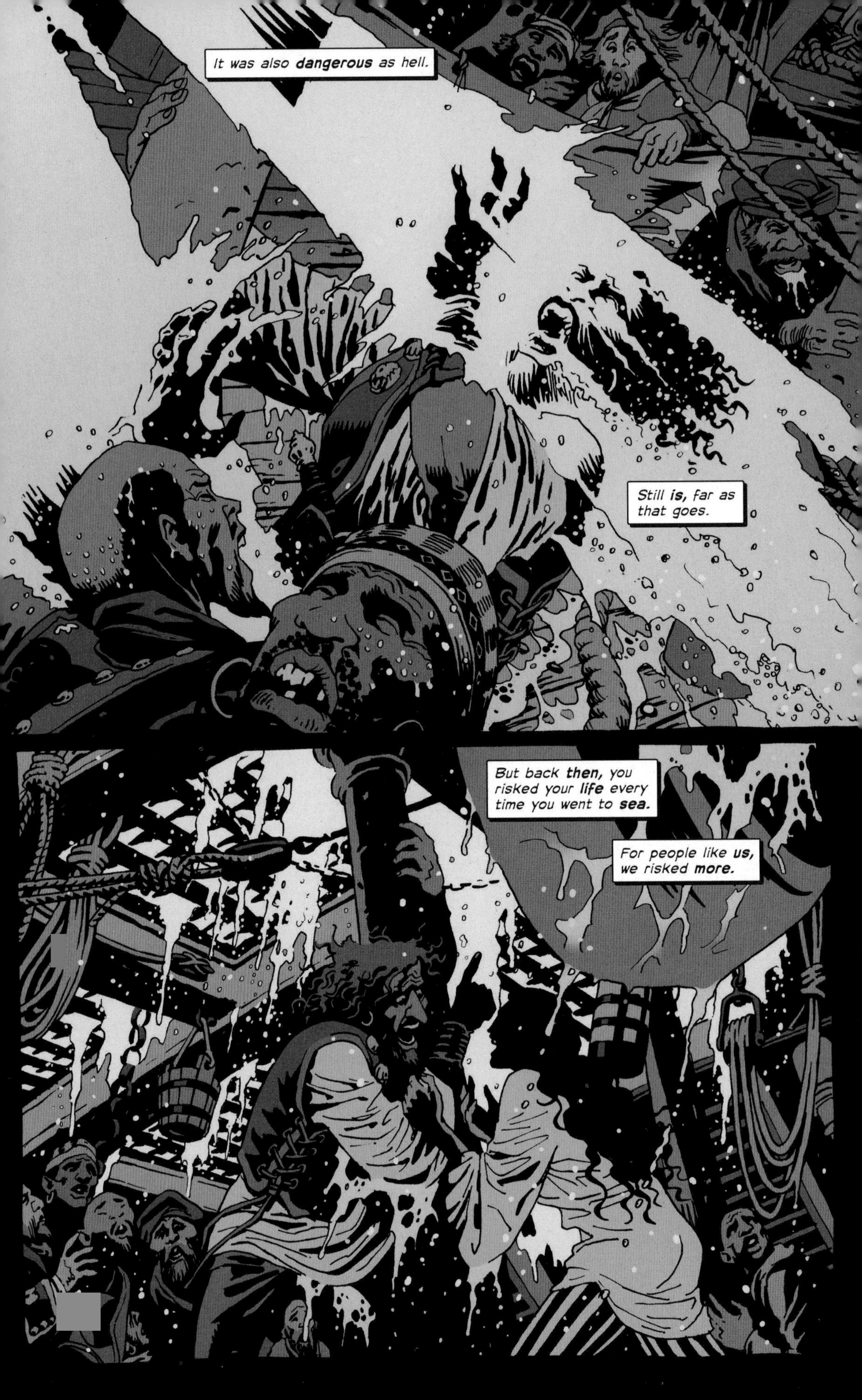
It was also dangerous as hell.
Still is, far as that goes.
But back then, you risked your life every time you went to sea.
For people like us, we risked more.

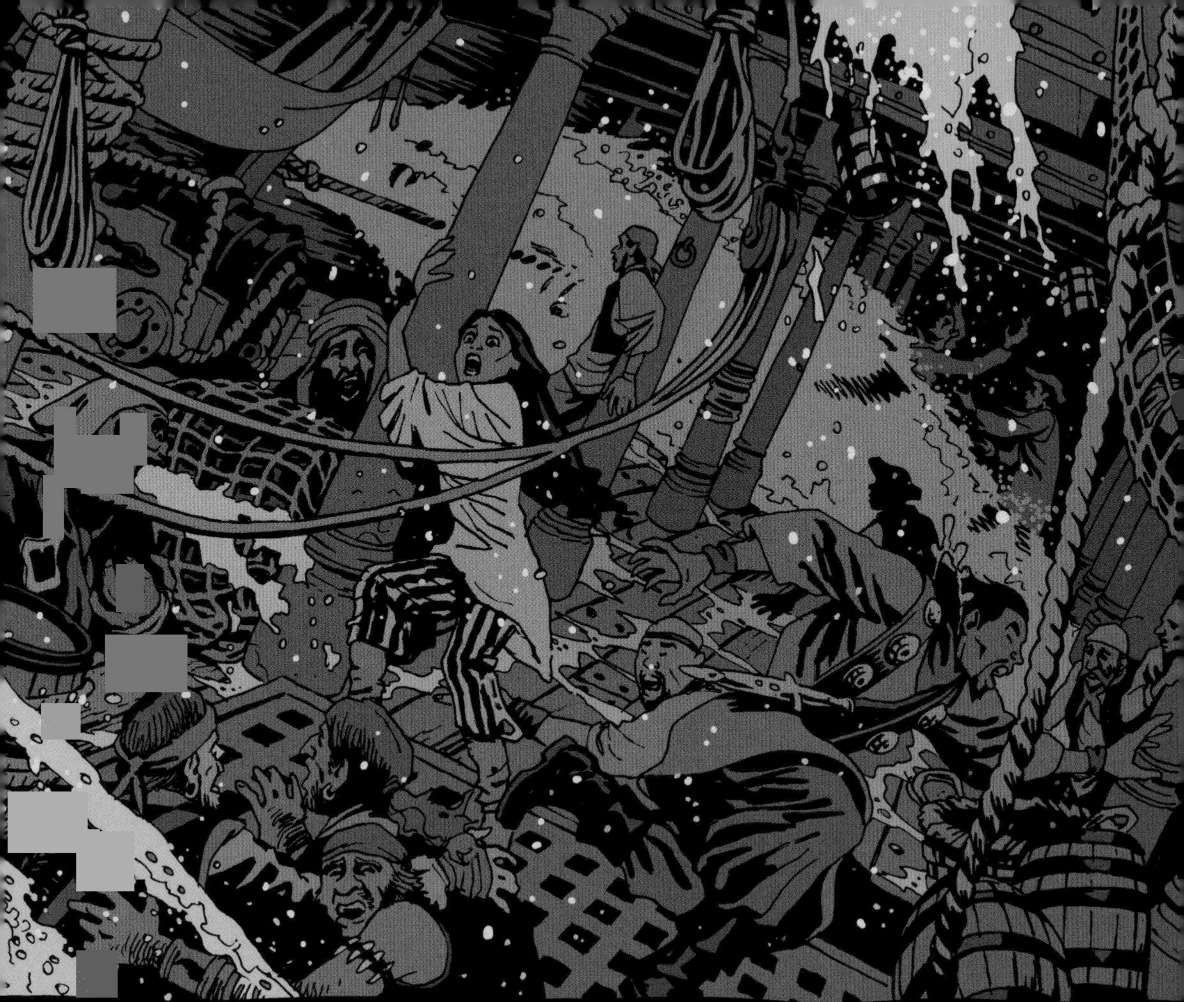

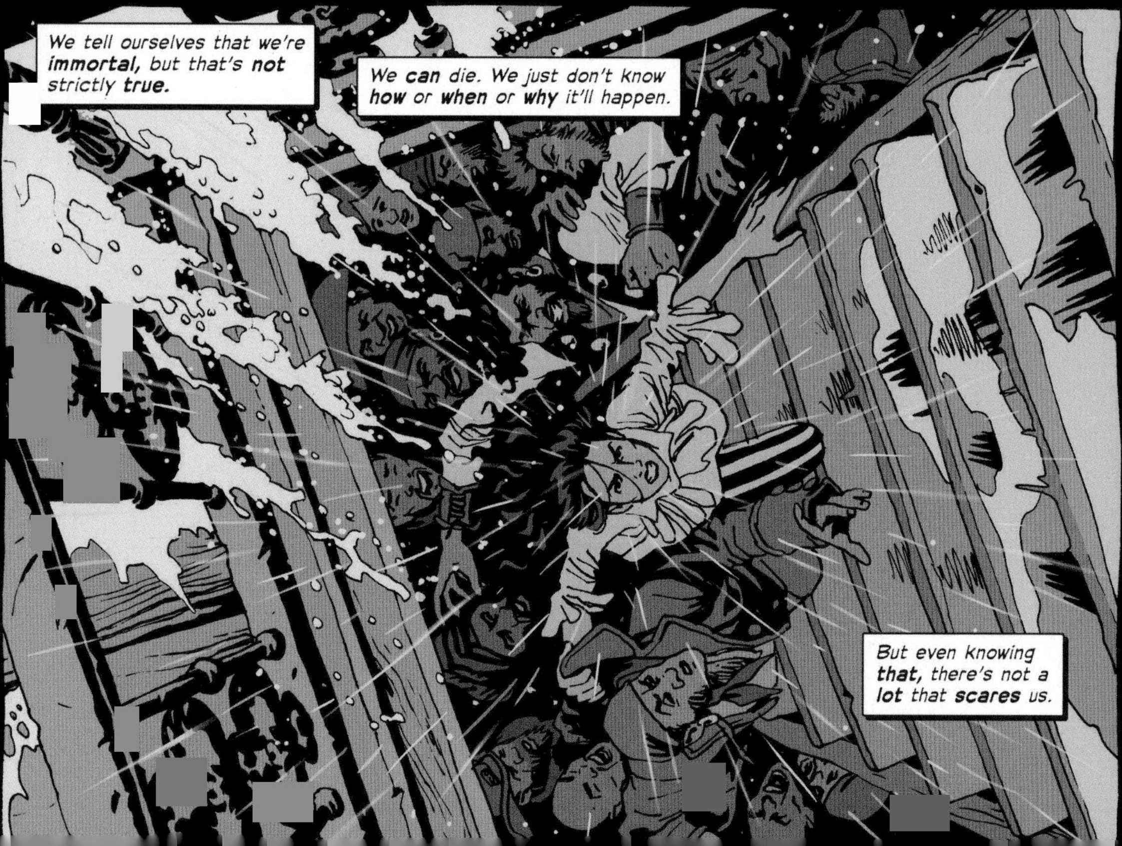

We tell ourselves that we're immortal, but that's not strictly true.
We can die. We just don't know how or when or why it'll happen.
But even knowing that, there's not a lot that scares us.

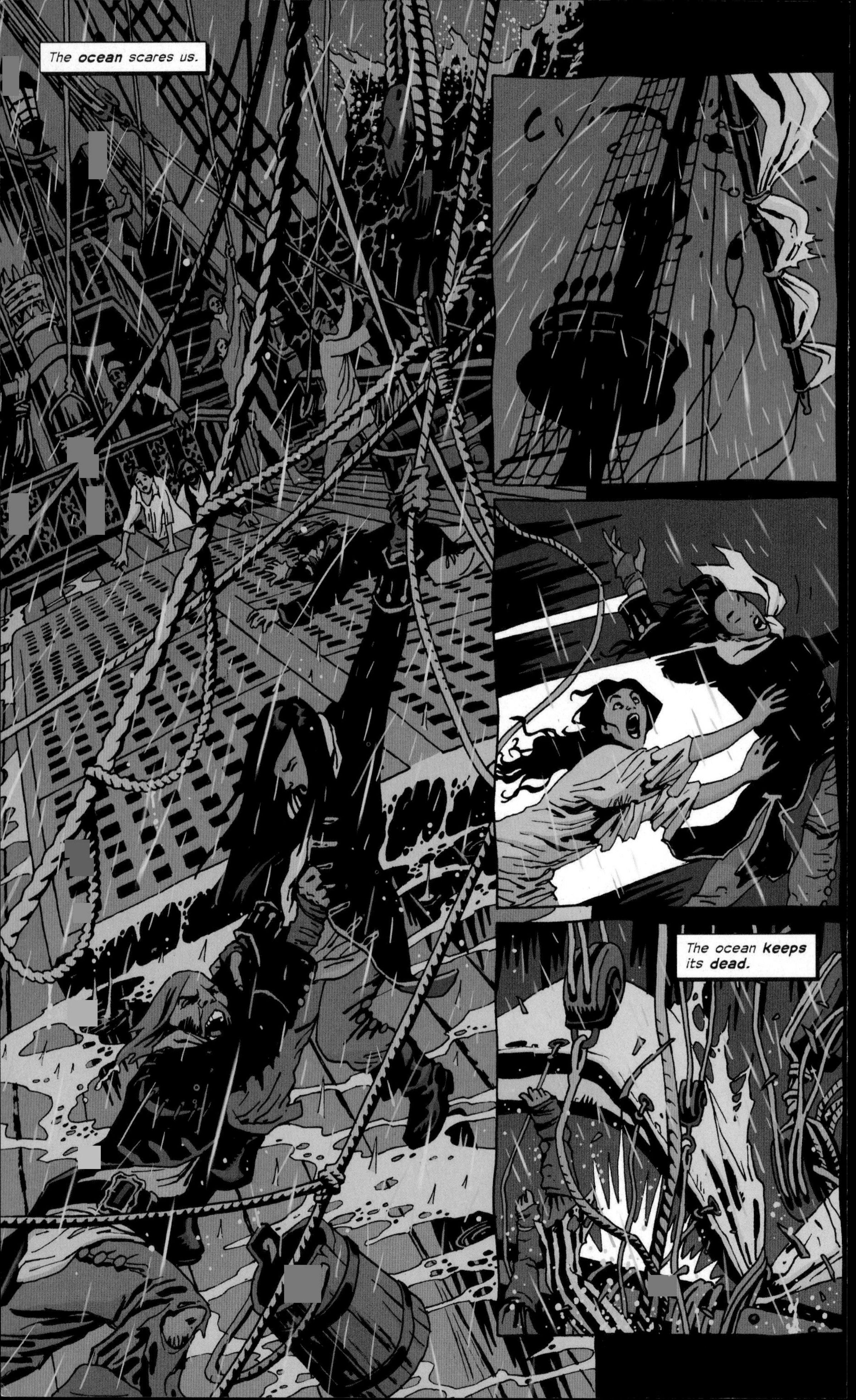
The ocean scares us.
The ocean keeps its dead.

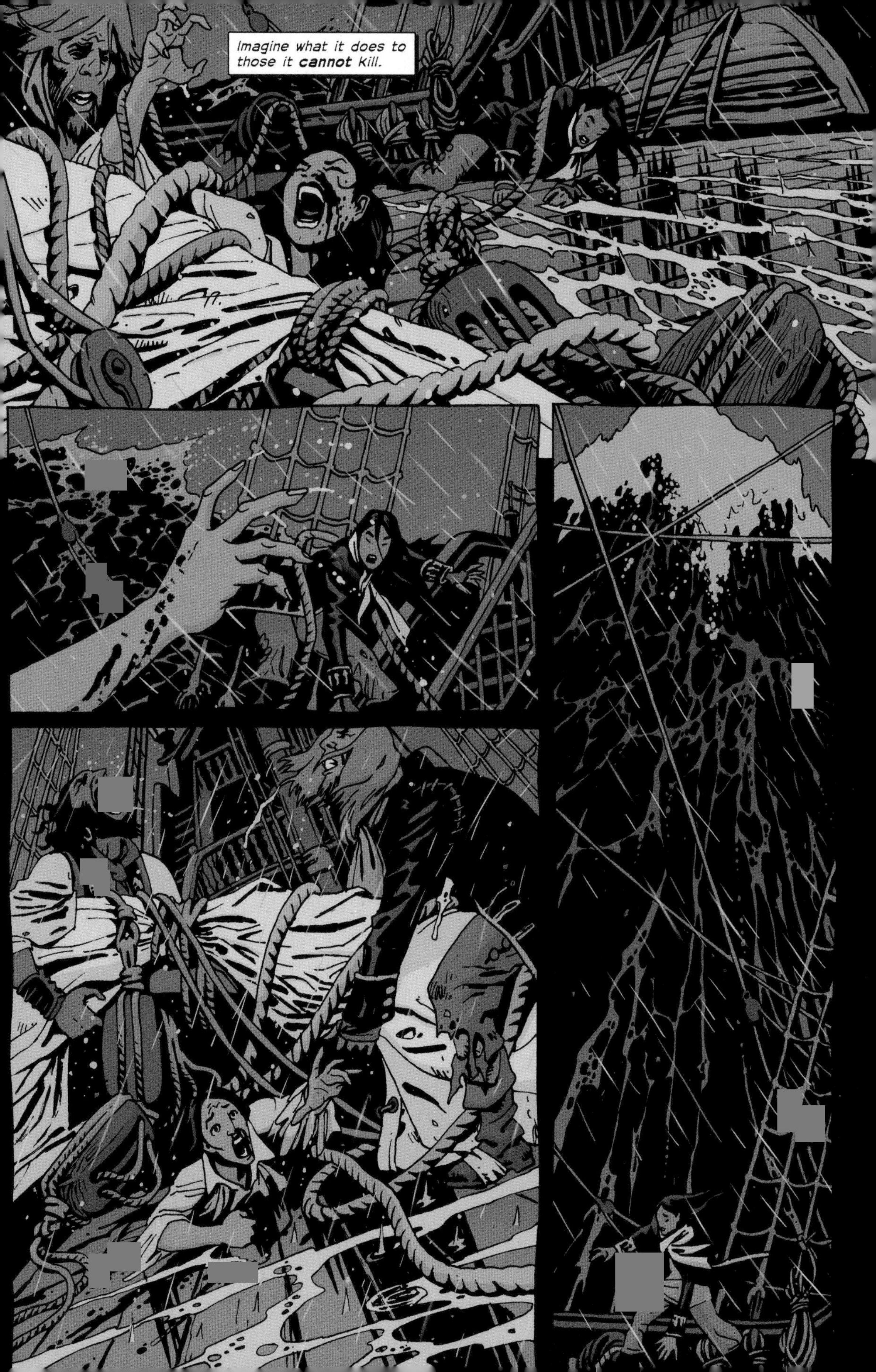
Imagine what it does to those it **cannot** kill.

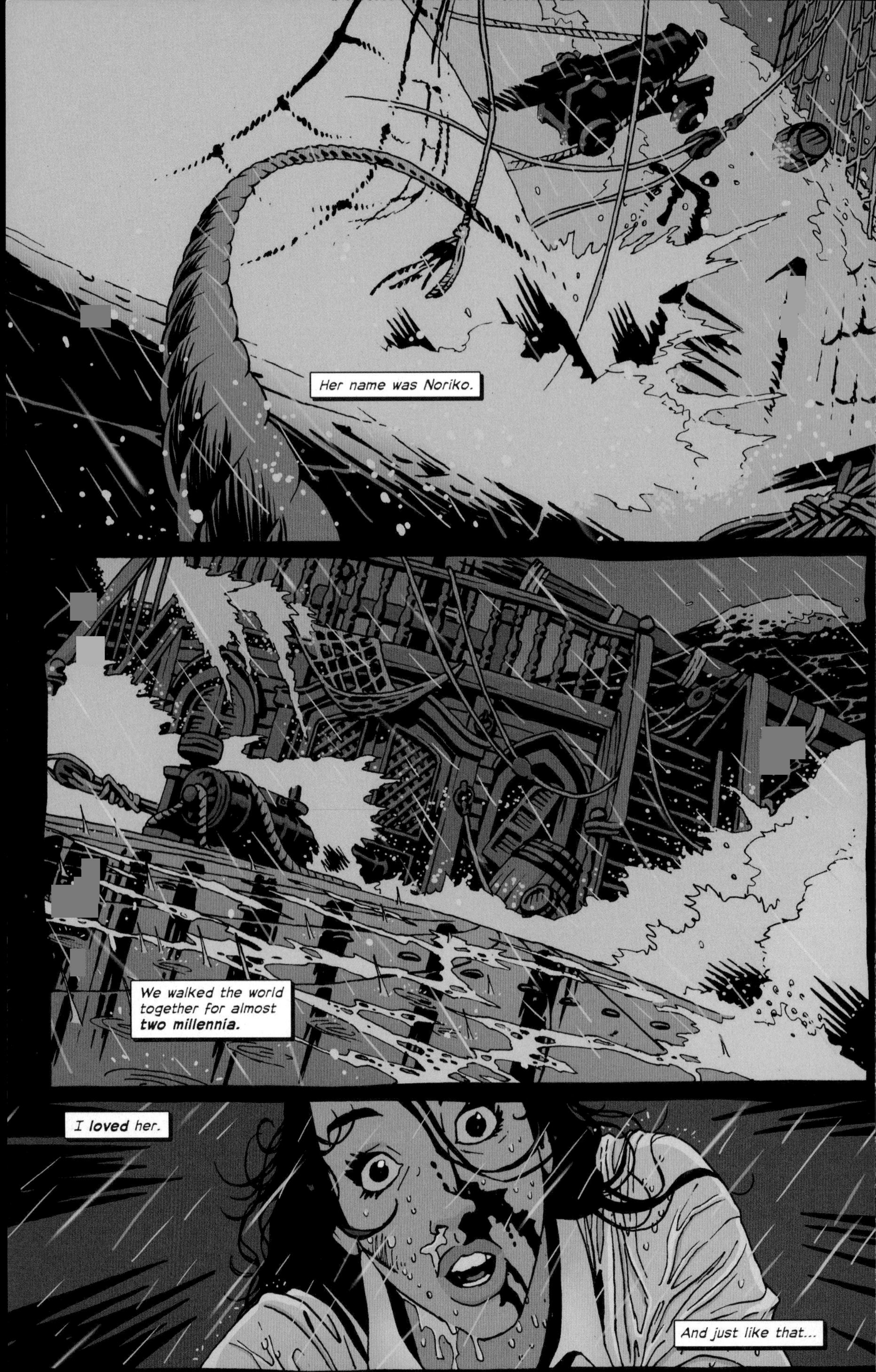
Her name was Noriko.
We walked the world together for almost **two millennia.**
I **loved** her.
And just like that...

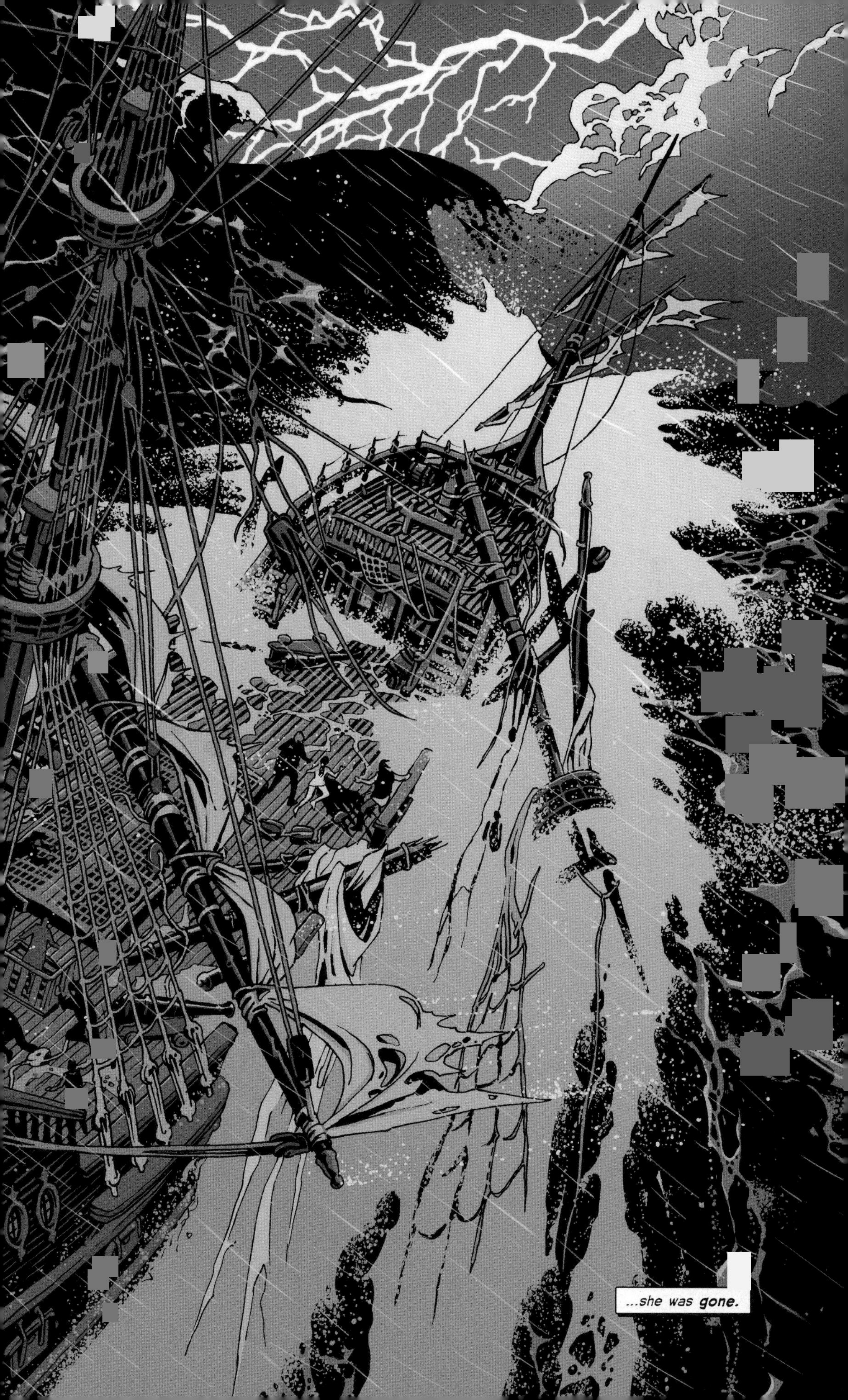
...she was gone.

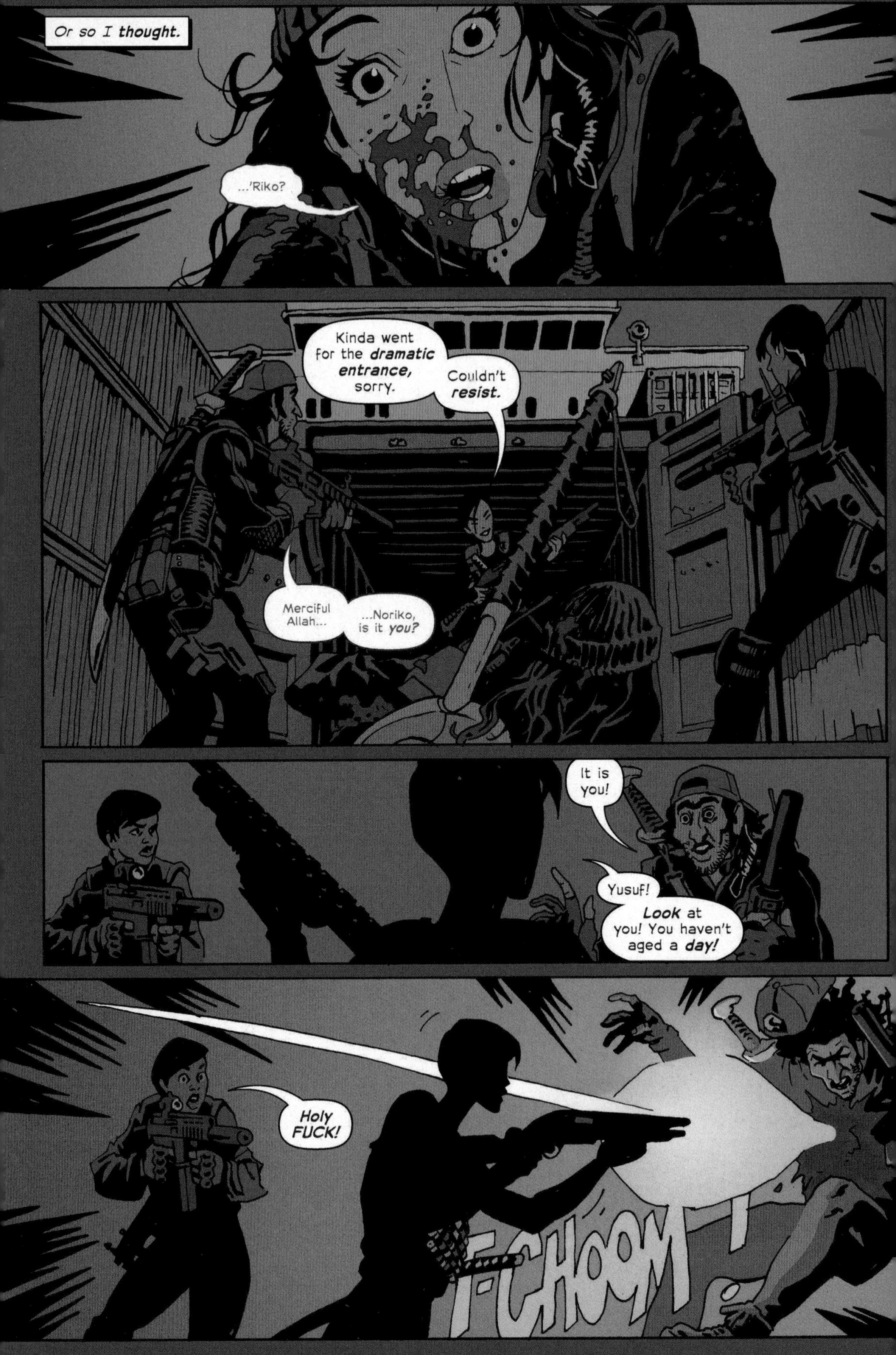
Or so I thought.
...'Riko?
Kinda went for the dramatic entrance, sorry.
Couldn't resist.
Merciful Allah...
...Noriko, is it you?
It is you!
Yusuf!
Look at you! You haven't aged a day!
Holy FUCK!
T-CHOOM

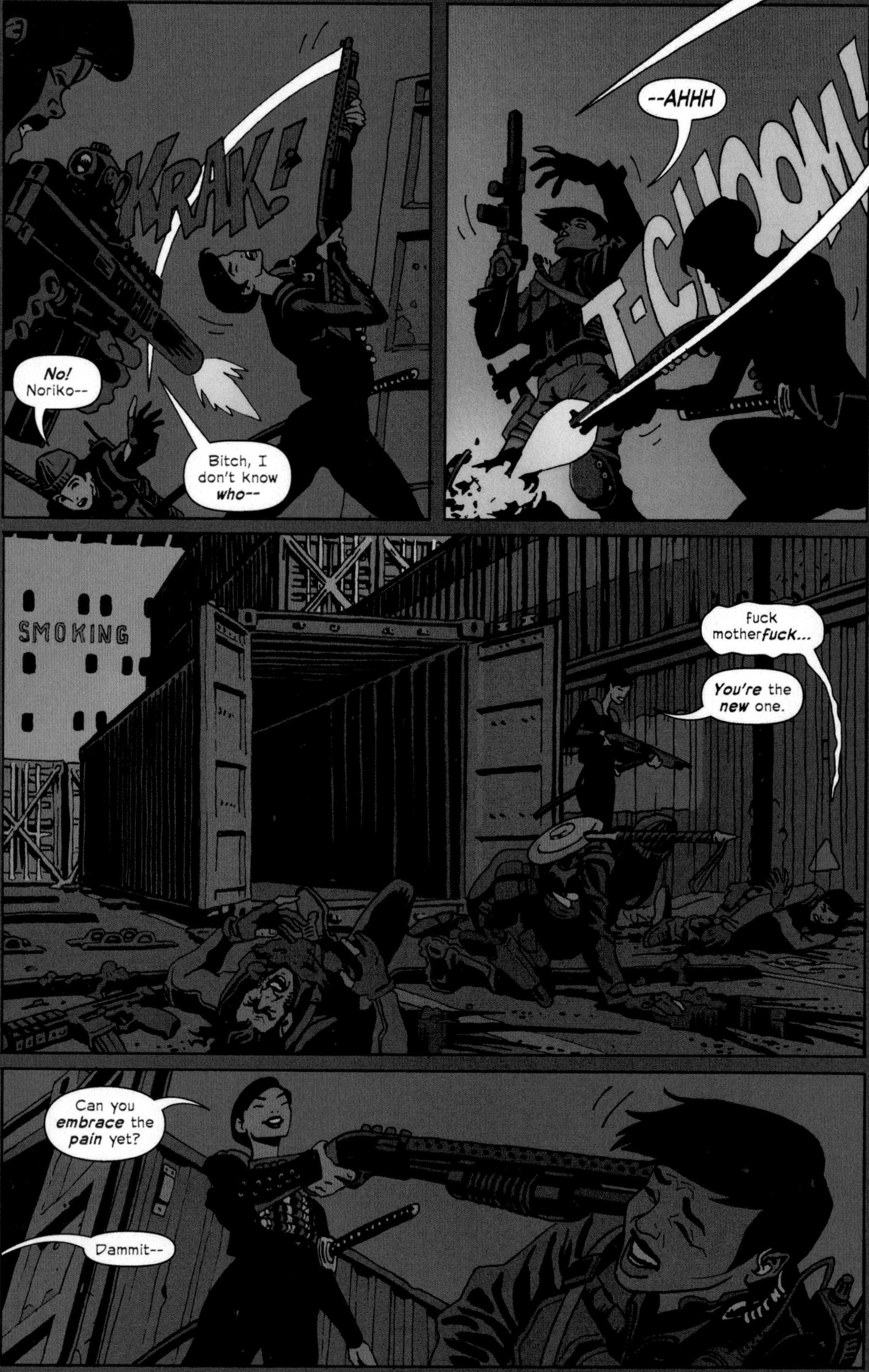
KRAK!
No! Noriko--
Bitch, I don't know who--
--AHHH
T-CHOOM!
SMOKING
fuck motherfuck...
You're the new one.
Can you embrace the pain yet?
Dammit--

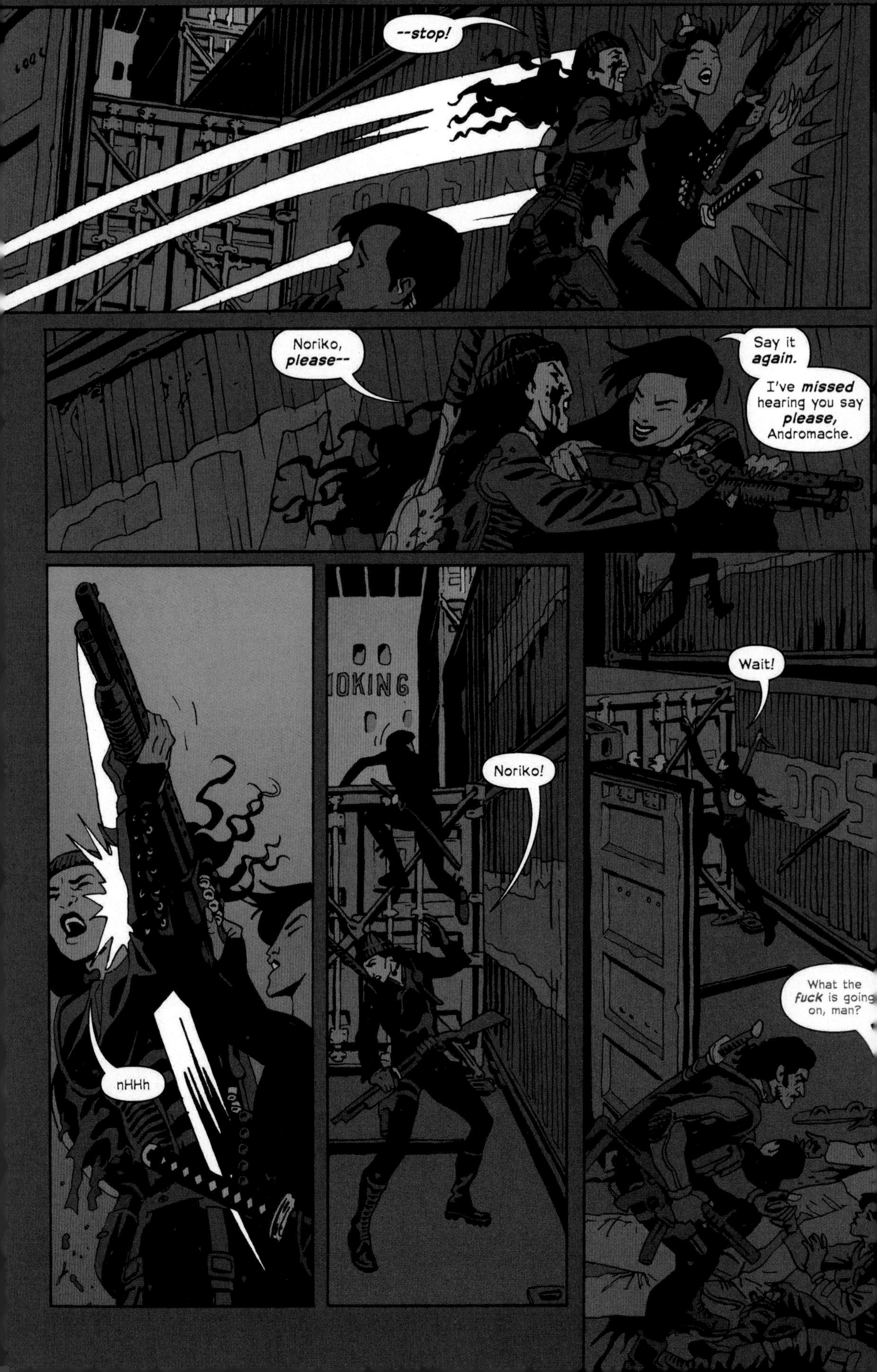
--stop!
Noriko, please--
Say it again.
I've missed hearing you say please, Andromache.
nHHh
Noriko!
Wait!
What the fuck is going on, man?

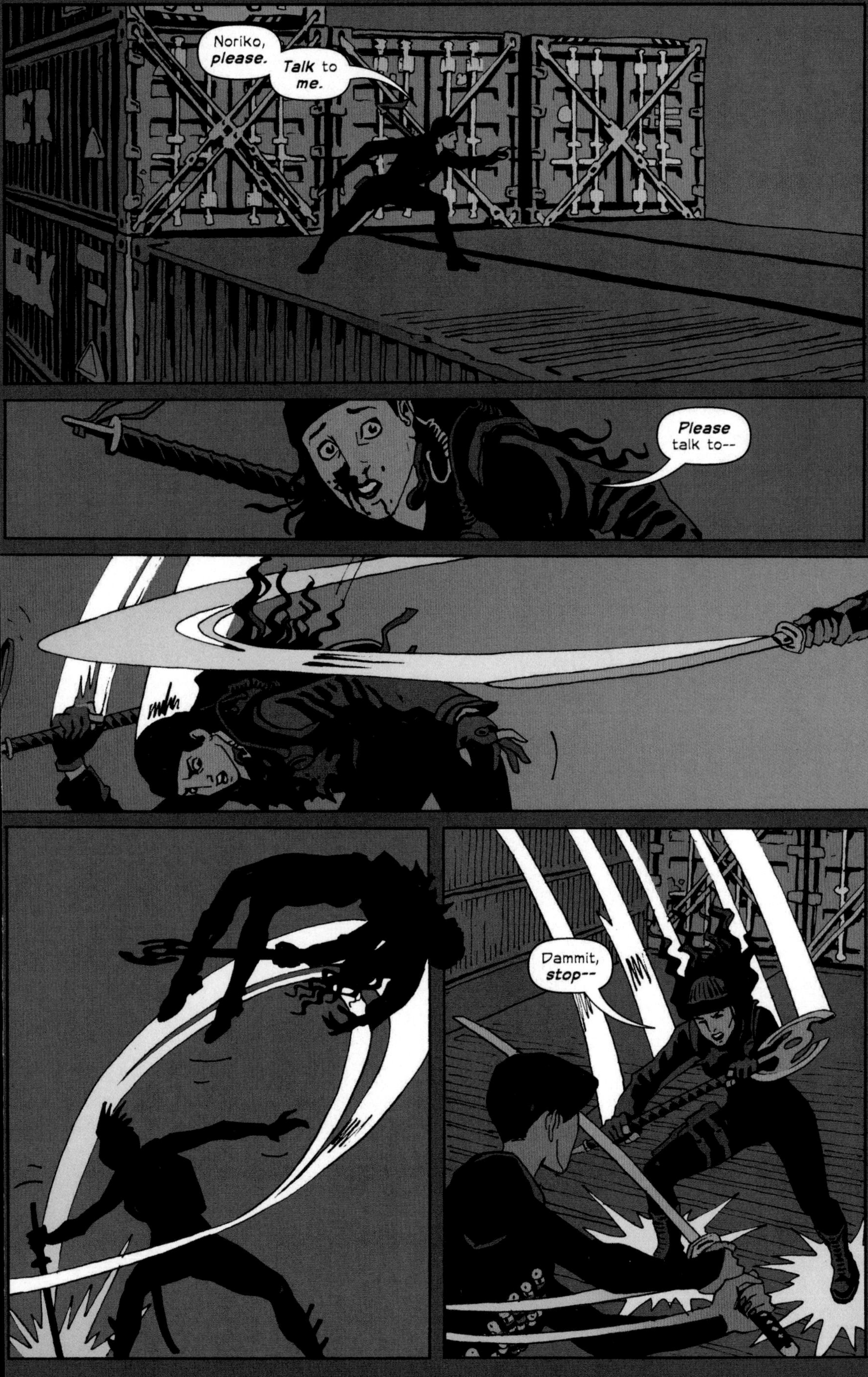
Noriko, please.
Talk to me.
Please talk to--
Dammit, stop--

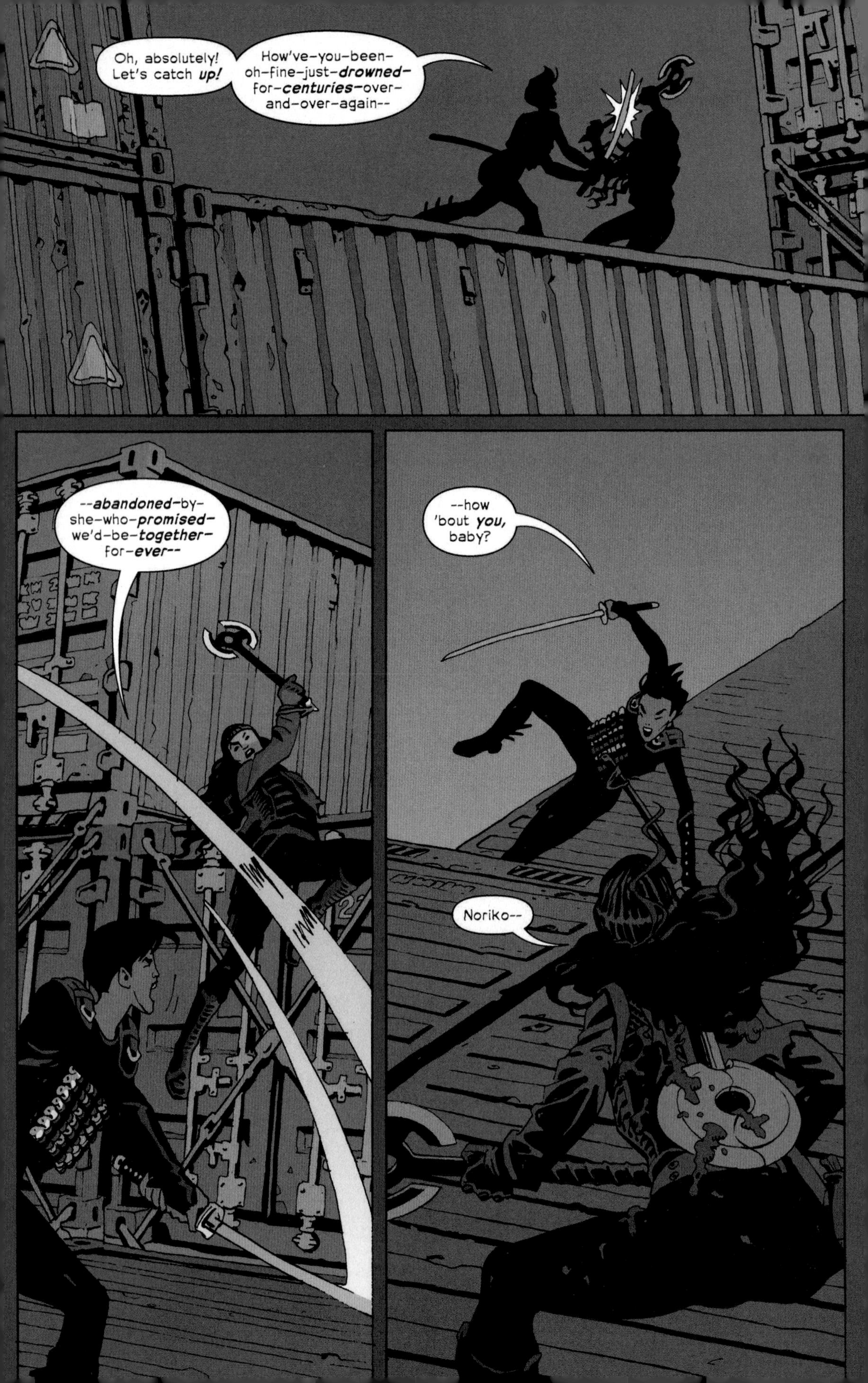
Oh, absolutely! Let's catch *up!*
How've-you-been-oh-fine-just-***drowned***-for-***centuries***-over-and-over-again--
--***abandoned***-by-she-who-***promised***-we'd-be-***together***-for-***ever***--
--how 'bout ***you,*** baby?
Noriko--

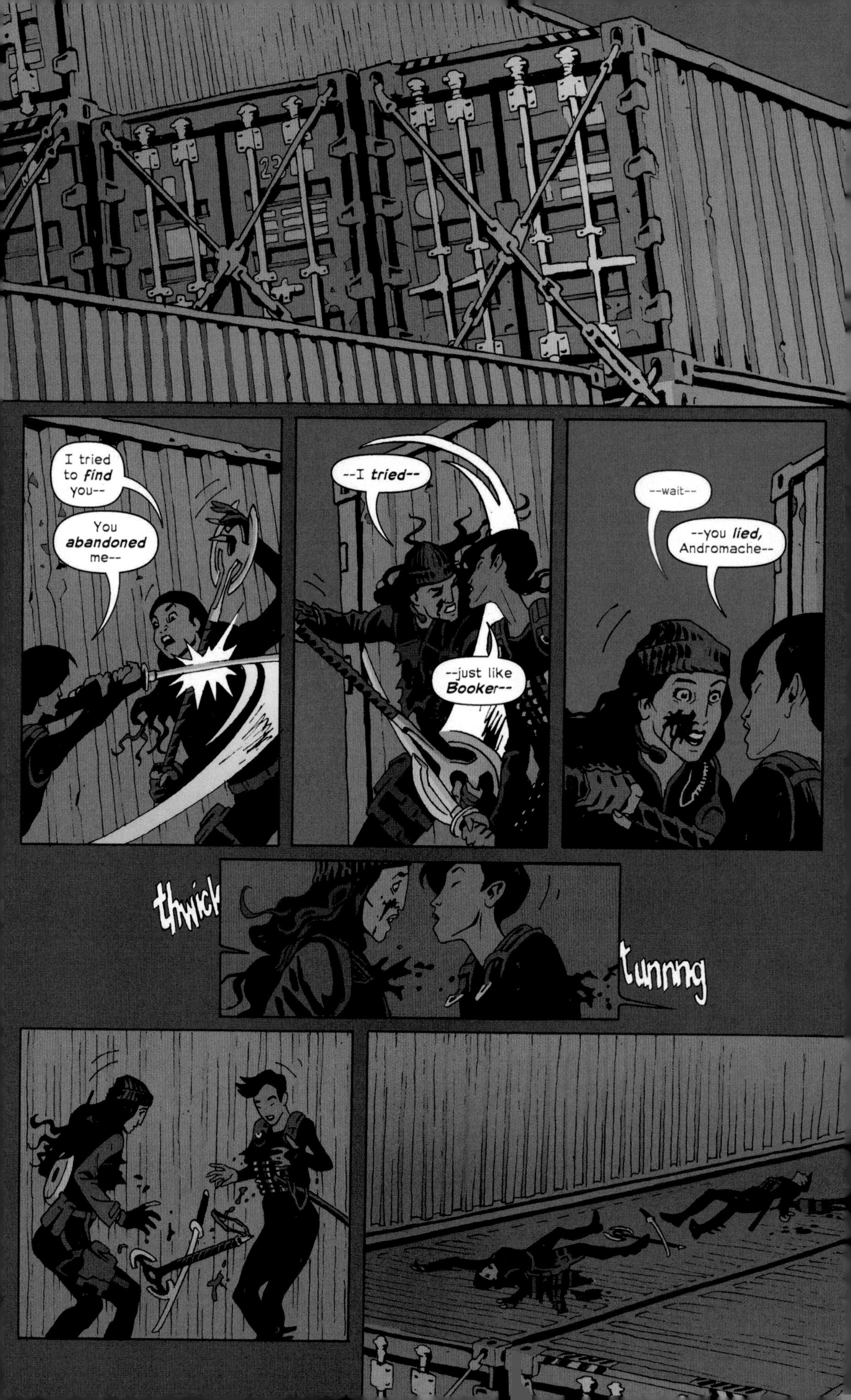
I tried to *find* you--
You ***abandoned*** me--
--I ***tried***--
--just like ***Booker***--
--wait--
--you ***lied,*** Andromache--
thwick
tunnng

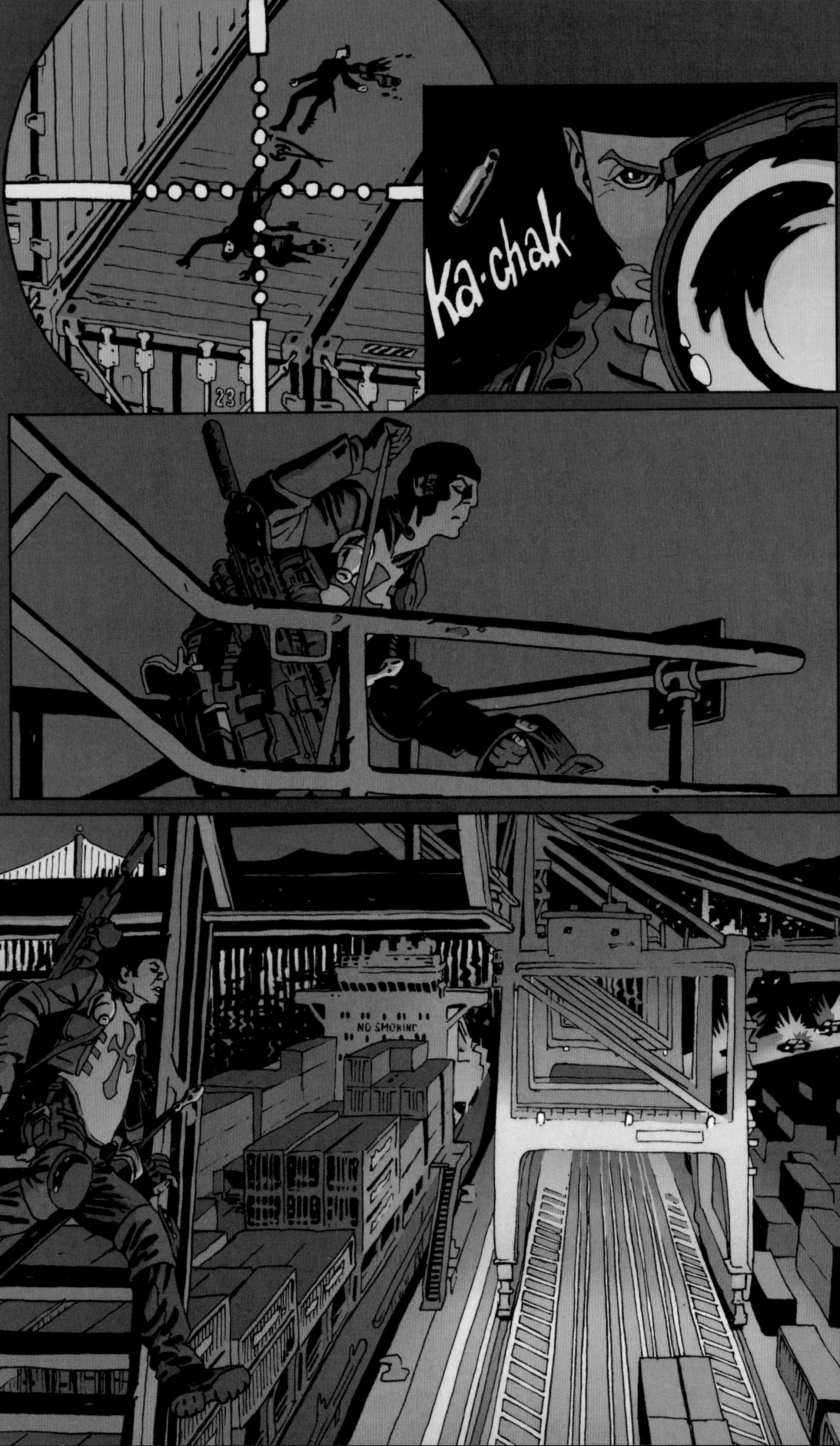
KA-CHAK
NO SMOKING

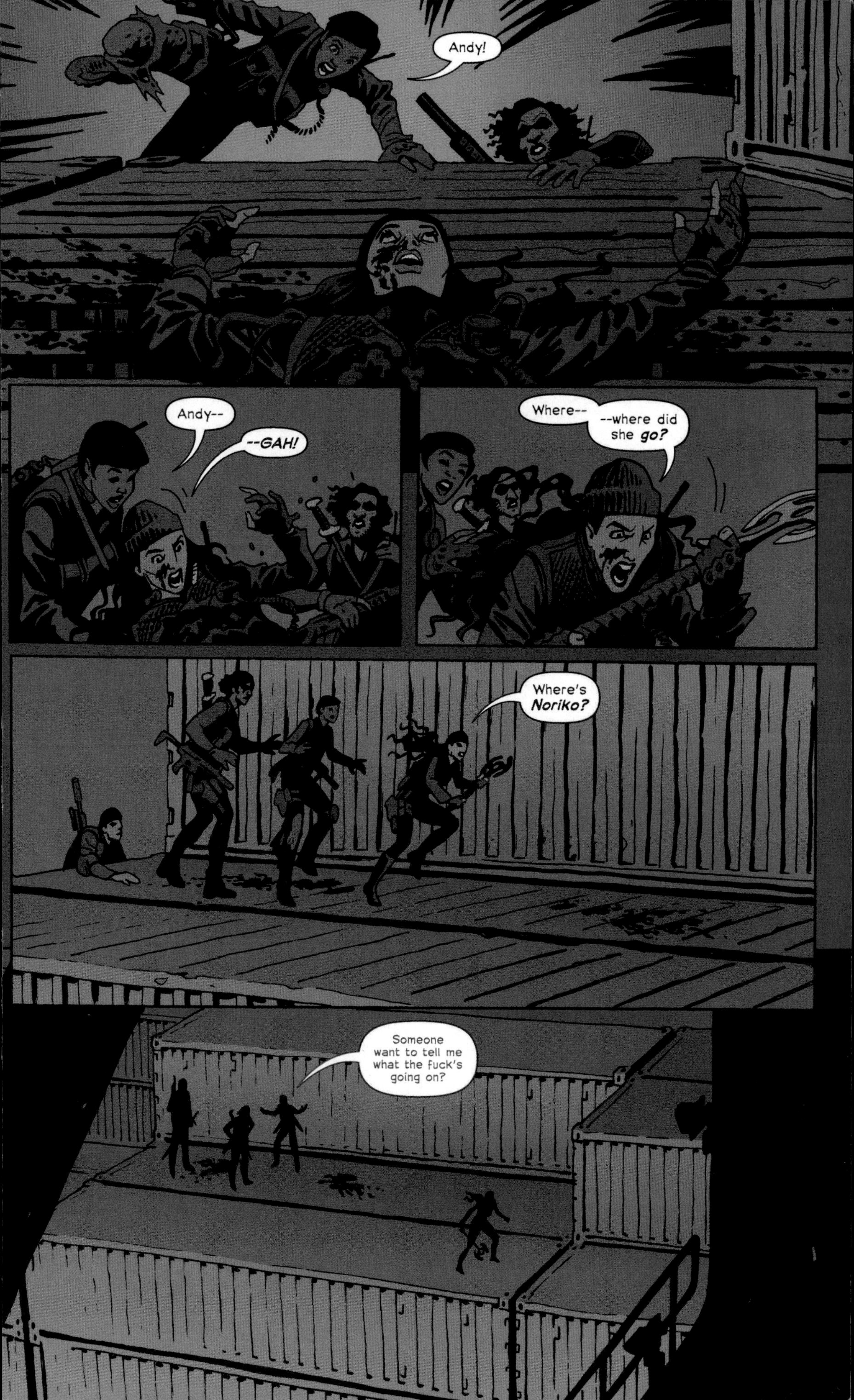
Andy!
Andy--
--GAH!
Where--
--where did she go?
Where's Noriko?
Someone want to tell me what the fuck's going on?

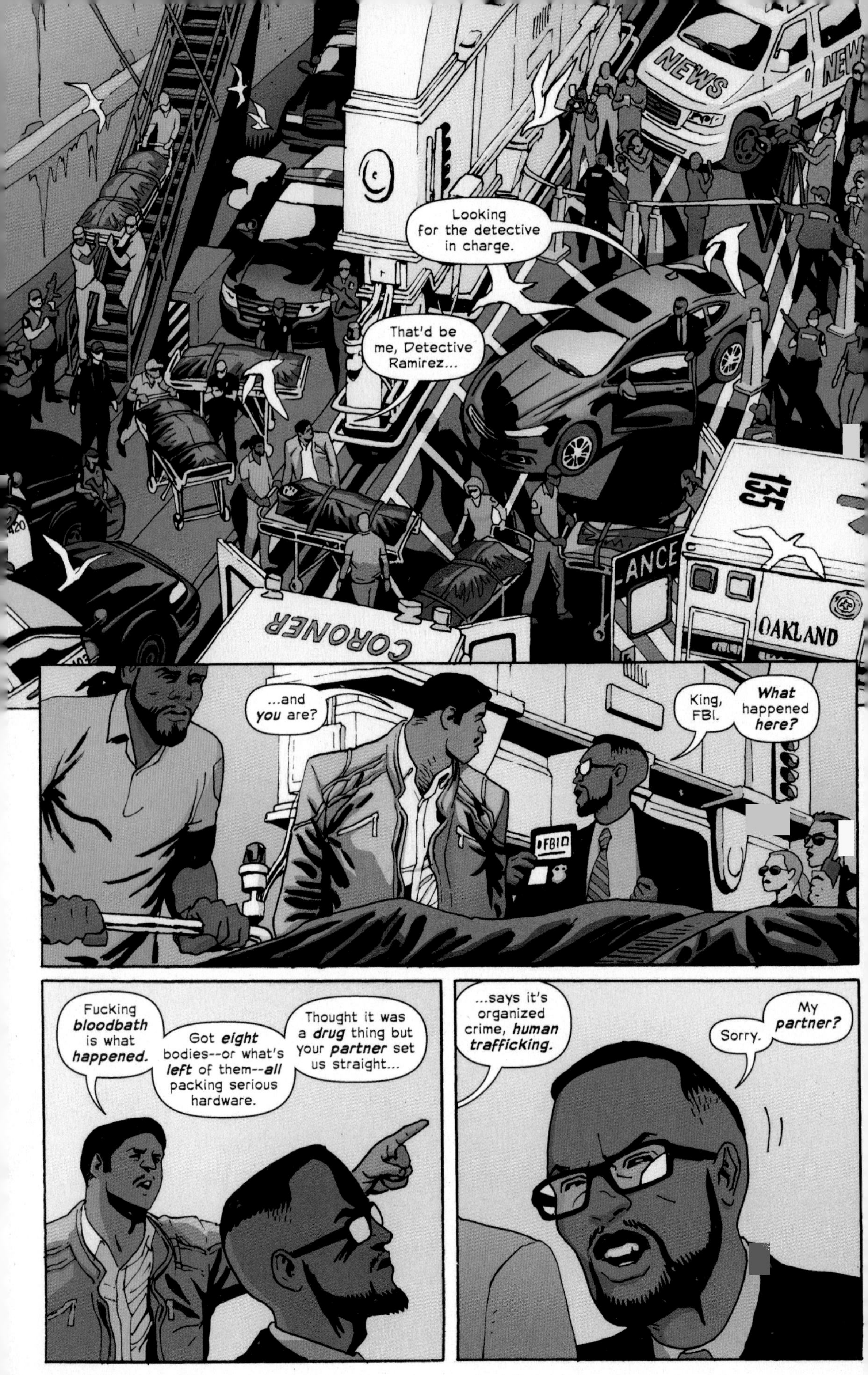
NEWS
Looking for the detective in charge.
That'd be me, Detective Ramirez...
CORONER
OAKLAND
...and *you* are?
King, FBI.
What happened *here?*
FBI
Fucking *bloodbath* is what *happened.*
Got *eight* bodies--or what's *left* of them--*all* packing serious hardware.
Thought it was a *drug* thing but your *partner* set us straight...
...says it's organized crime, *human trafficking.*
Sorry.
My *partner?*

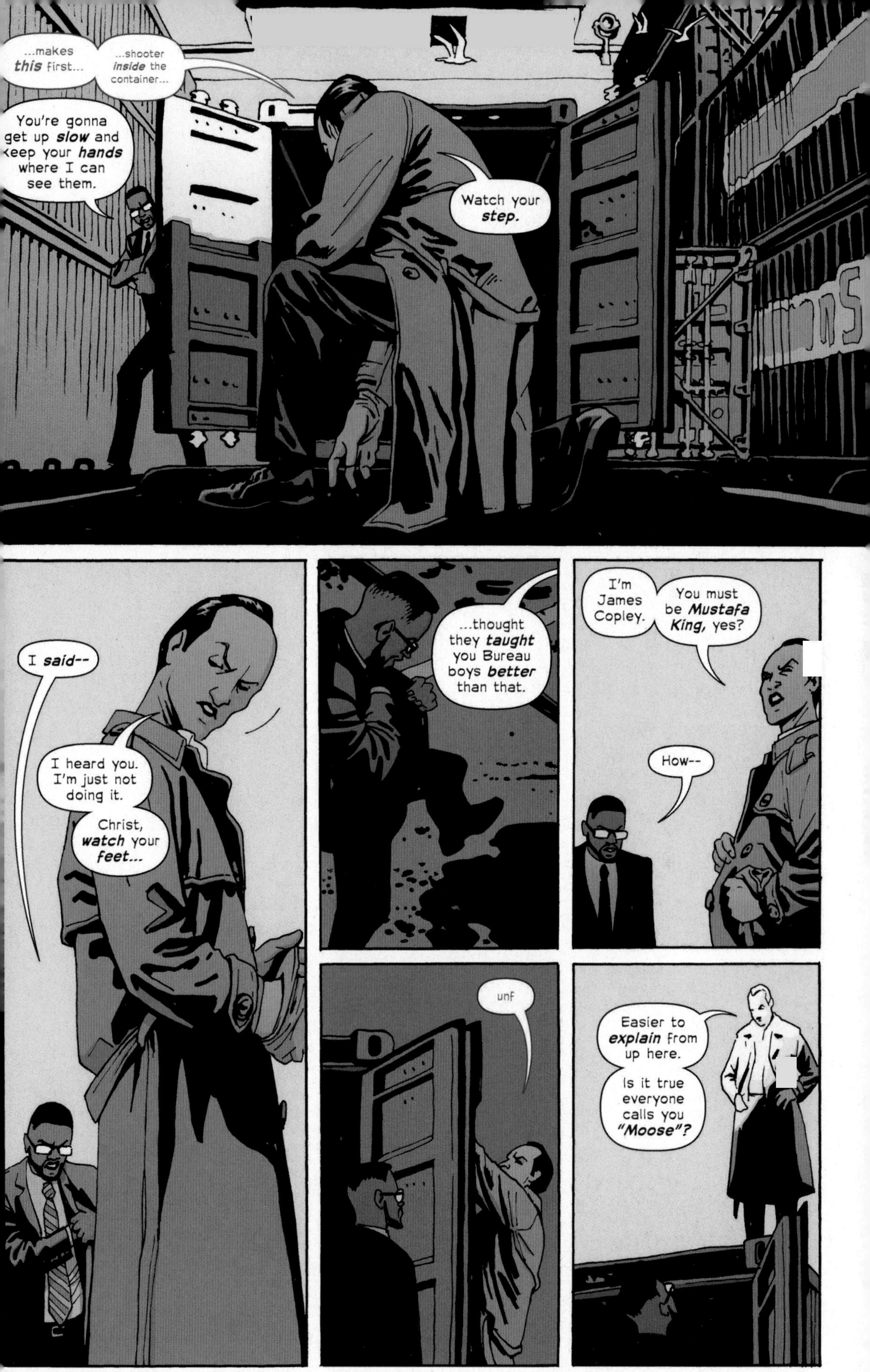
...makes this first...
...shooter inside the container...
You're gonna get up slow and keep your hands where I can see them.
Watch your step.
I said--
I heard you. I'm just not doing it.
Christ, watch your feet...
...thought they taught you Bureau boys better than that.
I'm James Copley.
You must be Mustafa King, yes?
How--
unf
Easier to explain from up here.
Is it true everyone calls you "Moose"?

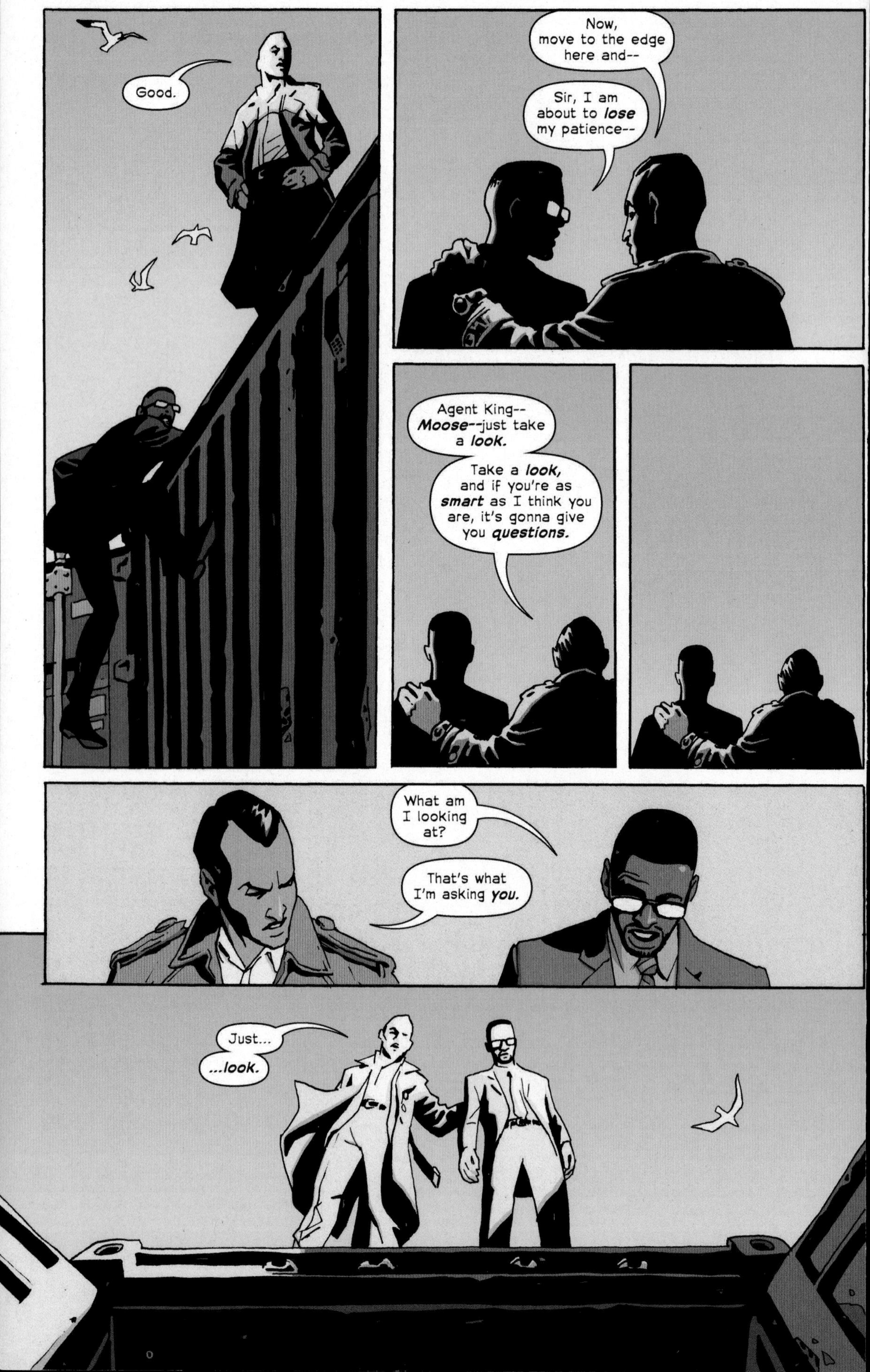
Good.
Now, move to the edge here and--
Sir, I am about to *lose* my patience--
Agent King-- *Moose*--just take a *look.*
Take a *look,* and if you're as *smart* as I think you are, it's gonna give you *questions.*
What am I looking at?
That's what I'm asking *you.*
Just...
...*look.*

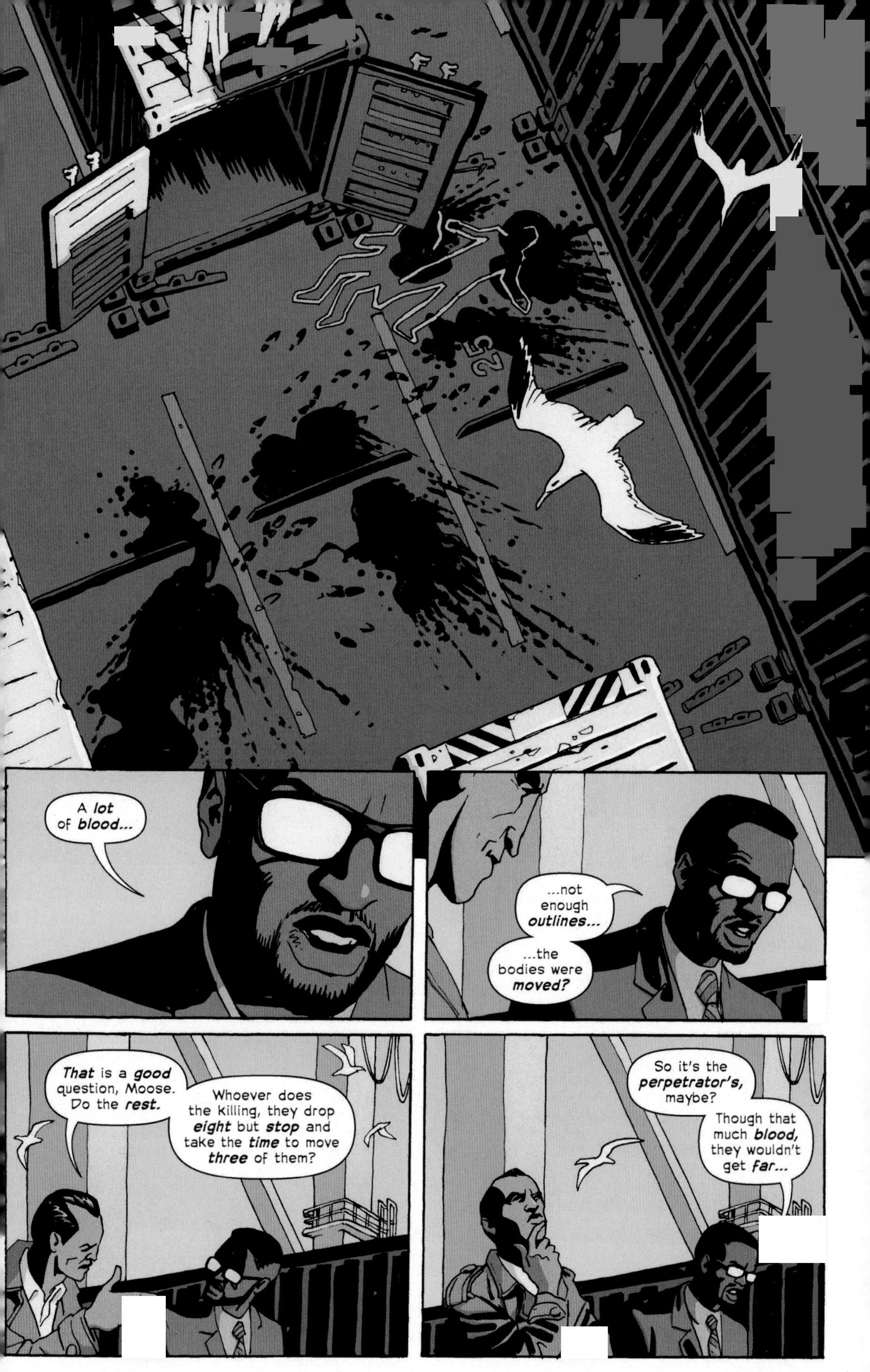
A lot of blood...
...not enough outlines...
...the bodies were moved?
That is a good question, Moose. Do the rest.
Whoever does the killing, they drop eight but stop and take the time to move three of them?
So it's the perpetrator's, maybe?
Though that much blood, they wouldn't get far...

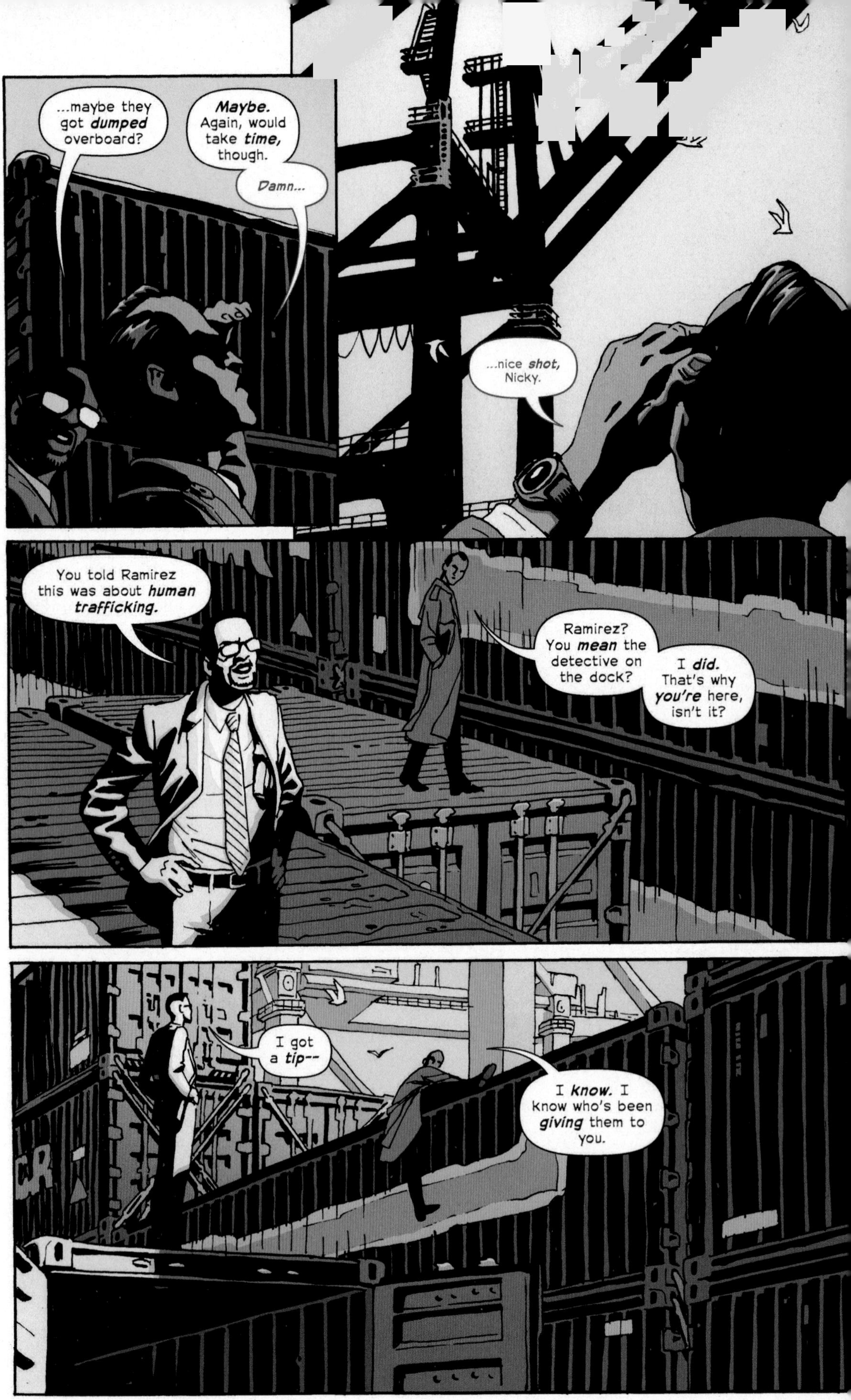
...maybe they got dumped overboard?
Maybe. Again, would take time, though.
Damn...
...nice shot, Nicky.
You told Ramirez this was about human trafficking.
Ramirez? You mean the detective on the dock?
I did. That's why you're here, isn't it?
I got a tip--
I know. I know who's been giving them to you.

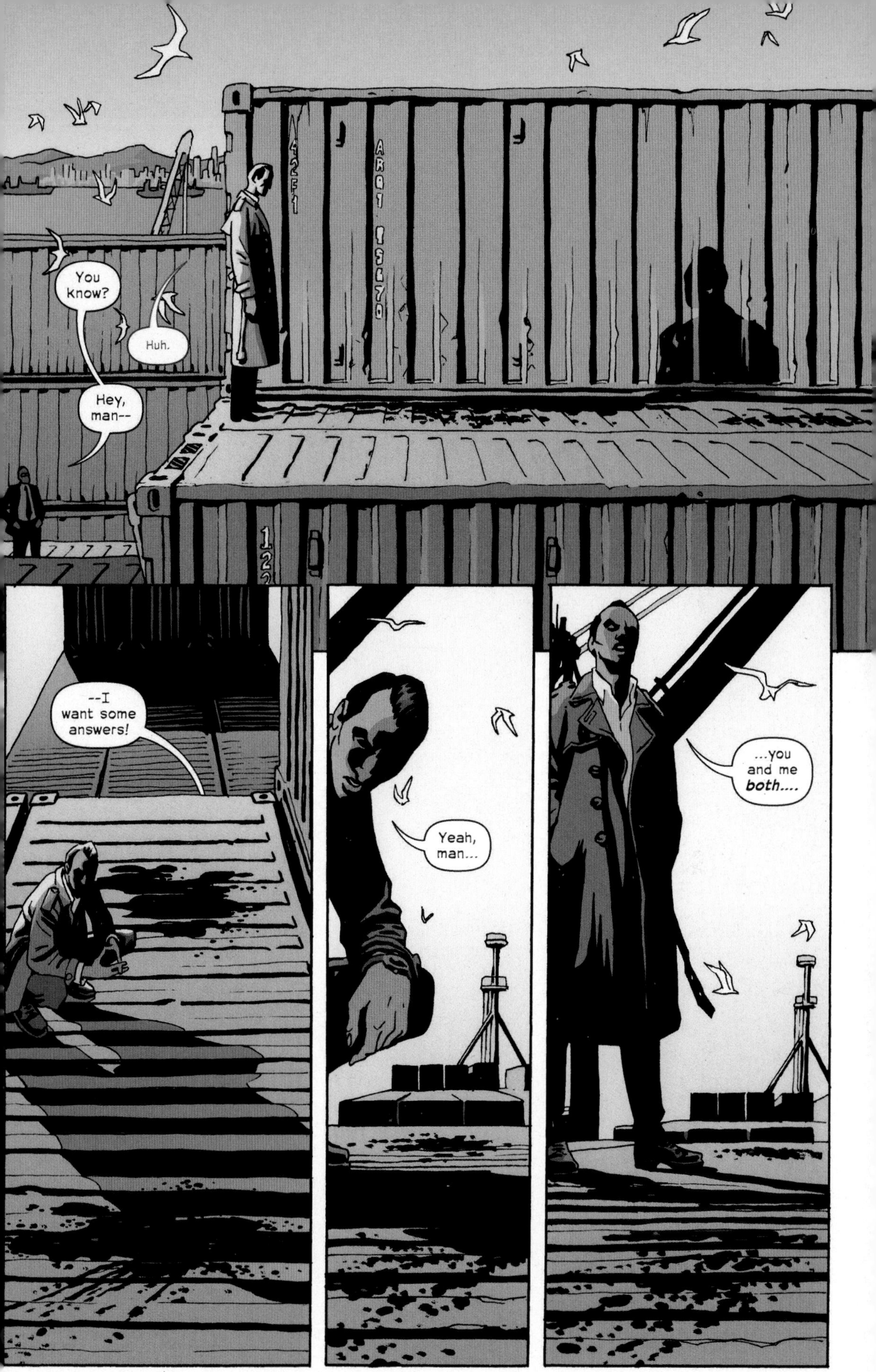
You know?
Huh.
Hey, man--
--I want some answers!
Yeah, man...
...you and me *both*....

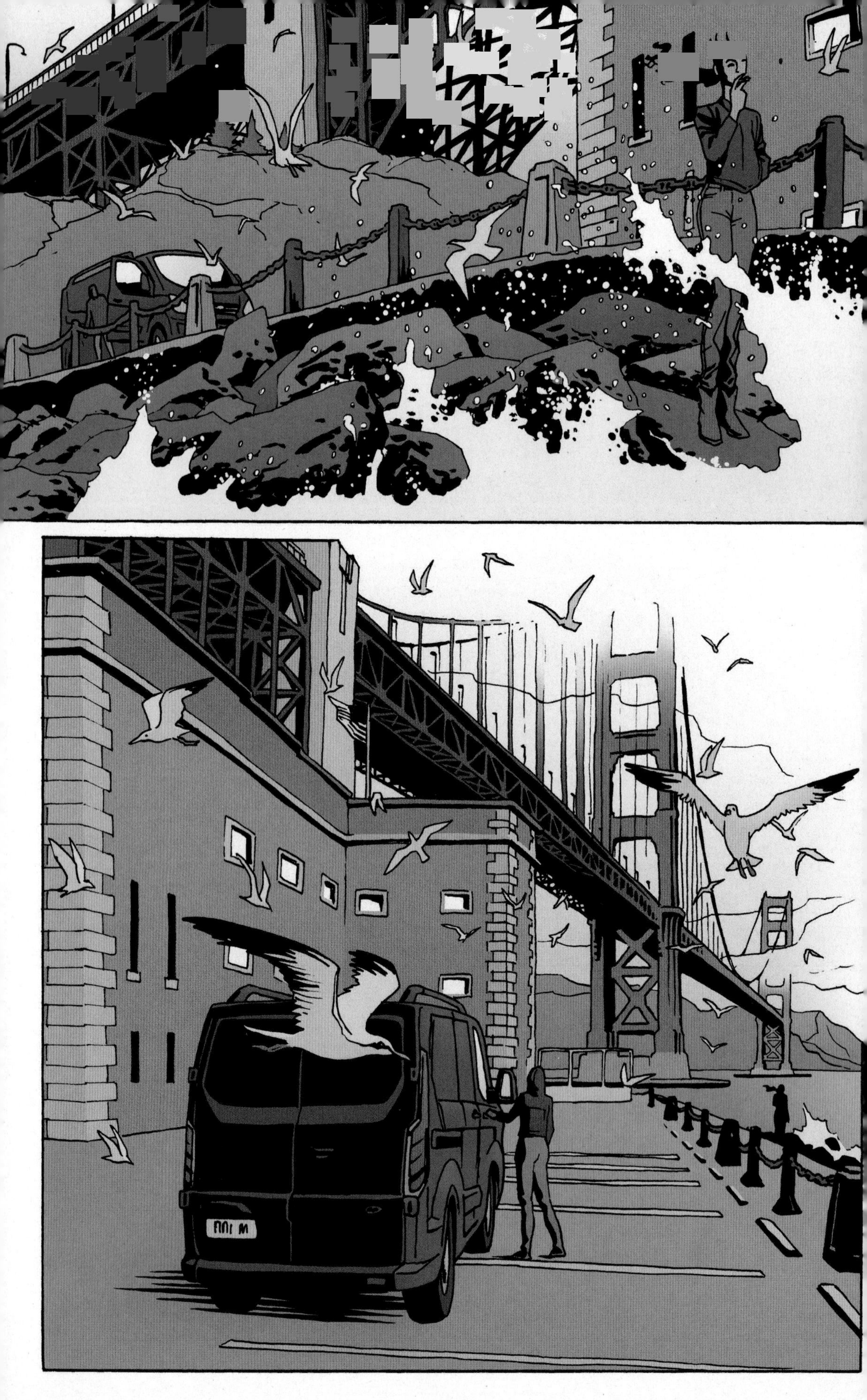

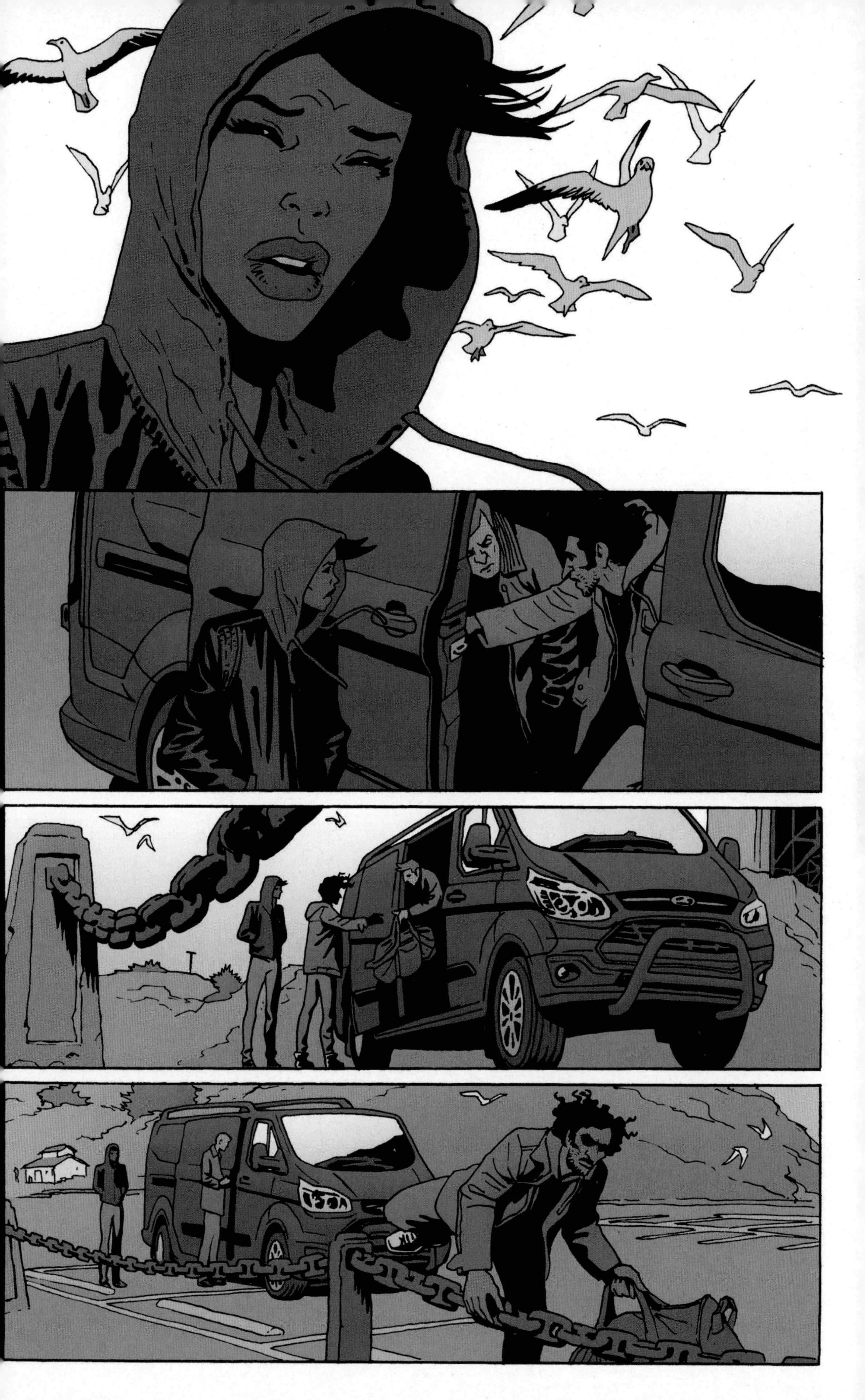

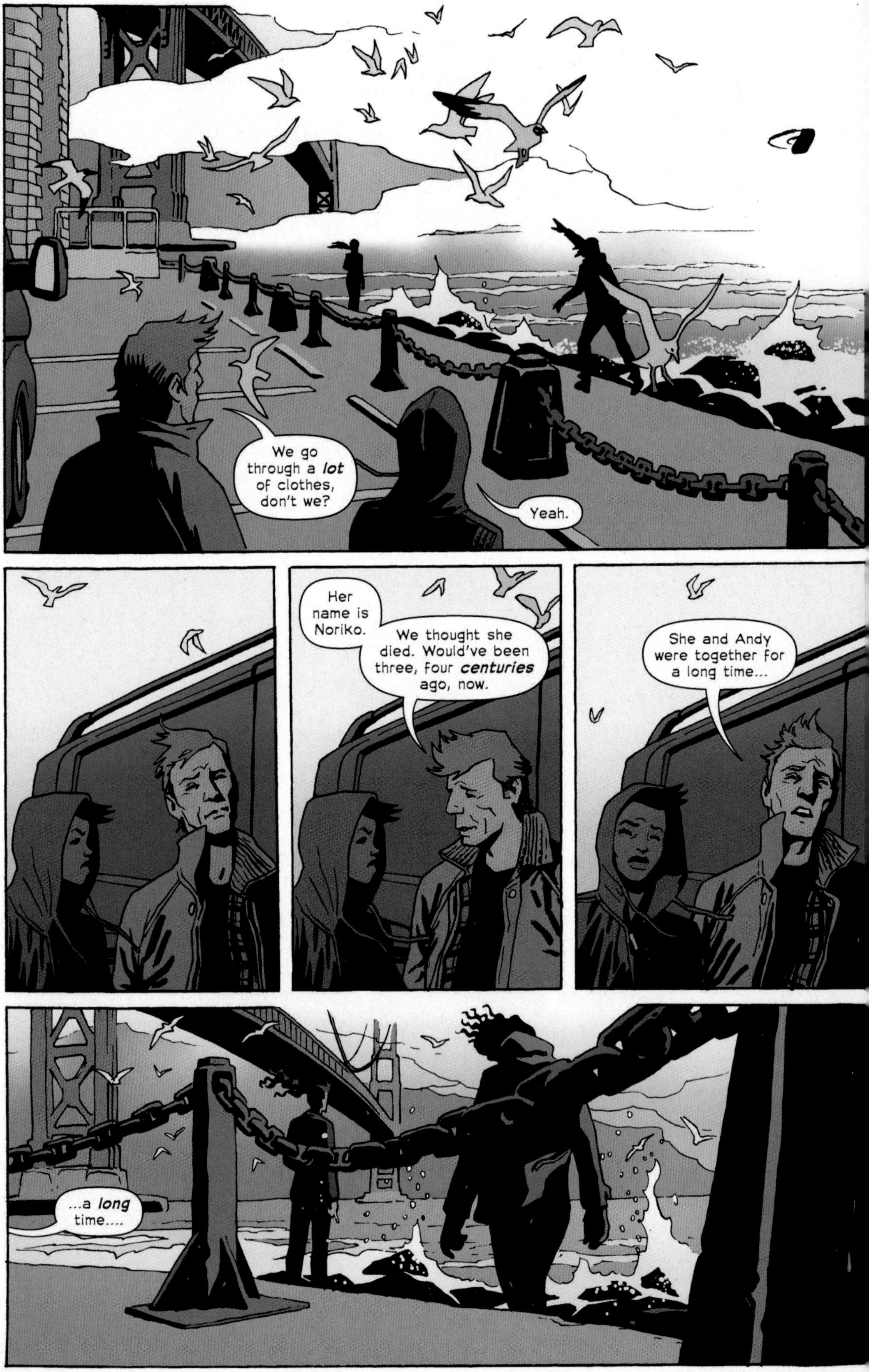

We go through a *lot* of clothes, don't we?
Yeah.
Her name is Noriko.
We thought she died. Would've been three, four *centuries* ago, now.
She and Andy were together for a long time...
...a *long* time....

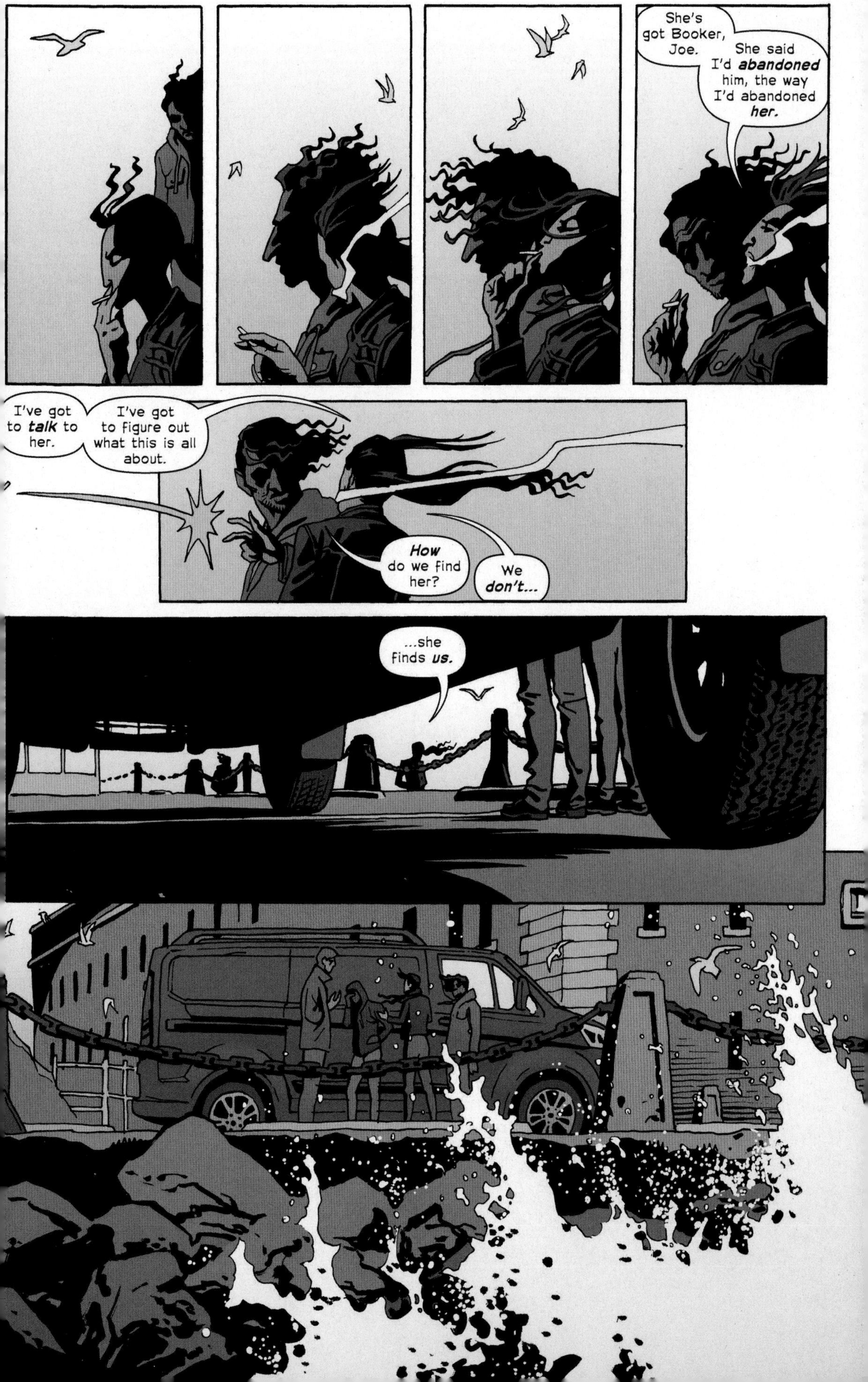
She's got Booker, Joe.
She said I'd abandoned him, the way I'd abandoned her.
I've got to talk to her.
I've got to figure out what this is all about.
How do we find her?
We don't...
...she finds us.

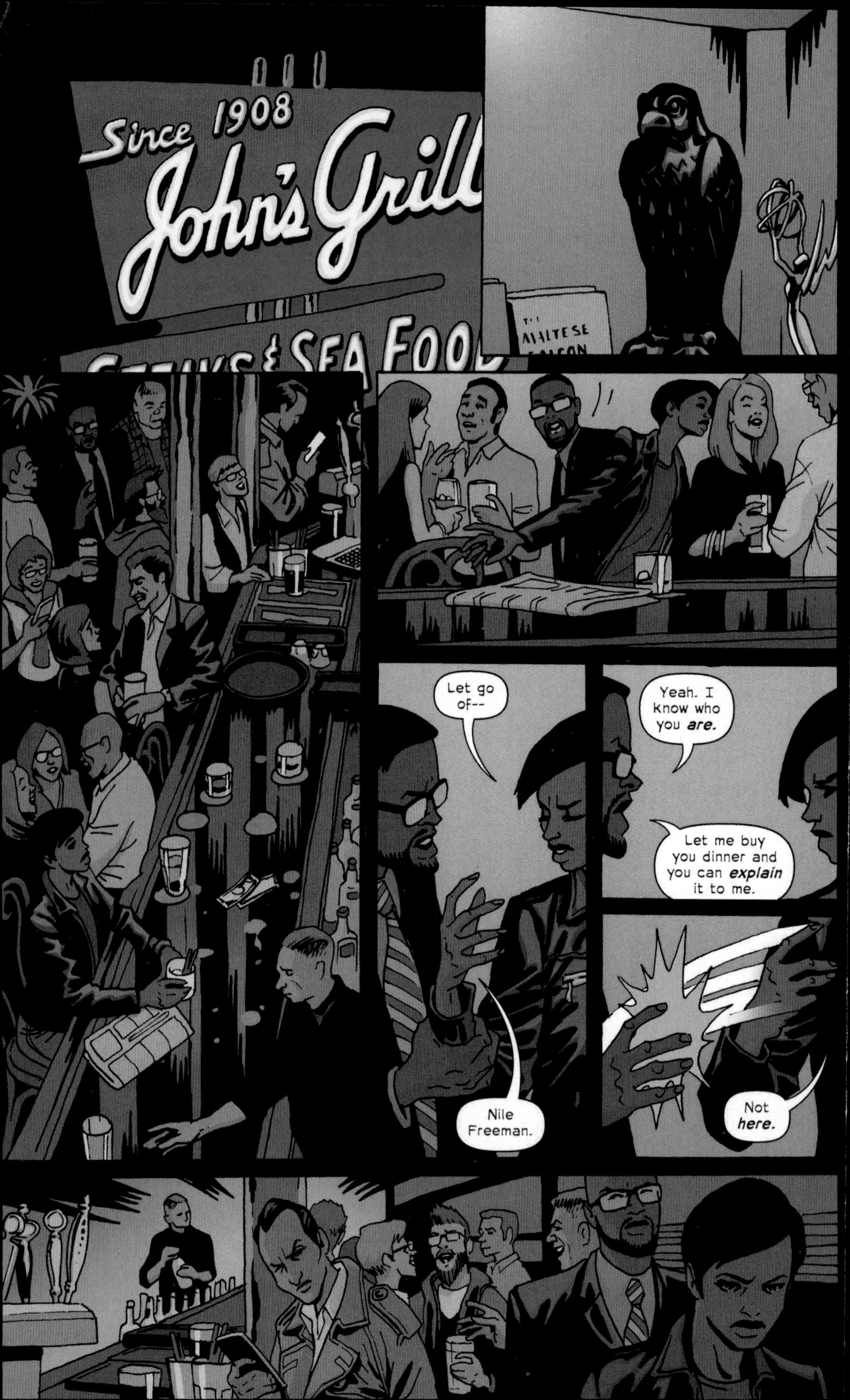
Since 1908
John's Grill
STEAKS & SEA FOOD
THE MALTESE FALCON
Let go of--
Nile Freeman.
Yeah. I know who you *are.*
Let me buy you dinner and you can *explain* it to me.
Not *here.*

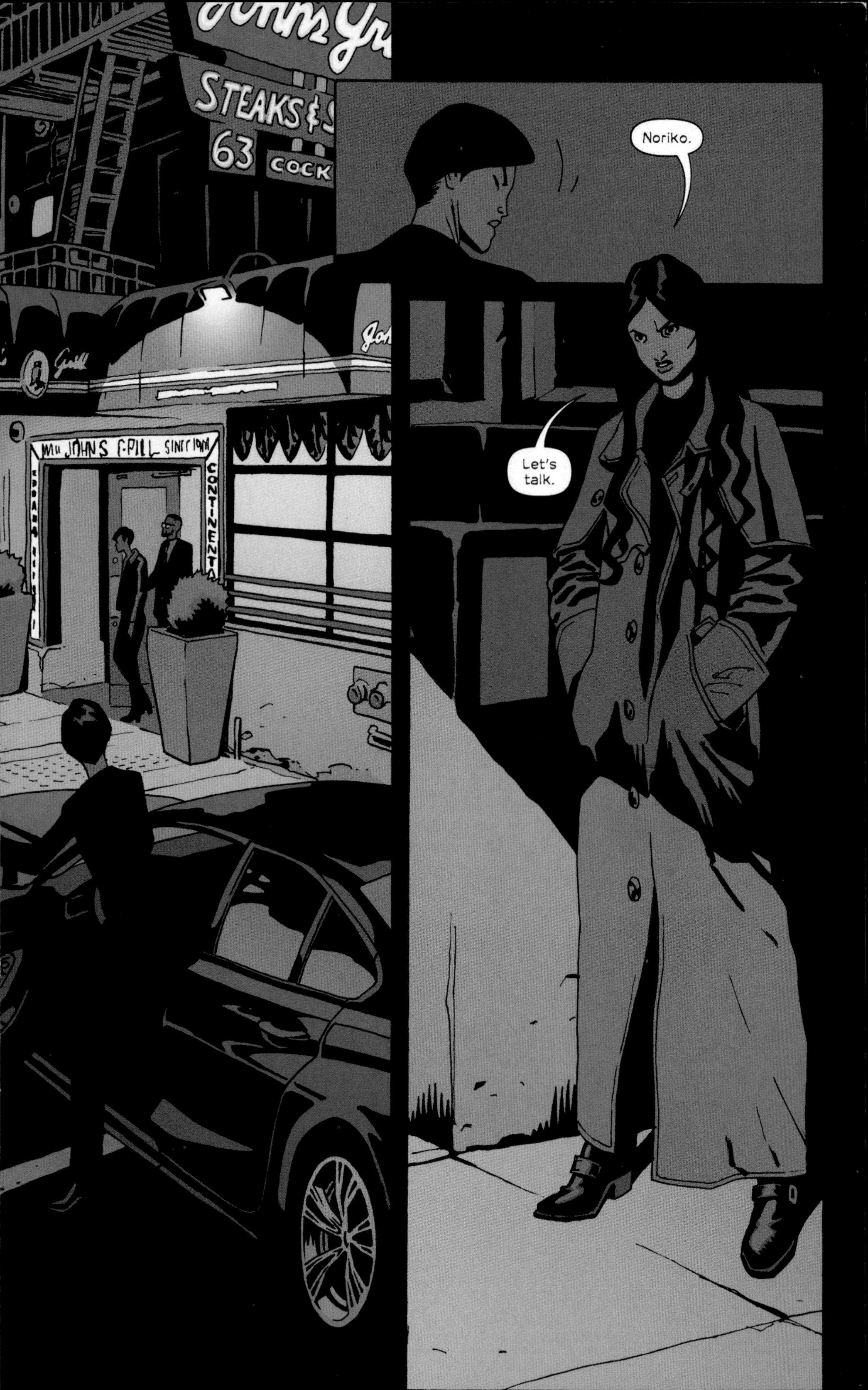
Noriko.
Let's talk.

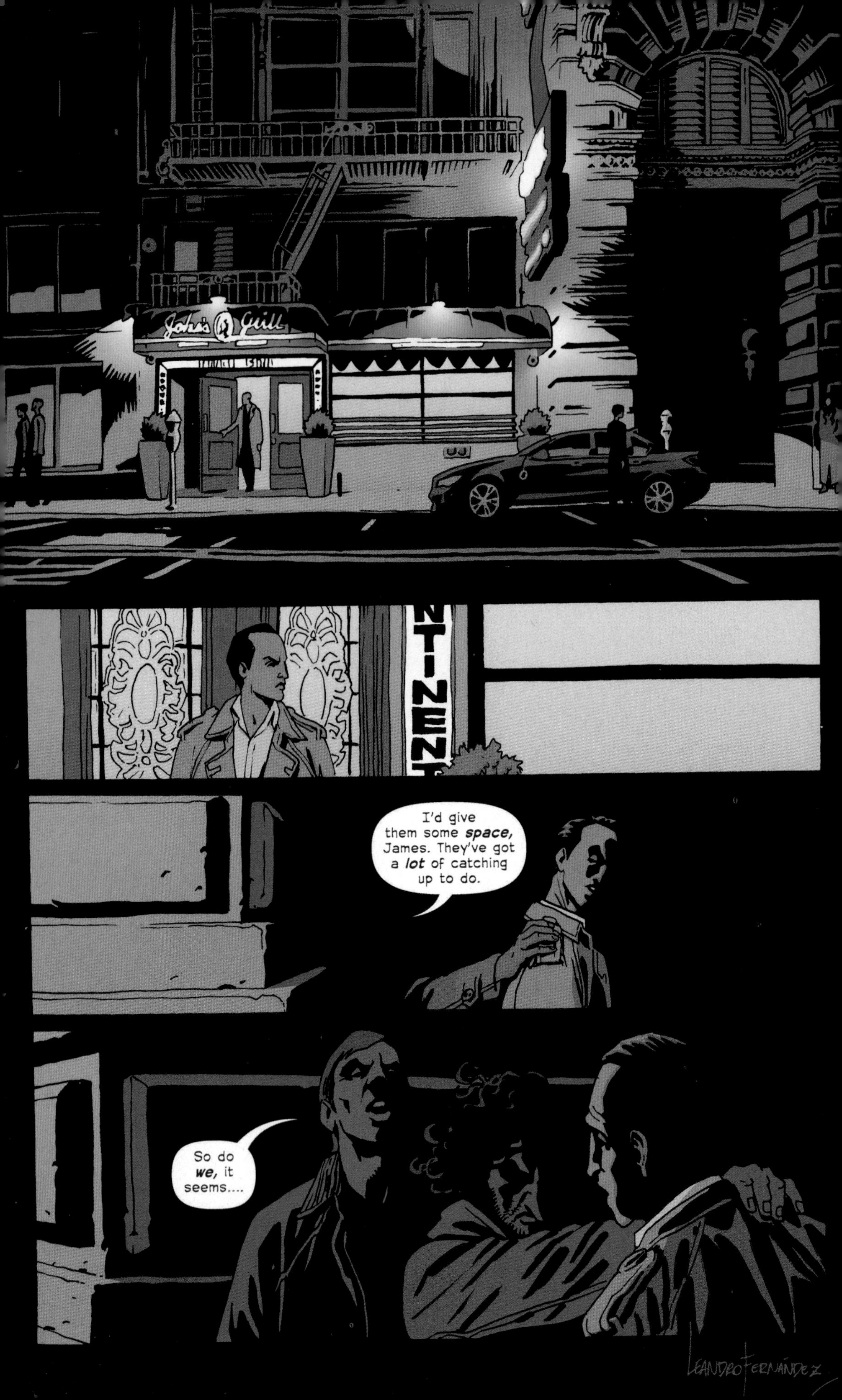
John's Grill
NTINENT
I'd give them some *space,* James. They've got a *lot* of catching up to do.
So do *we,* it seems....
LEANDRO FERNÁNDEZ

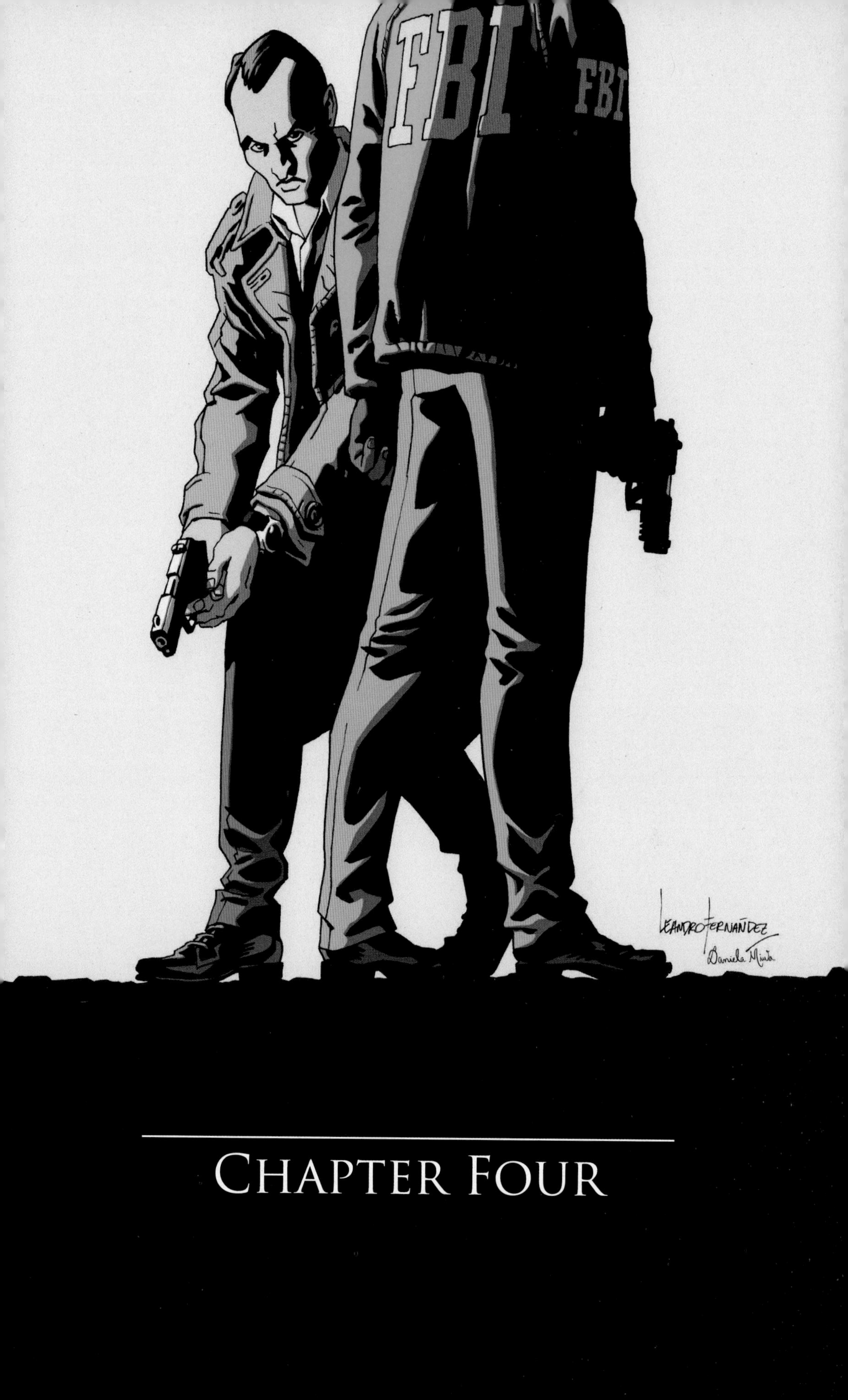
FBI
FBI
LEANDRO FERNÁNDEZ

CHAPTER FOUR

"BETRAYAL IS THE ONLY
TRUTH THAT STICKS."

~Arthur Miller

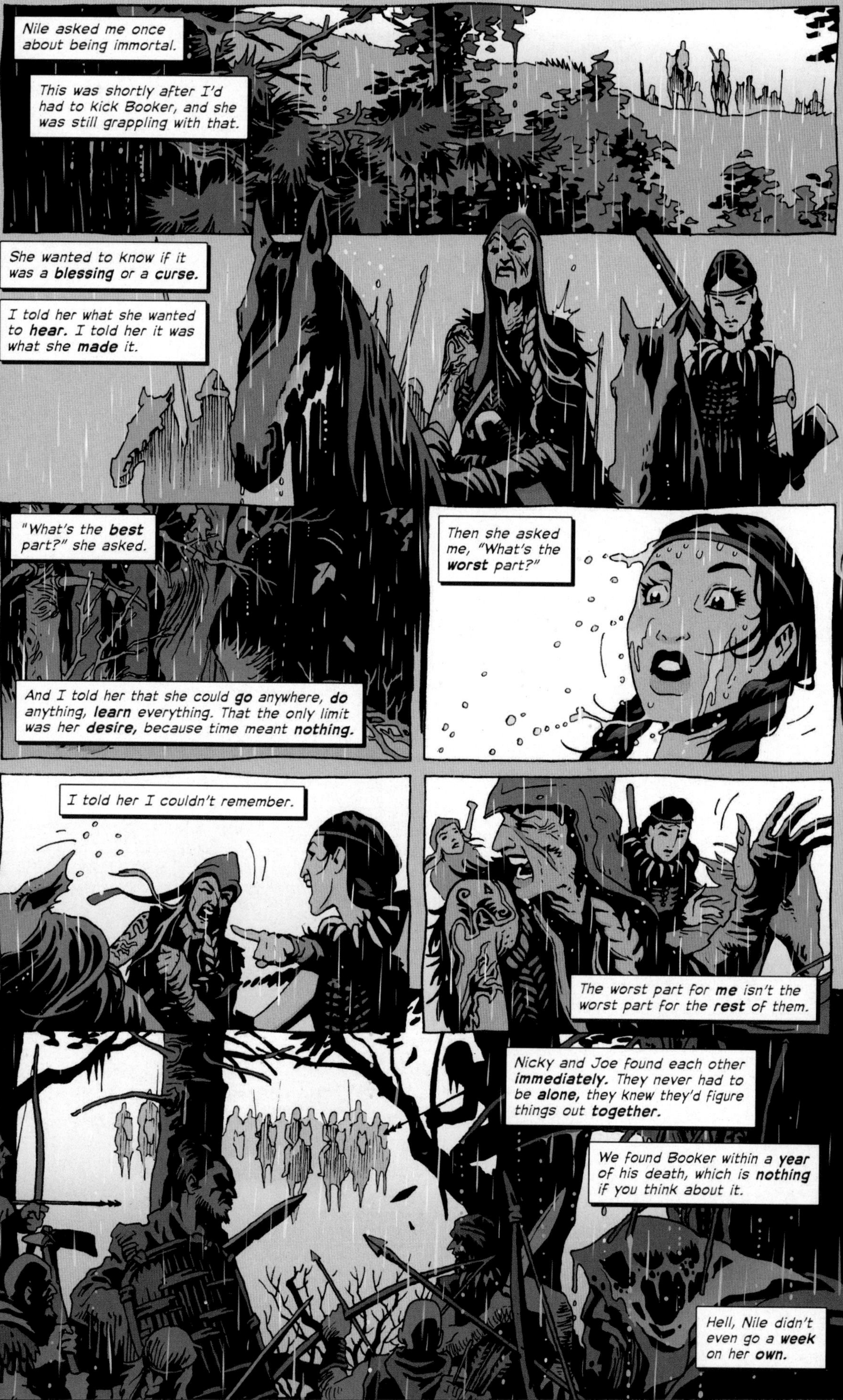

Nile asked me once about being immortal.
This was shortly after I'd had to kick Booker, and she was still grappling with that.
She wanted to know if it was a **blessing** or a **curse.**
I told her what she wanted to **hear.** I told her it was what she **made** it.
"What's the **best** part?" she asked.
And I told her that she could **go** anywhere, **do** anything, **learn** everything. That the only limit was her **desire,** because time meant **nothing.**
Then she asked me, "What's the **worst** part?"
I told her I couldn't remember.
The worst part for **me** isn't the worst part for the **rest** of them.
Nicky and Joe found each other **immediately.** They never had to be **alone,** they knew they'd figure things out **together.**
We found Booker within a **year** of his death, which is **nothing** if you think about it.
Hell, Nile didn't even go a **week** on her **own.**

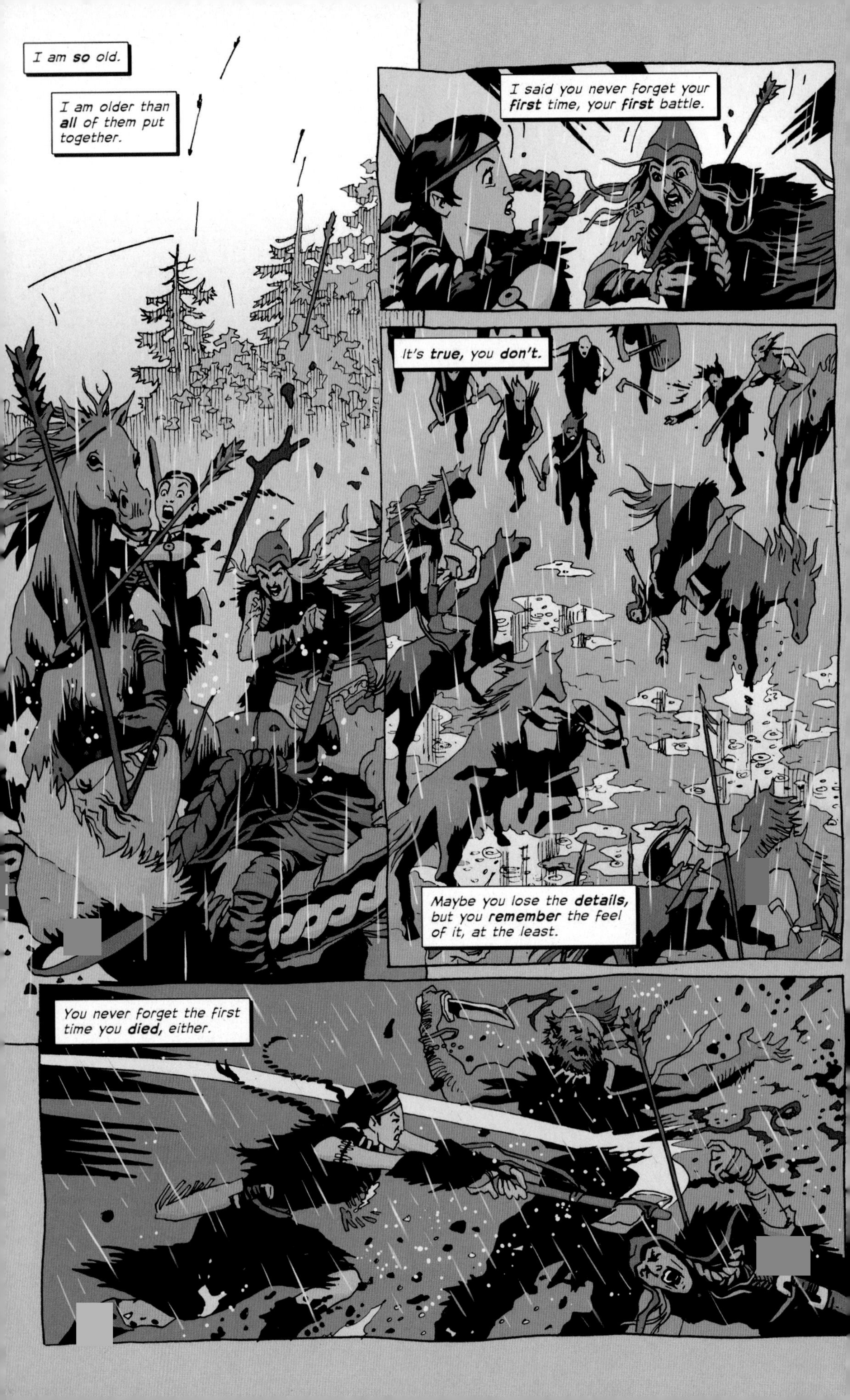
I am **so** old.
I am older than **all** of them put together.
I said you never forget your **first** time, your **first** battle.
It's **true,** you **don't.**
Maybe you lose the **details,** but you **remember** the feel of it, at the least.
You never forget the first time you **died,** either.

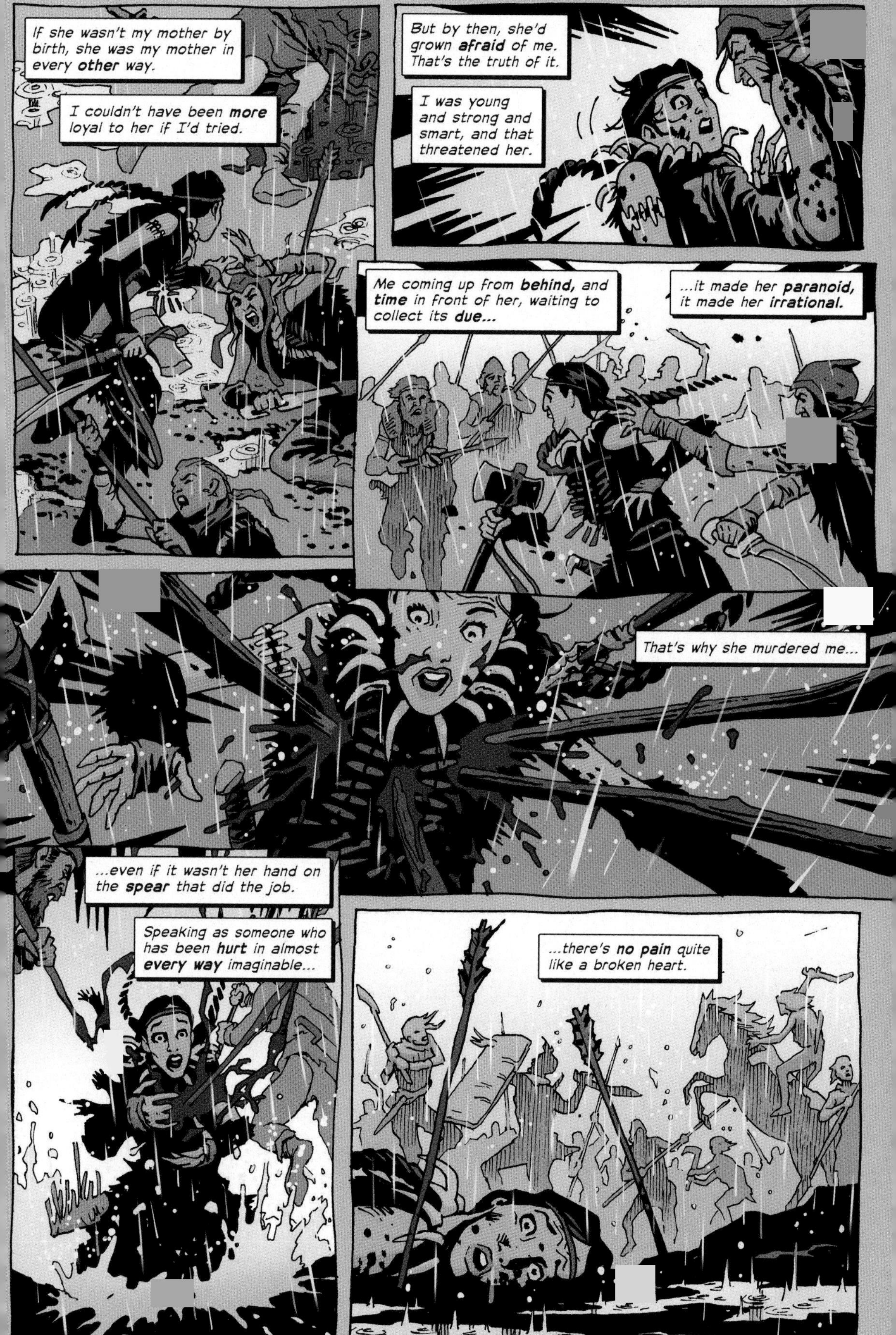
If she wasn't my mother by birth, she was my mother in every other way.
I couldn't have been more loyal to her if I'd tried.
But by then, she'd grown afraid of me. That's the truth of it.
I was young and strong and smart, and that threatened her.
Me coming up from behind, and time in front of her, waiting to collect its due...
...it made her paranoid, it made her irrational.
That's why she murdered me...
...even if it wasn't her hand on the spear that did the job.
Speaking as someone who has been hurt in almost every way imaginable...
...there's no pain quite like a broken heart.

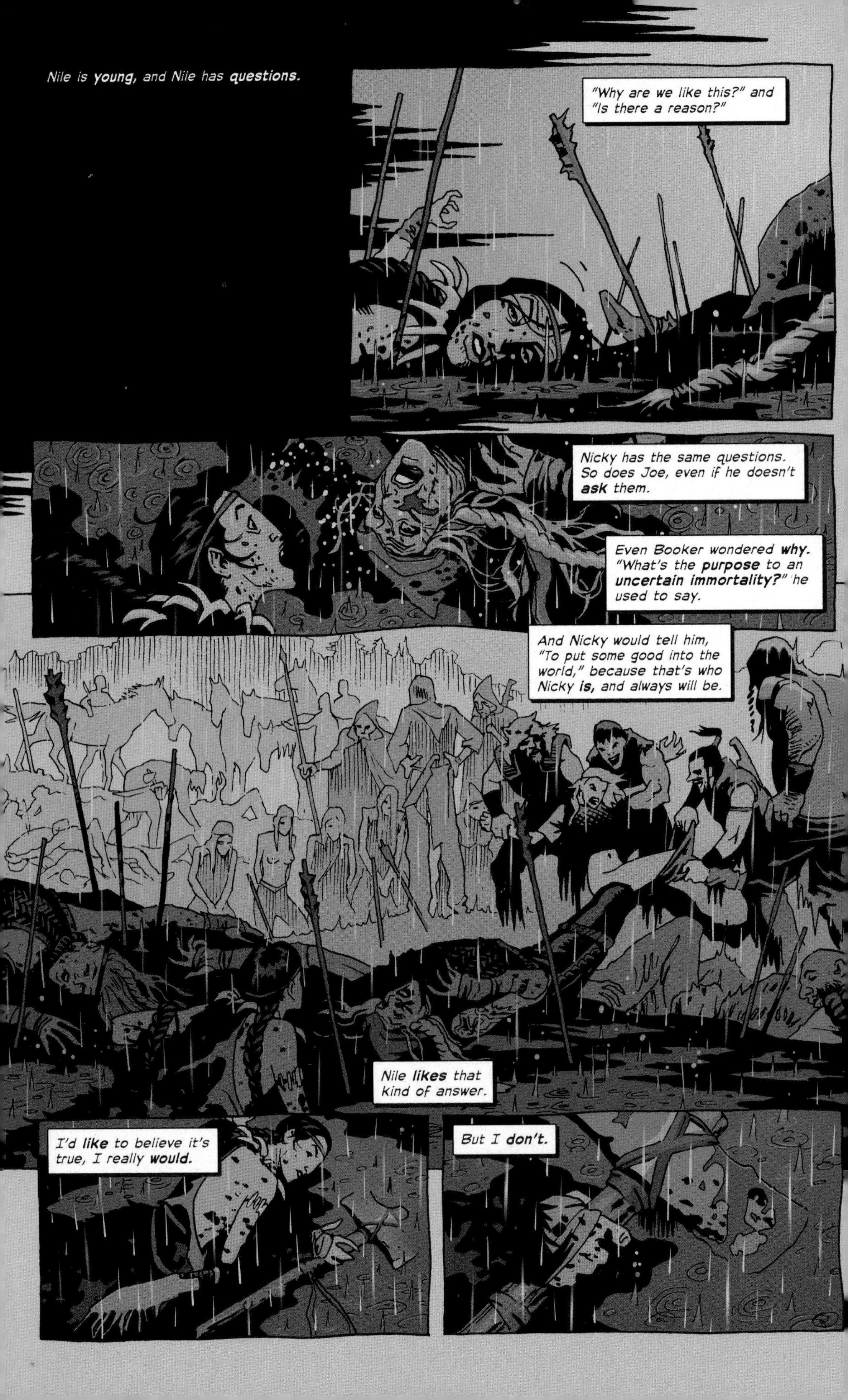

Nile is young, and Nile has questions.
"Why are we like this?" and "Is there a reason?"
Nicky has the same questions. So does Joe, even if he doesn't ask them.
Even Booker wondered why. "What's the purpose to an uncertain immortality?" he used to say.
And Nicky would tell him, "To put some good into the world," because that's who Nicky is, and always will be.
Nile likes that kind of answer.
I'd like to believe it's true, I really would.
But I don't.

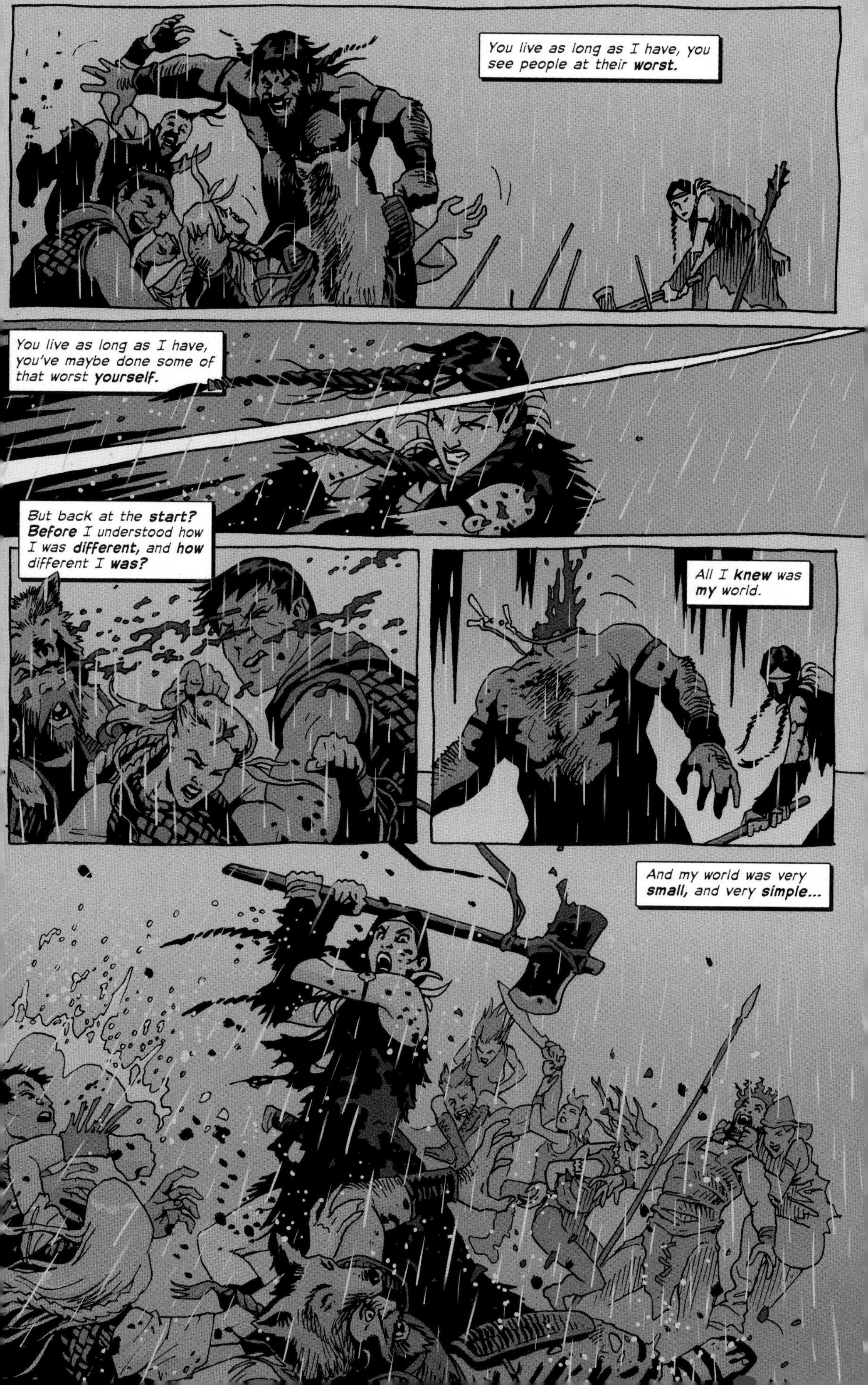
You live as long as I have, you see people at their **worst.**
You live as long as I have, you've maybe done some of that worst **yourself.**
But back at the **start? Before** I understood how I was **different,** and **how** different I **was?**
All I **knew** was **my** world.
And my world was very **small,** and very **simple...**

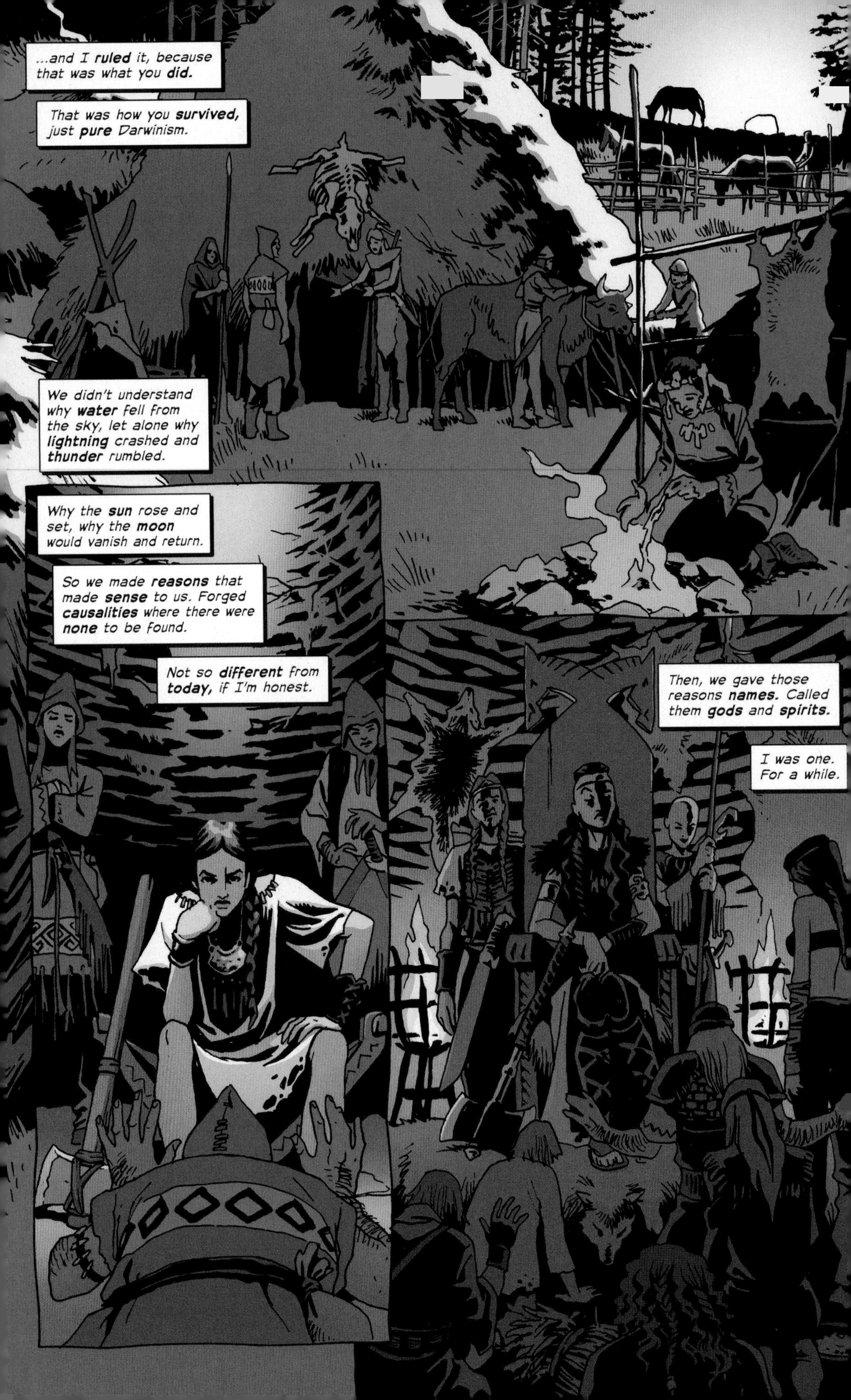

...and I ruled it, because that was what you did.
That was how you survived, just pure Darwinism.
We didn't understand why water fell from the sky, let alone why lightning crashed and thunder rumbled.
Why the sun rose and set, why the moon would vanish and return.
So we made reasons that made sense to us. Forged causalities where there were none to be found.
Not so different from today, if I'm honest.
Then, we gave those reasons names. Called them gods and spirits.
I was one. For a while.

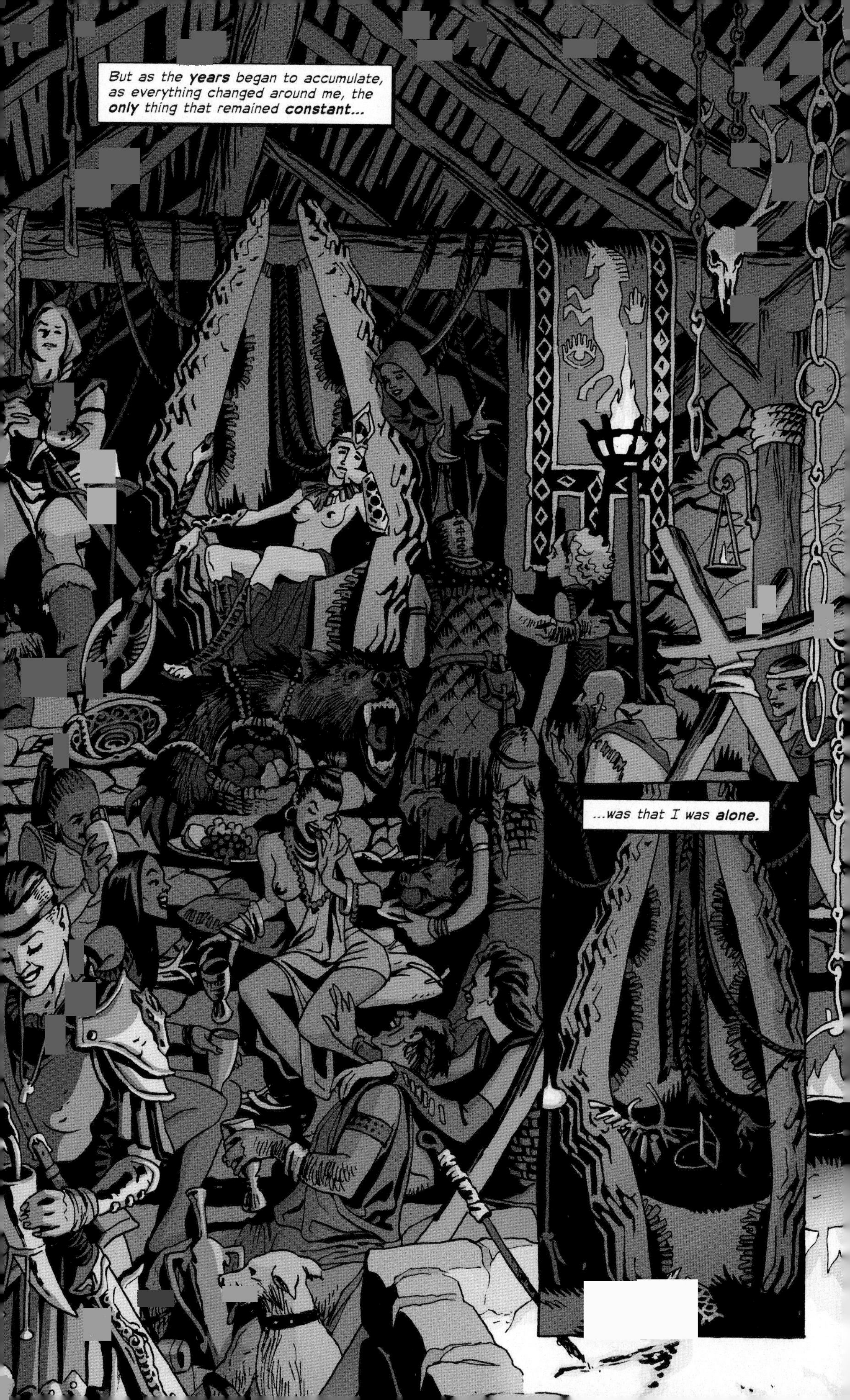
But as the years began to accumulate, as everything changed around me, the only thing that remained constant...
...was that I was alone.

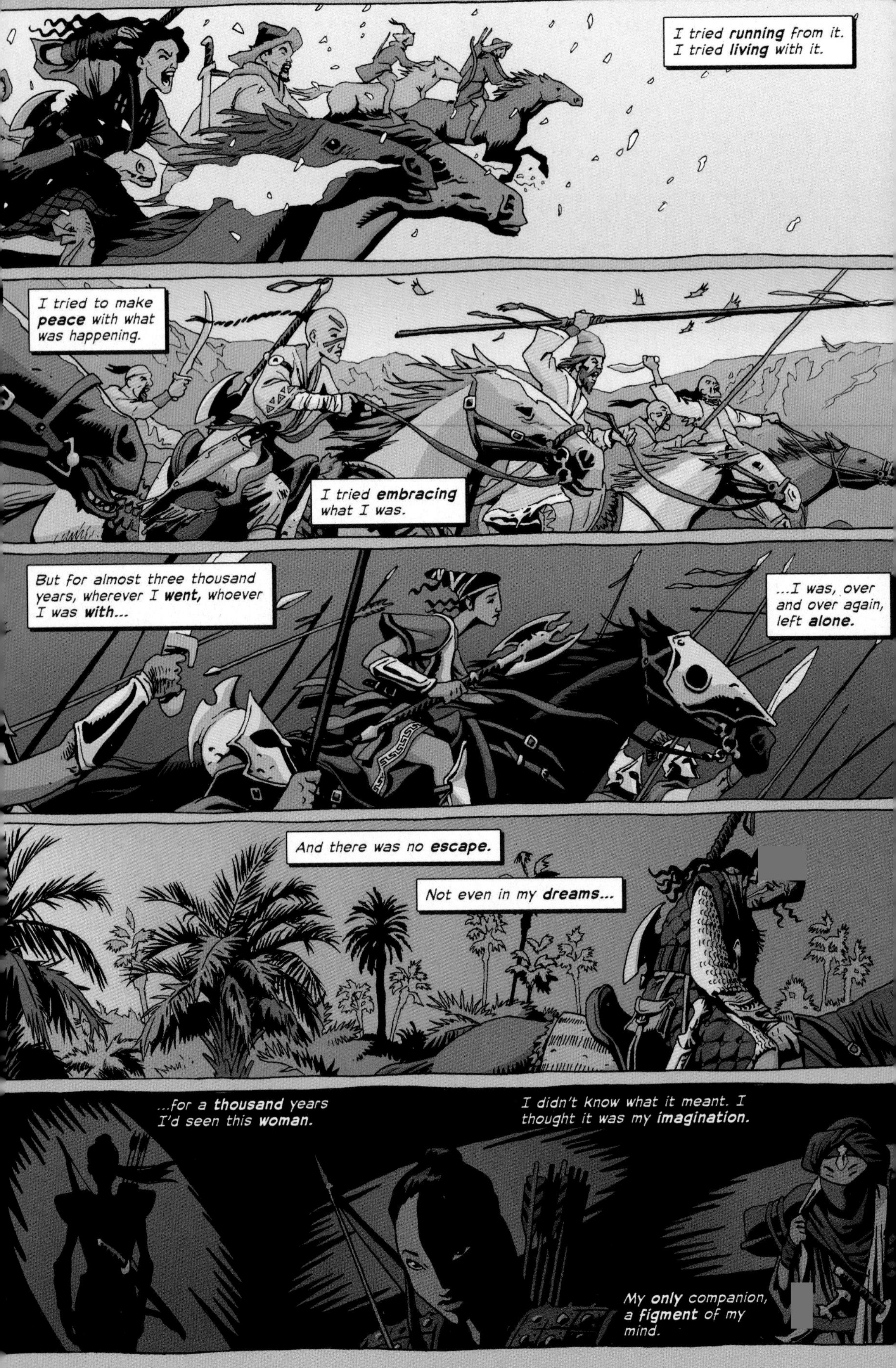

I tried running from it. I tried living with it.
I tried to make peace with what was happening.
I tried embracing what I was.
But for almost three thousand years, wherever I went, whoever I was with...
...I was, over and over again, left alone.
And there was no escape.
Not even in my dreams...
...for a thousand years I'd seen this woman.
I didn't know what it meant. I thought it was my imagination.
My only companion, a figment of my mind.

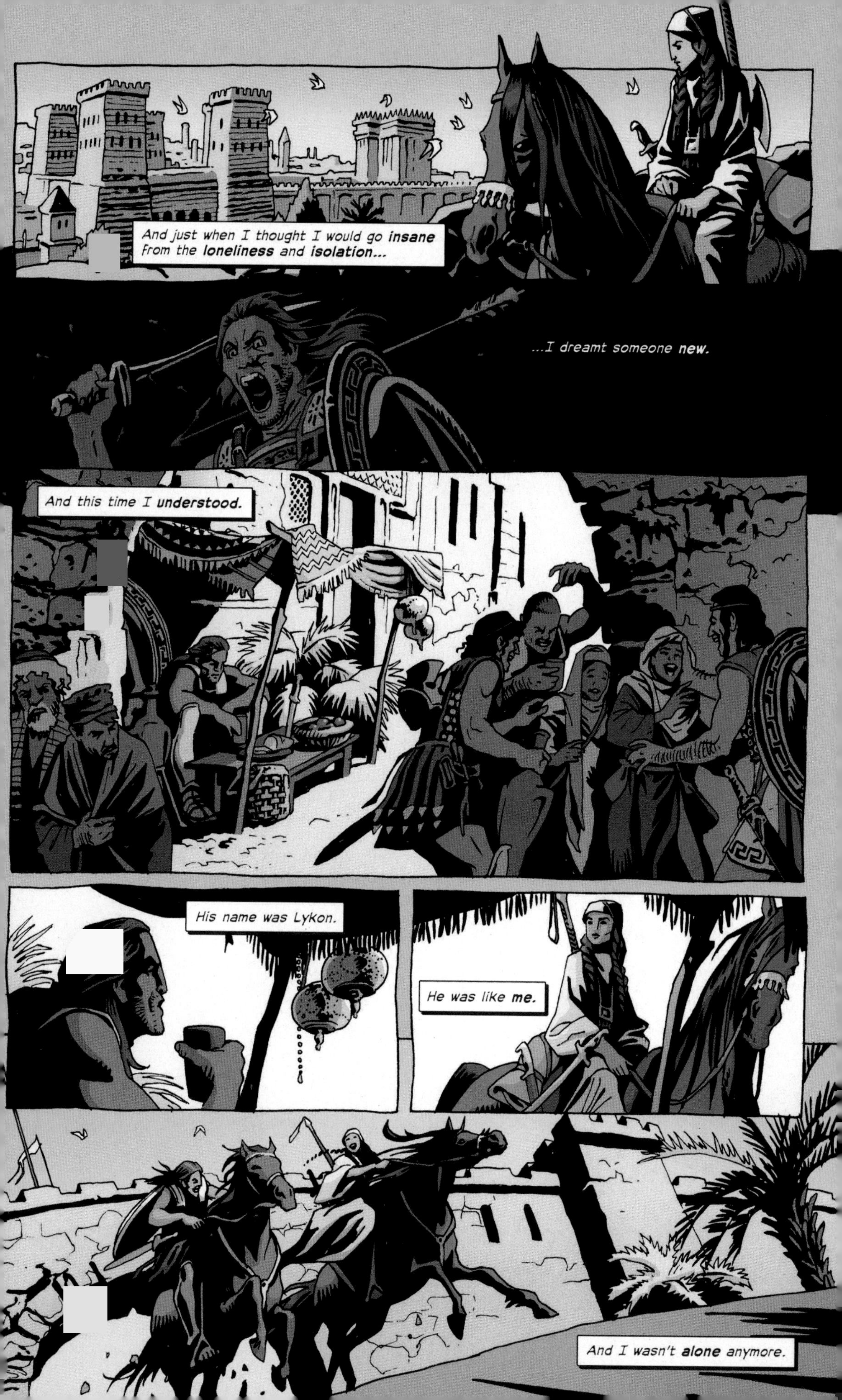
And just when I thought I would go insane from the loneliness and isolation...
...I dreamt someone new.
And this time I understood.
His name was Lykon.
He was like me.
And I wasn't alone anymore.

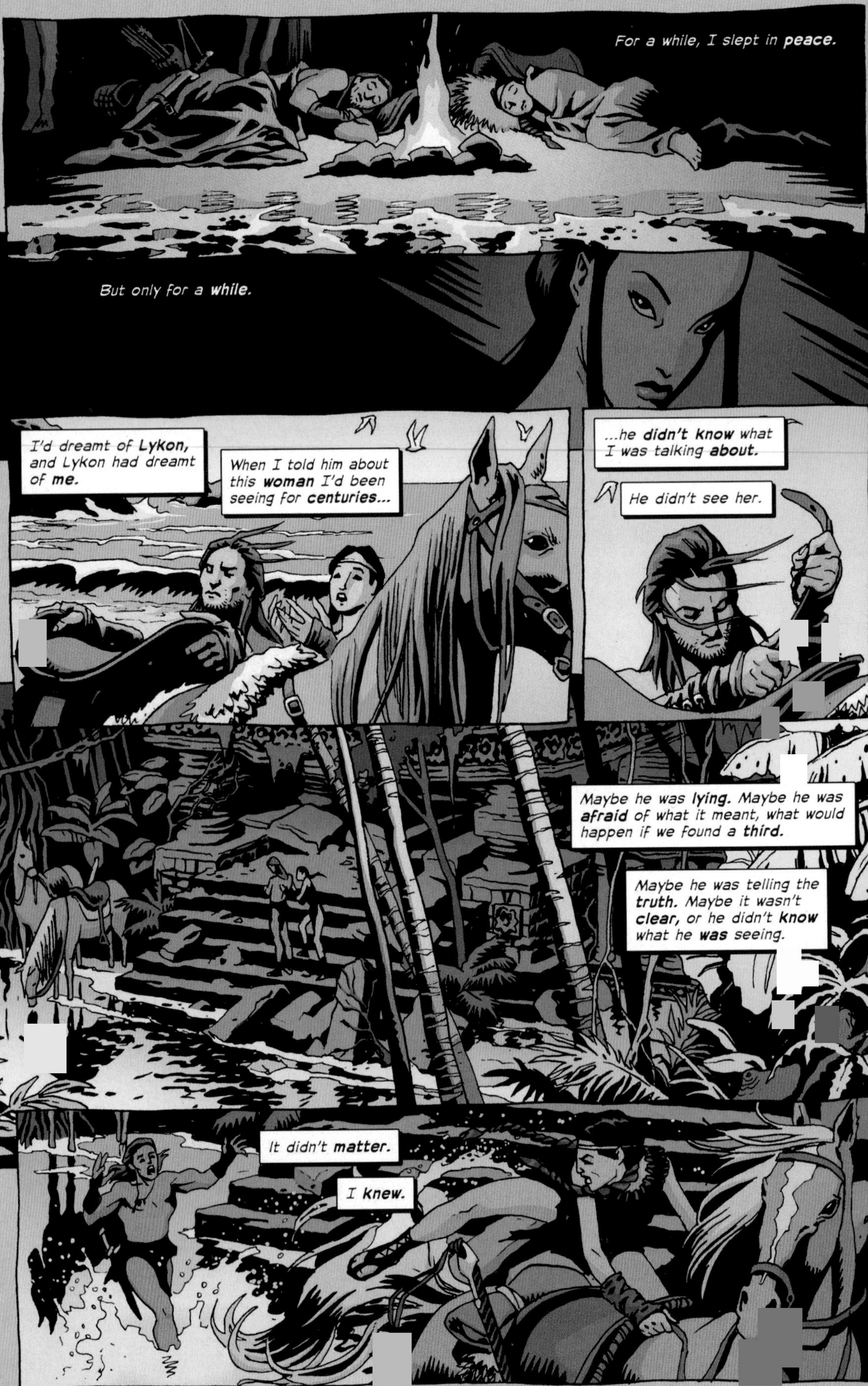
For a while, I slept in **peace.**
But only for a **while.**
I'd dreamt of **Lykon,** and Lykon had dreamt of **me.**
When I told him about this **woman** I'd been seeing for **centuries...**
...he **didn't know** what I was talking **about.**
He didn't see her.
Maybe he was **lying.** Maybe he was **afraid** of what it meant, what would happen if we found a **third.**
Maybe he was telling the **truth.** Maybe it wasn't **clear,** or he didn't **know** what he **was** seeing.
It didn't **matter.**
I **knew.**

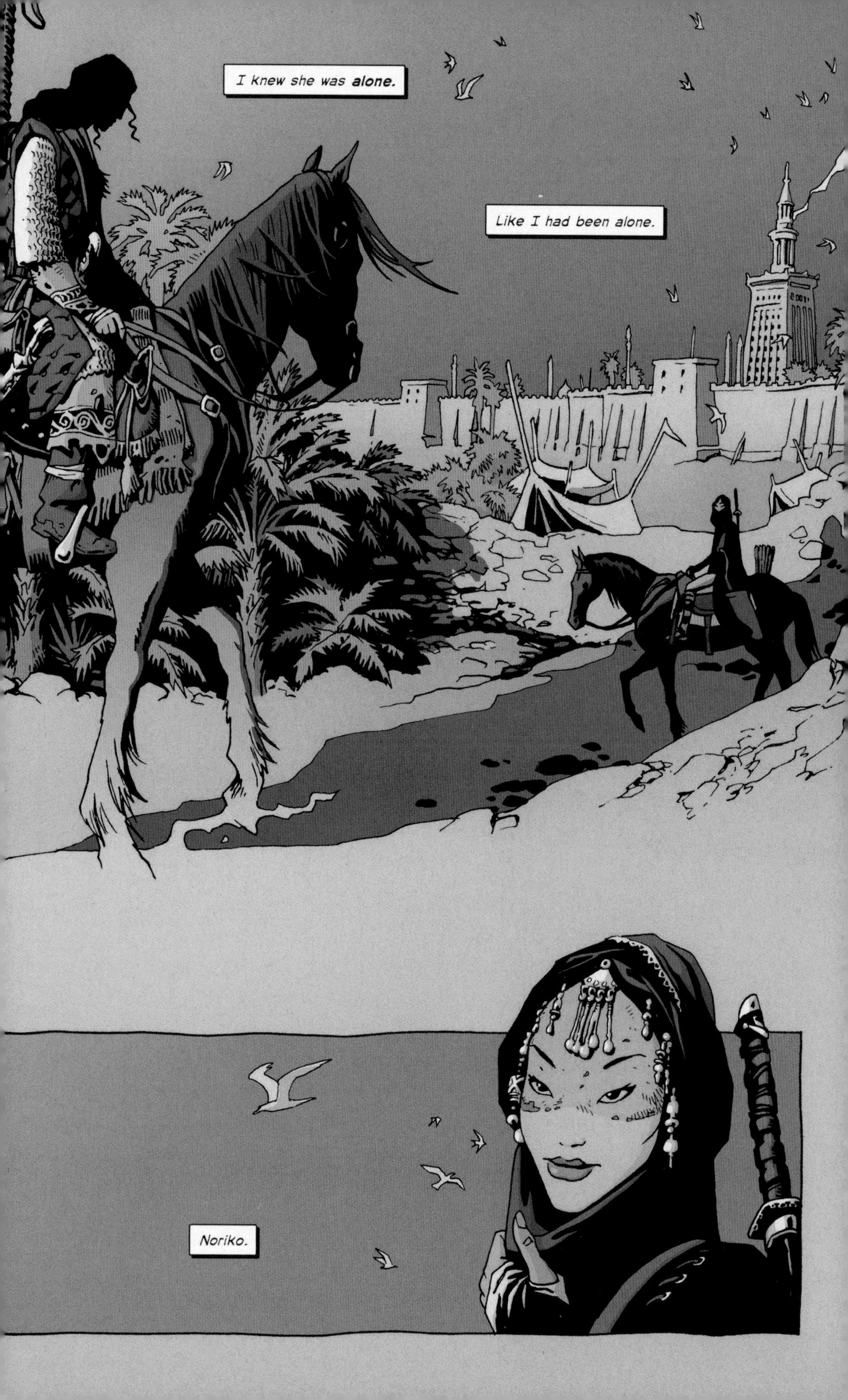
I knew she was alone.
Like I had been alone.
Noriko.

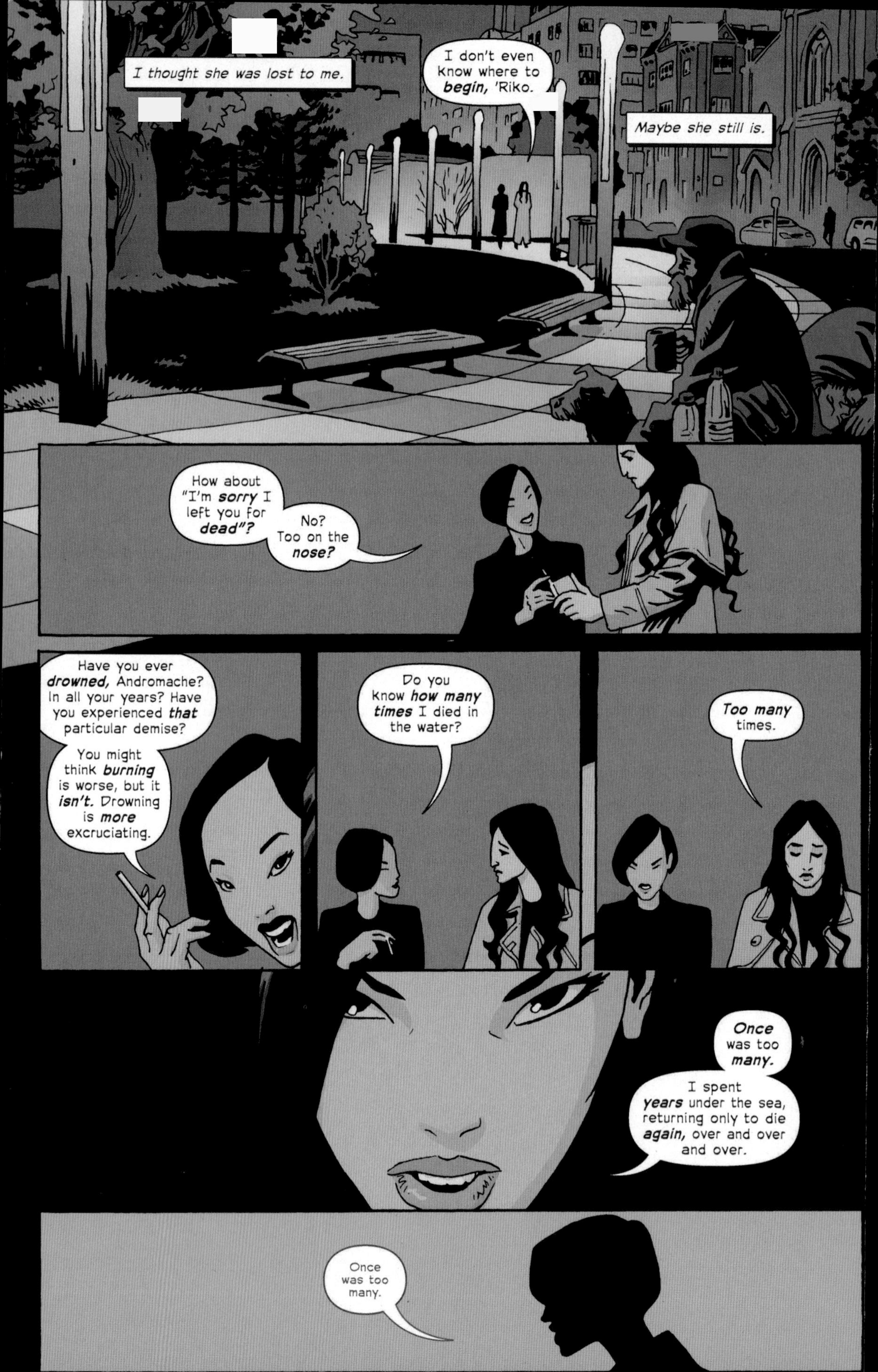
I thought she was lost to me.
I don't even know where to begin, 'Riko.
Maybe she still is.
How about "I'm sorry I left you for dead"?
No? Too on the nose?
Have you ever drowned, Andromache? In all your years? Have you experienced that particular demise?
You might think burning is worse, but it isn't. Drowning is more excruciating.
Do you know how many times I died in the water?
Too many times.
Once was too many.
I spent years under the sea, returning only to die again, over and over and over.
Once was too many.

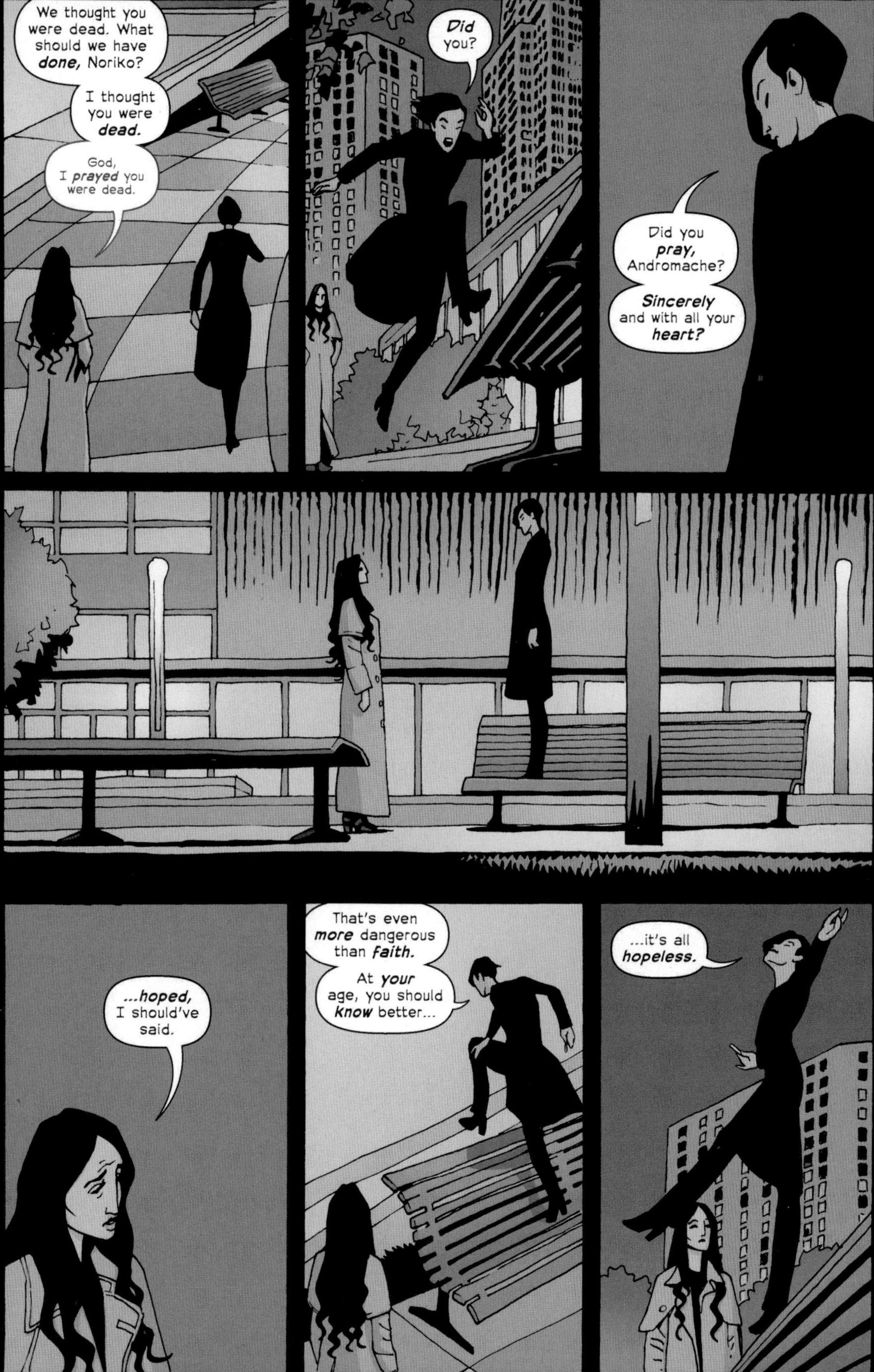
We thought you were dead. What should we have *done,* Noriko?
I thought you were *dead.*
God, I *prayed* you were dead.
Did you?
Did you *pray,* Andromache?
Sincerely and with all your *heart?*
...hoped, I should've said.
That's even *more* dangerous than *faith.*
At *your* age, you should *know* better...
...it's all *hopeless.*

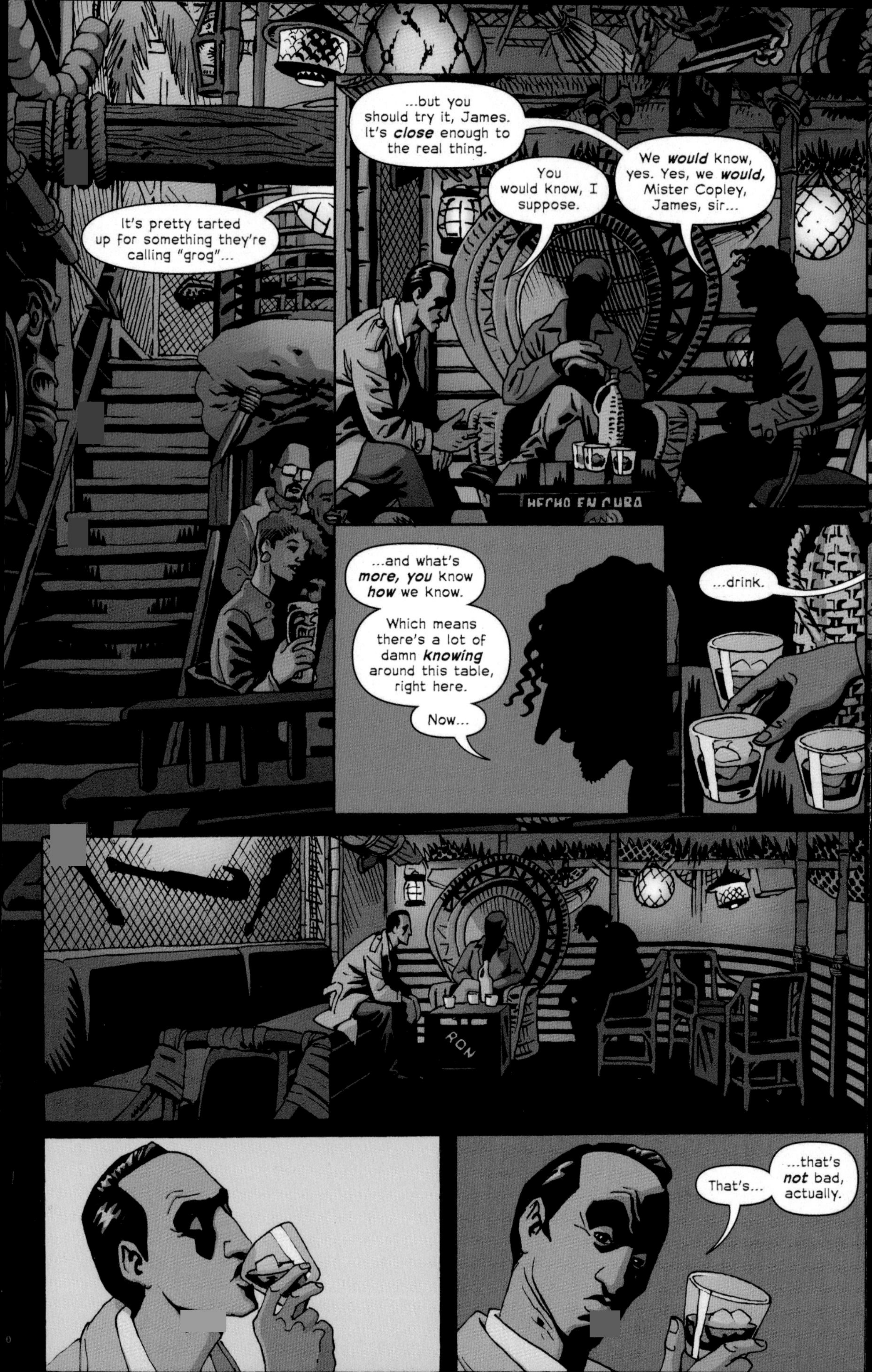

It's pretty tarted up for something they're calling "grog"...
...but you should try it, James. It's *close* enough to the real thing.
You would know, I suppose.
We *would* know, yes. Yes, we *would,* Mister Copley, James, sir...
HECHO EN CUBA
...and what's *more, you* know *how* we know.
Which means there's a lot of damn *knowing* around this table, right here.
Now...
...drink.
RON
That's...
...that's *not* bad, actually.

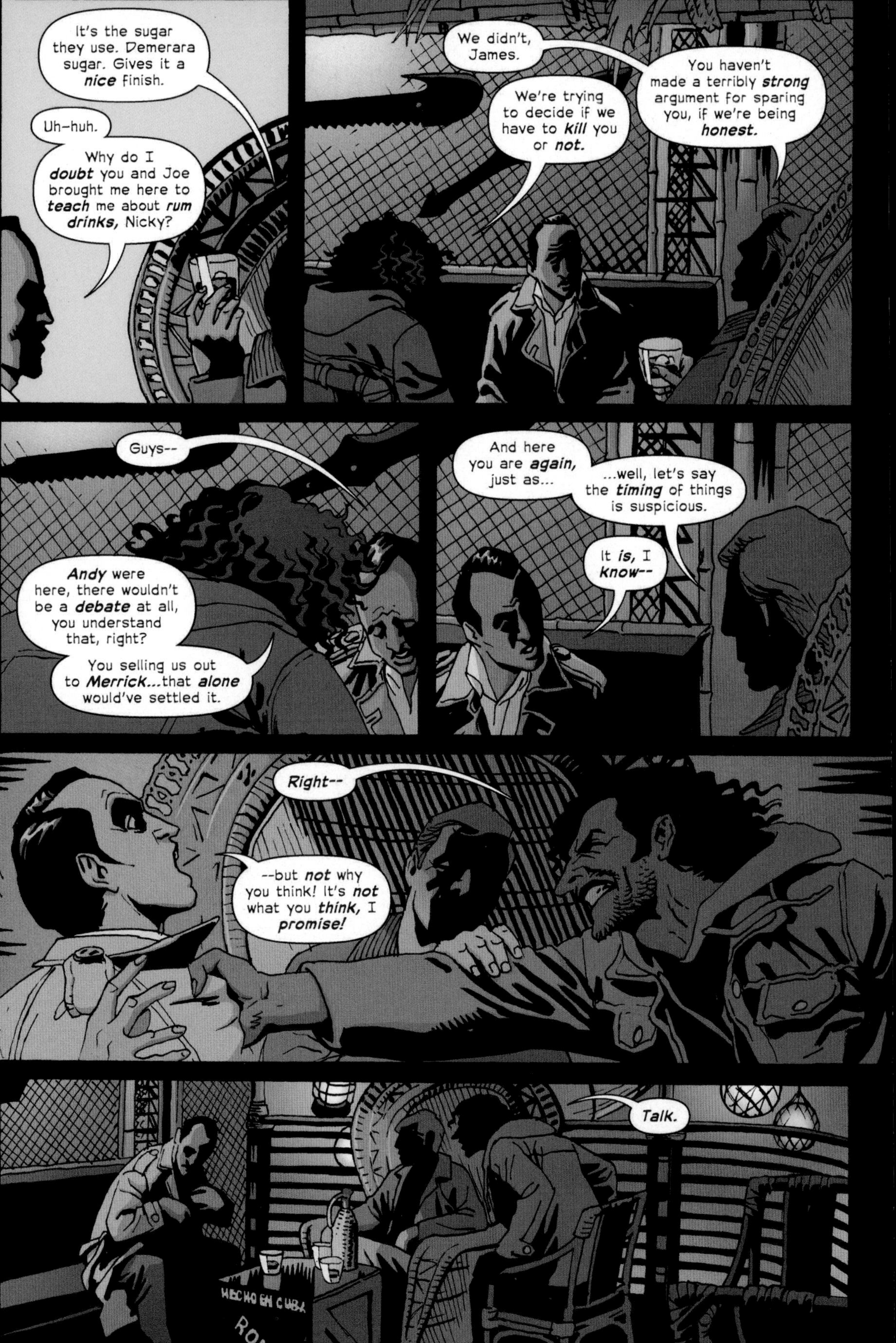
It's the sugar they use. Demerara sugar. Gives it a *nice* finish.
Uh-huh.
Why do I *doubt* you and Joe brought me here to *teach* me about *rum drinks,* Nicky?
We didn't, James.
We're trying to decide if we have to *kill* you or *not.*
You haven't made a terribly *strong* argument for sparing you, if we're being *honest.*
Guys--
Andy were here, there wouldn't be a *debate* at all, you understand that, right?
You selling us out to *Merrick*...that *alone* would've settled it.
And here you are *again,* just as...
...well, let's say the *timing* of things is suspicious.
It *is,* I *know*--
Right--
--but *not* why you think! It's *not* what you *think,* I *promise!*
Talk.
HECHO EN CUBA

It *isn't* hopeless. It *can't* be.

And is that *how* you've gotten through the *centuries* since we *parted*, my love?

Telling yourself *that*, over and over again?

You *know* it's not *true*. You know I'm *right*.

You're *older* than I am, you've seen it more *clearly*, certainly.

What have they *accomplished* that can give you *hope?*

Medicine. Technology. Education. *Sanitation*.

I mean, they invented *sports bras*, for fuck's sake, that's a damn *improvement*, 'Riko.

Mhm...

...and *these.*

Do you remember when *tobacco* was *rare?* When it was *holy?*

And now it's *mass-produced* and murders millions...

...more than you and I have done put *together*.

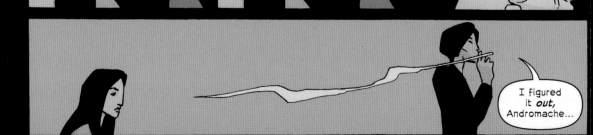

I figured it *out*, Andromache...

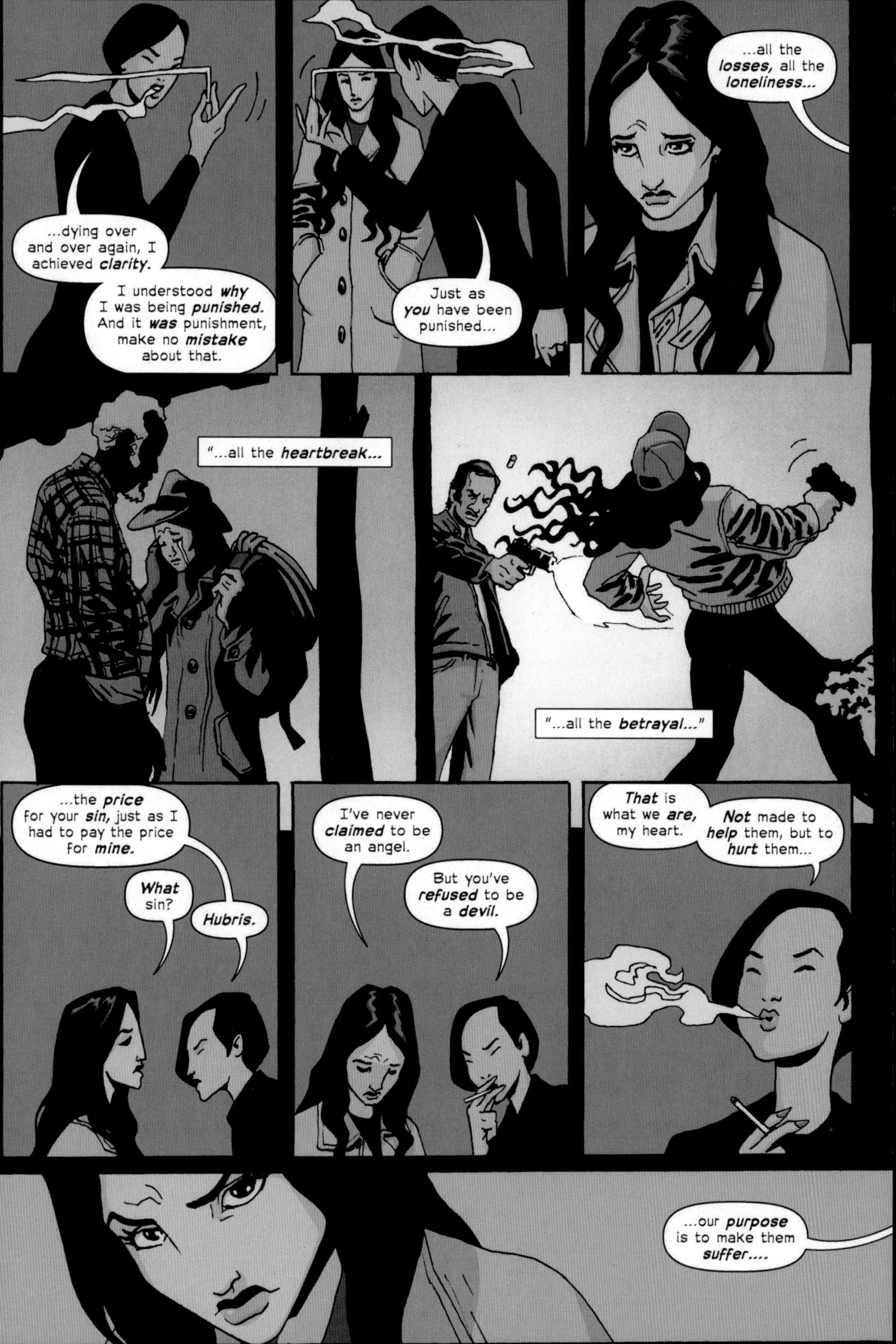

...dying over and over again, I achieved *clarity.*
I understood *why* I was being *punished.* And it *was* punishment, make no *mistake* about that.
Just as *you* have been punished...
...all the *losses,* all the *loneliness...*
"...all the *heartbreak...*
"...all the *betrayal...*"
...the *price* for your *sin,* just as I had to pay the price for *mine.*
What sin?
Hubris.
I've never *claimed* to be an angel.
But you've *refused* to be a *devil.*
That is what we *are,* my heart.
Not made to *help* them, but to *hurt* them...
...our *purpose* is to make them *suffer....*

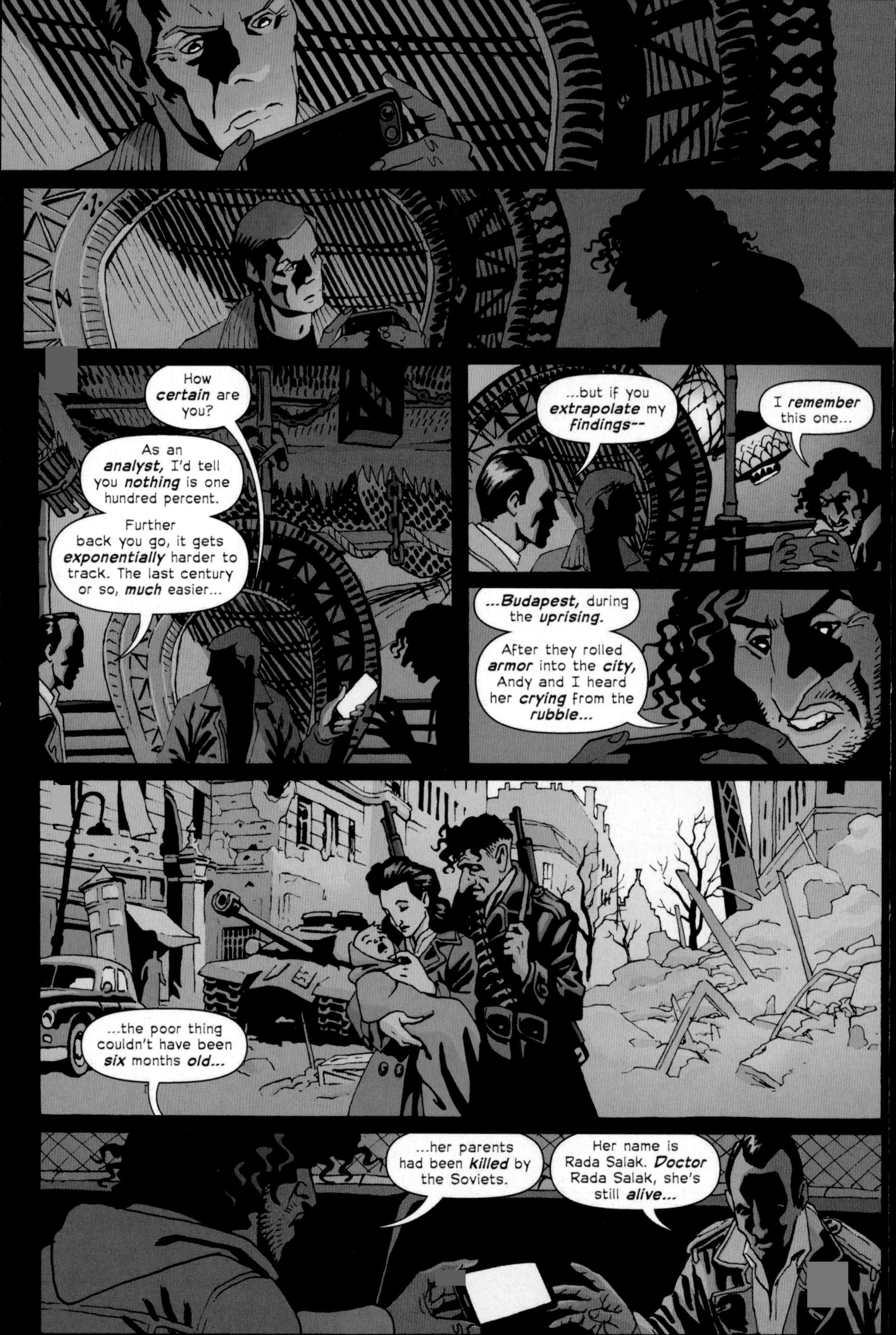
How certain are you?
As an analyst, I'd tell you nothing is one hundred percent.
Further back you go, it gets exponentially harder to track. The last century or so, much easier...
...but if you extrapolate my findings--
I remember this one...
...Budapest, during the uprising.
After they rolled armor into the city, Andy and I heard her crying from the rubble...
...the poor thing couldn't have been six months old...
...her parents had been killed by the Soviets.
Her name is Rada Salak. Doctor Rada Salak, she's still alive...

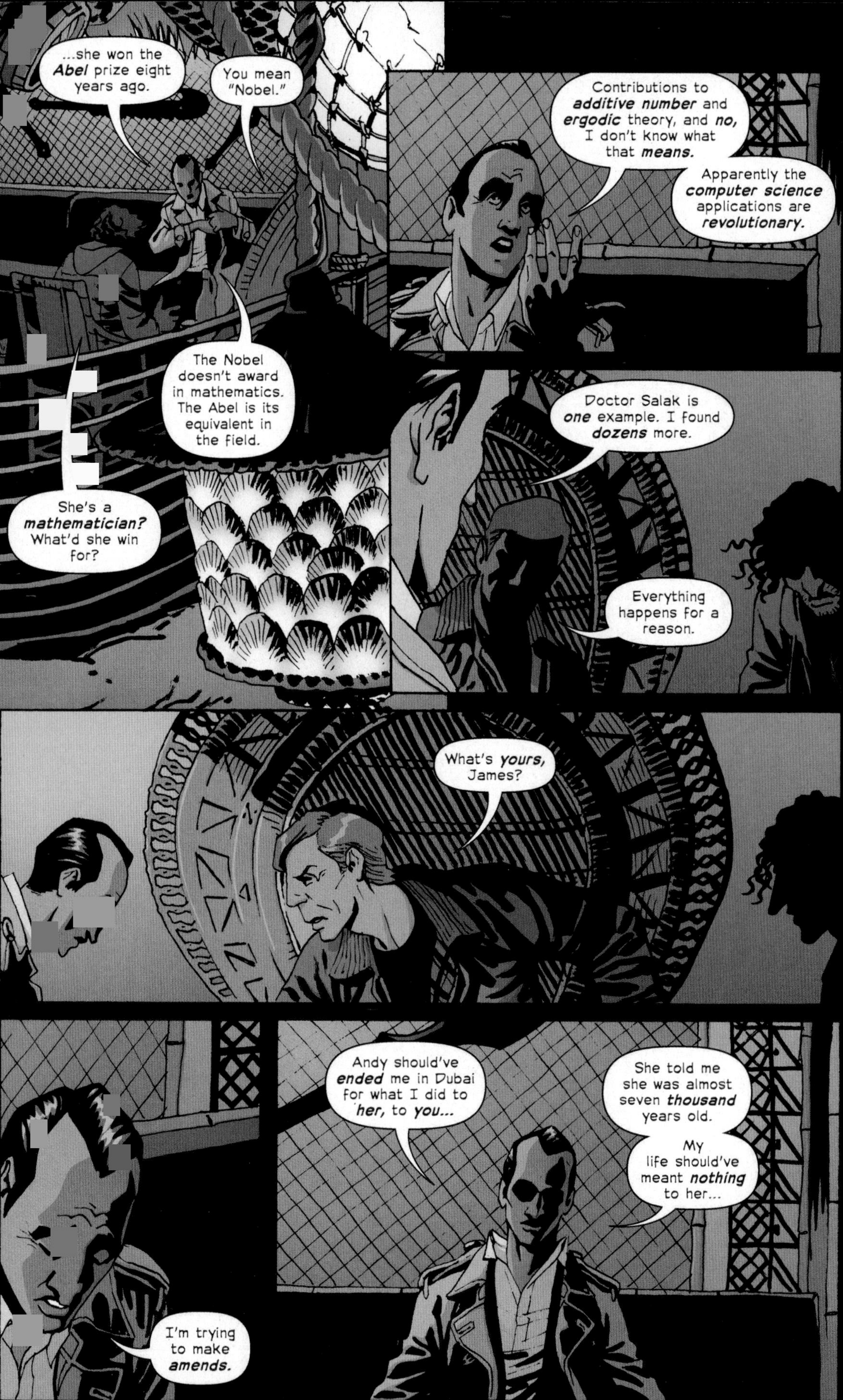
...she won the *Abel* prize eight years ago.
You mean "Nobel."
The Nobel doesn't award in mathematics. The Abel is its equivalent in the field.
She's a *mathematician?* What'd she win for?
Contributions to *additive number* and *ergodic* theory, and *no,* I don't know what that *means.*
Apparently the *computer science* applications are *revolutionary.*
Doctor Salak is *one* example. I found *dozens* more.
Everything happens for a reason.
What's *yours,* James?
Andy should've *ended* me in Dubai for what I did to *her,* to *you...*
She told me she was almost seven *thousand* years old.
My life should've meant *nothing* to her...
I'm trying to make *amends.*

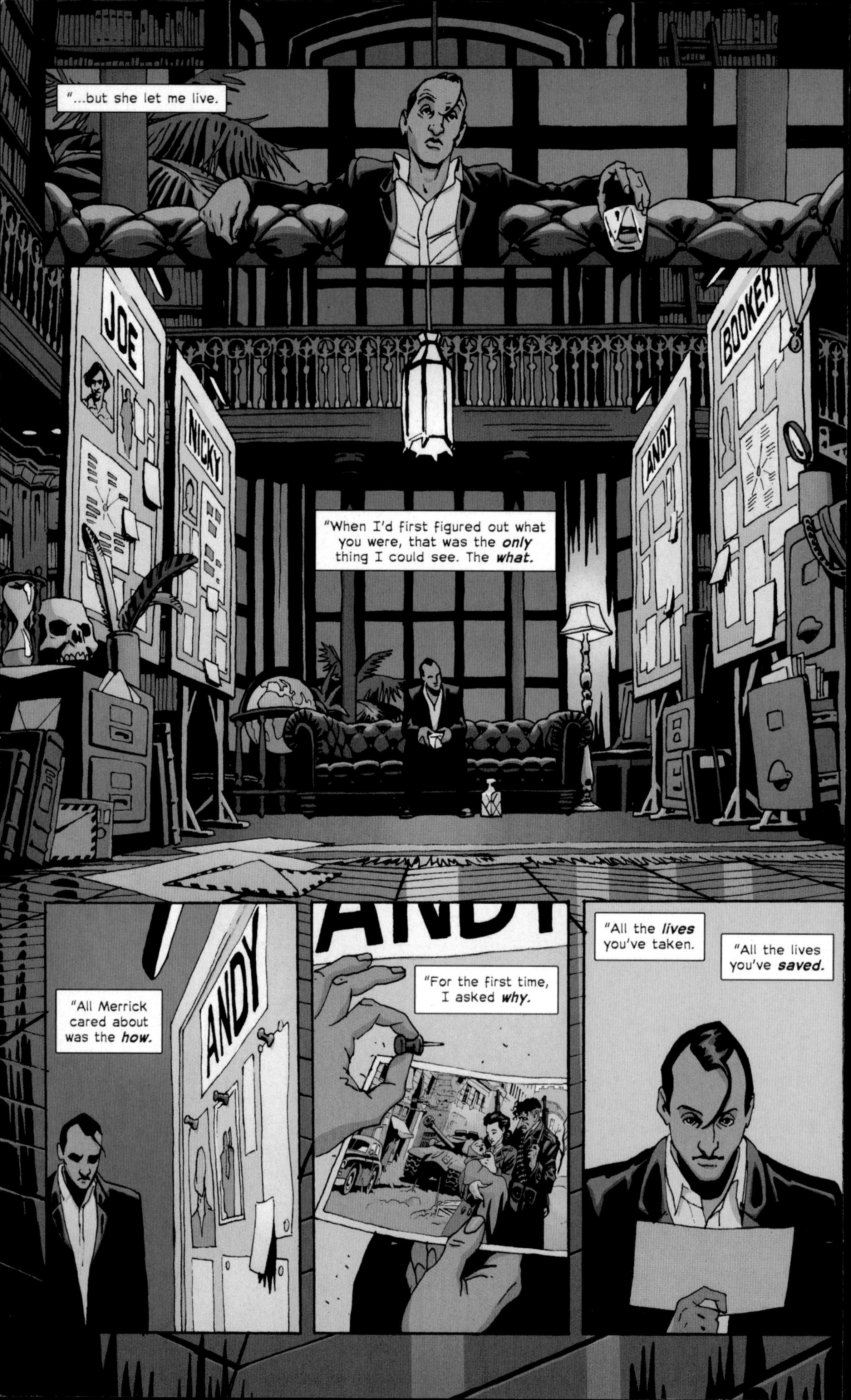
"...but she let me live.
JOE
NICKY
ANDY
BOOKER
"When I'd first figured out what you were, that was the *only* thing I could see. The ***what.***
"All Merrick cared about was the ***how.***
ANDY
"For the first time, I asked ***why.***
"All the *lives* you've taken.
"All the lives you've ***saved.***

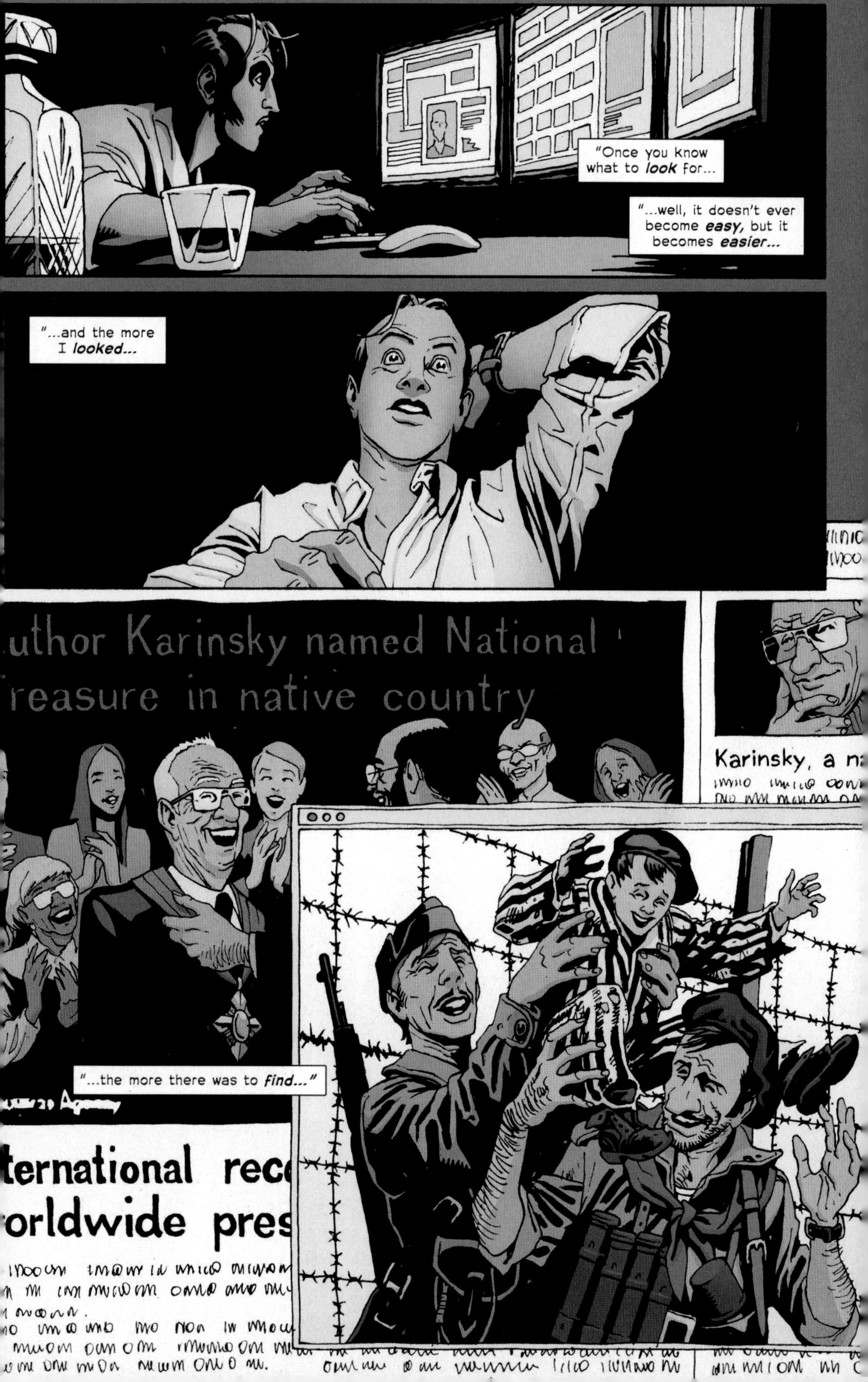
"Once you know what to *look* for...
"...well, it doesn't ever become *easy,* but it becomes *easier...*
"...and the more I *looked...*
uthor Karinsky named National
Treasure in native country
Karinsky, a n
"...the more there was to *find...*"
ternational rec
orldwide pres

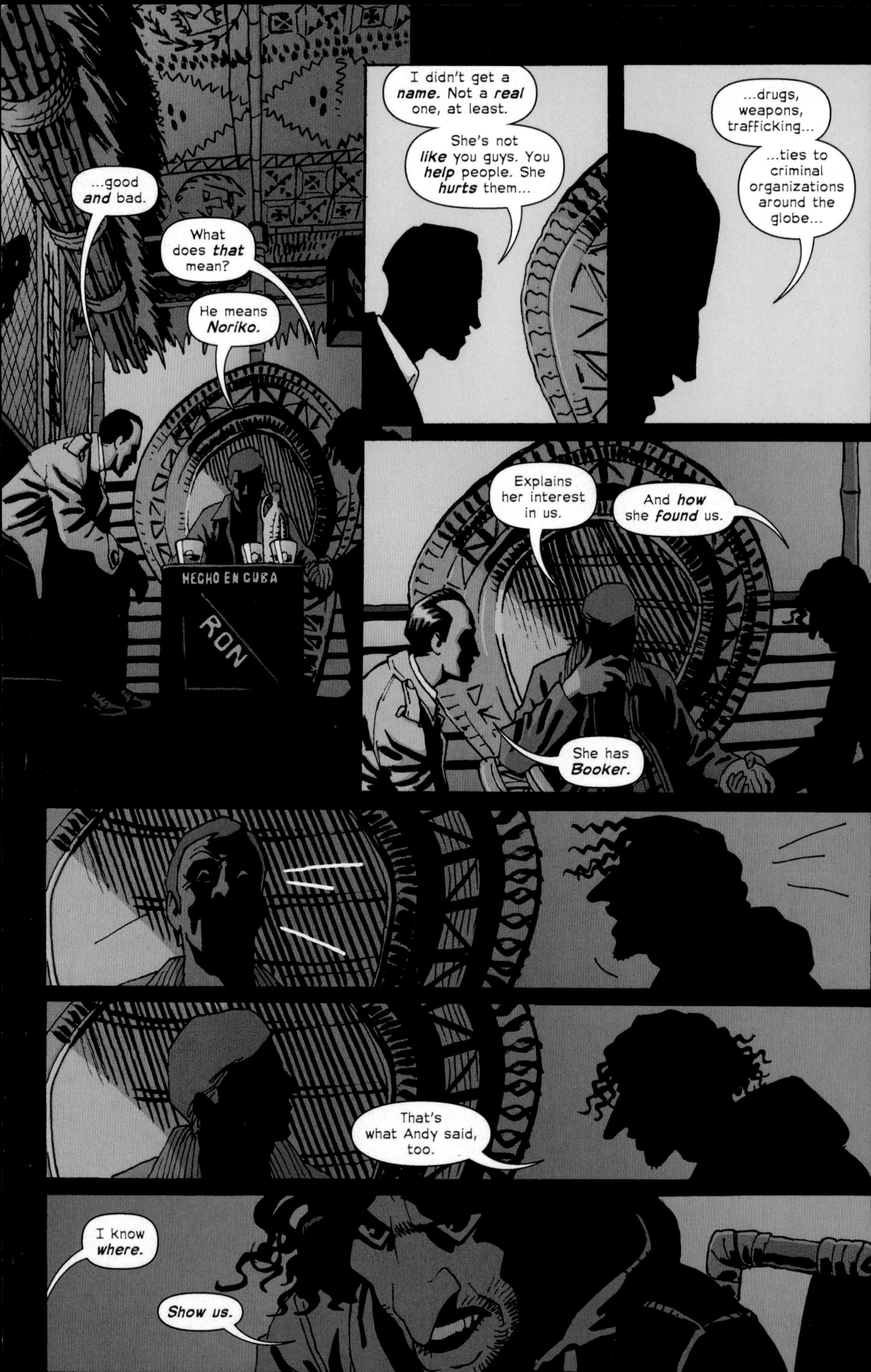
...good *and* bad.
What does *that* mean?
He means *Noriko.*
HECHO EN CUBA
RON
I didn't get a *name.* Not a *real* one, at least.
She's not *like* you guys. You *help* people. She *hurts* them...
...drugs, weapons, trafficking...
...ties to criminal organizations around the globe...
Explains her interest in us.
And *how* she *found* us.
She has *Booker.*
That's what Andy said, too.
I know *where.*
Show us.

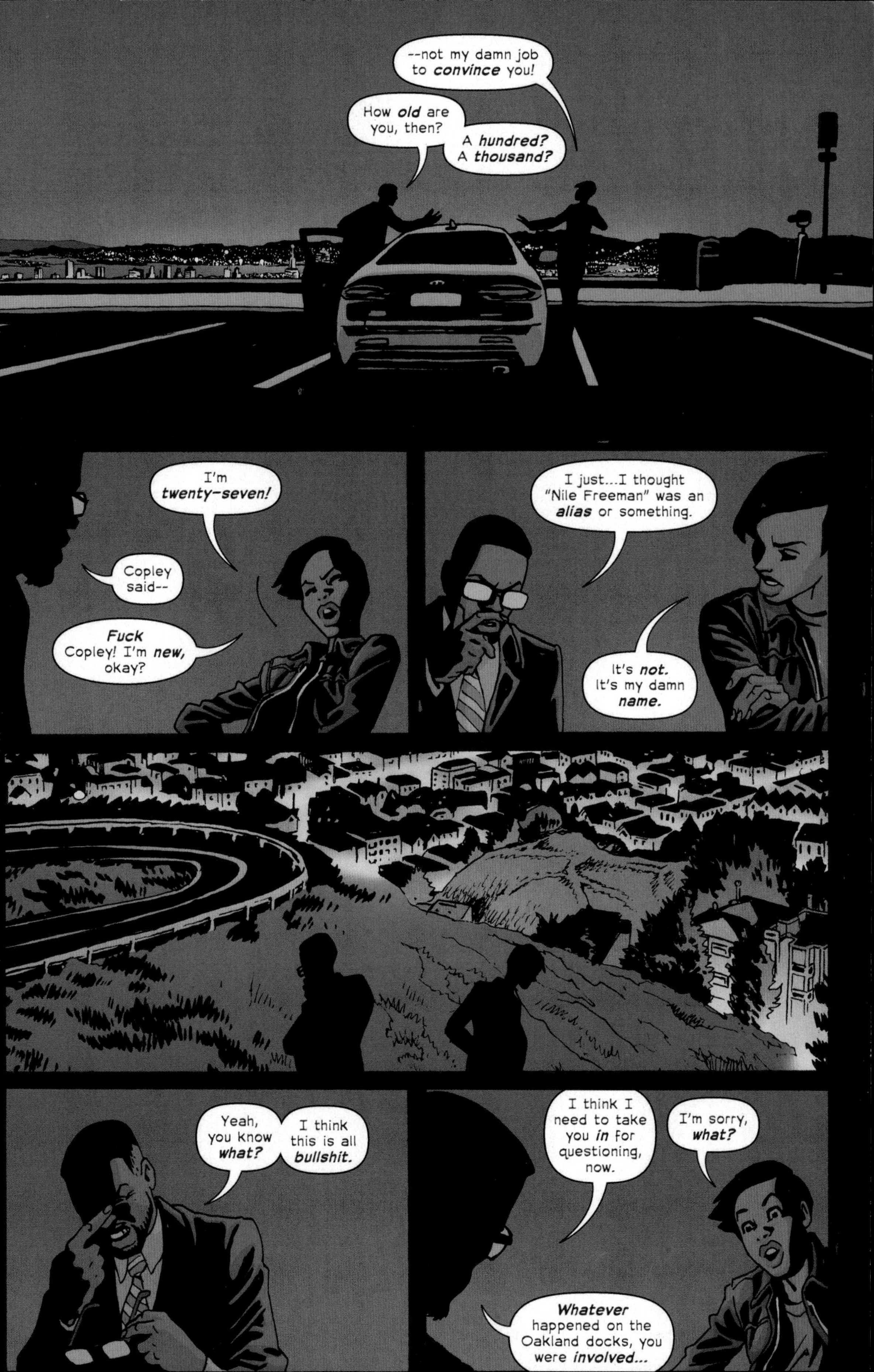
--not my damn job to *convince* you!
How *old* are you, then?
A *hundred?* A *thousand?*
I'm *twenty-seven!*
Copley said--
Fuck Copley! I'm *new,* okay?
I just...I thought "Nile Freeman" was an *alias* or something.
It's *not.* It's my damn *name.*
Yeah, you know *what?*
I think this is all *bullshit.*
I think I need to take you *in* for questioning, now.
I'm sorry, *what?*
Whatever happened on the Oakland docks, you were *involved...*

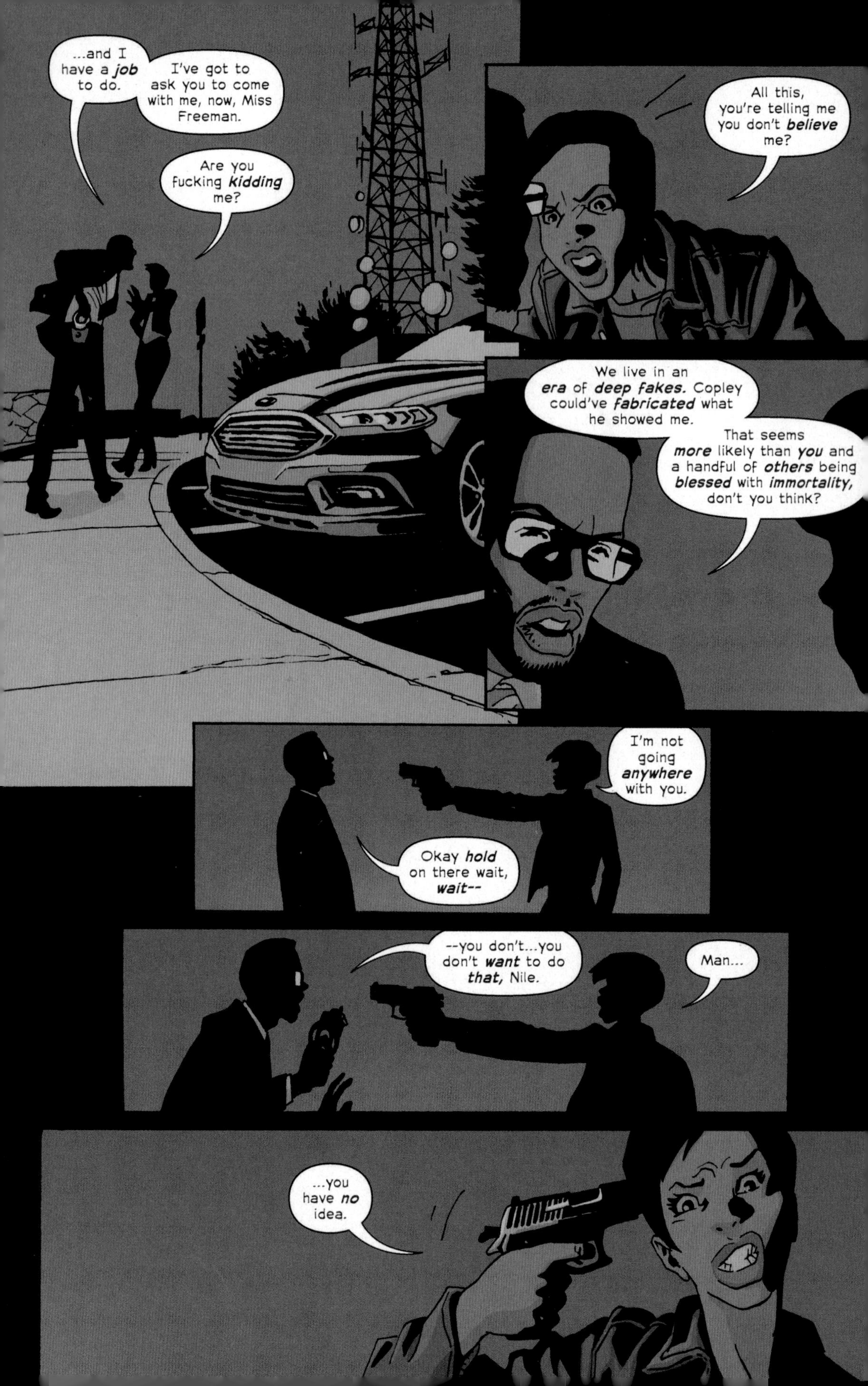
...and I have a job to do.
I've got to ask you to come with me, now, Miss Freeman.
Are you fucking kidding me?
All this, you're telling me you don't believe me?
We live in an era of deep fakes. Copley could've fabricated what he showed me.
That seems more likely than you and a handful of others being blessed with immortality, don't you think?
I'm not going anywhere with you.
Okay hold on there wait, wait--
--you don't...you don't want to do that, Nile.
Man...
...you have no idea.

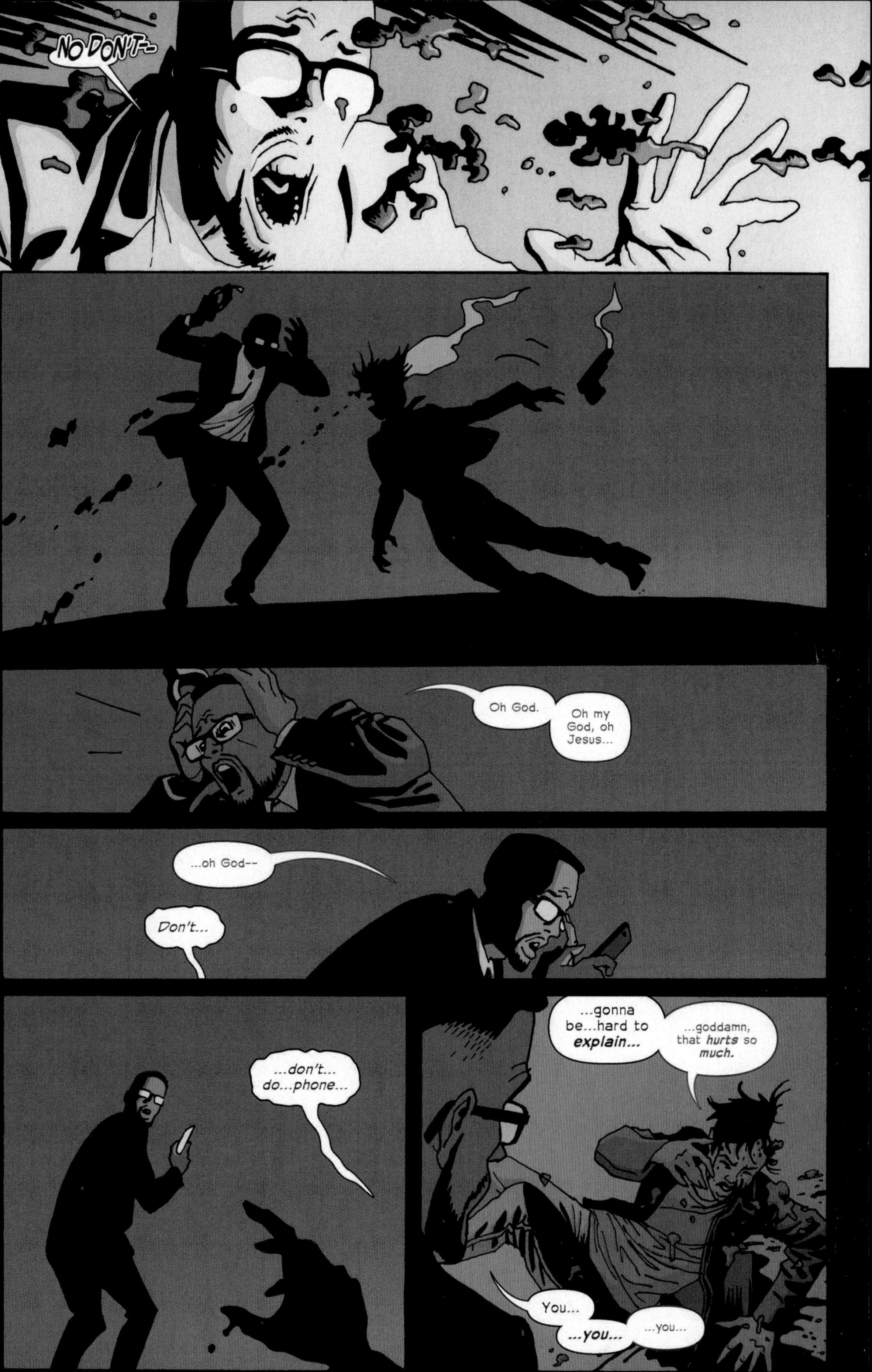
NO DON'T--
Oh God.
Oh my God, oh Jesus...
...oh God--
Don't...
...don't... do...phone...
...gonna be...hard to explain...
...goddamn, that hurts so much.
You...
...you...
...you...

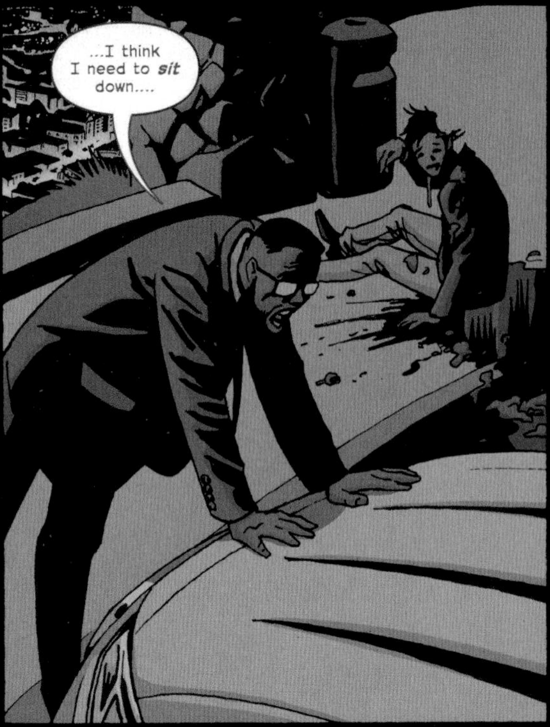
...I think I need to *sit* down....

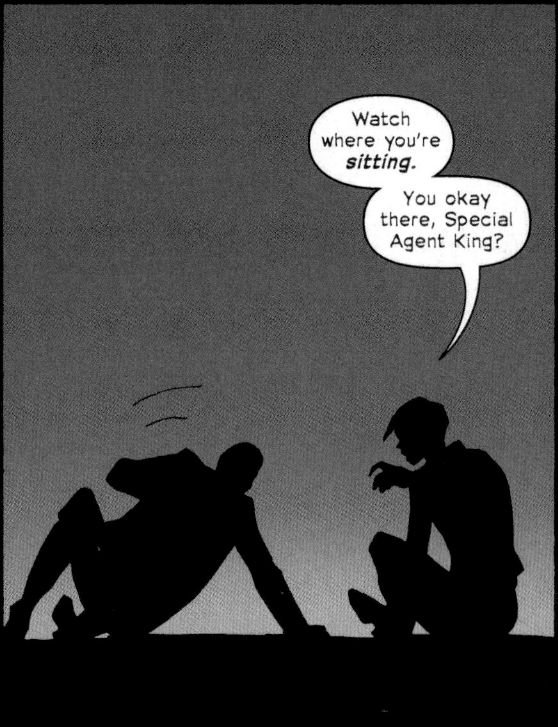
Watch where you're *sitting.*
You okay there, Special Agent King?

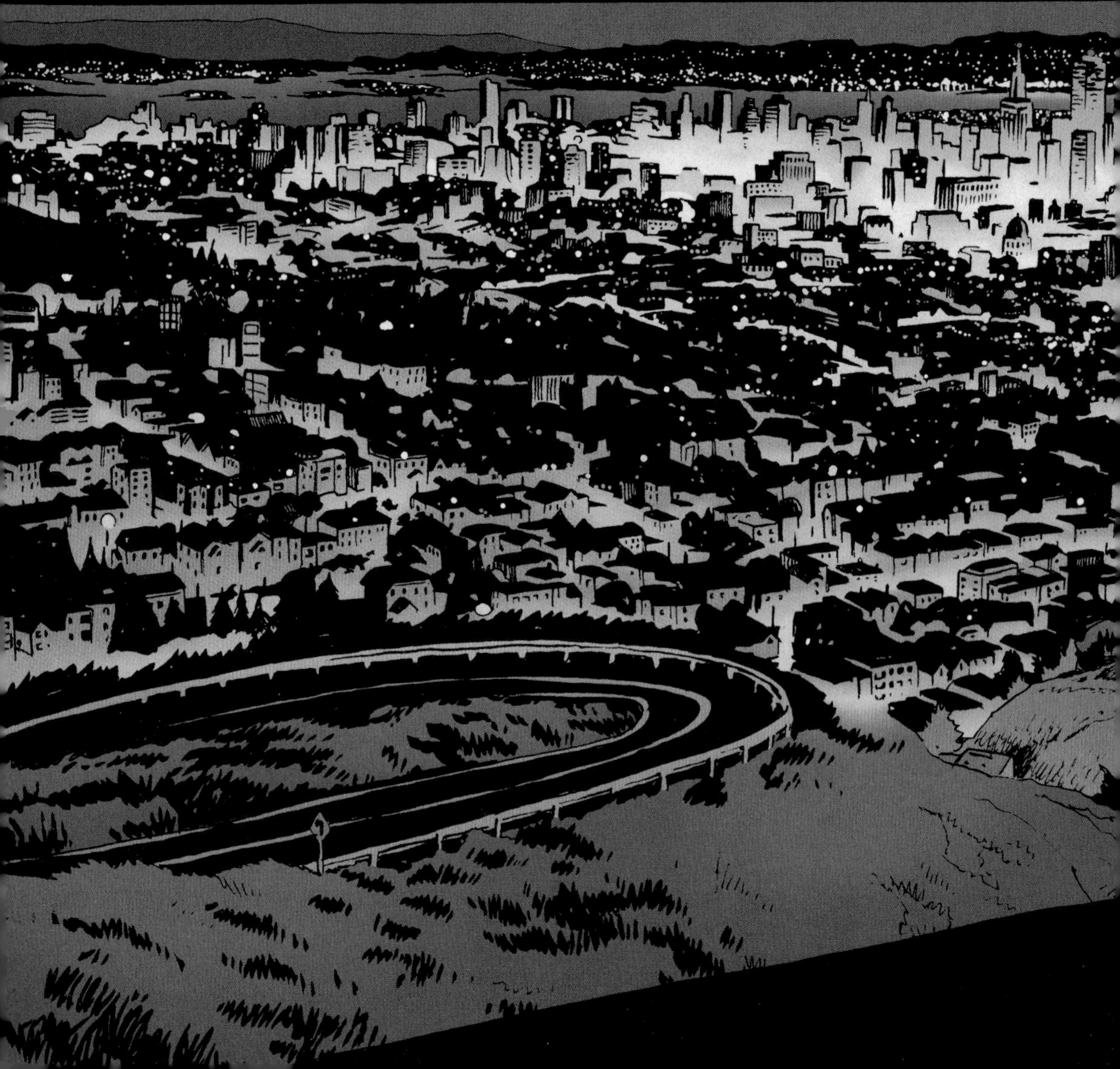

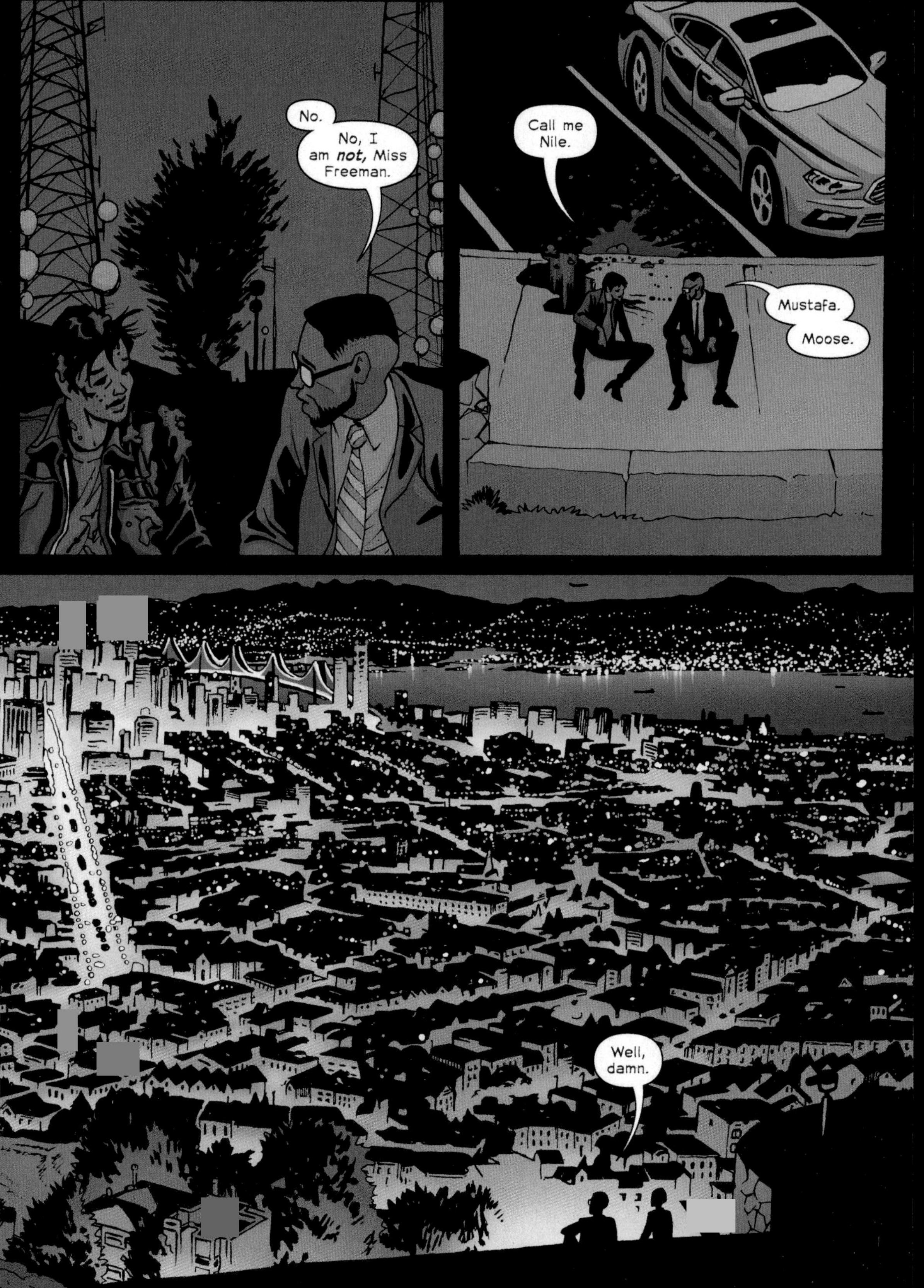
No.
No, I am *not,* Miss Freeman.
Call me Nile.
Mustafa.
Moose.
Well, damn.

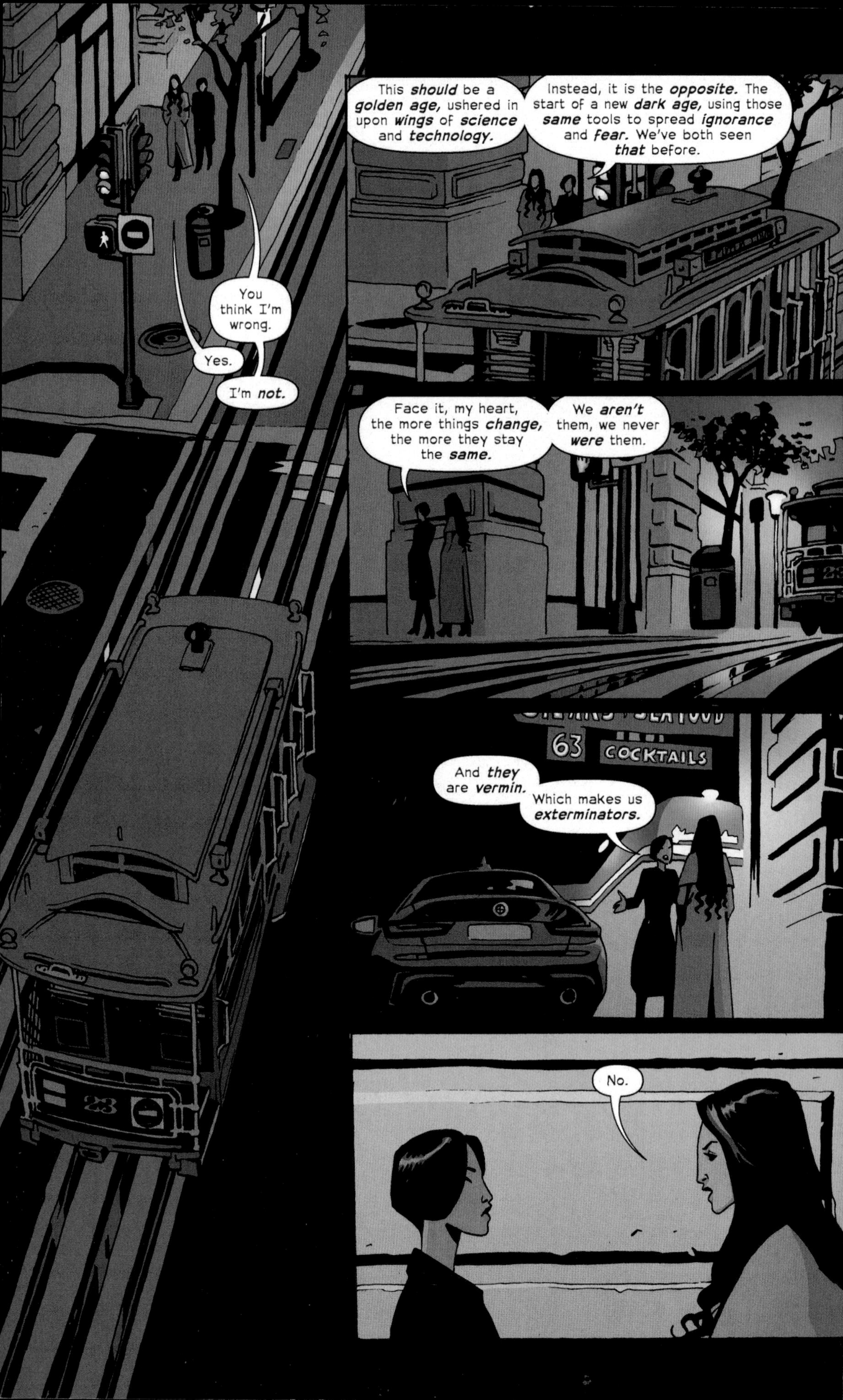

You think I'm wrong.
Yes.
I'm *not.*
This *should* be a *golden age,* ushered in upon *wings* of *science* and *technology.*
Instead, it is the *opposite.* The start of a new *dark age,* using those *same* tools to spread *ignorance* and *fear.* We've both seen *that* before.
Face it, my heart, the more things *change,* the more they stay the *same.*
We *aren't* them, we never *were* them.
63
COCKTAILS
And *they* are *vermin.*
Which makes us *exterminators.*
No.

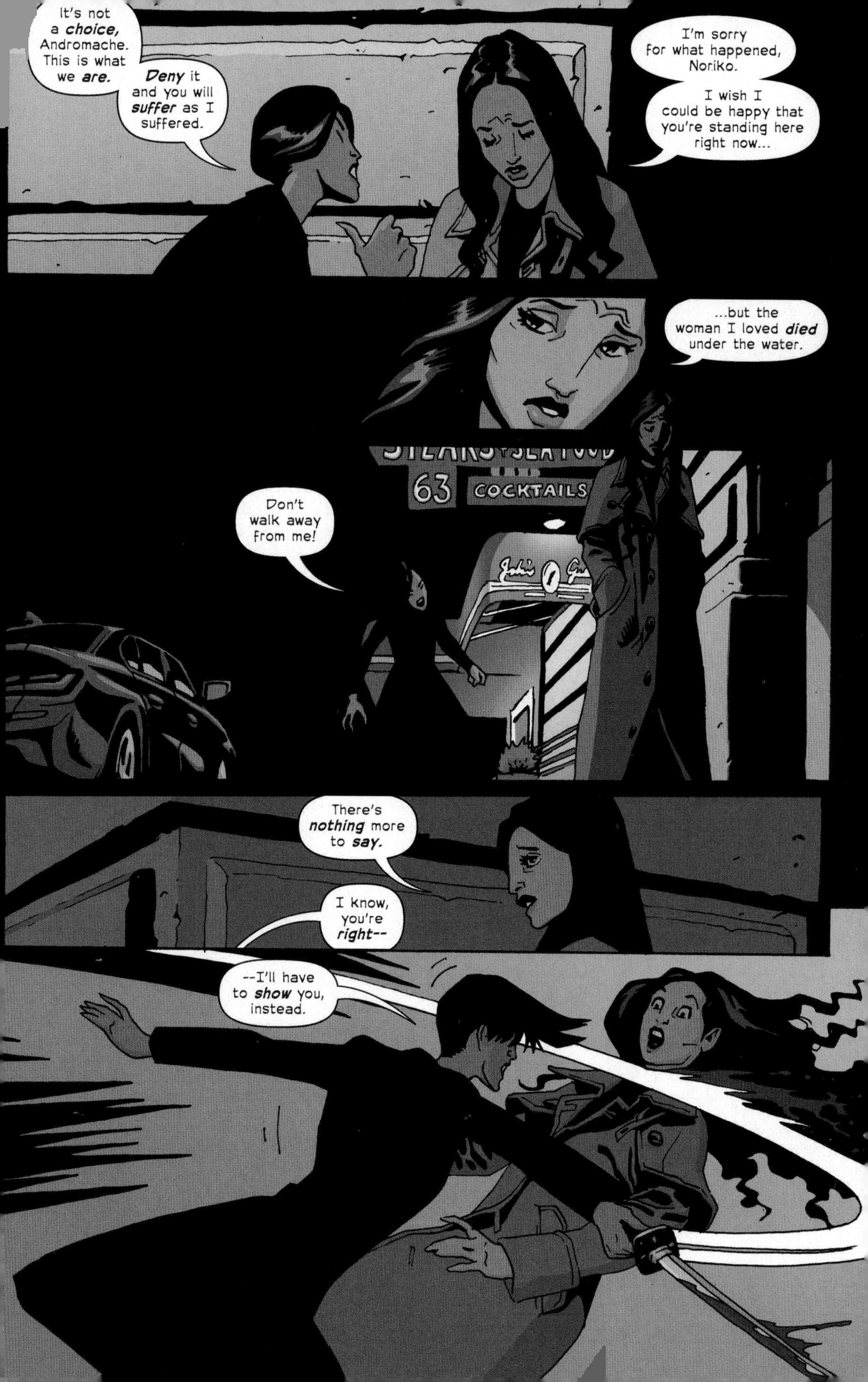

It's not a choice, Andromache. This is what we are.
Deny it and you will suffer as I suffered.
I'm sorry for what happened, Noriko.
I wish I could be happy that you're standing here right now...
...but the woman I loved died under the water.
63
COCKTAILS
Don't walk away from me!
There's nothing more to say.
I know, you're right--
--I'll have to show you, instead.

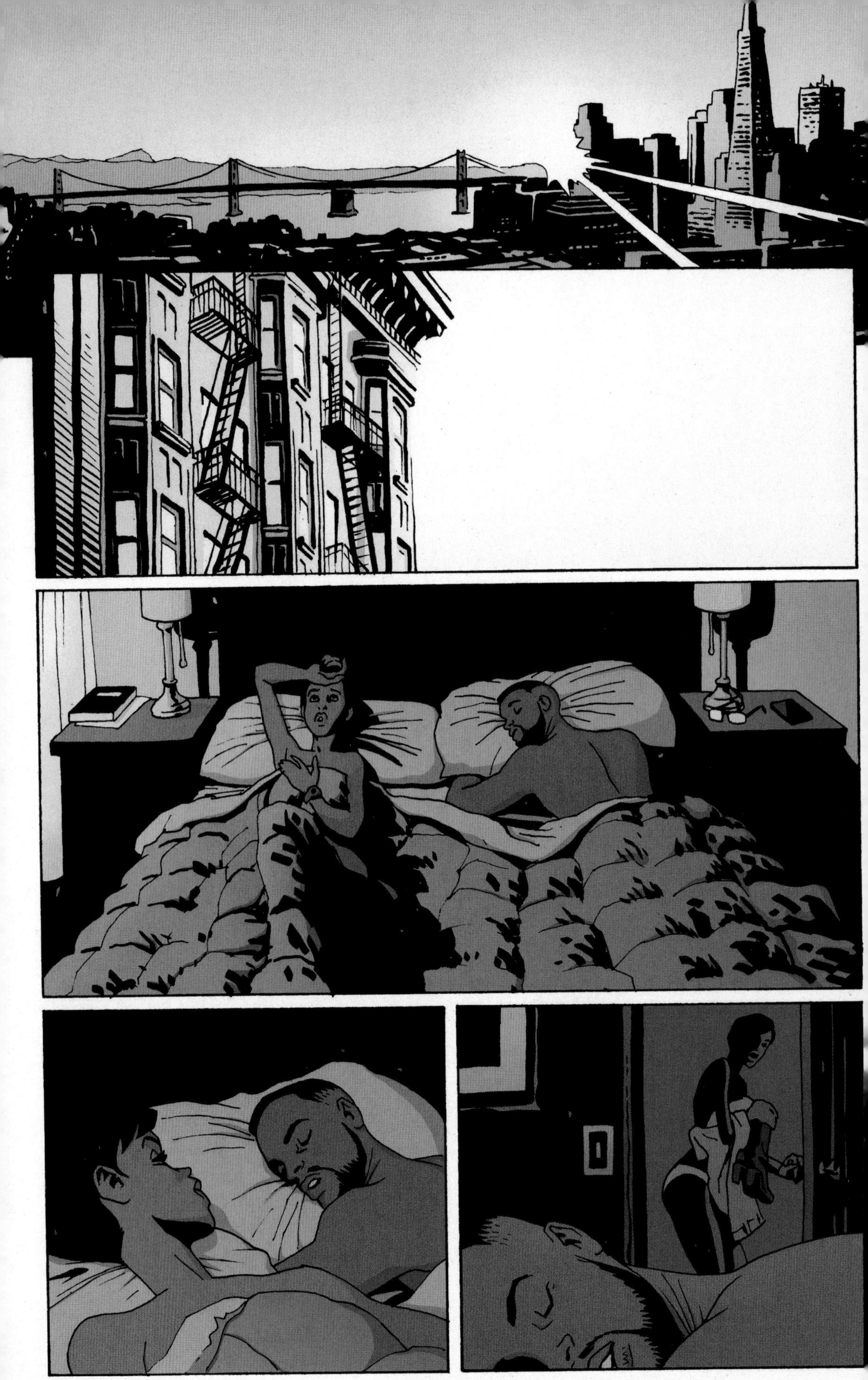

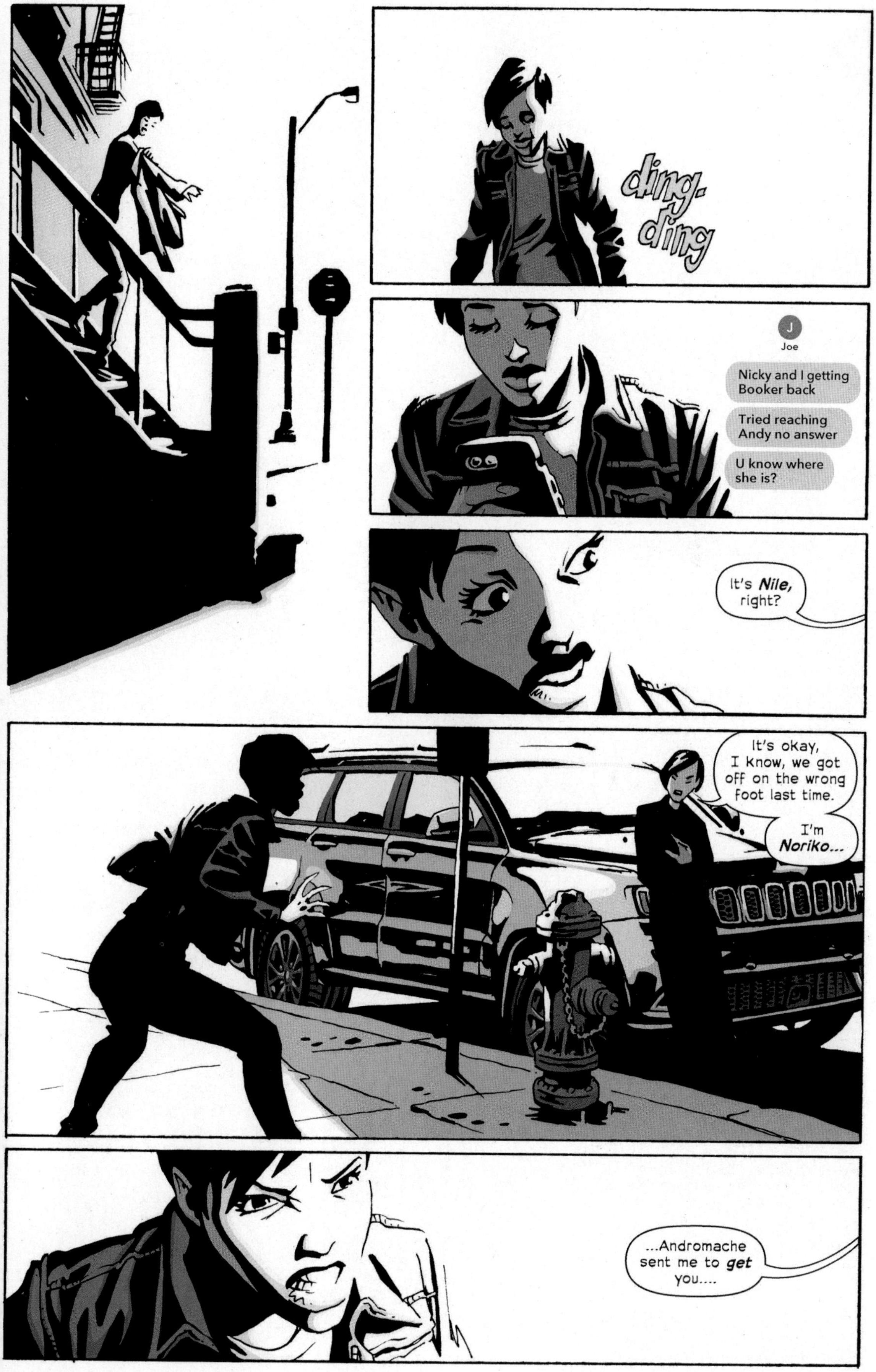
ding-
ding
J
Joe
Nicky and I getting Booker back
Tried reaching Andy no answer
U know where she is?
It's *Nile,* right?
It's okay, I know, we got off on the wrong foot last time.
I'm *Noriko...*
...Andromache sent me to *get* you....

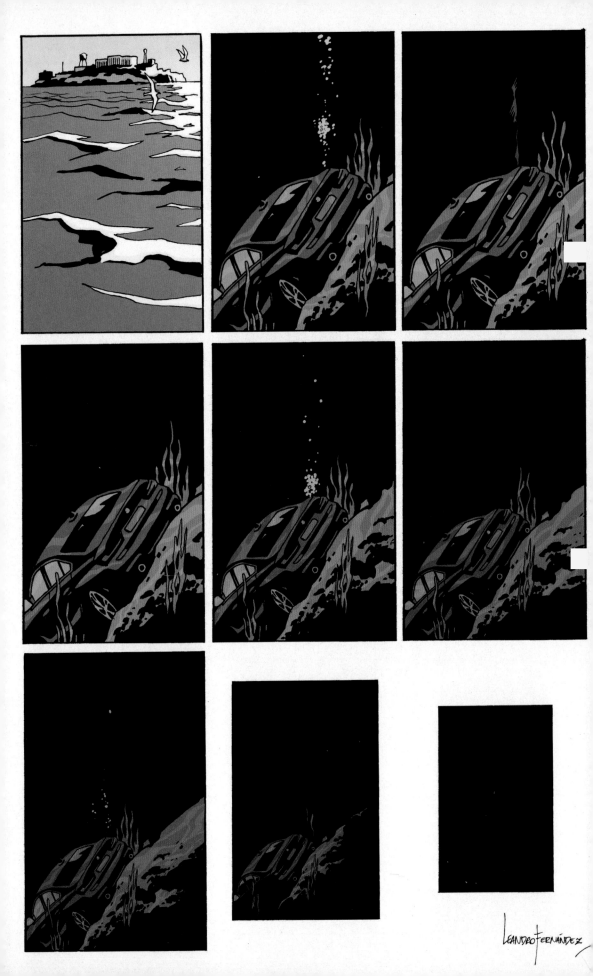

LEANDRO FERNÁNDEZ

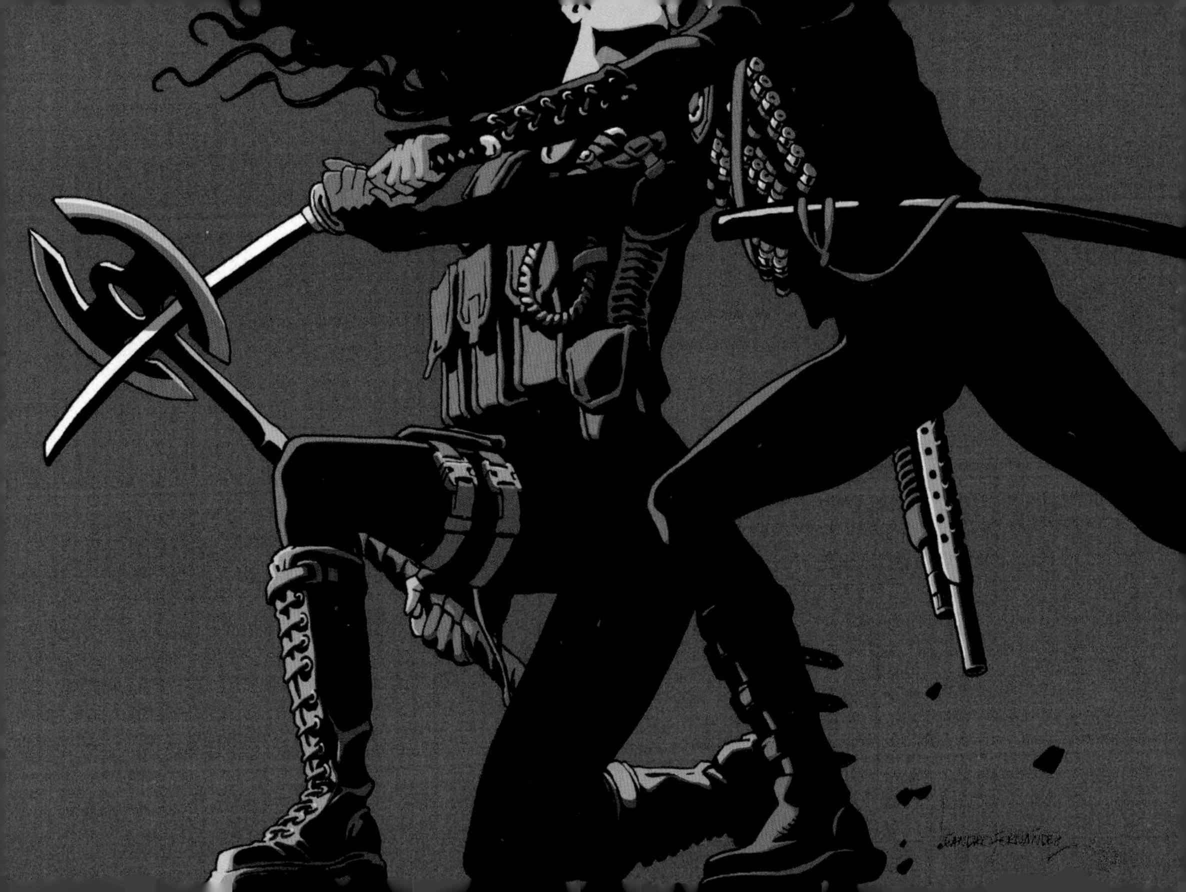

"Do you know what **LOVE** is?

I'll tell you: It is whatever

you can still **BETRAY.**"

~John Le Carré, **THE LOOKING GLASS WAR**

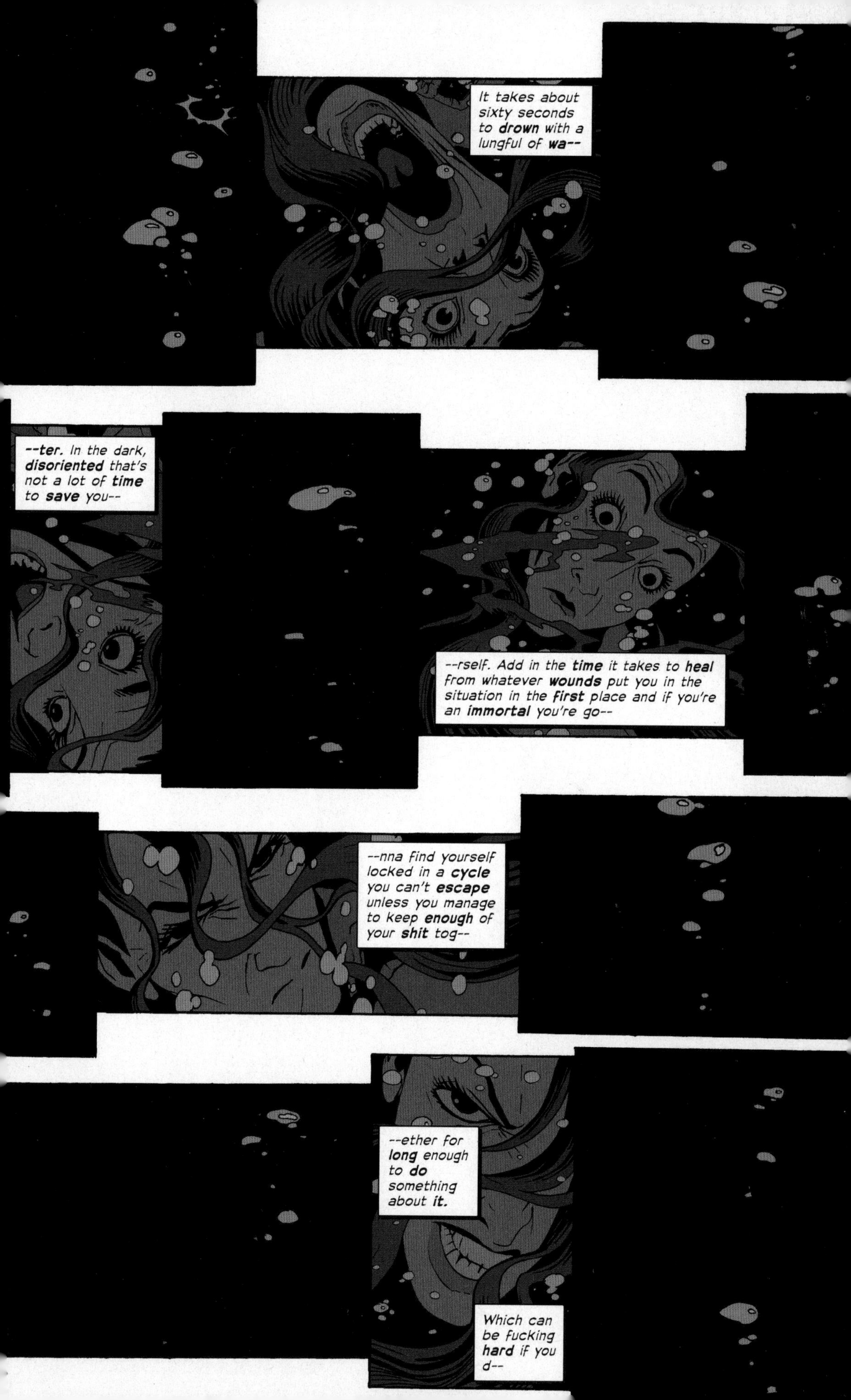

It takes about sixty seconds to **drown** with a lungful of **wa--**
--ter. In the dark, **disoriented** that's not a lot of **time** to **save** you--
--rself. Add in the **time** it takes to **heal** from whatever **wounds** put you in the situation in the **first** place and if you're an **immortal** you're go--
--nna find yourself locked in a **cycle** you can't **escape** unless you manage to keep **enough** of your **shit** tog--
--ether for **long** enough to **do** something about **it.**
Which can be fucking **hard** if you d--

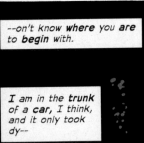

--on't know **where** you **are** to **begin** with.

I am in the **trunk** of a **car**, I think, and it only took dy--

--ve a glow-in-the-dark trunk **release** lever to open it from the **inside**, so all I need to do is keep it **toget**--

--but even **despite** that she's maybe **not** as up to speed on the **world** as she **should** be because she would **know** that since 2002 all cars must ha--

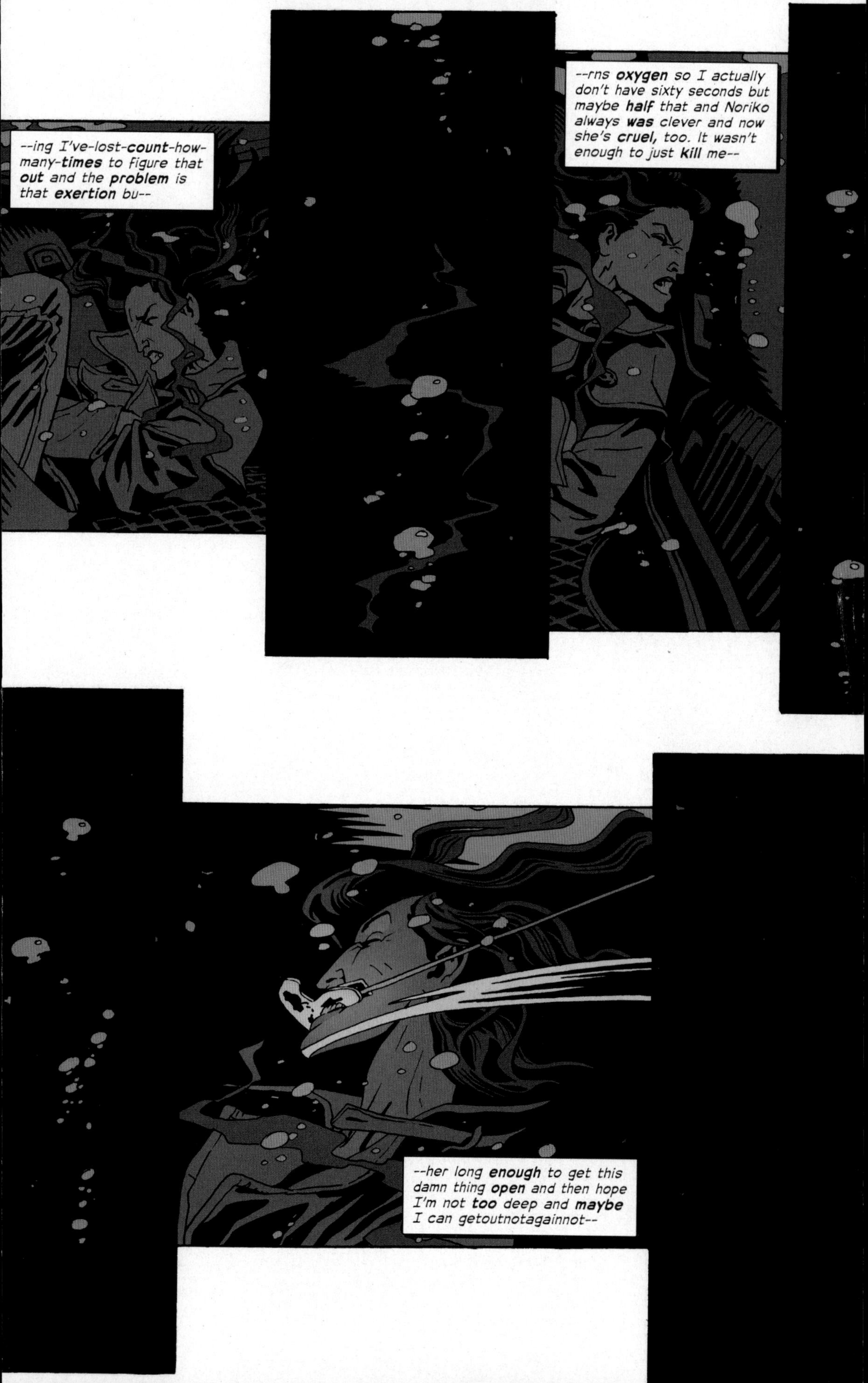
--ing I've-lost-**count**-how-many-**times** to figure that **out** and the **problem** is that **exertion** bu--
--rns **oxygen** so I actually don't have sixty seconds but maybe **half** that and Noriko always **was** clever and now she's **cruel,** too. It wasn't enough to just **kill** me--
--her long **enough** to get this damn thing **open** and then hope I'm not **too** deep and **maybe** I can getoutnotagainnot--

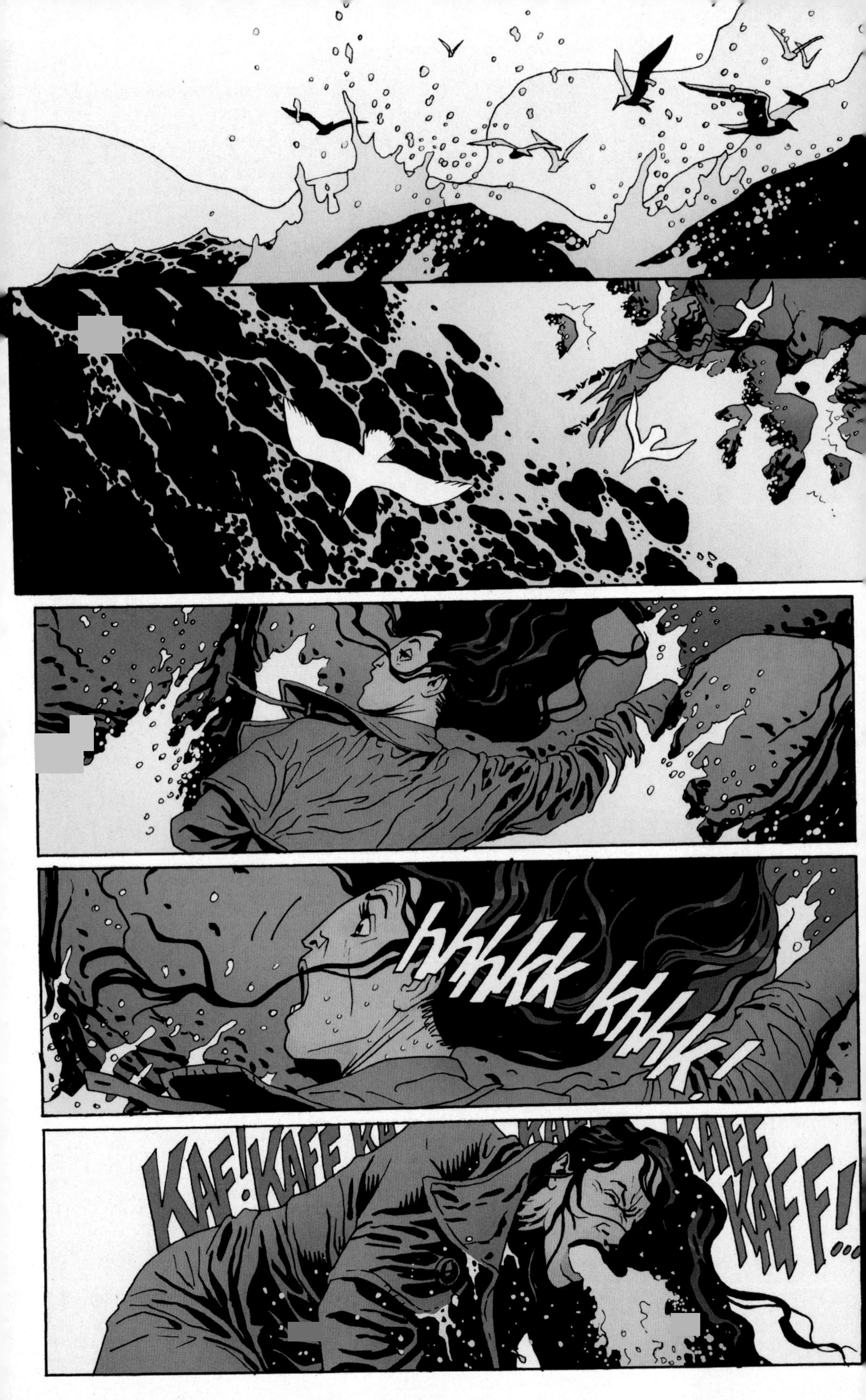
hhhkk khhk!
KAF! KAFF KAFF KAFF KAFF!...

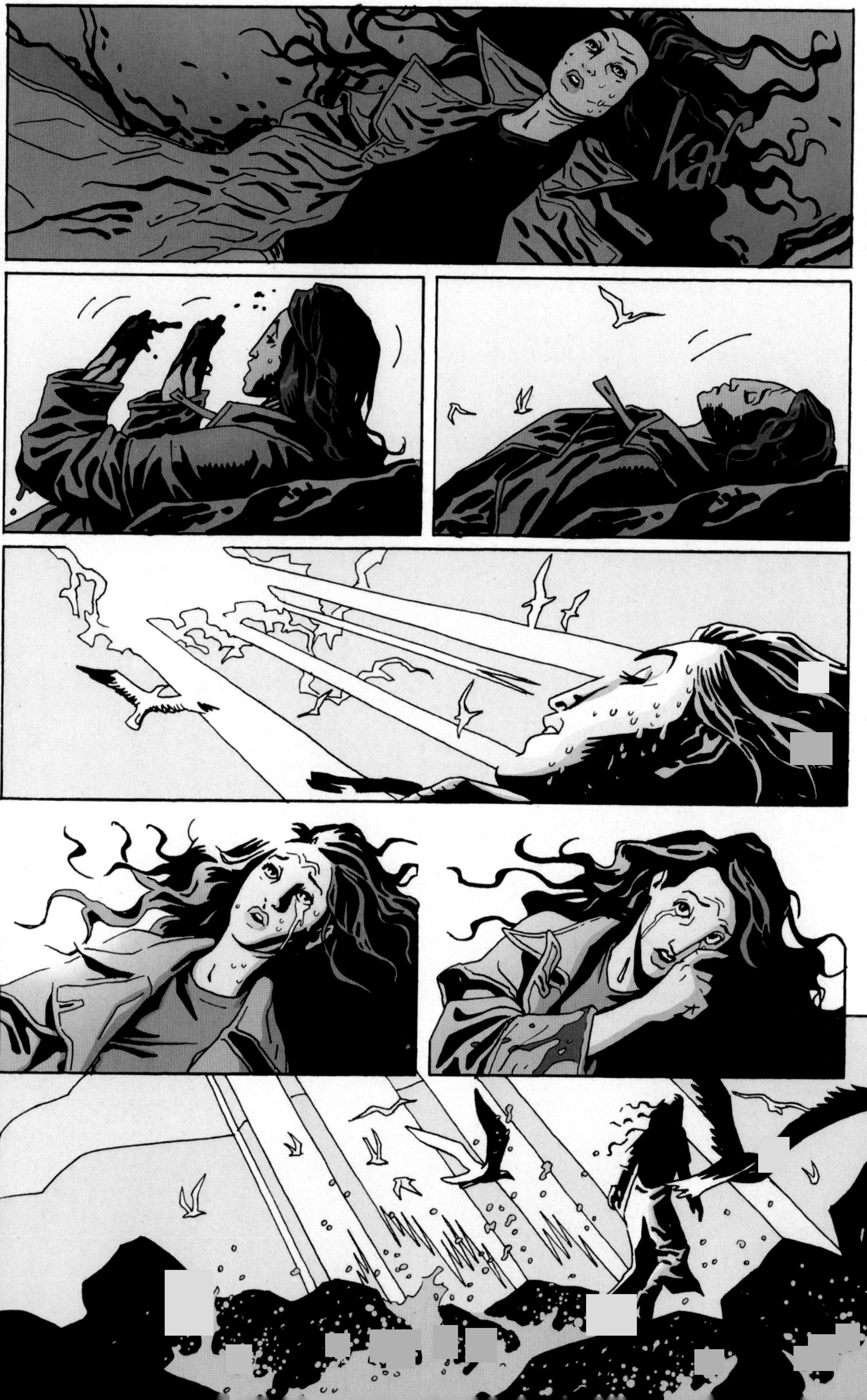
kaf

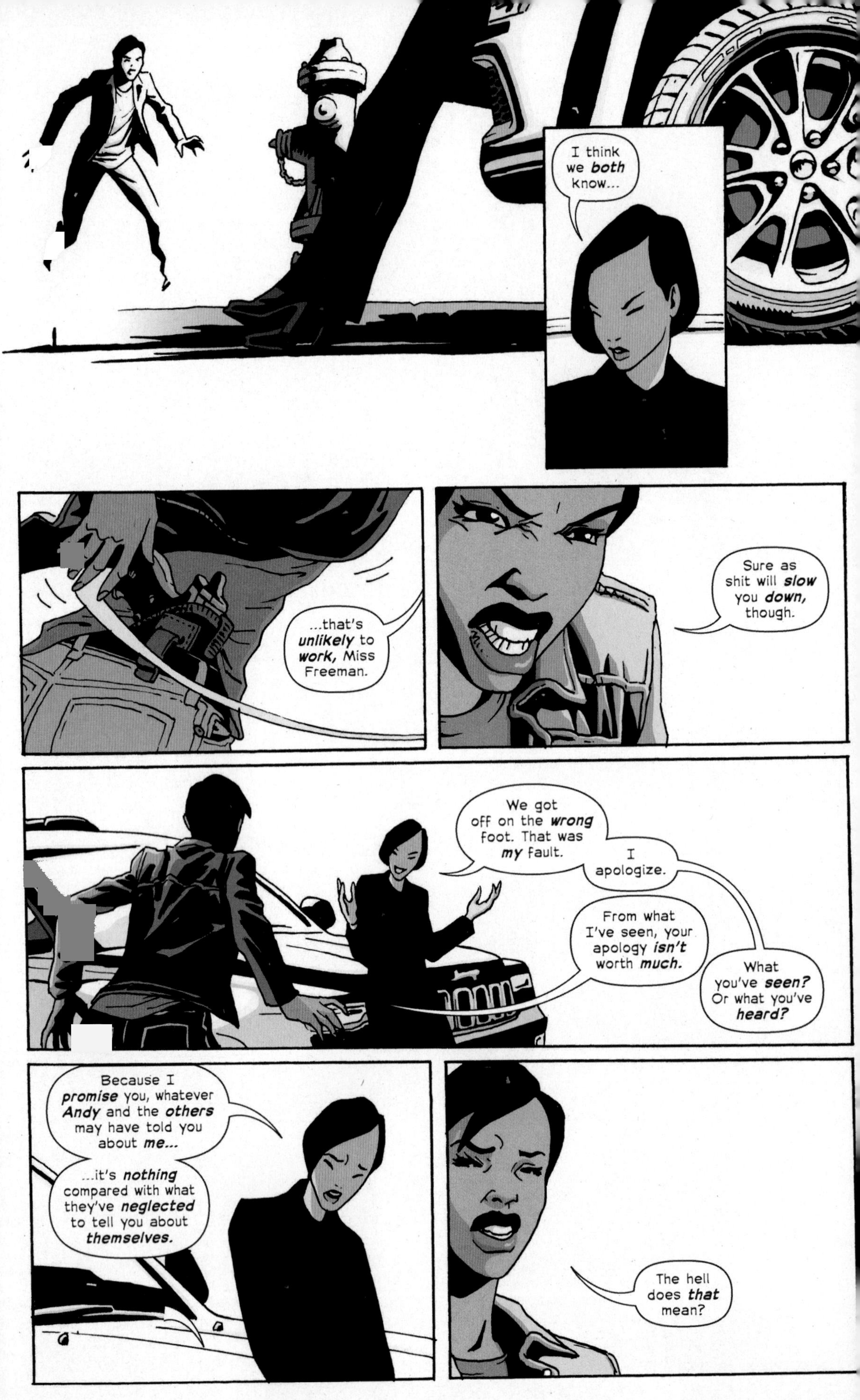
I think we both know...
...that's unlikely to work, Miss Freeman.
Sure as shit will slow you down, though.
We got off on the wrong foot. That was my fault.
I apologize.
From what I've seen, your apology isn't worth much.
What you've seen? Or what you've heard?
Because I promise you, whatever Andy and the others may have told you about me...
...it's nothing compared with what they've neglected to tell you about themselves.
The hell does that mean?

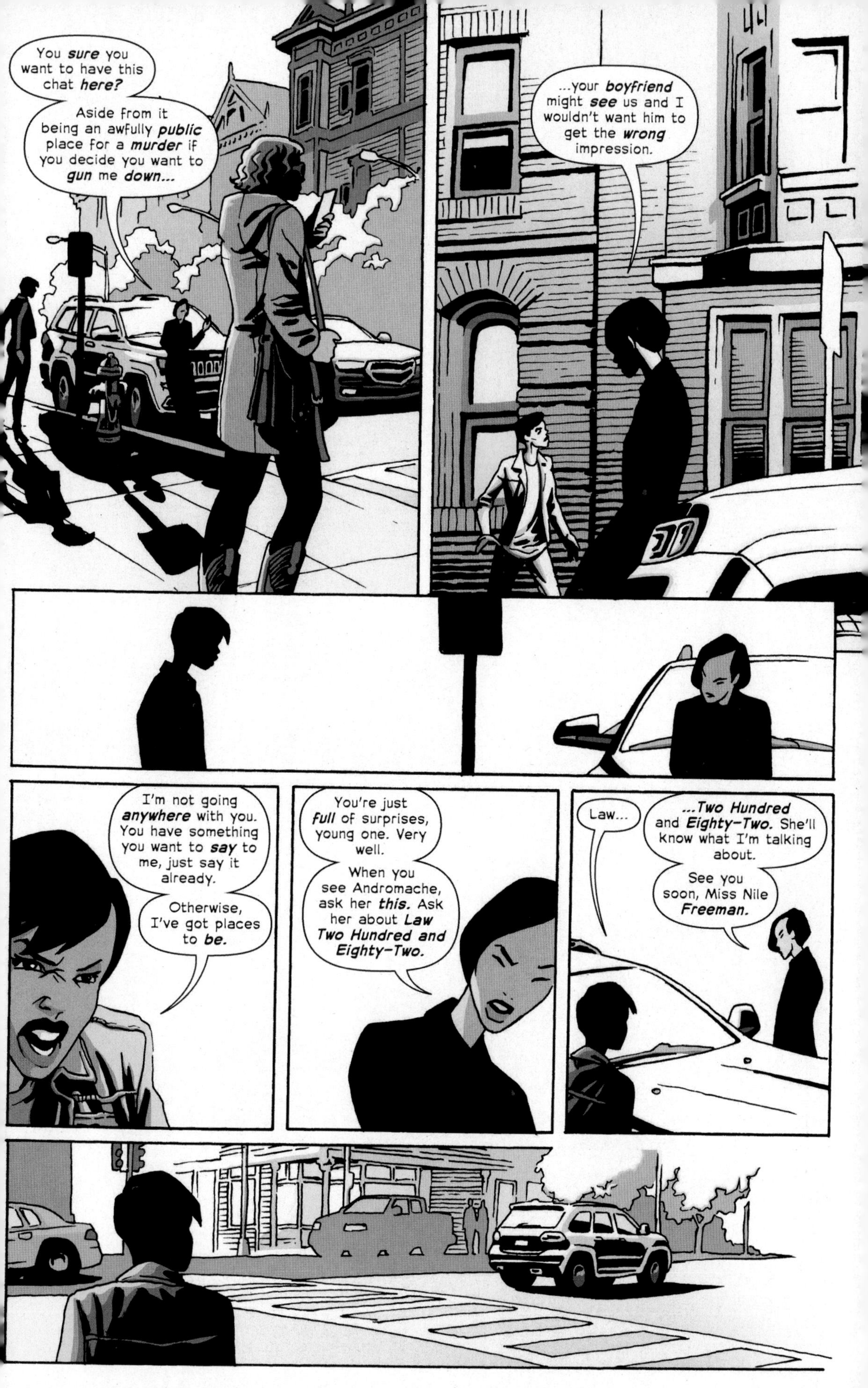
You sure you want to have this chat here?
Aside from it being an awfully public place for a murder if you decide you want to gun me down...
...your boyfriend might see us and I wouldn't want him to get the wrong impression.
I'm not going anywhere with you. You have something you want to say to me, just say it already.
Otherwise, I've got places to be.
You're just full of surprises, young one. Very well.
When you see Andromache, ask her this. Ask her about Law Two Hundred and Eighty-Two.
Law...
...Two Hundred and Eighty-Two. She'll know what I'm talking about.
See you soon, Miss Nile Freeman.

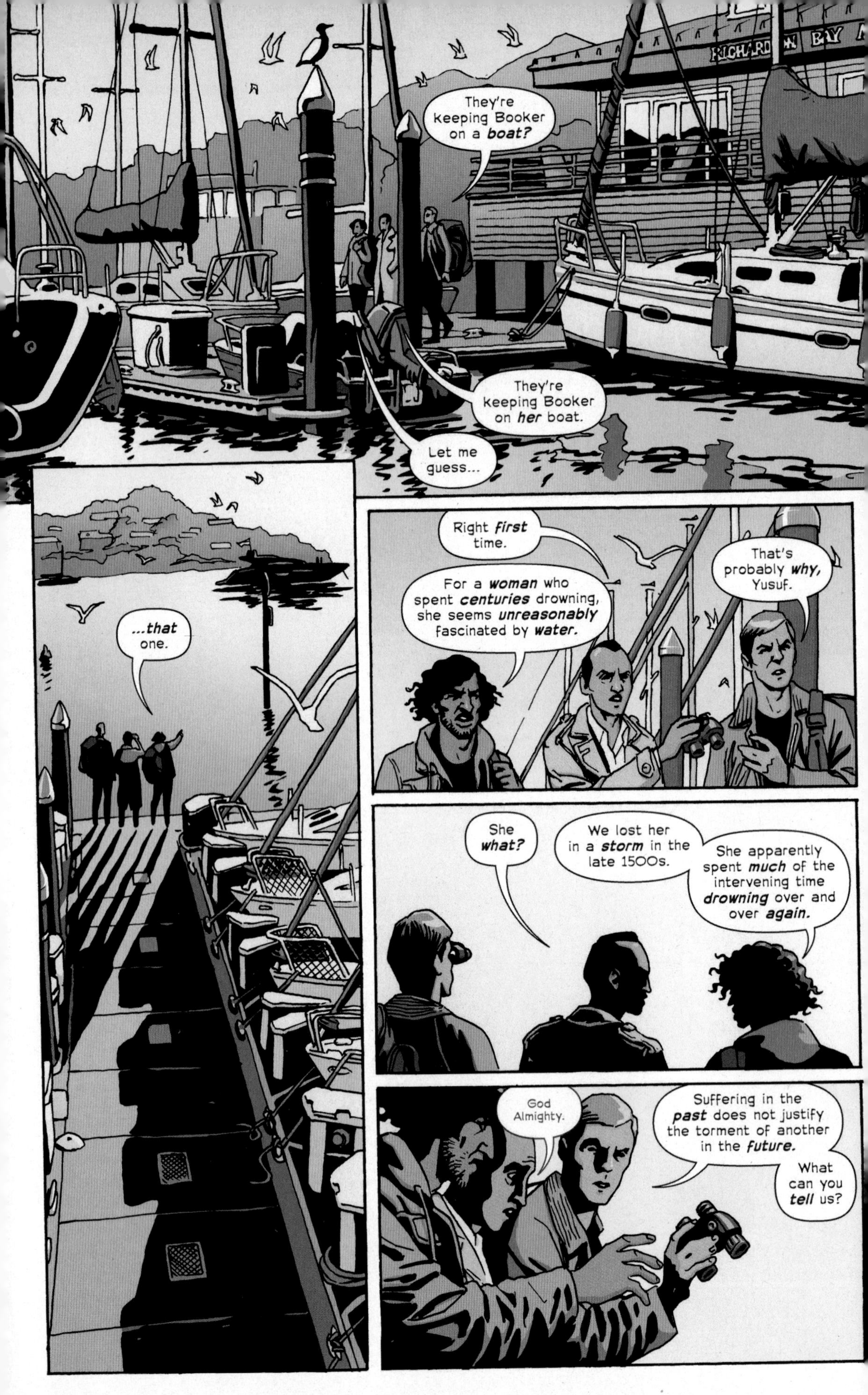
RICHARDSON BAY
They're keeping Booker on a *boat?*
They're keeping Booker on *her* boat.
Let me guess...
...that one.
Right *first* time.
For a *woman* who spent *centuries* drowning, she seems *unreasonably* fascinated by *water.*
That's probably *why,* Yusuf.
She *what?*
We lost her in a *storm* in the late 1500s.
She apparently spent *much* of the intervening time *drowning* over and over *again.*
God Almighty.
Suffering in the *past* does not justify the torment of another in the *future.*
What can you *tell* us?

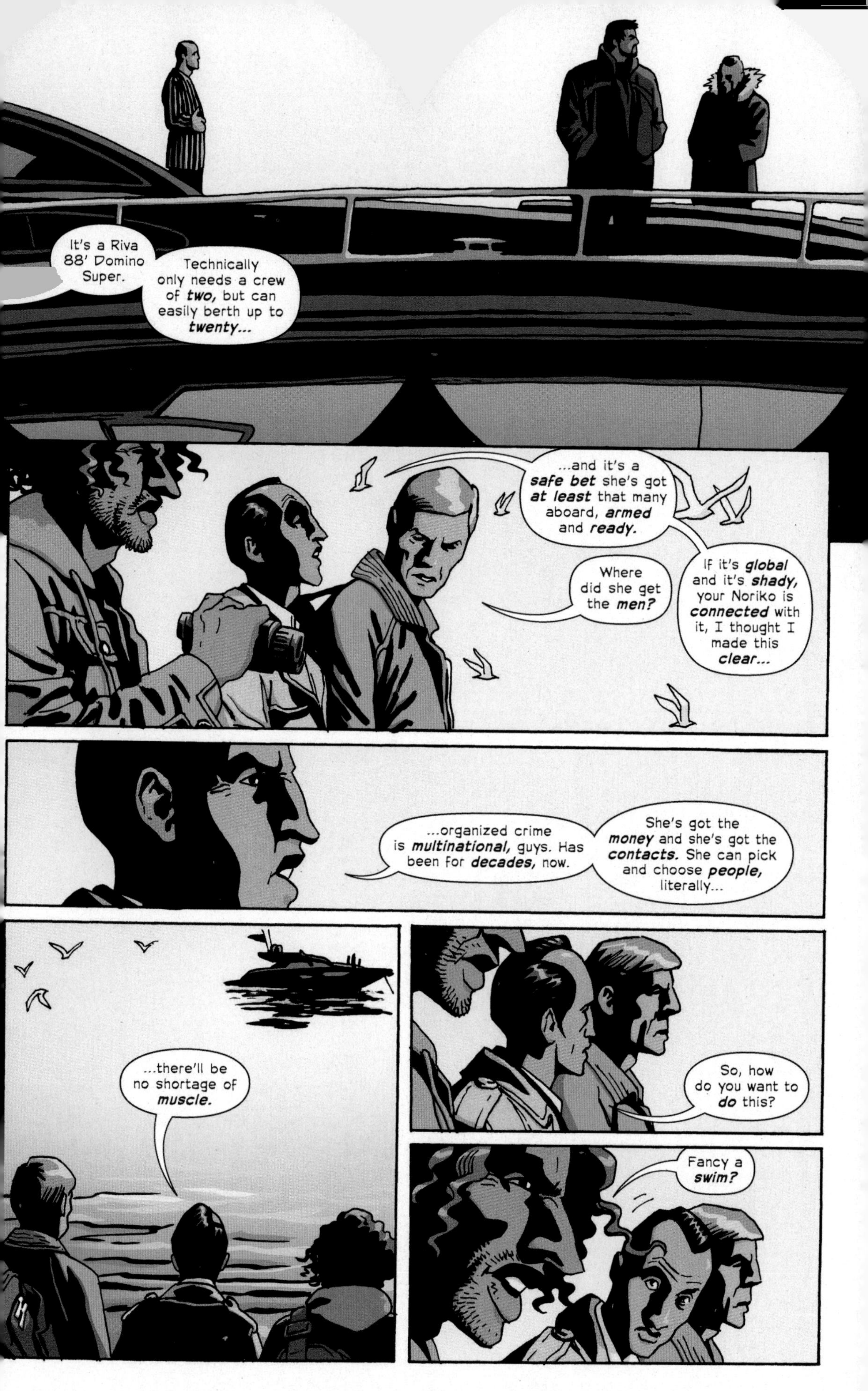
It's a Riva 88' Domino Super.
Technically only needs a crew of *two,* but can easily berth up to *twenty...*
...and it's a *safe bet* she's got *at least* that many aboard, *armed* and *ready.*
Where did she get the *men?*
If it's *global* and it's *shady,* your Noriko is *connected* with it, I thought I made this *clear...*
...organized crime is *multinational,* guys. Has been for *decades,* now.
She's got the *money* and she's got the *contacts.* She can pick and choose *people,* literally...
...there'll be no shortage of *muscle.*
So, how do you want to *do* this?
Fancy a *swim?*

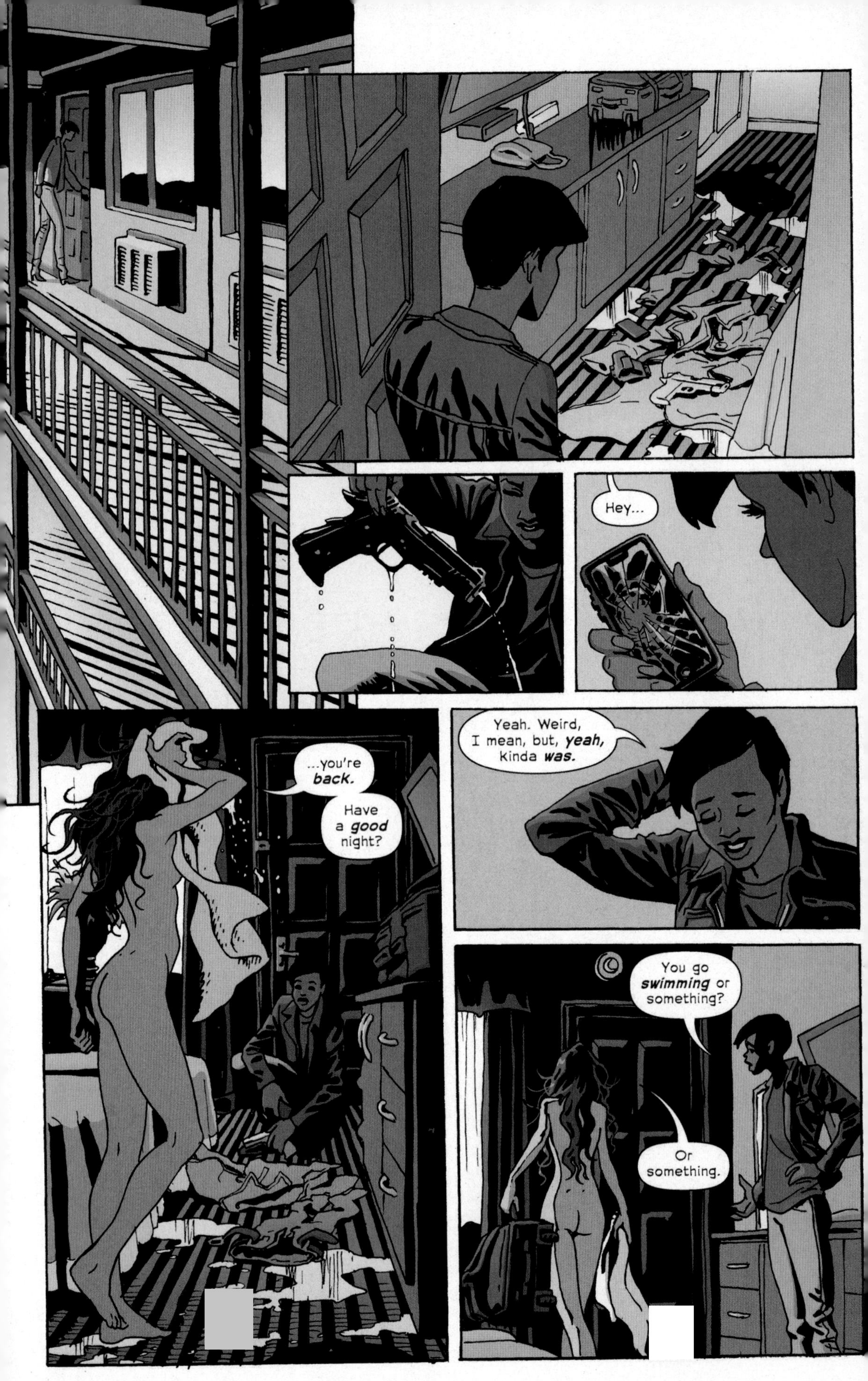
Hey...
...you're back.
Have a good night?
Yeah. Weird, I mean, but, yeah, kinda was.
You go swimming or something?
Or something.

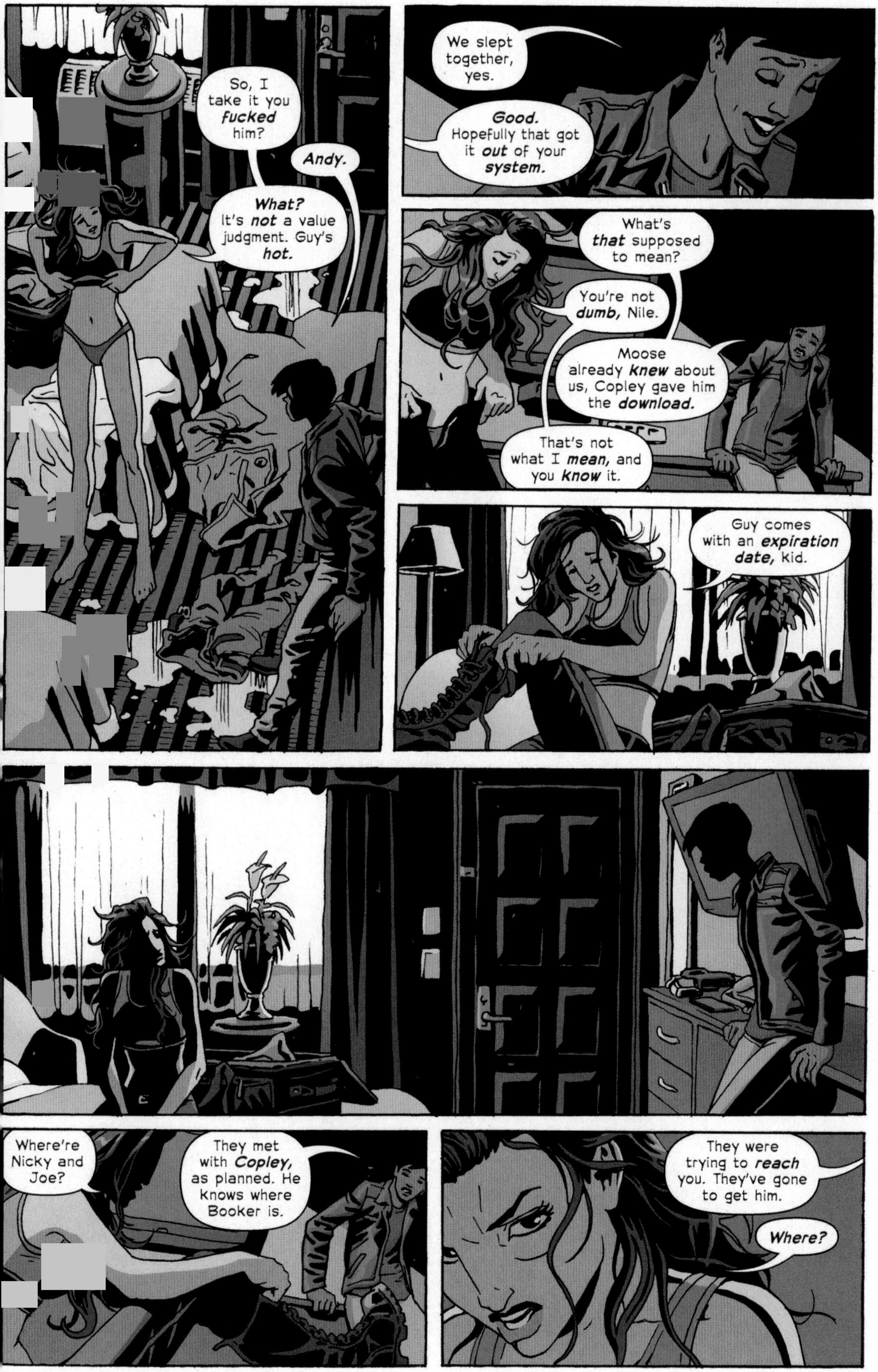
So, I take it you *fucked* him?
Andy.
What? It's *not* a value judgment. Guy's *hot.*
We slept together, yes.
Good. Hopefully that got it *out* of your *system.*
What's *that* supposed to mean?
You're not *dumb,* Nile.
Moose already *knew* about us, Copley gave him the *download.*
That's not what I *mean,* and you *know* it.
Guy comes with an *expiration date,* kid.
Where're Nicky and Joe?
They met with *Copley,* as planned. He knows where Booker is.
They were trying to *reach* you. They've gone to get him.
Where?

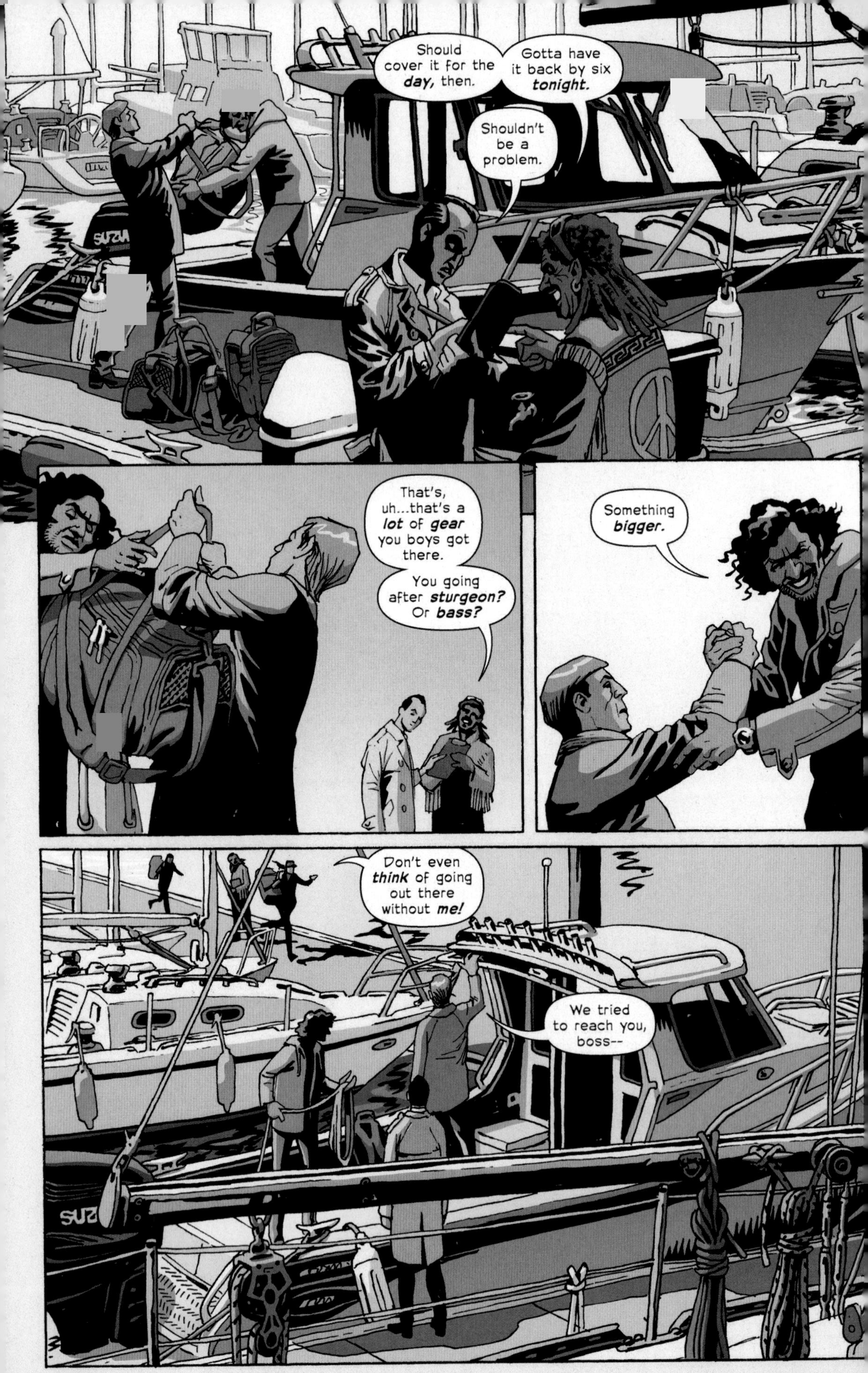
Should cover it for the *day,* then.
Gotta have it back by six *tonight.*
Shouldn't be a problem.
That's, uh...that's a *lot* of *gear* you boys got there.
You going after *sturgeon?* Or *bass?*
Something *bigger.*
Don't even *think* of going out there without *me!*
We tried to reach you, boss--

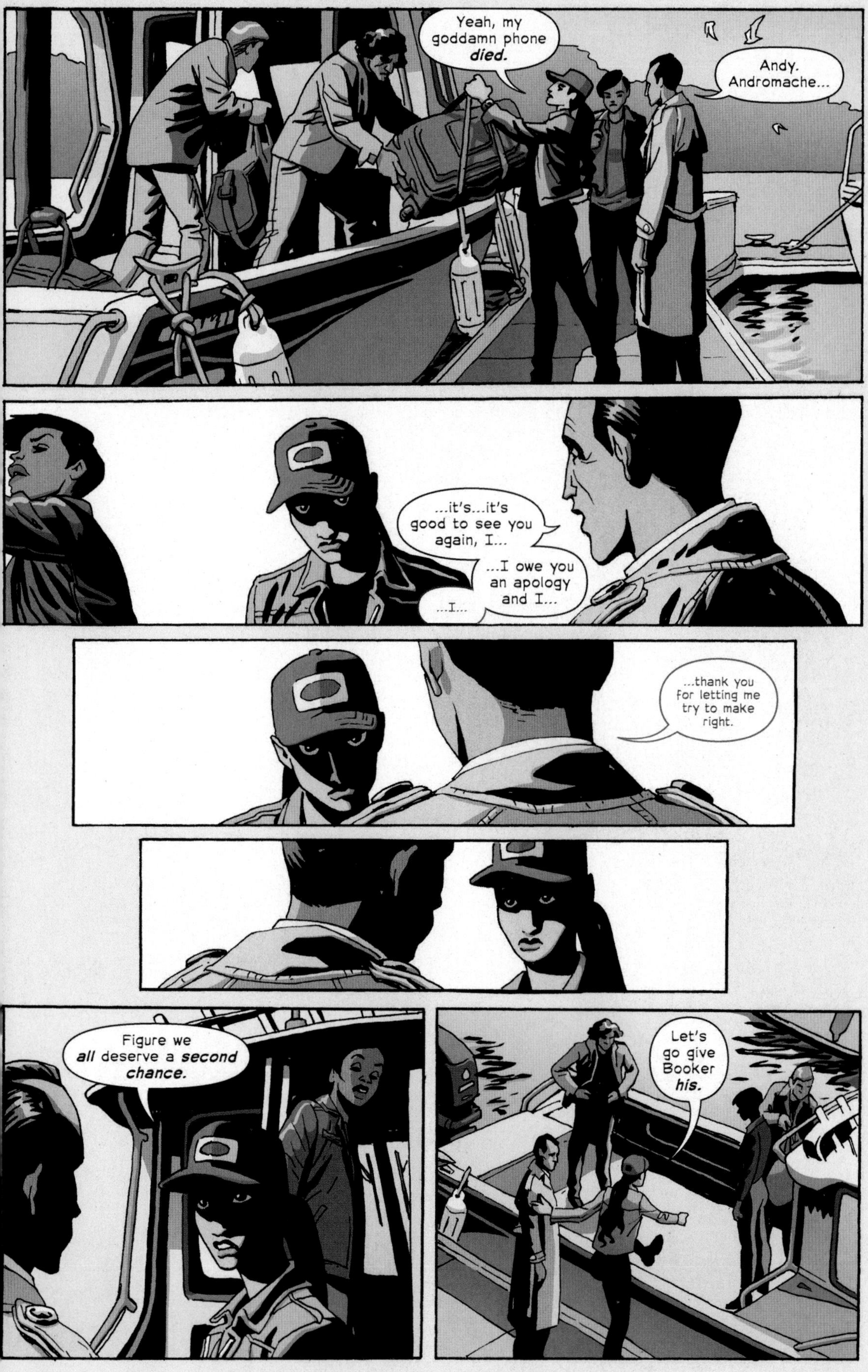
Yeah, my goddamn phone *died.*
Andy. Andromache...
...it's...it's good to see you again, I...
...I owe you an apology and I...
...I...
...thank you for letting me try to make right.
Figure we *all* deserve a *second chance.*
Let's go give Booker *his.*

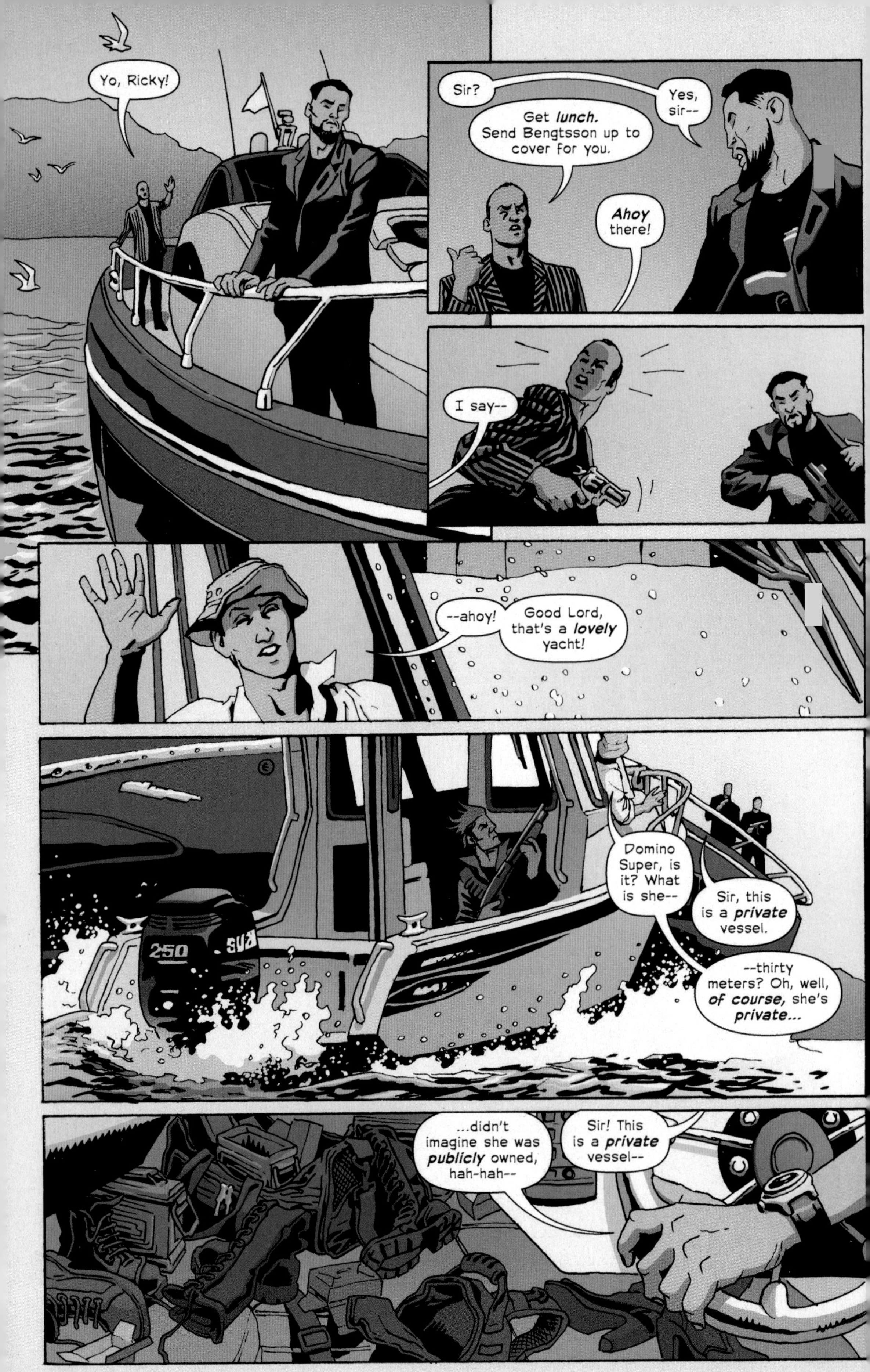

Yo, Ricky!
Sir?
Get lunch. Send Bengtsson up to cover for you.
Yes, sir--
Ahoy there!
I say--
--ahoy!
Good Lord, that's a lovely yacht!
Domino Super, is it? What is she--
Sir, this is a private vessel.
--thirty meters? Oh, well, of course, she's private...
...didn't imagine she was publicly owned, hah-hah--
Sir! This is a private vessel--

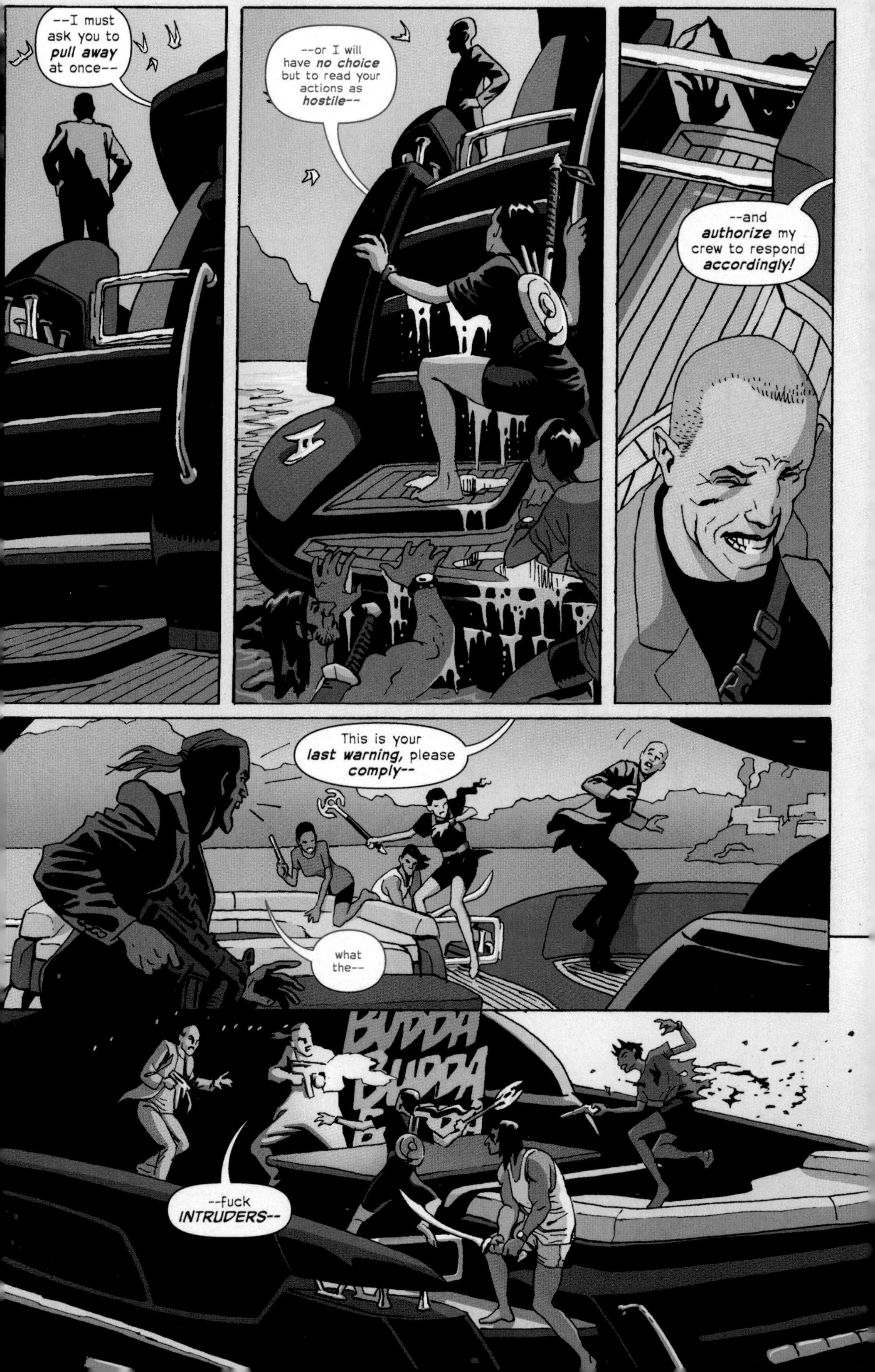
--I must ask you to pull away at once--
--or I will have no choice but to read your actions as hostile--
--and authorize my crew to respond accordingly!
This is your last warning, please comply--
what the--
BUDDA BUDDA
--fuck INTRUDERS--

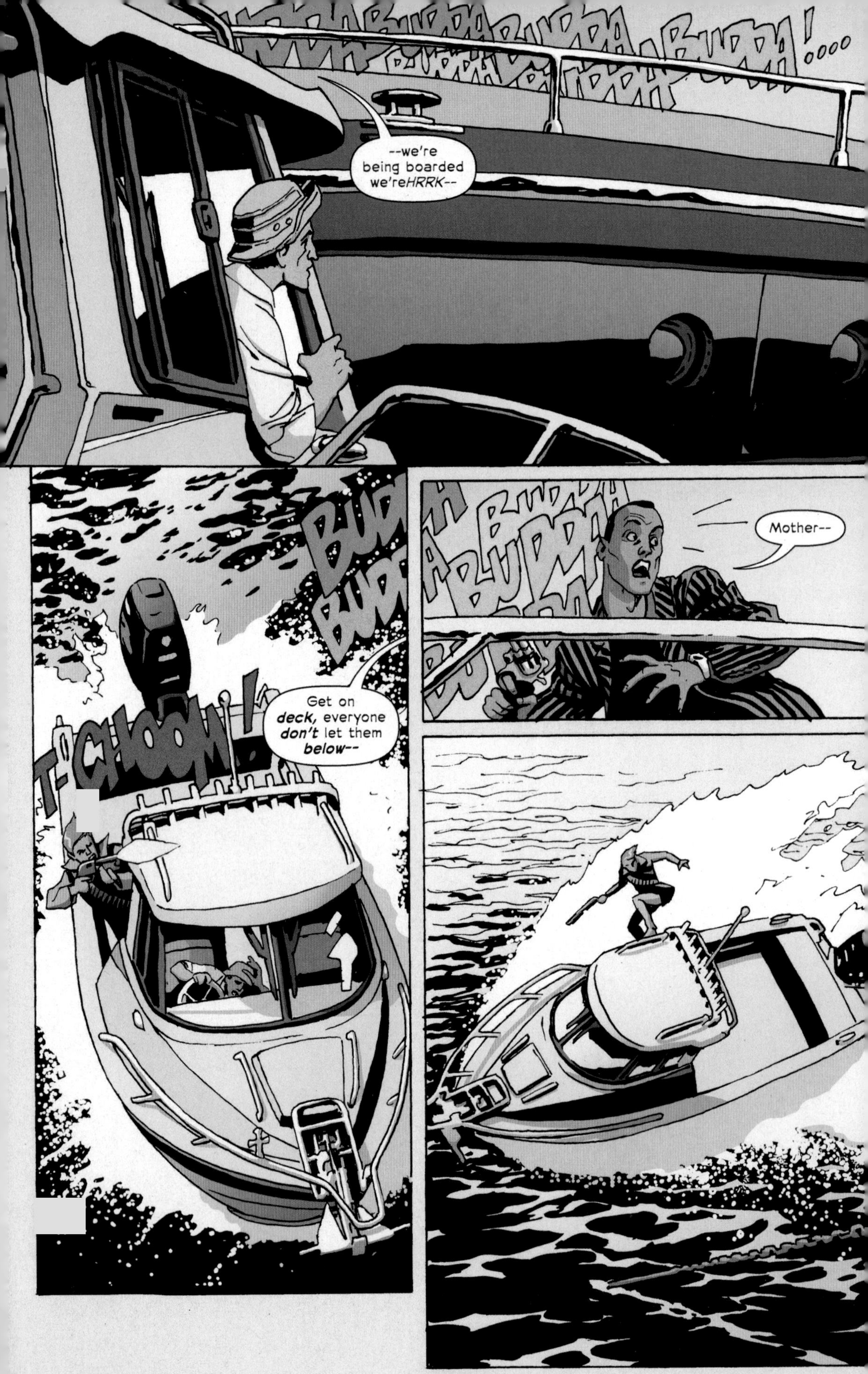

BUDDABUDDABUDDA!oooo
--we're being boarded we'reHRRK--
BUDDA BUDDA
T-CHOOM!
Get on *deck,* everyone *don't* let them *below--*
BUDDA BUDDA
Mother--

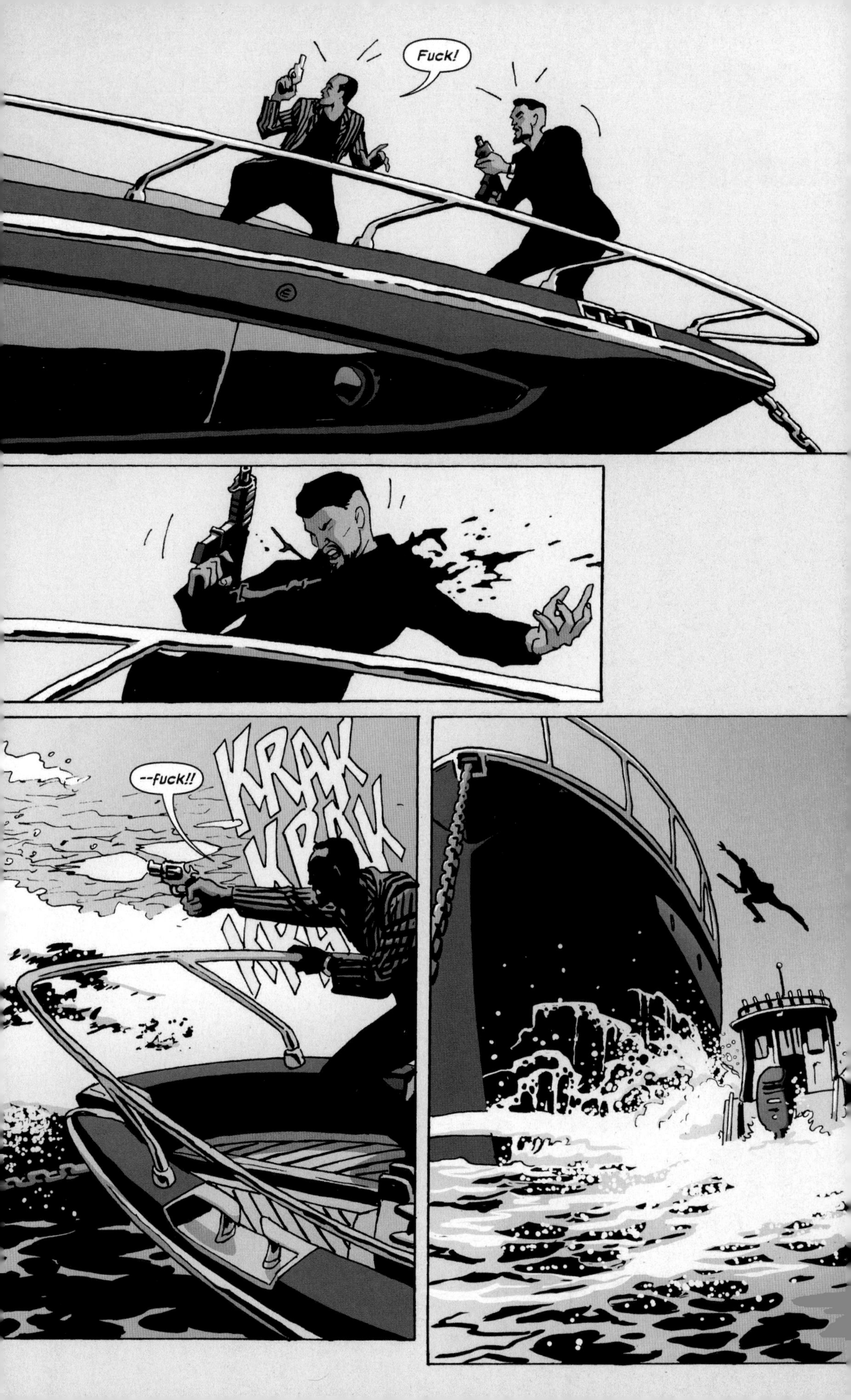

Fuck!
--fuck!!
KRAK
KRAK

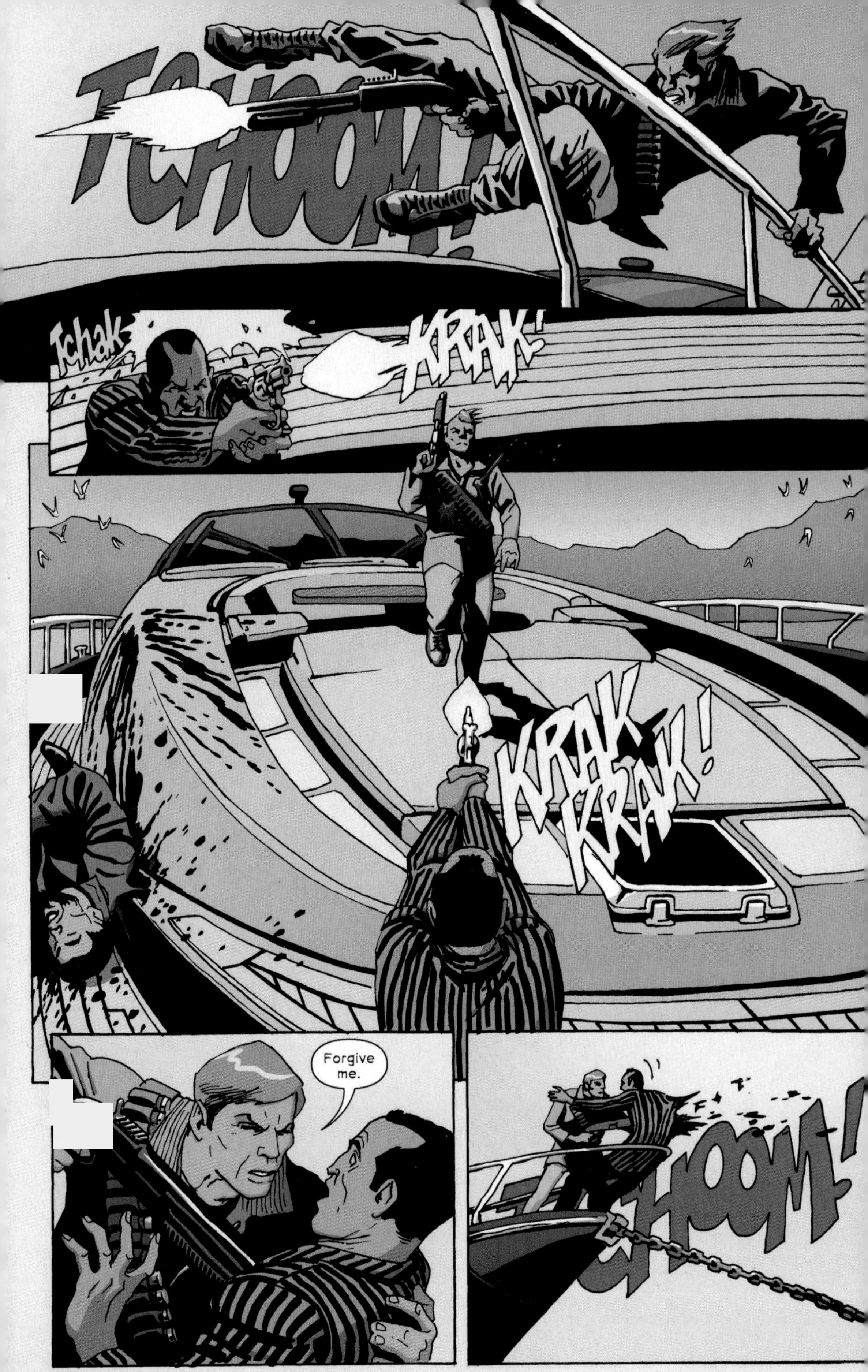
TCHOOM!
Tchak
KRAK!
KRAK KRAK!
Forgive me.
CHOOM!

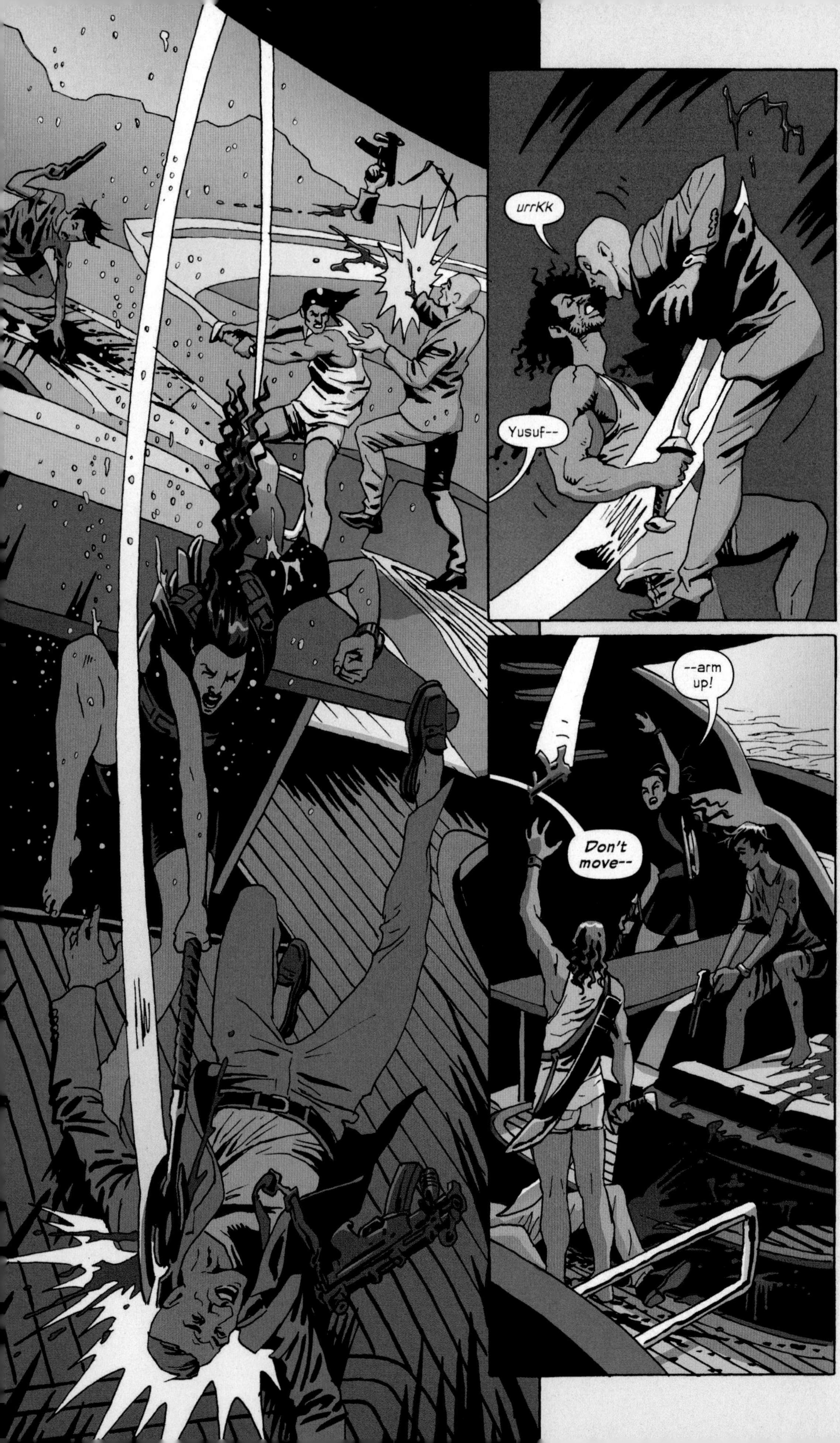
urrKk
Yusuf--
--arm up!
Don't move--

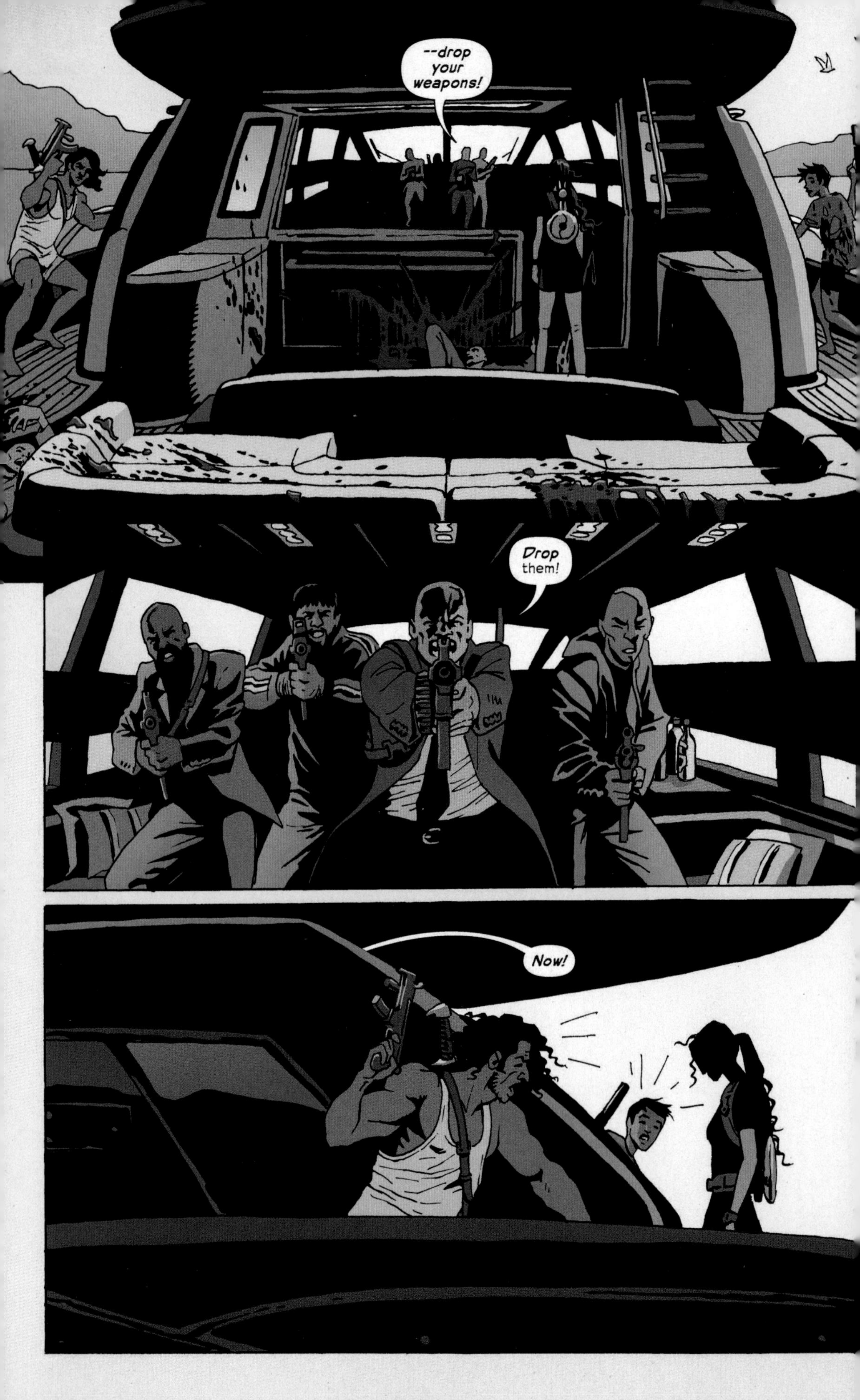
--drop your weapons!
Drop them!
Now!

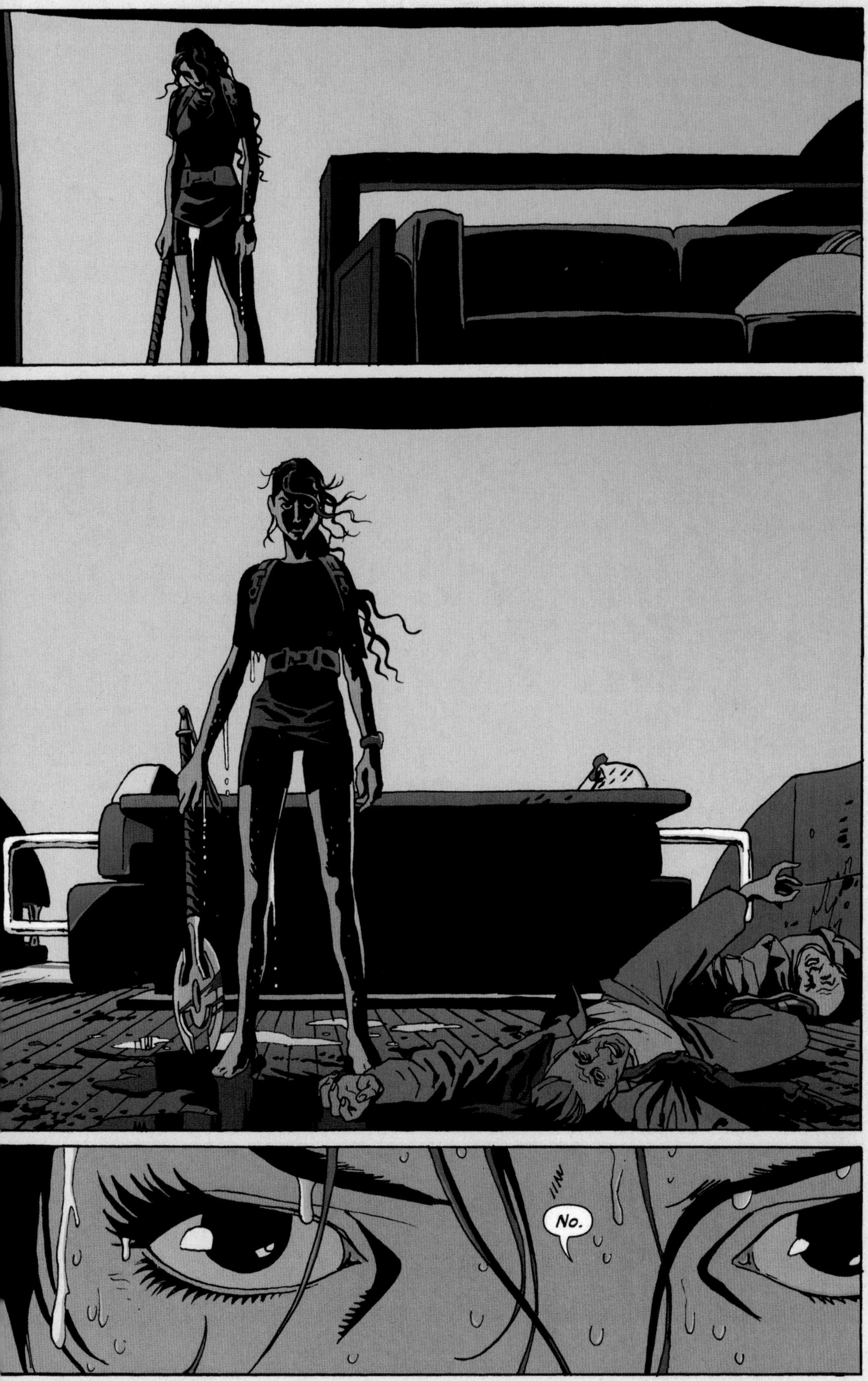
No.

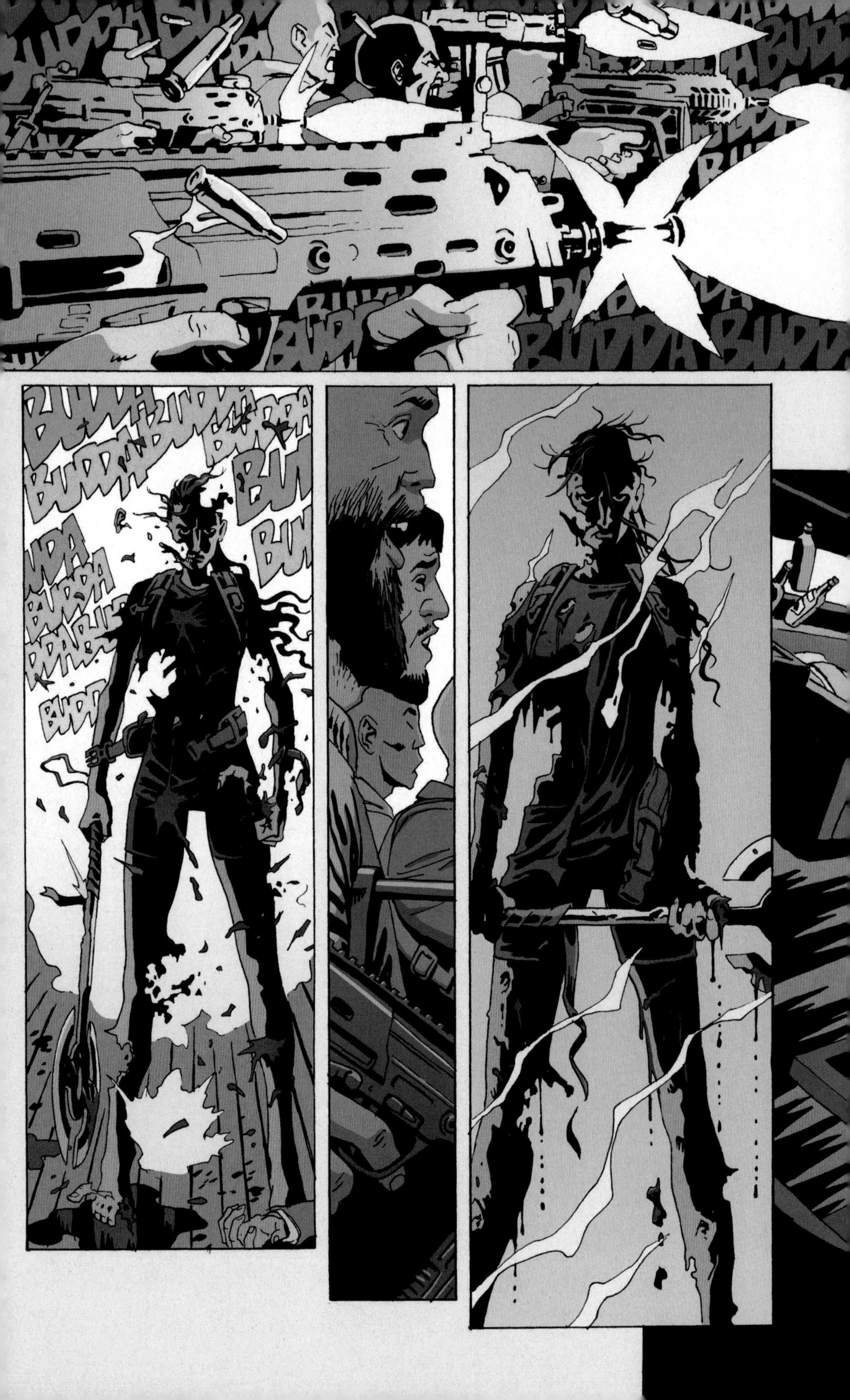
BUDDA
BUDDA BUDDA
BUDDA

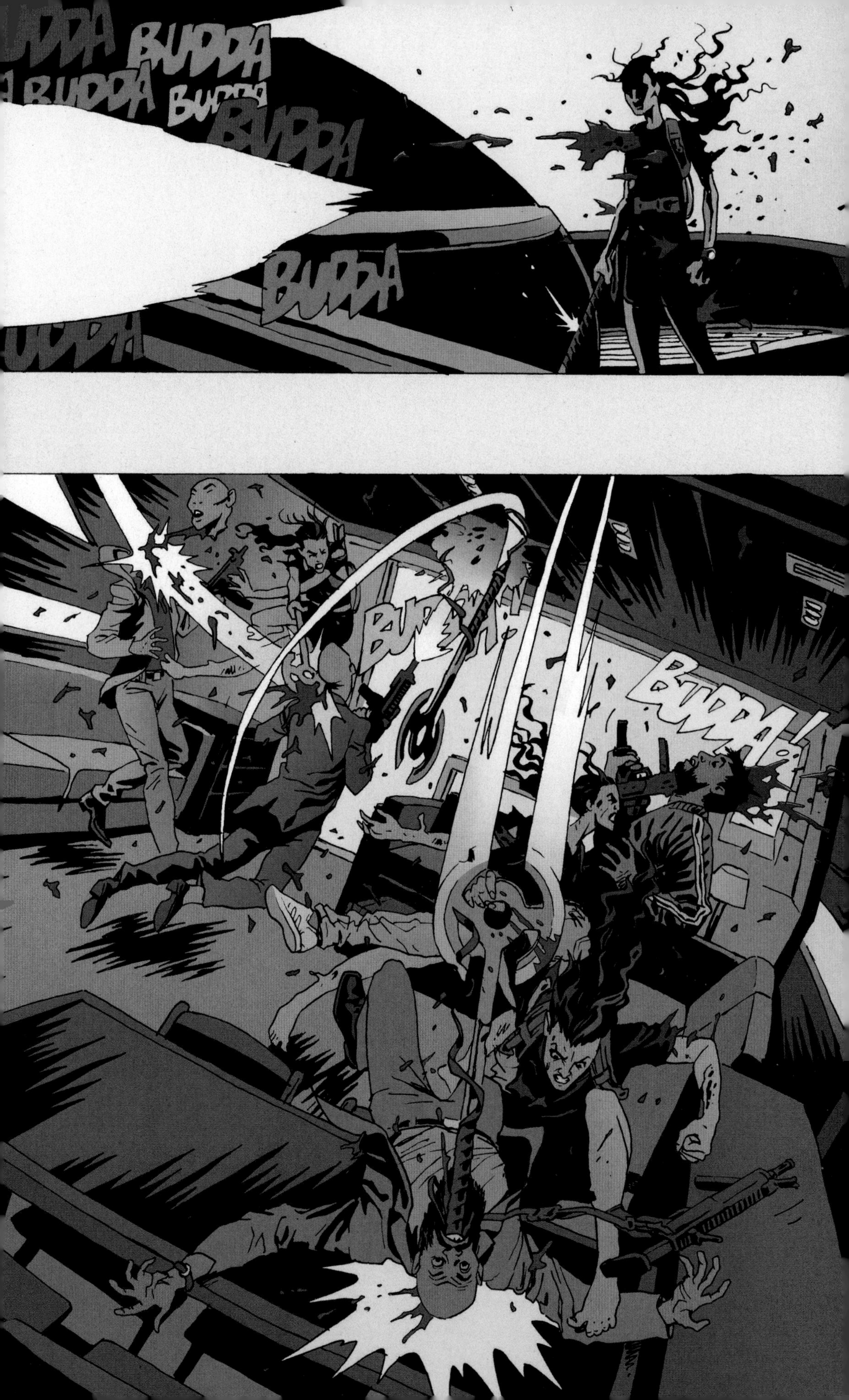
BUDDA
BUDDA
BUDDA
BUDDA
BUDDA
BUDDA!

Jesus Christ, Andy.

You wanted me to give them a *spanking* and send them to *bed* without *supper?*

Of course *not!*

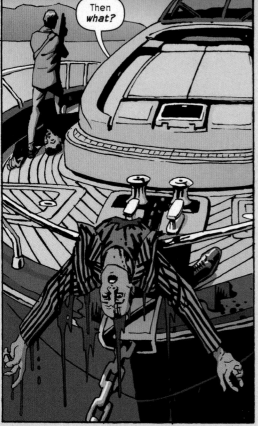

Then *what?*

Andy, you took them *apart!*

This... this *isn't* like you.

Maybe you don't *know* me, Nile.

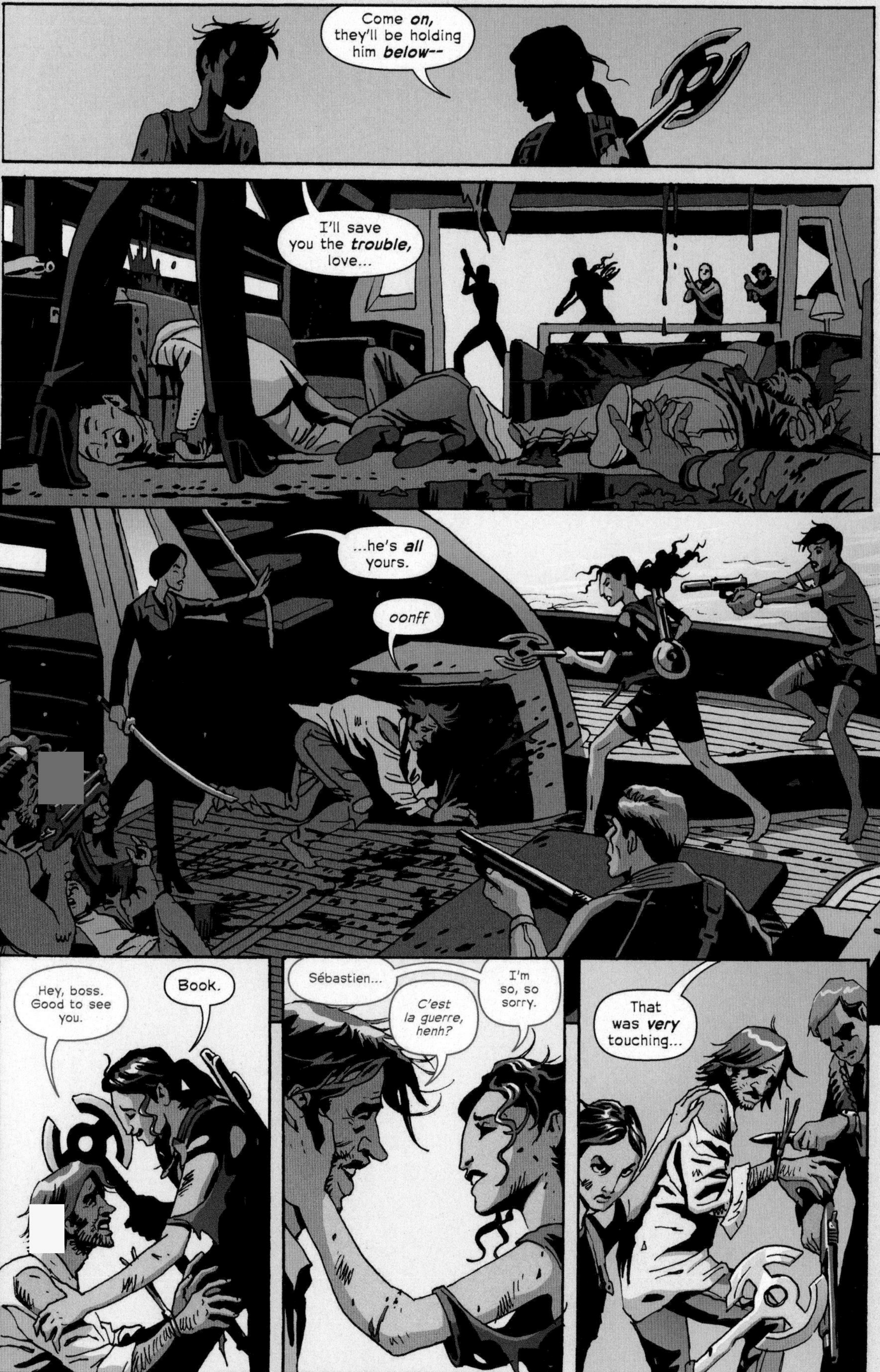
Come *on*, they'll be holding him *below*--
I'll save you the *trouble*, love...
...he's *all* yours.
oonff
Hey, boss. Good to see you.
Book.
Sébastien...
C'est la guerre, henh?
I'm so, so sorry.
That was *very* touching...

...I'd like to think, once upon a *time*, you'd have welcomed *me* home the *same* way.

But I somehow *doubt* it.

So, *how* do we want to *do* this?

A pitched *battle* on the deck of my yacht? *Old* school and *new,* blades and bullets?

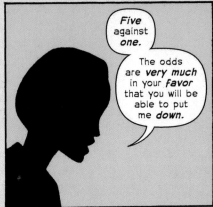

Five against *one.*

The odds are *very much* in your *favor* that you will be able to put me *down.*

So I'll *lose.*

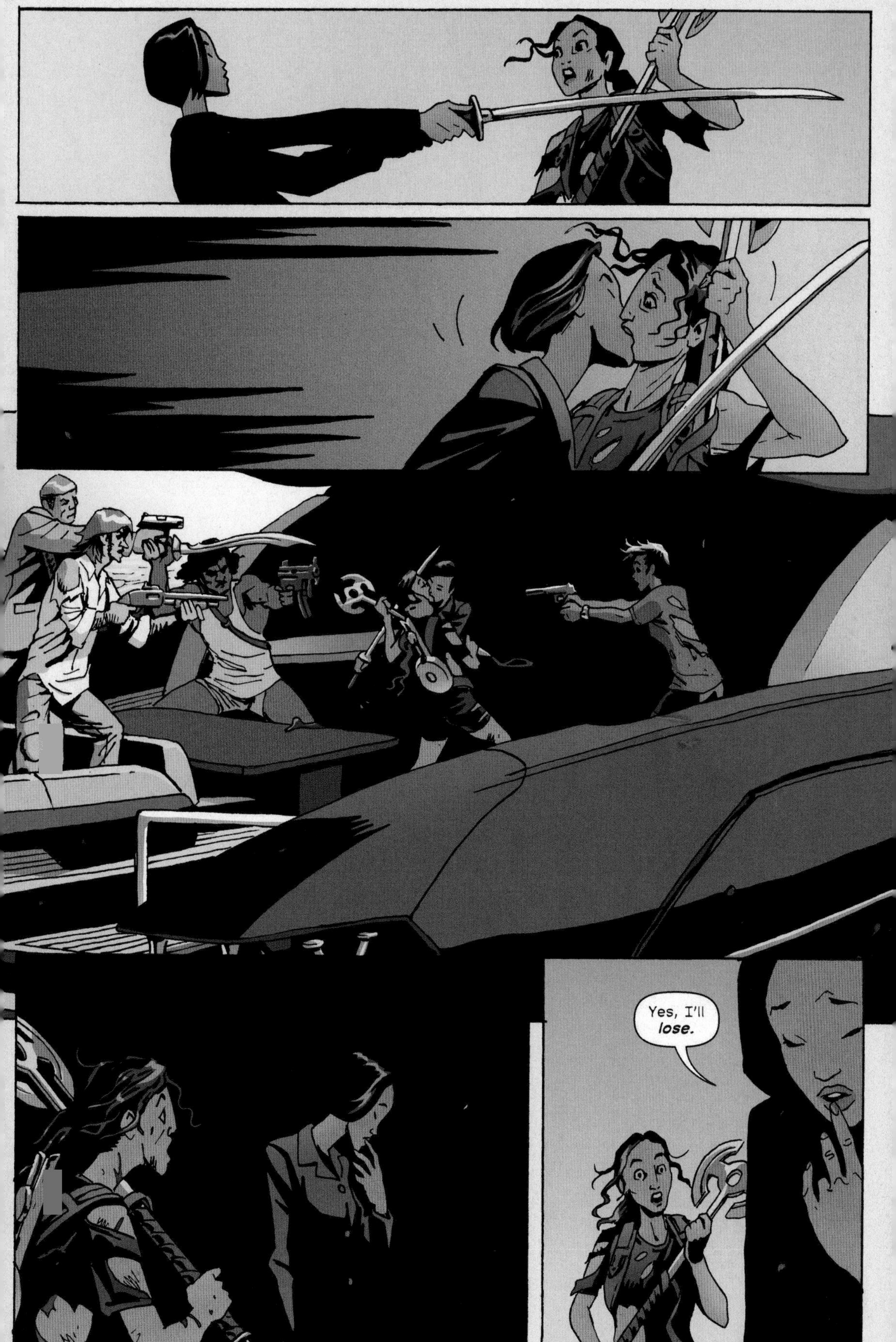
Yes, I'll
lose.

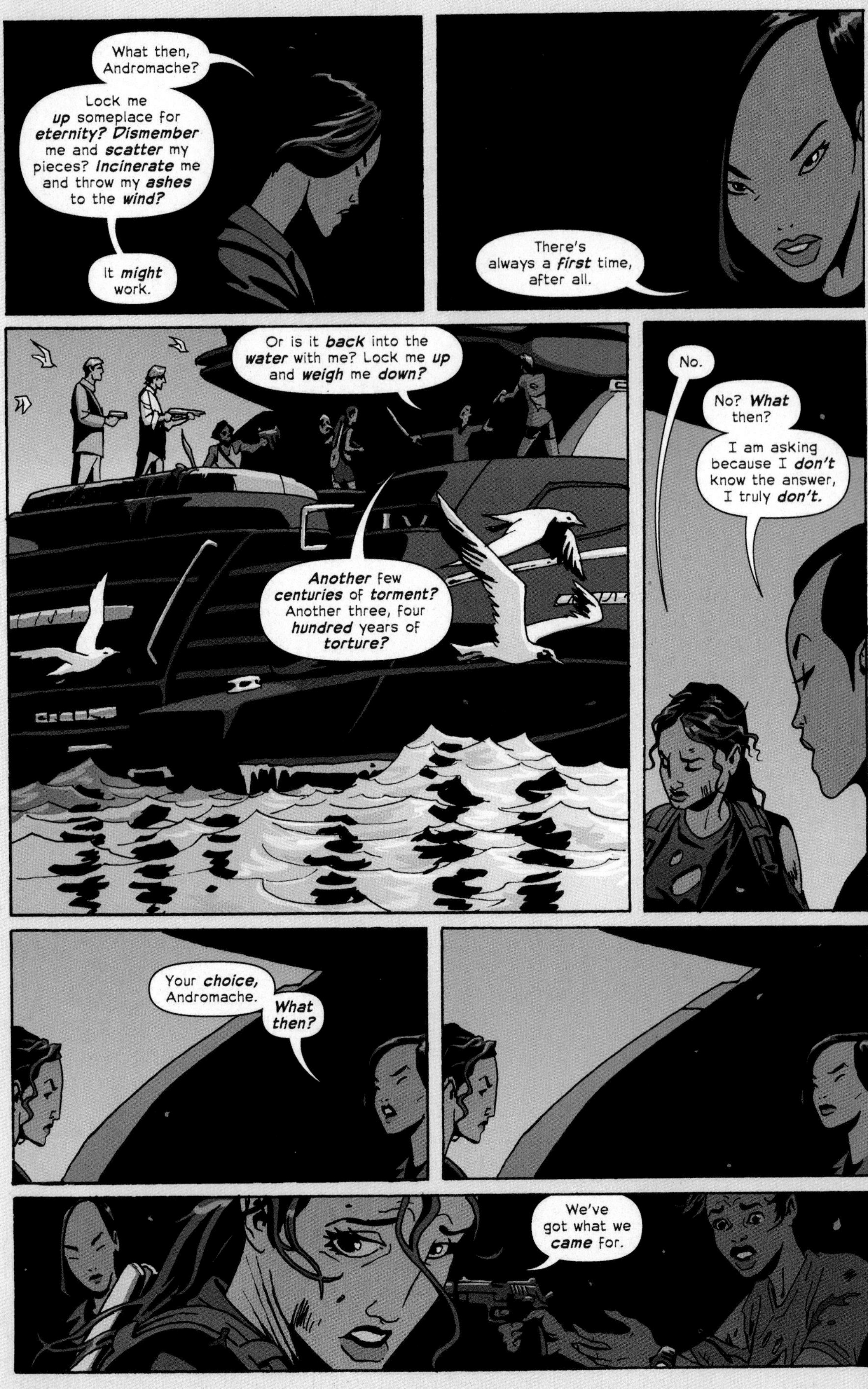
What then, Andromache?
Lock me up someplace for eternity? Dismember me and scatter my pieces? Incinerate me and throw my ashes to the wind?
It might work.
There's always a first time, after all.
Or is it back into the water with me? Lock me up and weigh me down?
Another few centuries of torment? Another three, four hundred years of torture?
No.
No? What then?
I am asking because I don't know the answer, I truly don't.
Your choice, Andromache.
What then?
We've got what we came for.

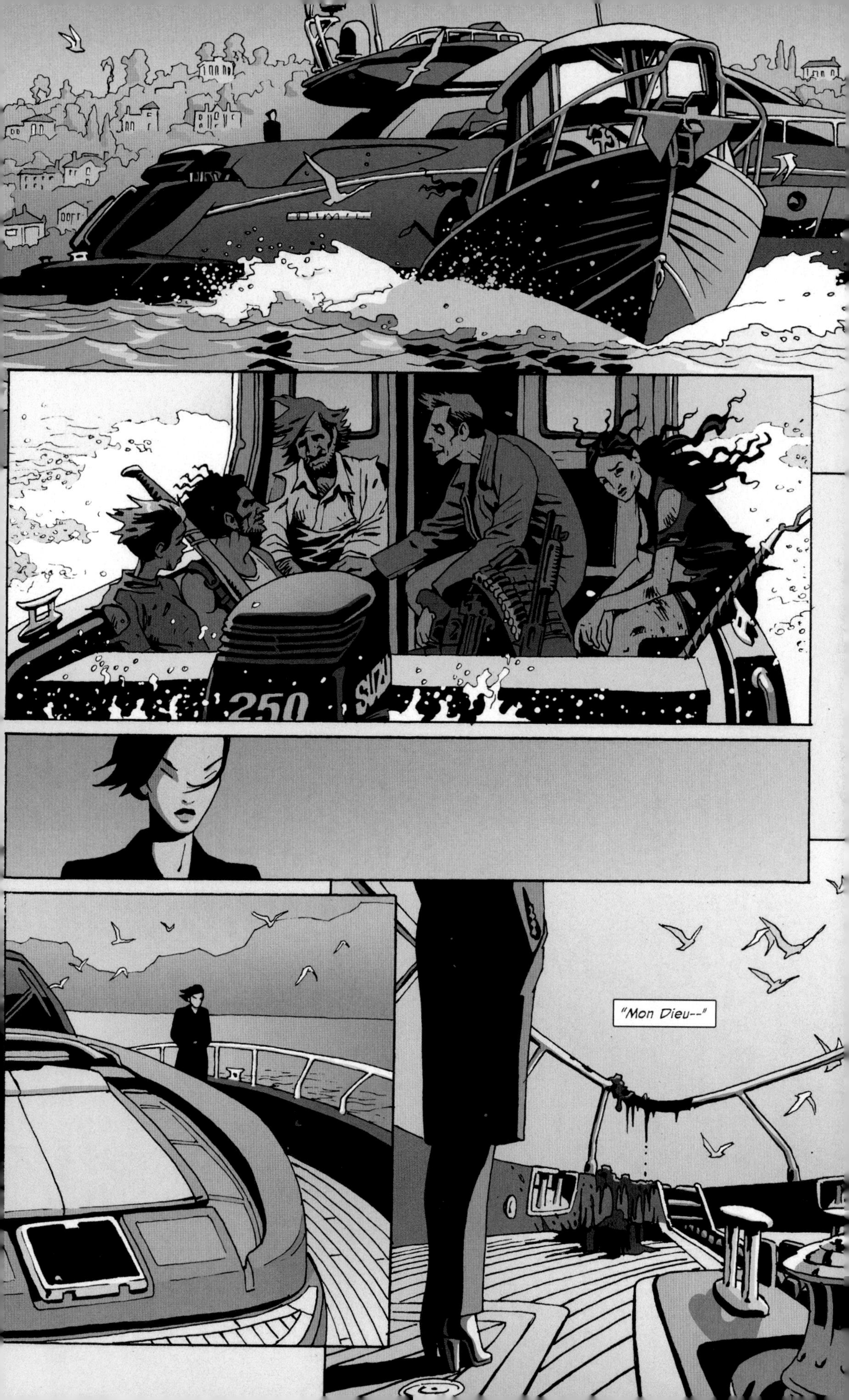
250
"Mon Dieu--"

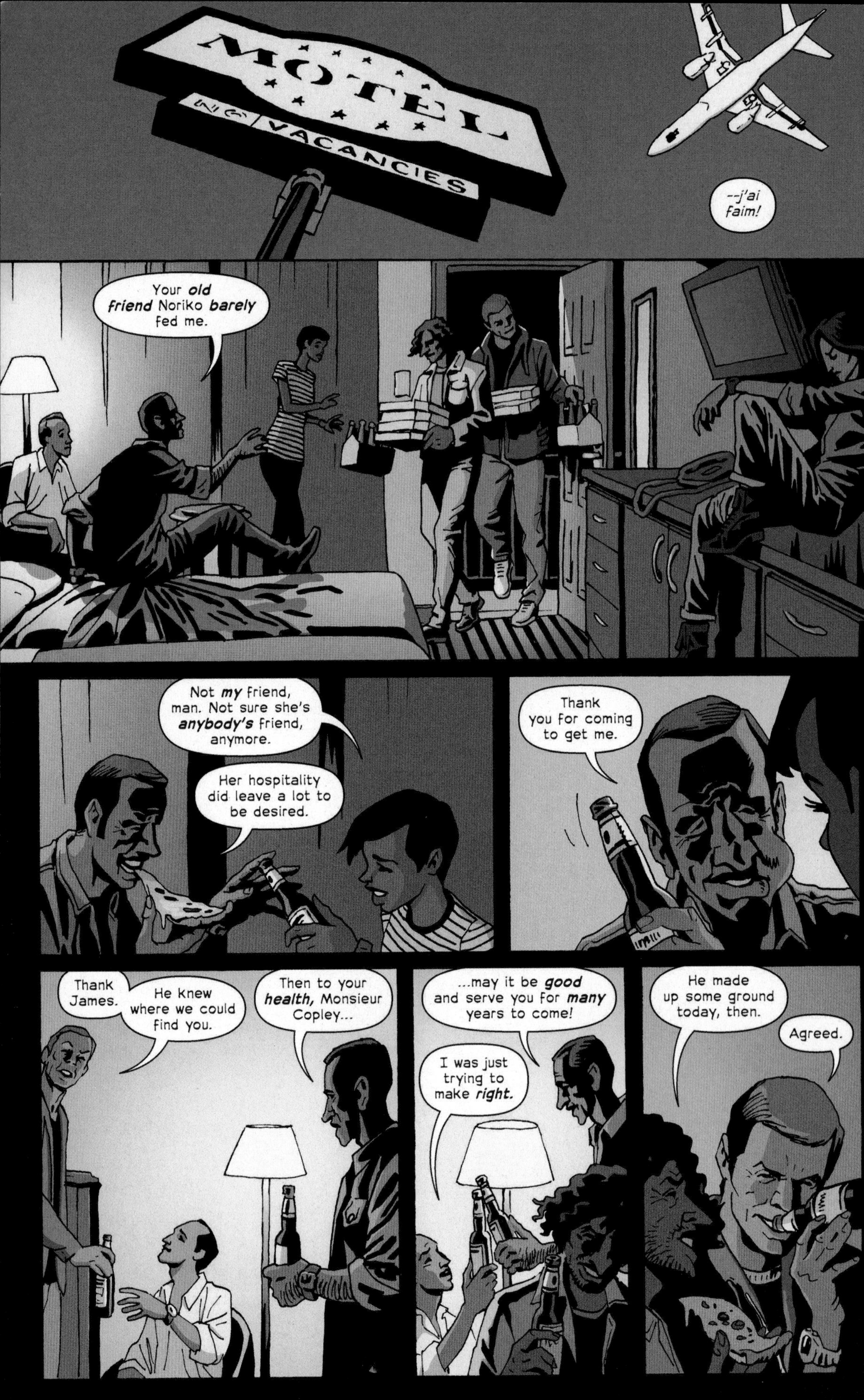
MOTEL
VACANCIES
--j'ai faim!
Your old friend Noriko barely fed me.
Not my friend, man. Not sure she's anybody's friend, anymore.
Her hospitality did leave a lot to be desired.
Thank you for coming to get me.
Thank James.
He knew where we could find you.
Then to your health, Monsieur Copley...
...may it be good and serve you for many years to come!
I was just trying to make right.
He made up some ground today, then.
Agreed.

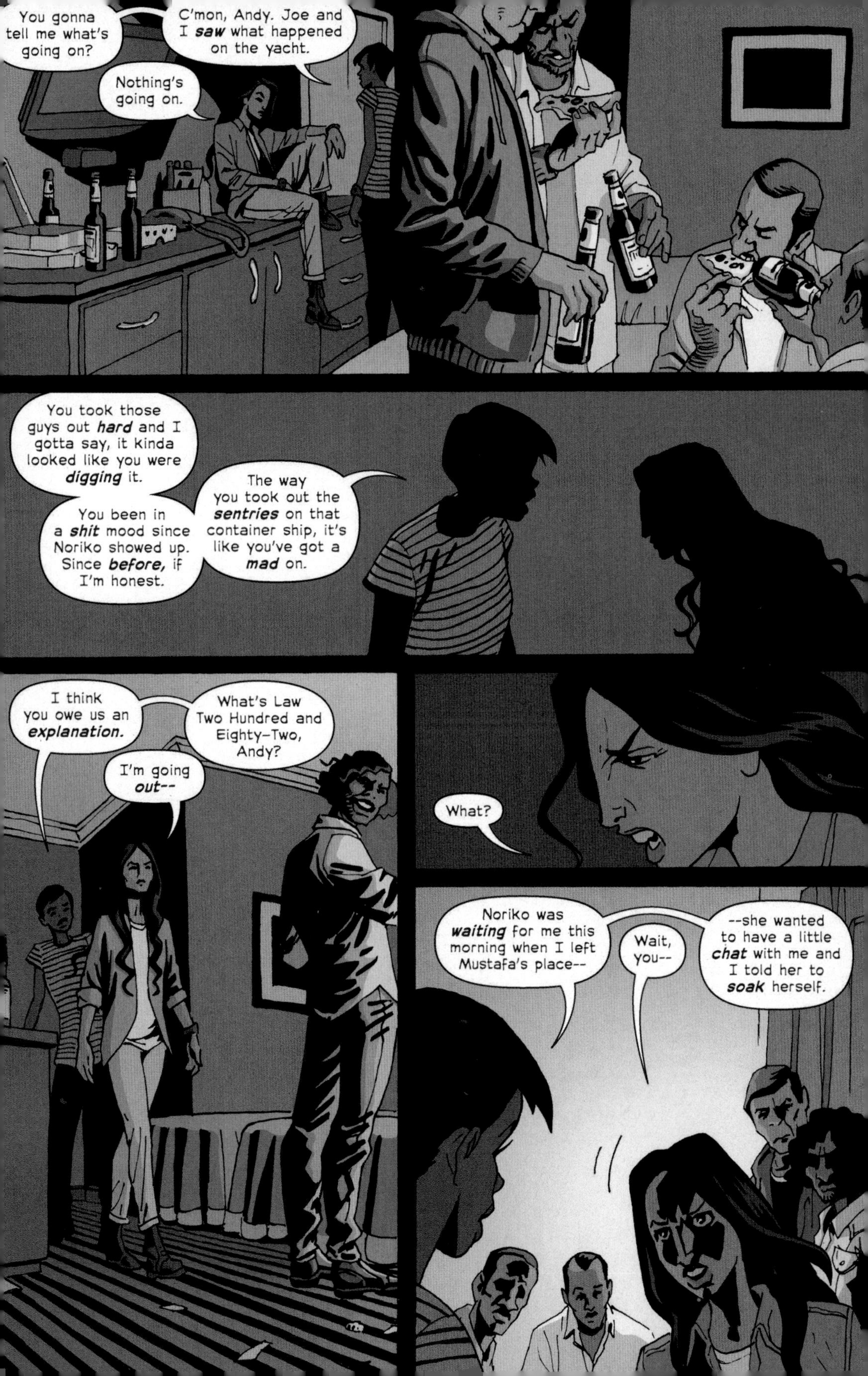
You gonna tell me what's going on?
C'mon, Andy. Joe and I saw what happened on the yacht.
Nothing's going on.
You took those guys out hard and I gotta say, it kinda looked like you were digging it.
You been in a shit mood since Noriko showed up. Since before, if I'm honest.
The way you took out the sentries on that container ship, it's like you've got a mad on.
I think you owe us an explanation.
What's Law Two Hundred and Eighty-Two, Andy?
I'm going out--
What?
Noriko was waiting for me this morning when I left Mustafa's place--
Wait, you--
--she wanted to have a little chat with me and I told her to soak herself.

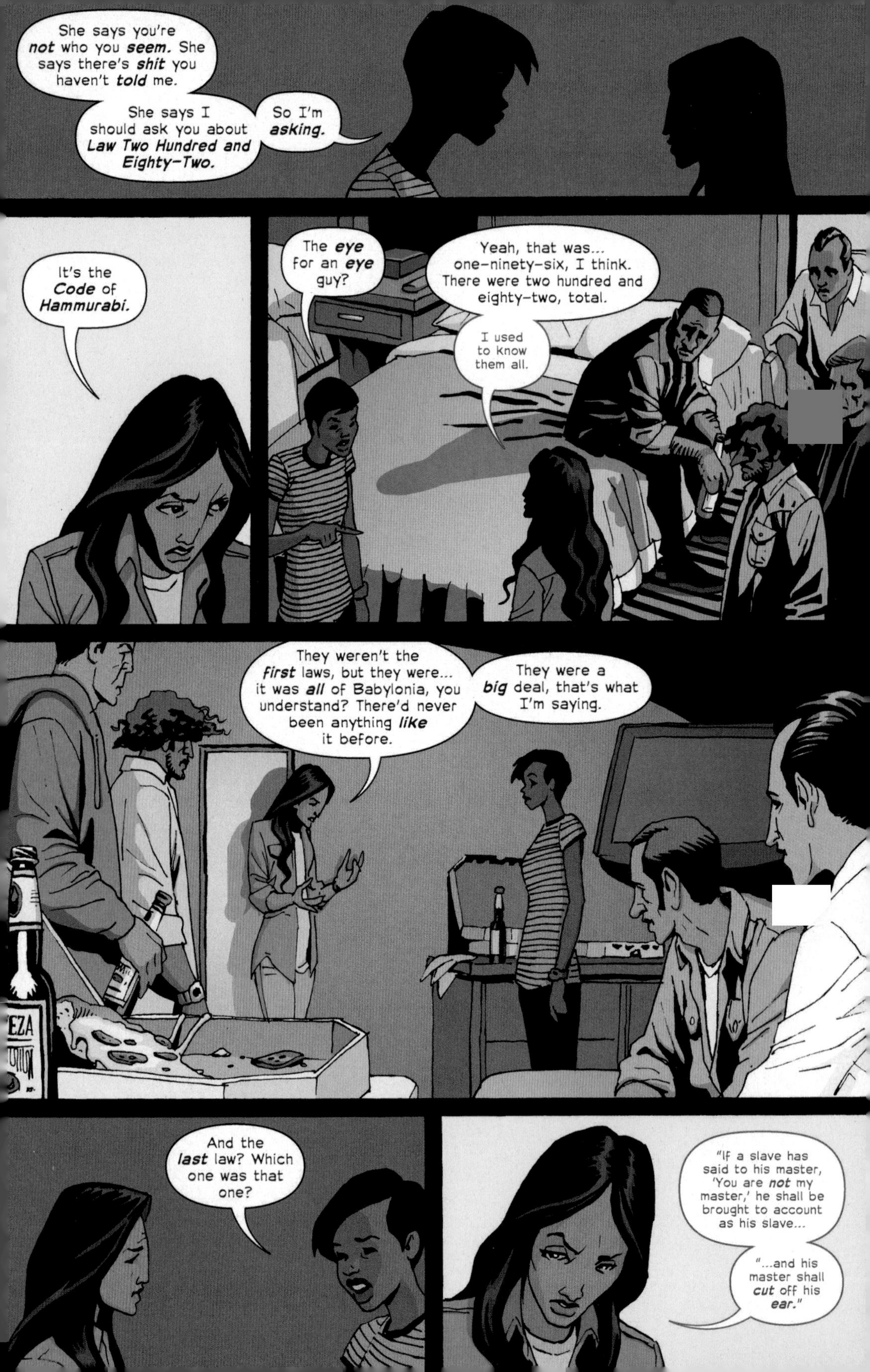
She says you're *not* who you *seem.* She says there's *shit* you haven't *told* me.
She says I should ask you about *Law Two Hundred and Eighty-Two.*
So I'm *asking.*
It's the *Code* of *Hammurabi.*
The *eye* for an *eye* guy?
Yeah, that was... one-ninety-six, I think. There were two hundred and eighty-two, total.
I used to know them all.
They weren't the *first* laws, but they were... it was *all* of Babylonia, you understand? There'd never been anything *like* it before.
They were a *big* deal, that's what I'm saying.
And the *last* law? Which one was that one?
"If a slave has said to his master, 'You are *not* my master,' he shall be brought to account as his slave...
"...and his master shall *cut* off his *ear.*"

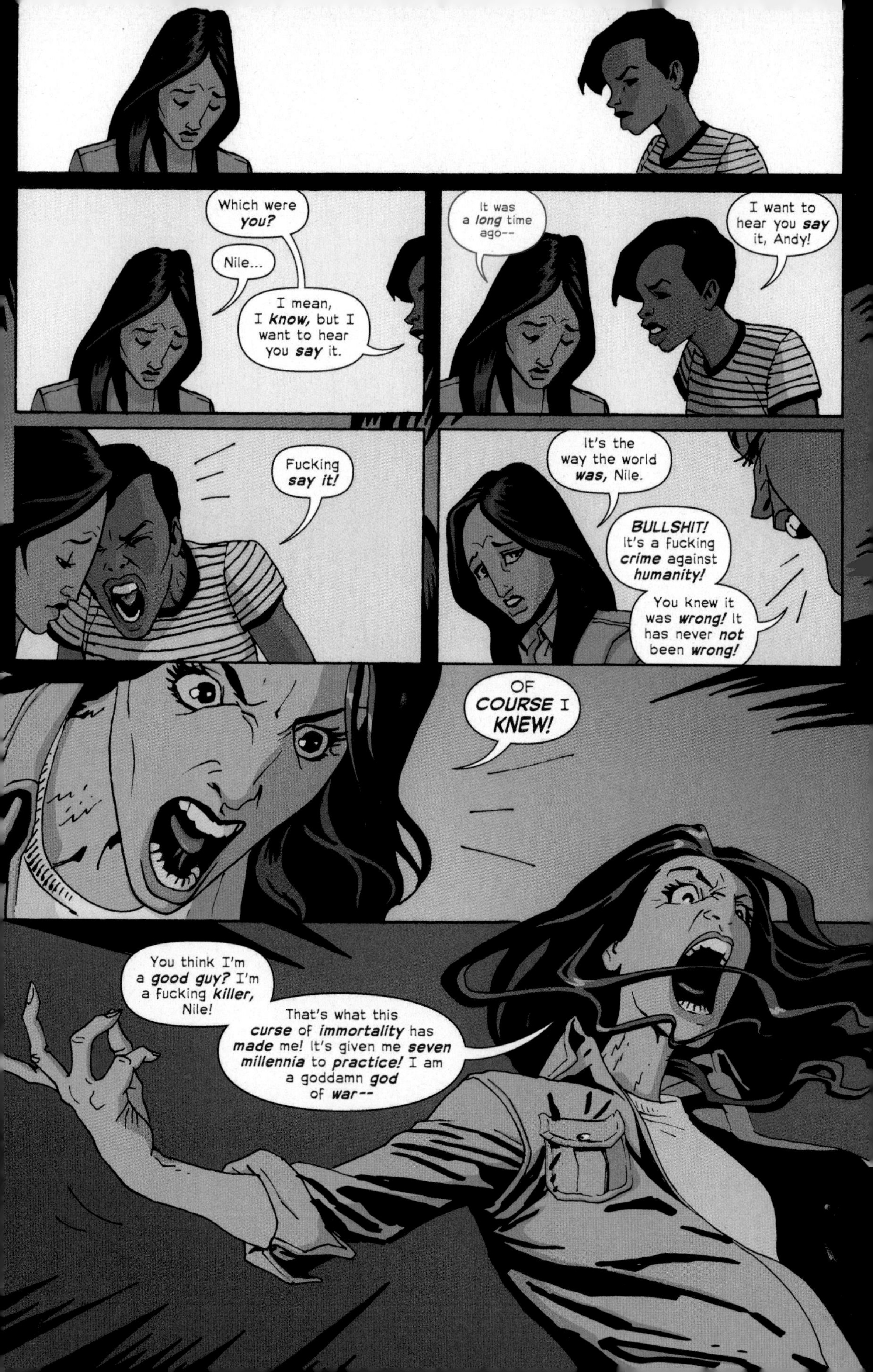
Which were *you?*
Nile...
I mean, I *know,* but I want to hear you *say* it.
It was a *long* time ago--
I want to hear you *say* it, Andy!
Fucking *say it!*
It's the way the world *was,* Nile.
BULLSHIT! It's a fucking *crime* against *humanity!*
You knew it was *wrong!* It has never *not* been *wrong!*
OF *COURSE* I *KNEW!*
You think I'm a *good guy?* I'm a fucking *killer,* Nile!
That's what this *curse* of *immortality* has *made* me! It's given me *seven millennia* to *practice!* I am a goddamn *god* of *war--*

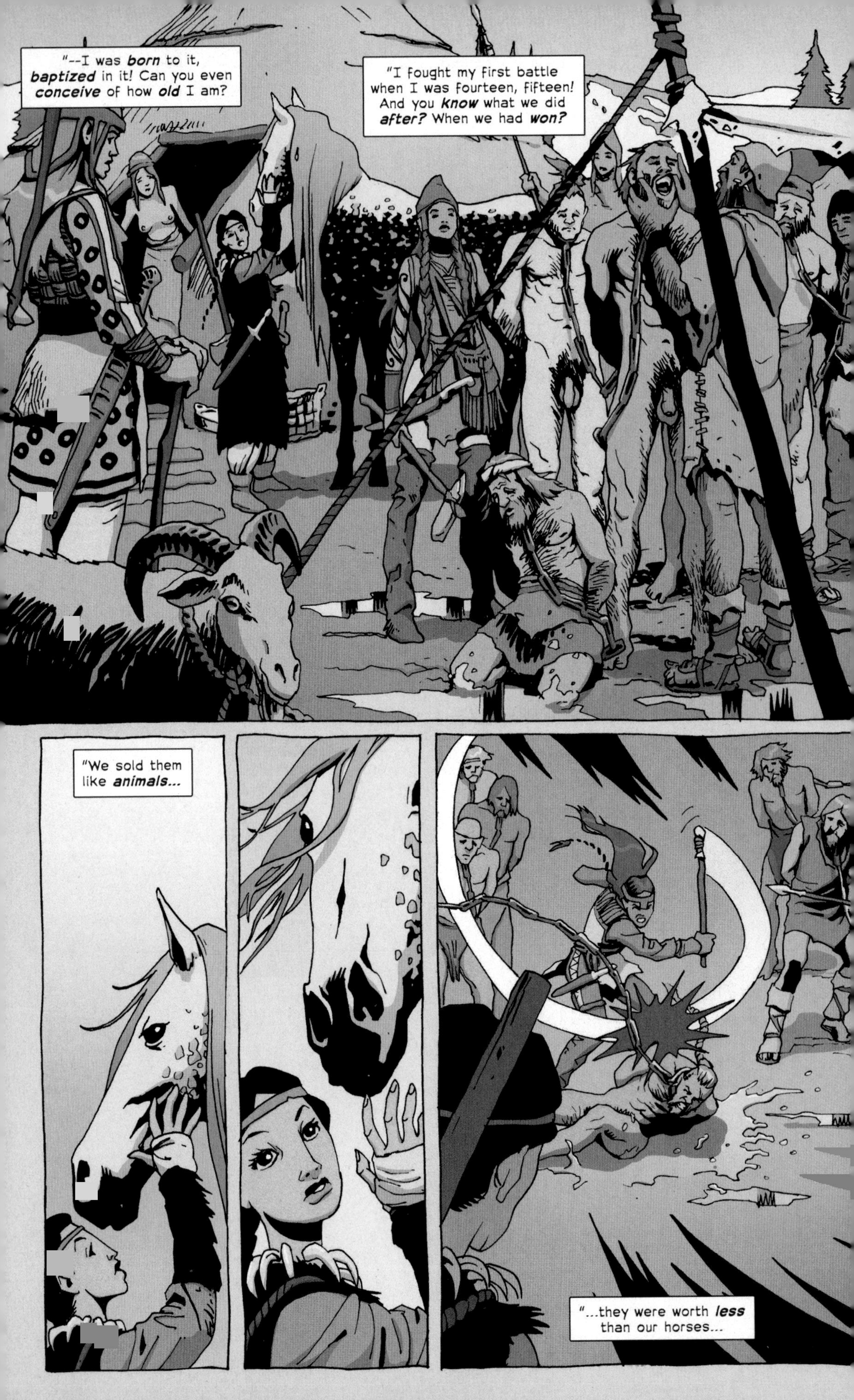
"--I was *born* to it, *baptized* in it! Can you even *conceive* of how *old* I am?
"I fought my first battle when I was fourteen, fifteen! And you *know* what we did *after?* When we had *won?*
"We sold them like *animals...*
"...they were worth *less* than our horses...

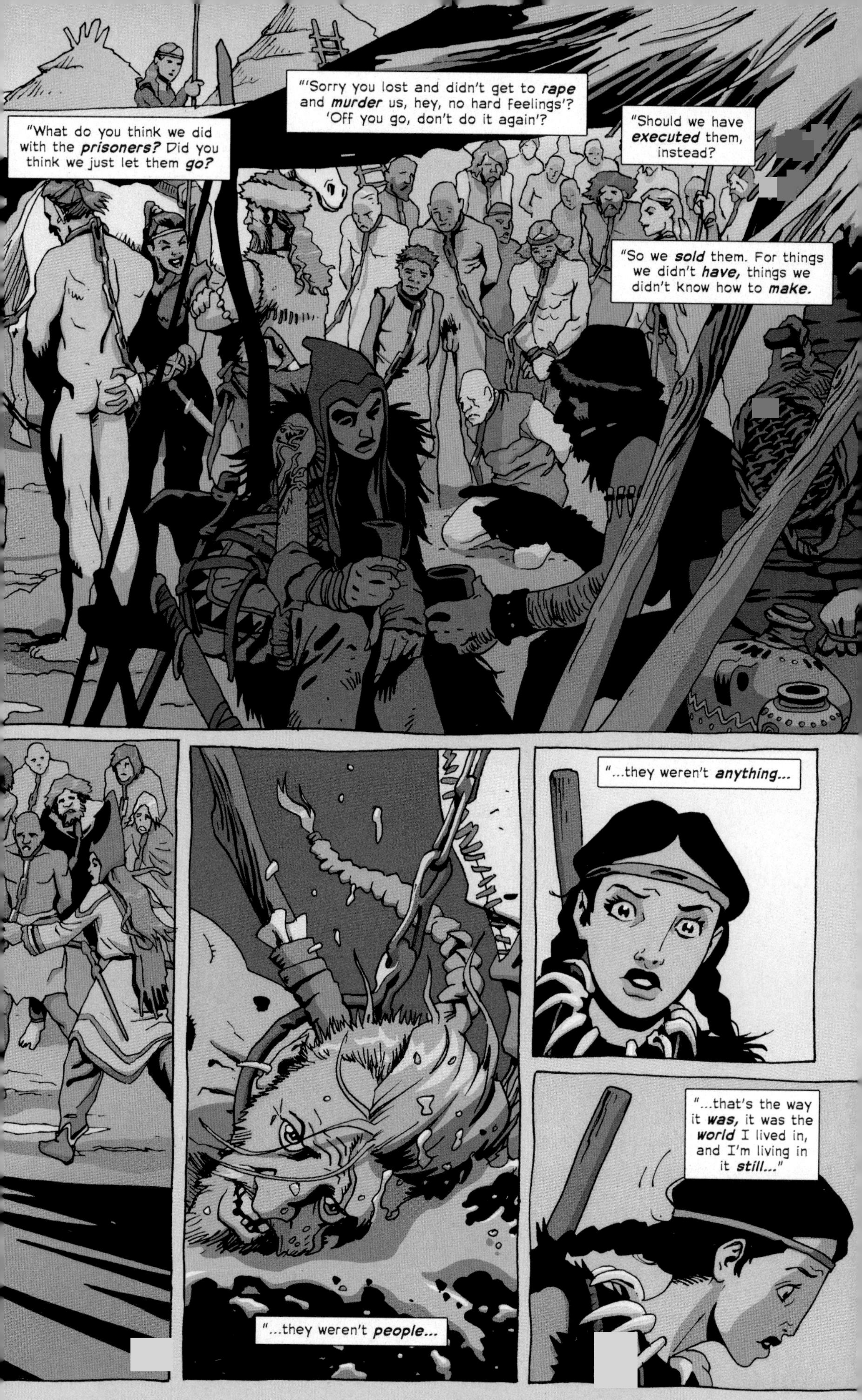
"What do you think we did with the prisoners? Did you think we just let them go?
"'Sorry you lost and didn't get to rape and murder us, hey, no hard feelings'? 'Off you go, don't do it again'?
"Should we have executed them, instead?
"So we sold them. For things we didn't have, things we didn't know how to make.
"...they weren't anything...
"...they weren't people...
"...that's the way it was, it was the world I lived in, and I'm living in it still..."

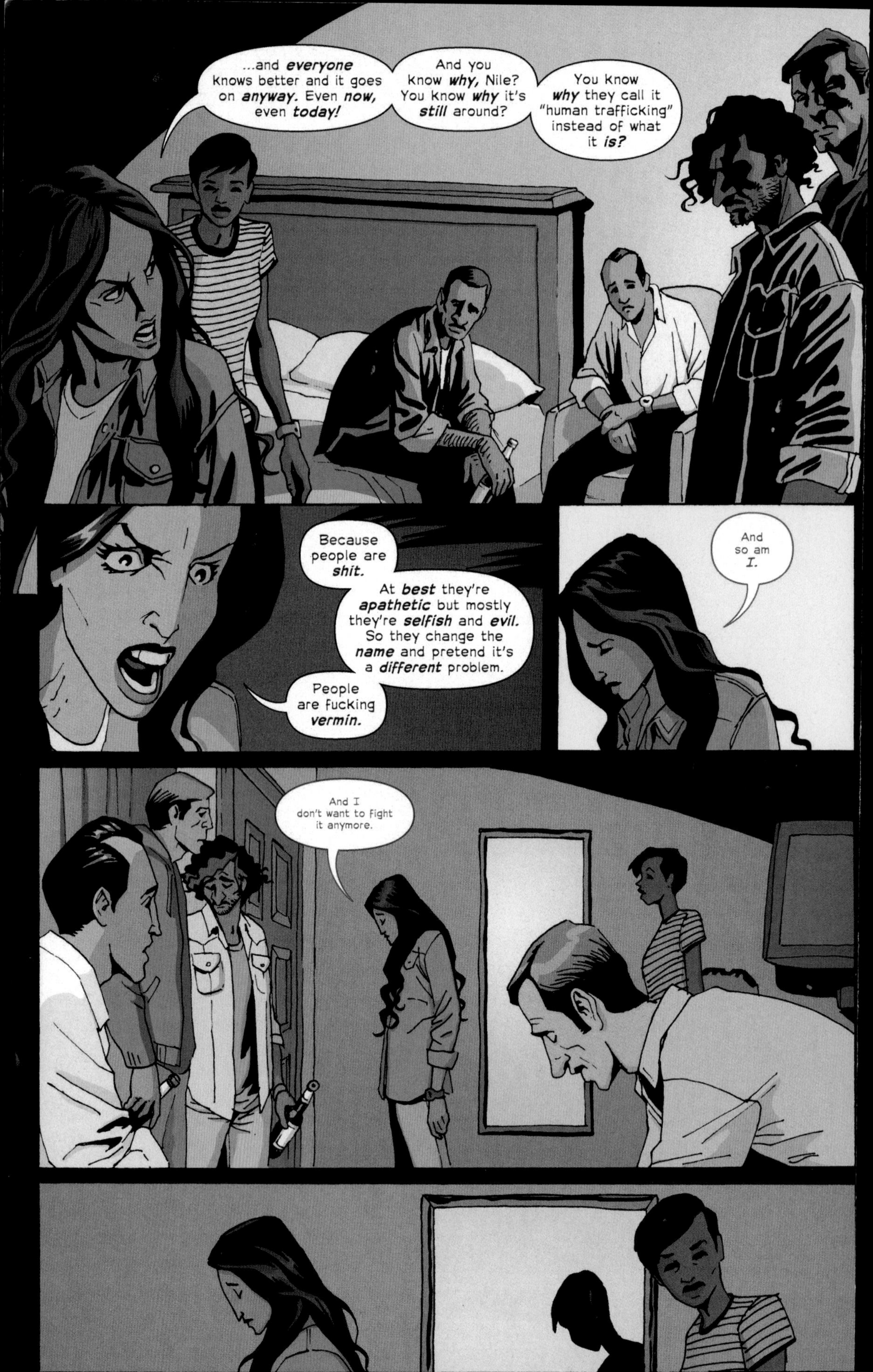
...and everyone knows better and it goes on anyway. Even now, even today!
And you know why, Nile? You know why it's still around?
You know why they call it "human trafficking" instead of what it is?
Because people are shit.
At best they're apathetic but mostly they're selfish and evil. So they change the name and pretend it's a different problem.
People are fucking vermin.
And so am I.
And I don't want to fight it anymore.

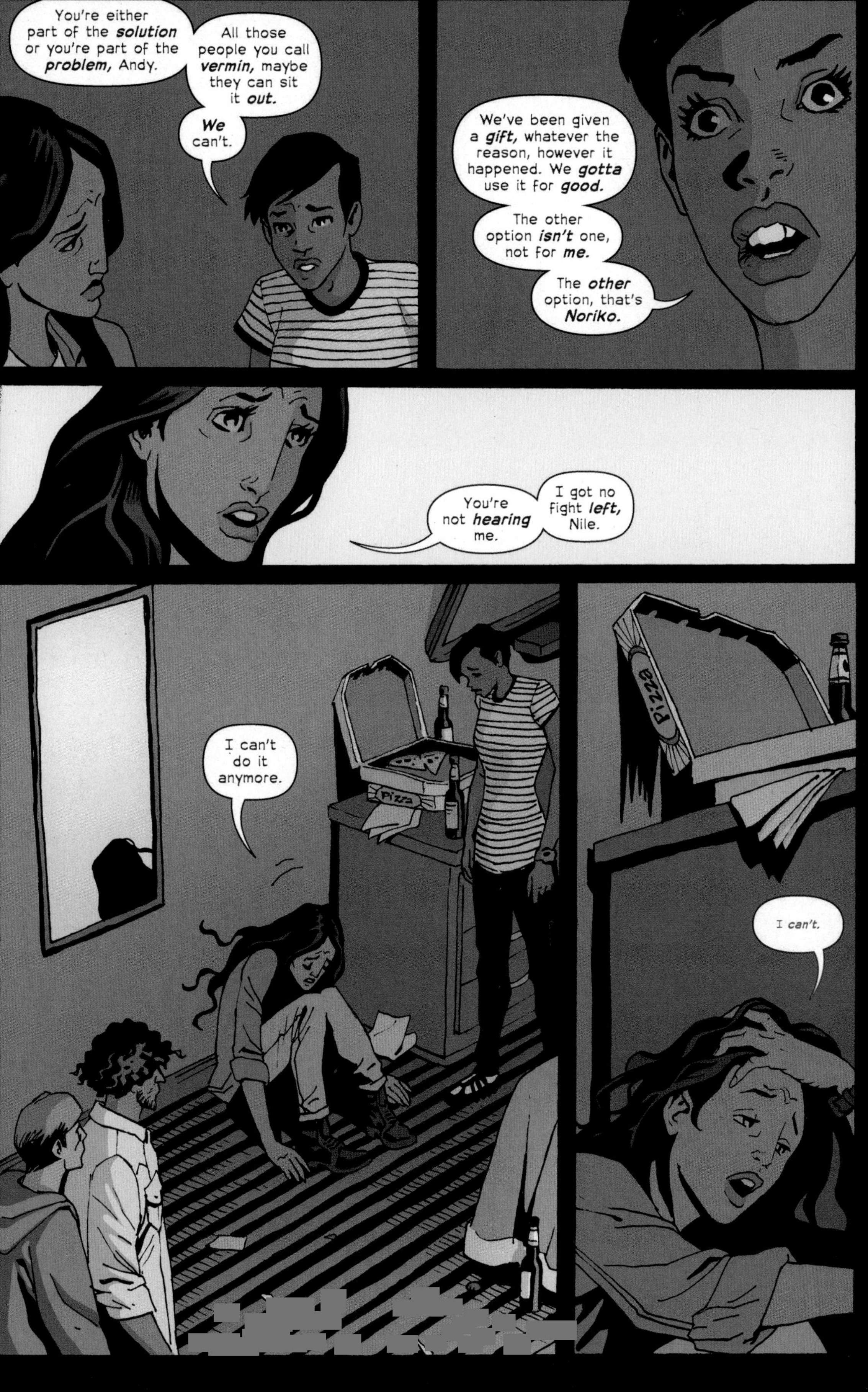
You're either part of the solution or you're part of the problem, Andy.
All those people you call vermin, maybe they can sit it out.
We can't.
We've been given a gift, whatever the reason, however it happened. We gotta use it for good.
The other option isn't one, not for me.
The other option, that's Noriko.
I got no fight left, Nile.
You're not hearing me.
Pizza
I can't do it anymore.
Pizza
I can't.

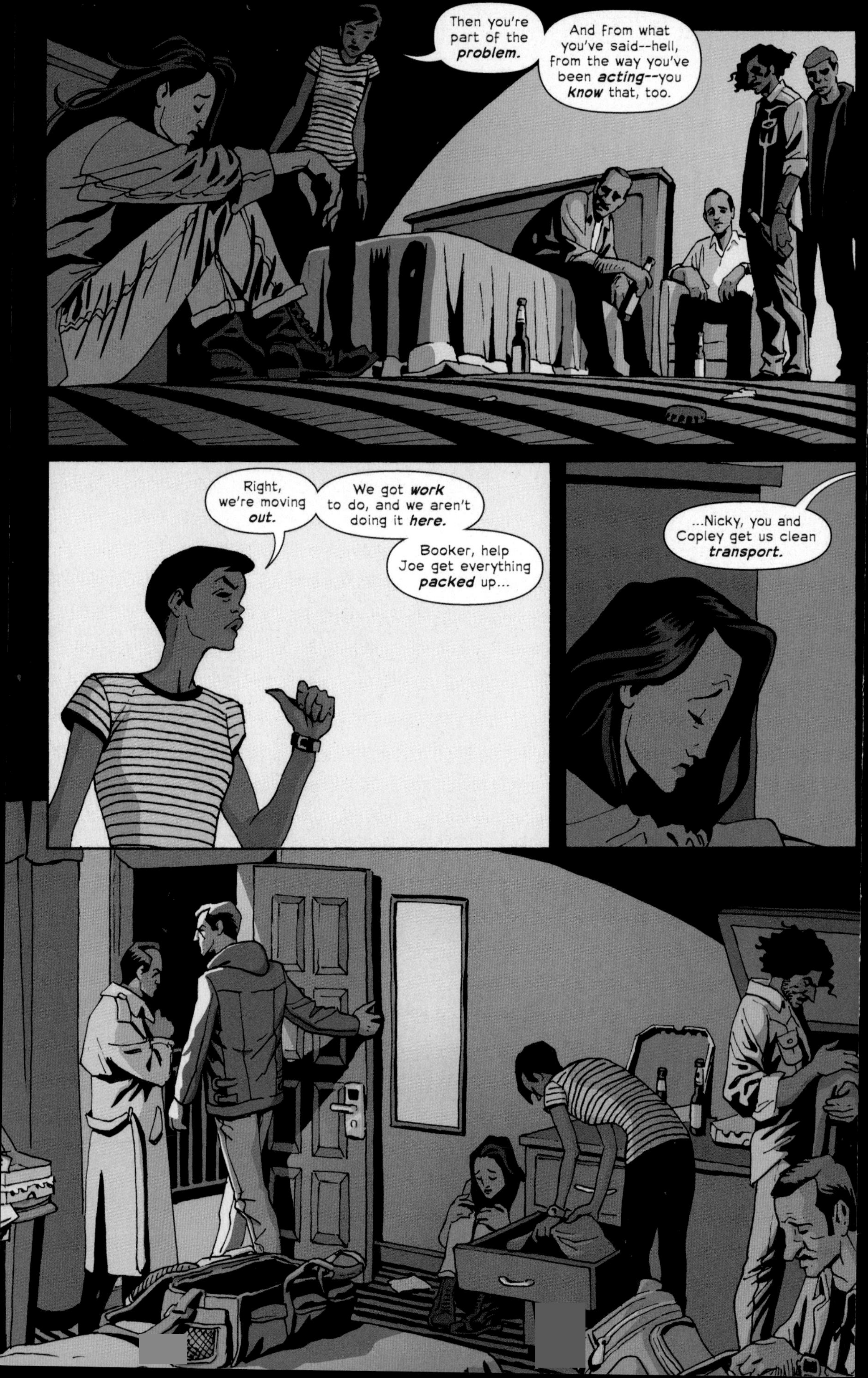
Then you're part of the problem.
And from what you've said--hell, from the way you've been acting--you know that, too.
Right, we're moving out.
We got work to do, and we aren't doing it here.
Booker, help Joe get everything packed up...
...Nicky, you and Copley get us clean transport.

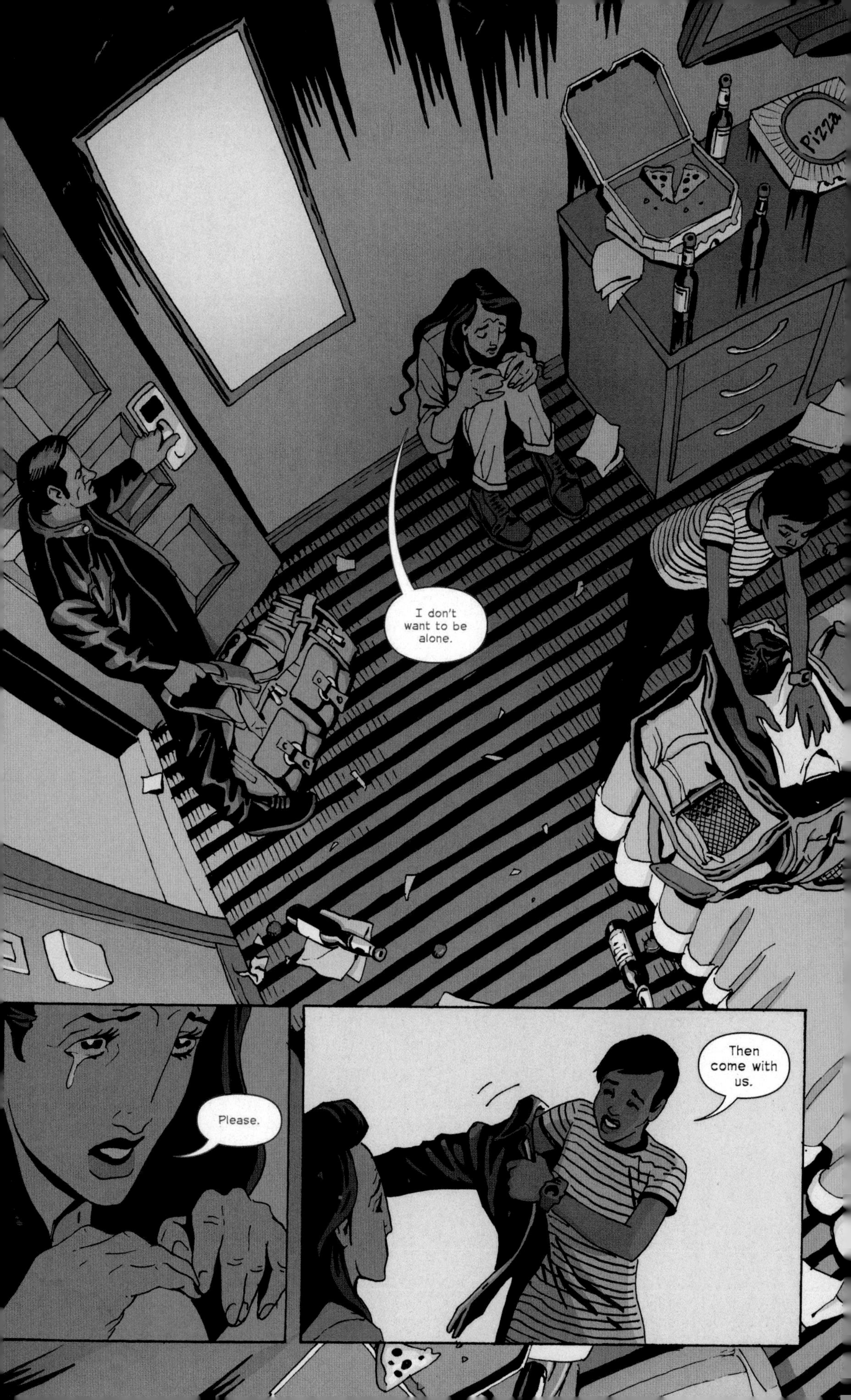
I don't want to be alone.
Please.
Then come with us.
Pizza

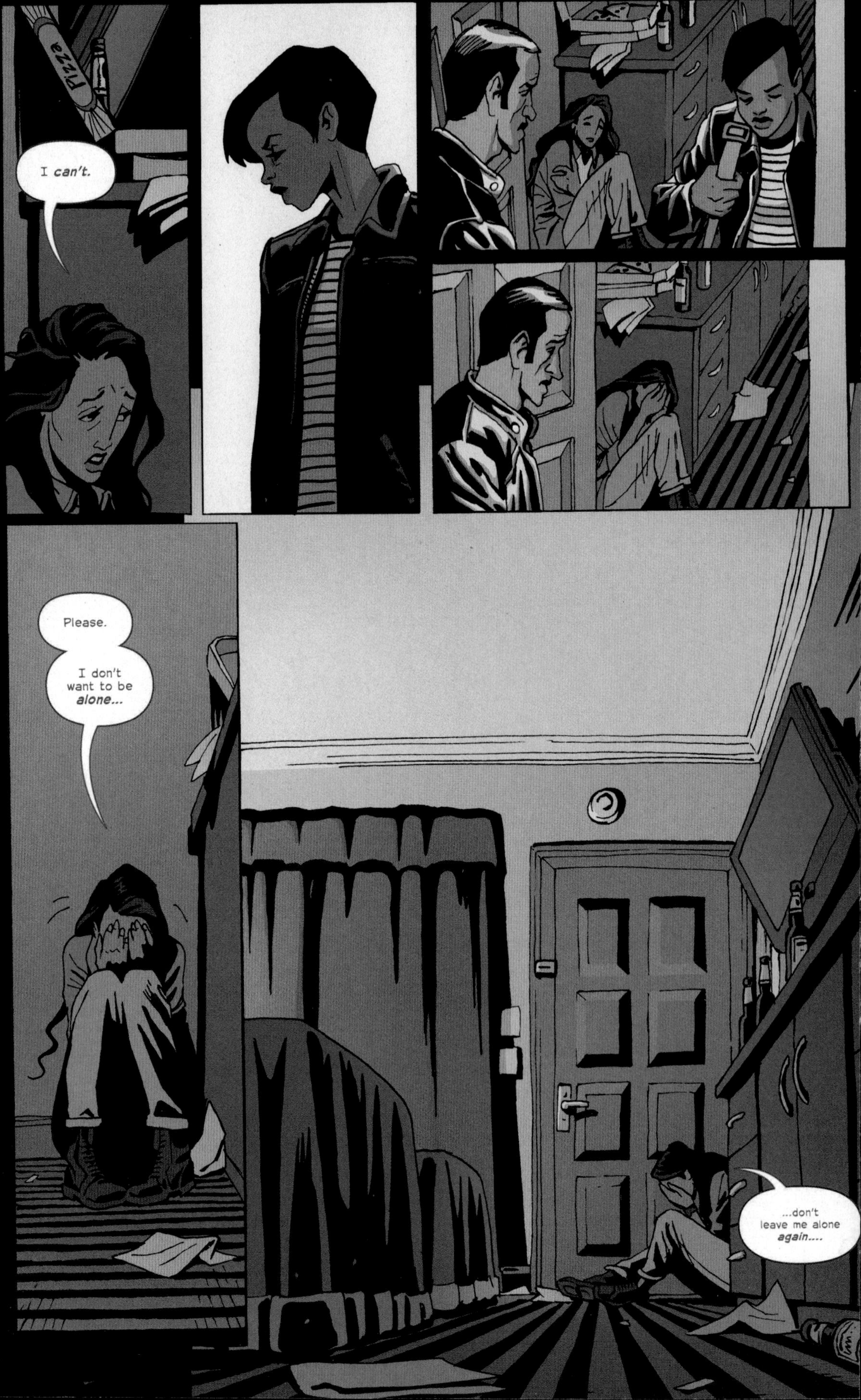
Pizza
I *can't.*
Please.
I don't want to be *alone...*
...don't leave me alone *again....*

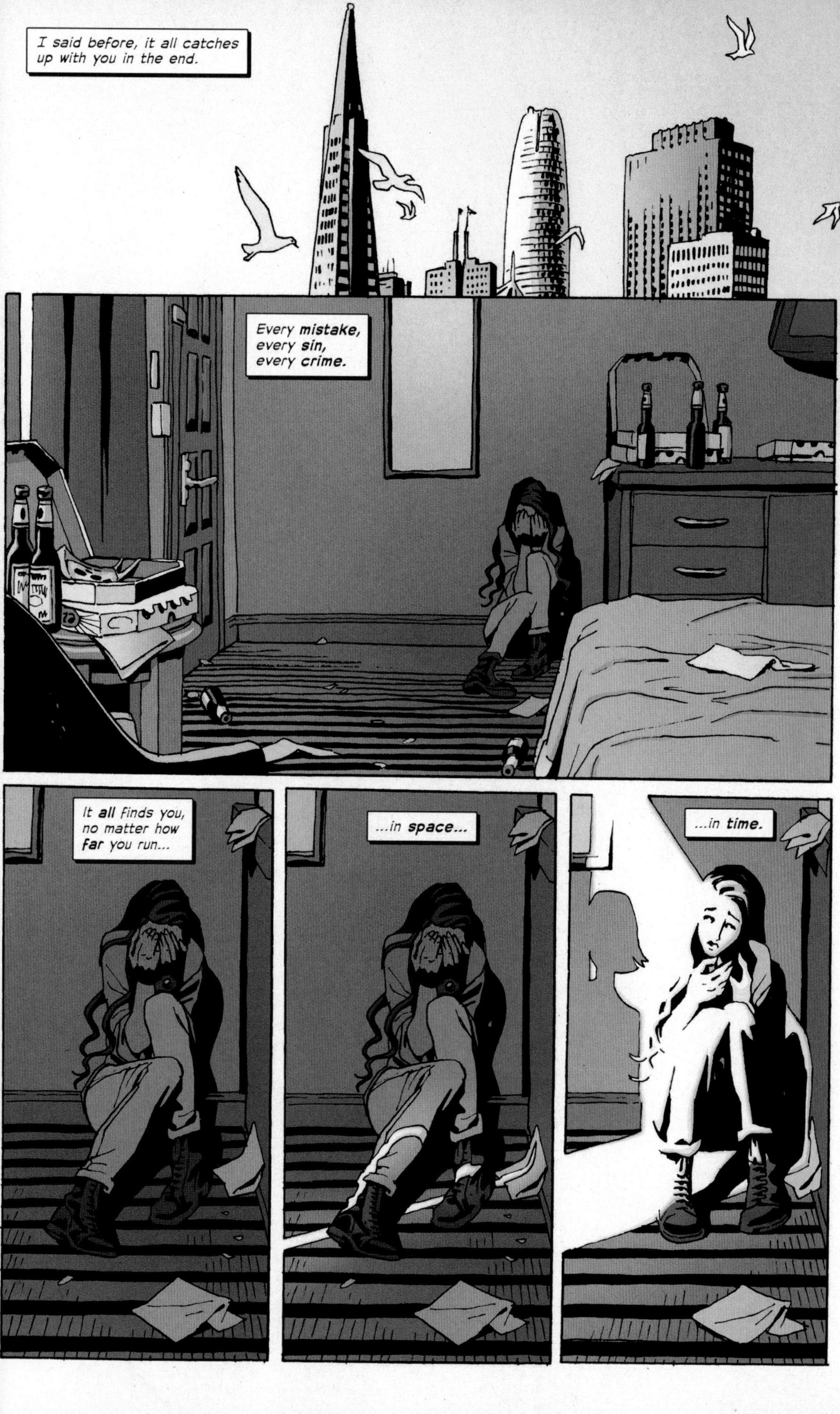
I said before, it all catches up with you in the end.
Every mistake, every sin, every crime.
It all finds you, no matter how far you run...
...in space...
...in time.

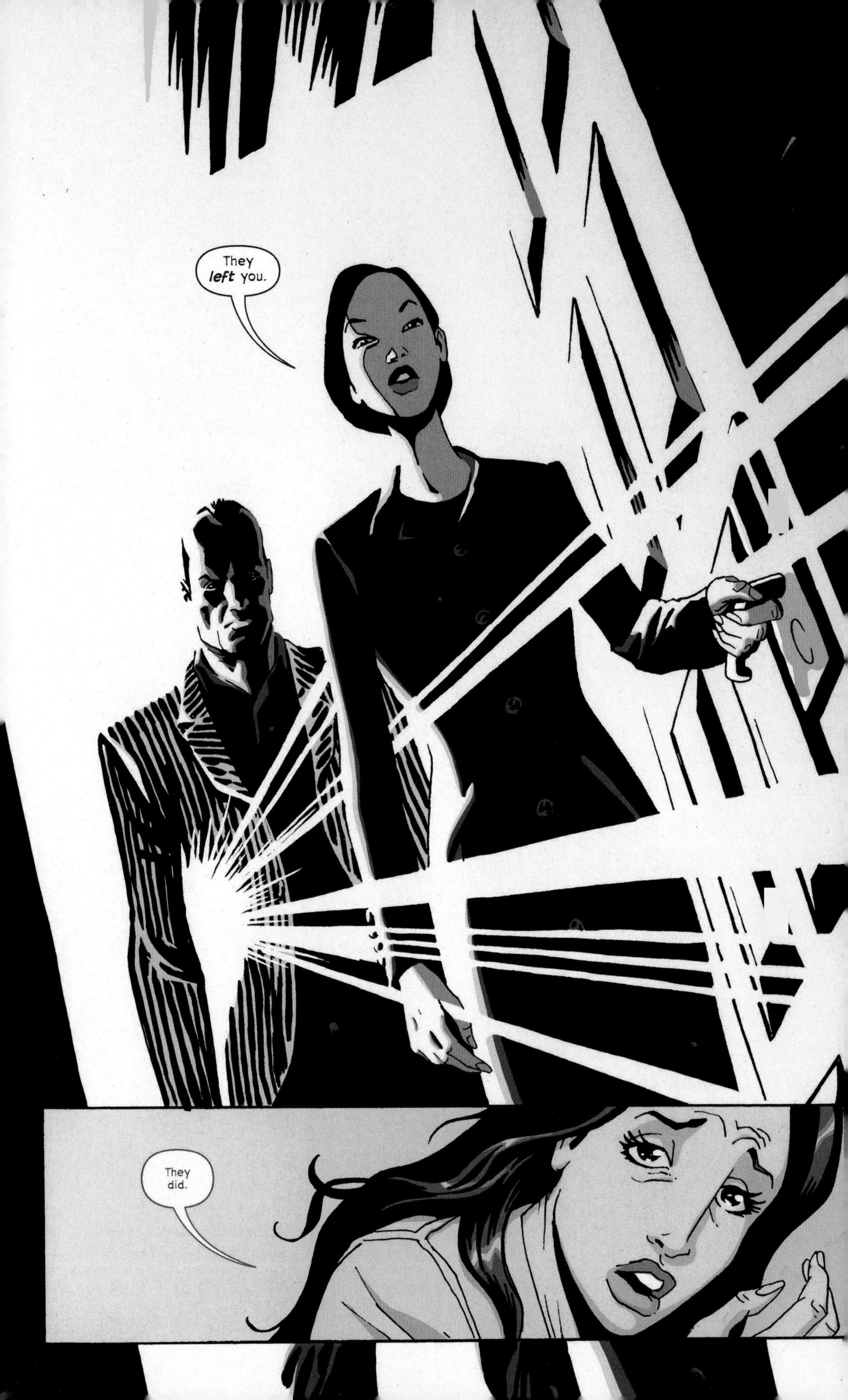
They *left* you.
They did.

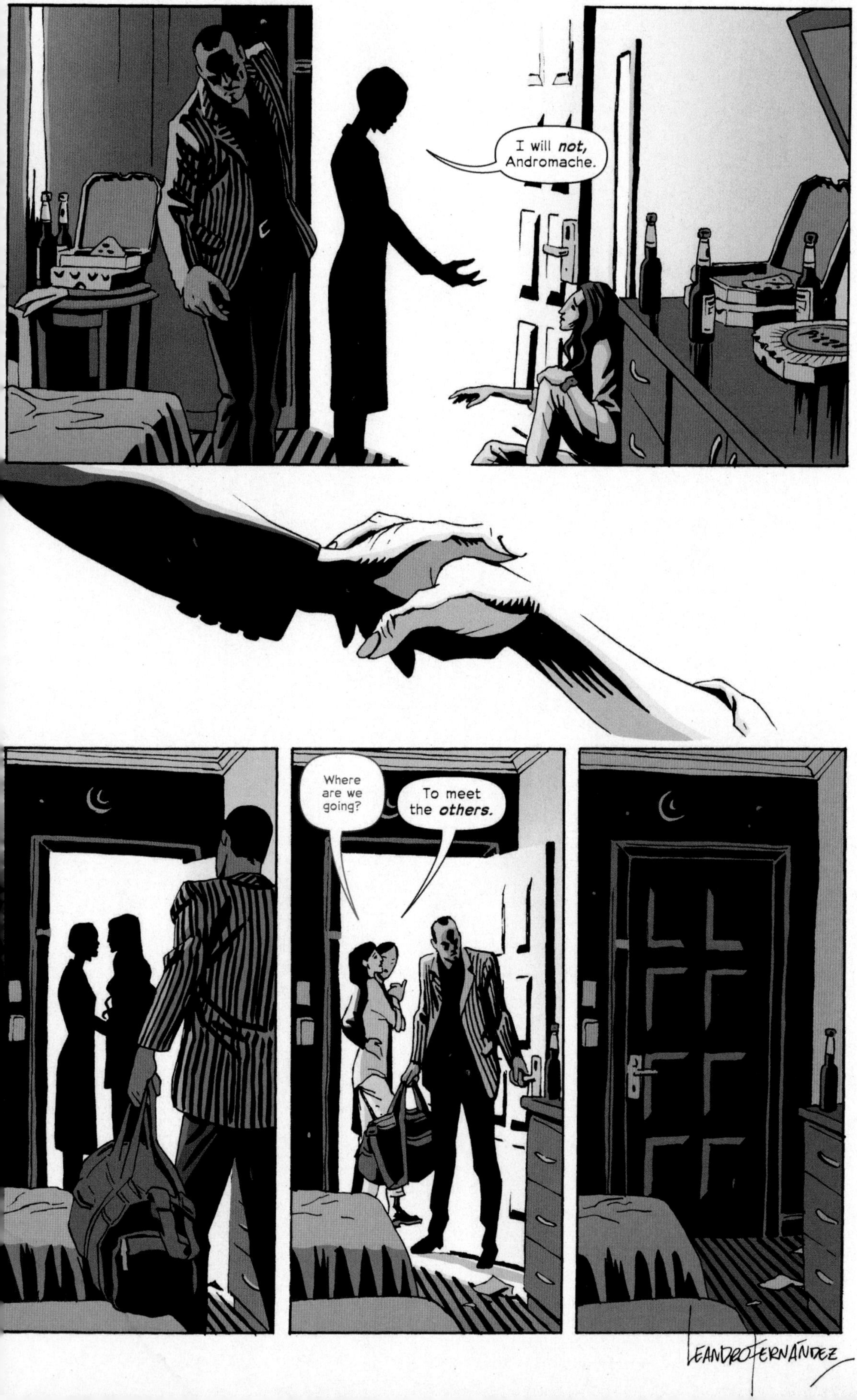
I will *not,* Andromache.
Where are we going?
To meet the *others.*
LEANDRO FERNÁNDEZ

"The dominant feeling on the battlefield is **LONELINESS.**"

~Field Marshal William Slim, 1st Viscount Slim

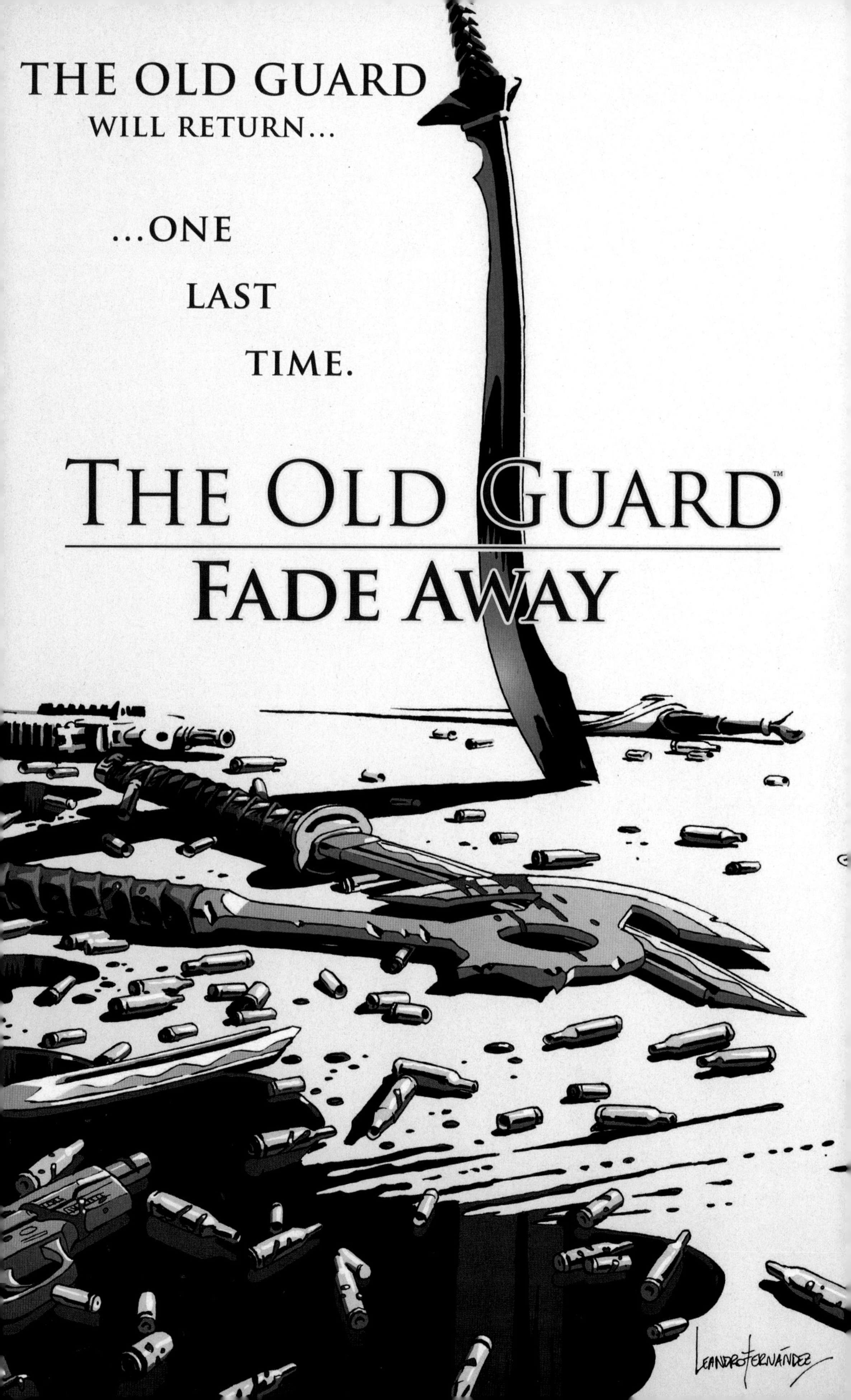

THE OLD GUARD
WILL RETURN...
...ONE
LAST
TIME.
THE OLD GUARD™
FADE AWAY
LEANDRO FERNÁNDEZ

LEANDRO FERNÁNDEZ

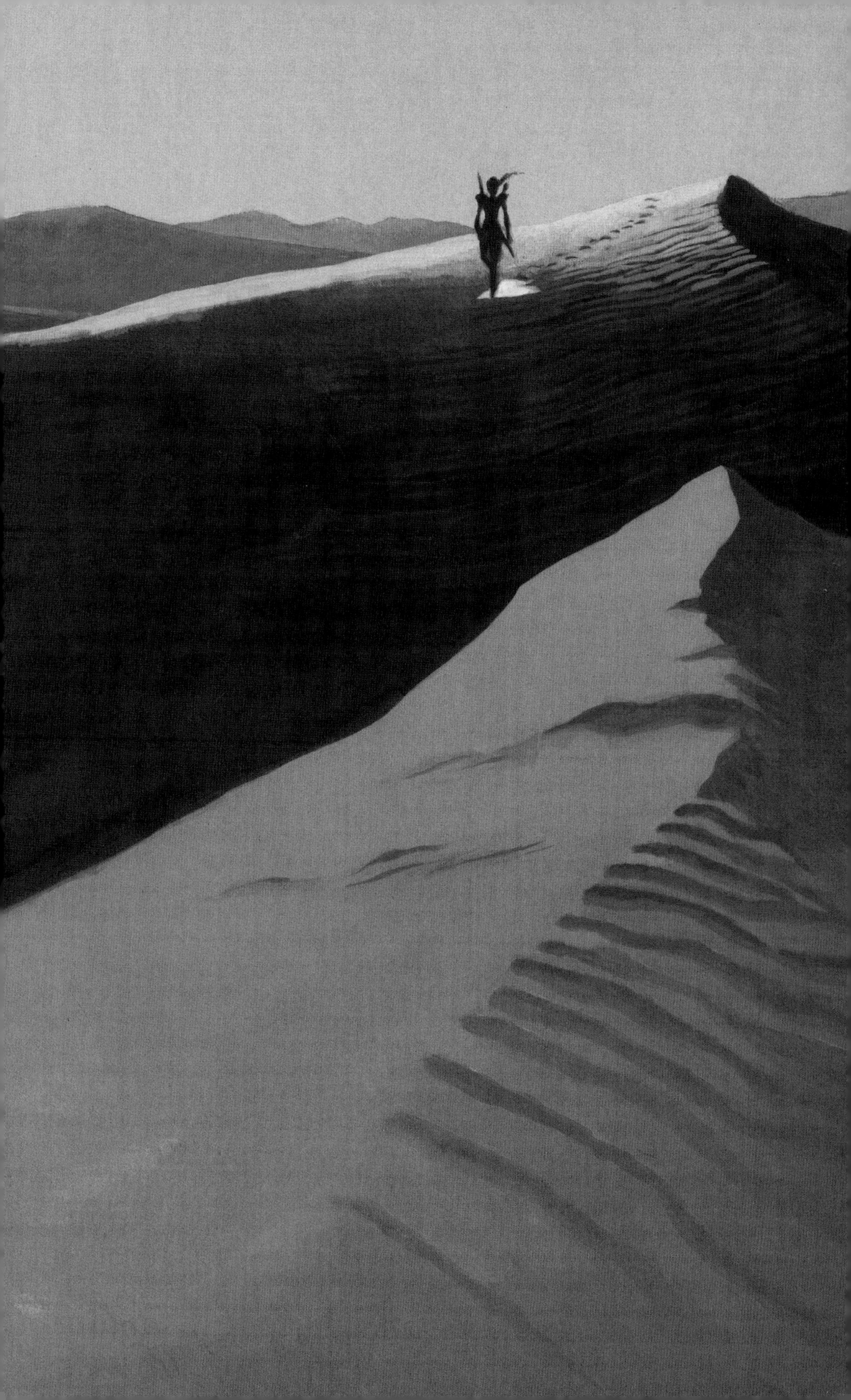

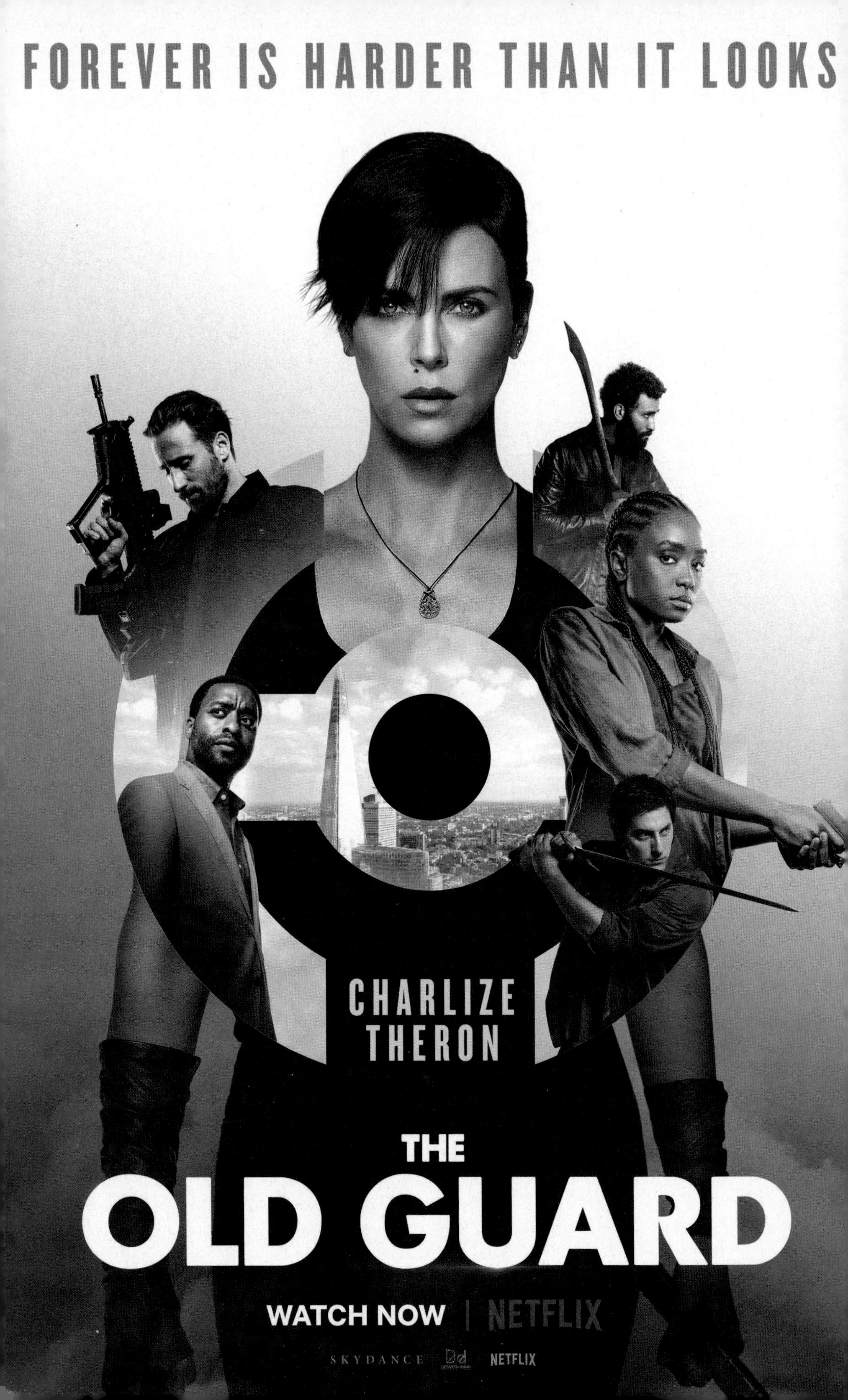
FOREVER IS HARDER THAN IT LOOKS
CHARLIZE THERON
THE OLD GUARD
WATCH NOW | NETFLIX
SKYDANCE
NETFLIX